A Flood of Passion . . .

Just then a particularly large wave rushed up the beach and caught Cece unaware. The splashing water doused her, from her face all the way to her toes. At first she stared at the ocean, as if questioning its daring, and then she began to laugh. Matthew could do no more than join in.

Until she licked the water from her lips. The sight of that rosy tongue sweeping the fullness of her mouth made him hunger for a taste—a taste of sea salt and woman's sweetness. His gut clenched with the longing, the want . . .

Love Evergreen

Ginny Aiken

JOVE BOOKS, NEW YORK

LOVE EVERGREEN

A Jove Book / published by arrangement with
the author

PRINTING HISTORY
Jove edition / December 1993

ISBN: 0-515-11249-6

A JOVE BOOK®
Jove Books are published by The Berkley Publishing Group,
200 Madison Avenue, New York, New York 10016.
JOVE and the "J" design are trademarks
belonging to Jove Publications, Inc.

PRINTED IN THE UNITED STATES OF AMERICA

10 9 8 7 6 5 4 3 2 1

TO GEORGE

Acknowledgments

For her unbelievable patience, support, and boundless knowledge, I am indebted to Susan Cozzens of the Avon Lake Public Library in Avon Lake, Ohio. Every author should be blessed with a research librarian like you, Sue.

The germ of an idea is very precious, as is my research assistant in Washington State. A special thank-you goes to Lou Schmitz for all the questions she answered, regardless of how late at night or how early in the morning they were asked. Thanks, sis.

My people are few. They resemble the scattering of trees on a storm-swept plain. There was a time when our people covered the land as the waves of a wind-ruffled sea cover its shell-paved floor, but that time long since passed away with the greatness of tribes that are now but a mournful memory.

—CHIEF SEALTH (Seattle)
From a speech at the Point
Elliot Treaty Council in
1855.

Chapter One

—— • ——

Home. After those six interminable years in San Francisco,
Cecelia Scanlon was finally on her way home. Gripping
the railing around the deck of the paddle wheeler *Pacific,*
Cece smiled, unable to suppress the rush of excitement
she felt at the sight of the majestic shoreline of the
Washington Territory.

Awed by nature's beauty, Cece turned to the passenger to her right. "Oh, Mrs. Sanders, isn't this just
magnificent? The most beautiful place in the whole
world?"

Mrs. Sanders clutched her ornately carved mahogany
cane—as if by doing so she could counteract the pitch-
ing and rolling of the deck below her arthritic feet—and
looked where Cece was pointing. "Oh, I don't know,
dear. It seems a mite too wild for my taste. I cannot
say I understand my son's penchant for moving himself
all the way out here."

Cece gasped, astounded by Mrs. Sanders's lack of
appreciation for her home. After another glance at the
raw splendor of the coastline, she knew she had to
come to Washington's defense. "The territory is growing
rapidly. We need good physicians. Your son must have
seen merit in coming this way."

Nodding, Mrs. Sanders took one hand off the silver
handle of her cane and grasped the deck railing. "I

daresay you are right. But I still cannot understand the appeal. It is all so . . . so rugged, I guess."

Stepping aside to avoid being jostled by a curious passenger, Cece turned her gaze back to the coast. Craggy outcroppings of rock were topped by towering evergreens, their rich color even more intense a green when viewed against the backdrop of the Pacific-blue sky. Where rock met the ocean, pure white froth bubbled and churned. The foam seemed to be trying to climb all the way up in an effort to bathe the trees. As she continued to reacquaint herself with the view, Cece watched a wily sea gull swoop down from the sky, drop to the cresting waters, and dip his head to come up with his prize. In an instant, the hunter took off, his silvery prey still struggling to escape its fate.

Yes, it was true. The Washington Territory was indeed still wild. Rugged, as Mrs. Sanders had called it. But to Cece that wildness merely meant freedom. Freedom from the rigid structures at the Convent of the Holy Cross and School for Young Ladies.

Poor Sister Marietta. She had tried to turn Cece into a lady. Unfortunately, as Cece well knew, she had shown no aptitude for the ladylike arts the good nuns had tried to teach her. Because she would rather gaze out the window at the birds in the bushes around the school, embroidery had been a nightmare of missed stitches and tangled silks. Since her voice rivaled a crow's, she had soon been allowed to miss those horrid singing lessons. And as far as musical instruments went . . . Well, it seemed Cece was tone-deaf.

She closed her eyes, relishing the feel of the ocean's motion below the paddle wheeler. With each roll, the soft serge of her navy skirt brushed her legs from thigh to ankle. She breathed deeply of the tangy, salt-laden air and felt the moisture in the breeze kiss her cheeks. The soft *slap-slap* of the waves against the side of the boat seemed to match the rhythmic beat of her heart.

With her eyes closed to the beauty around her, Cece envisioned her welcome. Father, who had been too busy to visit her in San Francisco, would most assuredly be stunned when he saw she had grown so.

"Cecelia!" Father would exclaim. "My, my . . . You are indeed grown up. I am ever so pleased to have you by my side again."

Cece would smile lovingly. *"Thank you, Father. I have waited all this time to come home. I want very much to be of help to you."*

Father would rub his gnarled fingers. *"Yes, child. The arthritis has become a burden in the past few years. A daughter who so cares for me is, most assuredly, a joy. You will be my right hand. I shall rely upon you. Utterly."*

A gentle touch upon Cece's arm brought her sharply out of her reverie. "Cecelia, my dear," said Mrs. Sanders, pointing to their left. "If you would be so kind, I would appreciate your assistance in reaching the deck chair in that shaded corner. I don't care for the glare of the sunlight."

Cece bit her lip in embarrassment. Sister Marietta had often complained to Aunt Prudence about what she called "Cecelia's lack of interest in the here and now." After all these years of trying to keep her attention from drifting, she still hated being caught in a daydream.

She collected herself. Slipping a hand under Mrs. Sanders's elbow, Cece led the frail lady around a group of chattering passengers to the shade she sought. "My father also has arthritis, you know. Last year, when he had planned to visit me in San Francisco, the pain became so bad he was forced to cancel the trip."

Although she could speak of it quite calmly, Cece still felt the sting of disappointment the cancellation of that visit had caused. She had so looked forward to seeing her beloved father.

Mrs. Sanders took great care in sitting down under the awning. She arranged her black flannel skirt on the lounge and settled back, making sure her small bustle was placed just so. When she motioned for Cece to bring her a plaid woolen deck blanket, Cece hastened to do so, then wrapped the warm fabric about the tiny lady.

Before she was done, Mrs. Sanders laid her blue-veined fingers on Cece's arm again. "You missed your father tremendously, did you not?"

Nodding, Cece smiled. "Yes. He is all I have. Mama died when I was born."

A frown creased the paper-thin skin between Mrs. Sanders's gray eyebrows. "And it has been how long since you last saw him?"

The familiar stab of pain pierced Cece's heart before she could brace herself against it. "Four years," she answered, her voice almost a whisper.

Mrs. Sanders shook her head, the stiff white lace on the upstanding collar of her blouse rubbing her slender neck. Her faded blue eyes peered at Cece while her fingers tugged at the lapels of her fitted black jacket. "He never came to visit in four years?" she asked.

Cece hated that question, especially when asked with the tender compassion Mrs. Sanders used. Pity felt horrid. Pulling out the brave smile she used for just such occasions, she offered her usual blithe explanation.

"He came when he could, four years ago. You see, Father is a very busy man, Mrs. Sanders. He is the manager of the Pope and Talbot timber mill in Port Gamble. He has much to do, and I look forward to being of great help to him." Cece took a deep breath, then decided to confide in the kind old lady. "I want to become his right hand."

Mrs. Sanders sighed, then patted Cece's hand. "You are a very sweet child. Very, very sweet. I hope he realizes that."

Cece looked at her companion, questions running in riotous confusion through her mind. But the vision of her father's serious face materialized before her, and she suddenly lacked the courage to ask any of the disturbing questions after all.

She leaned closer to Mrs. Sanders and placed a soft kiss upon the translucent skin of her cheek. A sweet powdery scent reached Cece's nostrils, the same scent that followed Mrs. Sanders everywhere she went. Cece wondered if the fragrance was cinnamon or sweet clove, but even after another sniff she still could not tell.

The ship took a pitch on a large wave, and Cece glanced at the shoreline again. "Since you are settled, I shall go back to the railing," Cece said. "I can't wait to see Seattle."

Mrs. Sanders waved her along. "Go, go, child. But make sure your hat covers your face adequately. You wouldn't want any more freckles. The sprinkle on your nose is charming, but more would be unseemly."

Cece nodded, then, taking care not to bump into any of the other passengers fascinated by the spectacular scenery before them, walked back to the railing, her thumb rubbing the offending dots of color on her nose. A gust of brisk ocean air lifted the brim of her straw boater, ruffling the cluster of curls on her temples. She had tried to tame her unruly locks by tying them into a low chignon at the base of her neck with a wide satin bow, but the wind had defied each and every one of her attempts. And the humid air had brought out the most amazing twists and turns in each strand of hair. As a result, the wildly curling red-gold mass appeared to have a life of its own.

As Cece admired the passing coastline time slowed to a snail's pace. Perhaps her anticipation made the time seem to pass so slowly. Finally, after hours of bobbing along on the waves of the Strait of Juan de Fuca, the ship reached Port Townsend. Those passengers debarking at the town on the tip of the peninsula left the paddle wheeler, and soon others replaced them. After an excruciating amount of time, Cece felt the huge wheel begin to turn, pushing the boat through the waters again.

They left behind the spit of land on which Port Townsend was situated, and entered Admiralty Inlet. Excitement churned in Cece's belly, making it impossible for her to eat. Soon, she thought. Very, very soon.

Then they entered Puget Sound.

The dense timber on the nearby shore was more lush than Cece remembered. Taller, denser, greener. Here and there she noted where logging had shorn some of the majestic cedars, and she felt a pang of sadness. She recognized the importance of Father's position, but she was not quite certain how she felt about the trees Pope and Talbot cut down.

A flurry of activity broke out on deck a while later, and Cece looked south. There! Finally. Seattle. And in Seattle, Father.

She breathed a prayer of relief, then went to find Mrs. Sanders. She felt somewhat responsible for the gentle lady and would not feel right rushing off without helping her friend find her doctor son.

She reached Mrs. Sanders's side after being bumped and pushed in every possible direction. All the passengers seemed to be as excited as Cece to reach Seattle. Even Mrs. Sanders was in a stir, trying to debark and having a terrible time of it.

"Here," Cece said. "Let me hold your cane. Take my arm and see if that does not make rising a bit easier."

Mrs. Sanders did as Cece suggested, and soon the two were headed toward their staterooms. Cece notified the room steward there would be someone awaiting her, and since she was unable to heft her heavy case off the ship, paid him handsomely for doing so.

In the room, Cece spared a glance into the looking glass. Shaking her head, she removed the pearl-topped hatpin from the crown of her boater and tried to calm her curls. Moments later she conceded defeat. Only a thorough washing to remove the brine the ocean breezes had deposited there would truly help. A good brushing would do no harm, either.

She donned her plum-colored jacket, buttoning the black bone buttons, then fluffing the leg-of-mutton sleeves. A swift run of her palms down the straight front of her skirt assured her she had not put too many creases there. A firm twist to the perky bow at the plain collar of her shirtwaist put the navy decoration back in its proper position, and Cece felt ready to show Father what a grown-up daughter he had.

When planks had been set in the gangway, the butterflies in Cece's stomach fluttered about her midsection in a rowdy rush. Grown up, she repeated in her head. "Grown up," she whispered one more time.

As she forced herself to walk sedately down to the dock, her eyes flew over the crowd gathered there, hoping to spot Edward Scanlon's imposing presence. Nowhere did she see the full head of white waves. Nowhere did she see forest-green eyes that exactly matched her own.

She paused halfway down and caught her breath. Mount Rainier, off to the south and a bit to the east, looked like something in a dream. Topped by stark white snow, it reached the heavens. Toward earth, though, the intense green of its blanket of forest seemed richer than anything she'd ever seen. Nothing else was so beautiful, so impressive, yet so ethereal.

A sharp elbow to her back broke into her enjoyment of the view. She cast another look at the crowd on the pier, and dismay began to work its way through her. This could not be. Cece had seen Aunt Prudence write to Father some time ago to inform him of her arrival. Being the organized type, Father would never have forgotten that today was the day. Then she heard a familiar voice.

"Missy Cece! Missy Cece, am he-ah."

A lump rushed to her throat at the sound of Lee Fung's familiar singsong voice. "Lee!" she called when she was finally able to speak. "I am ever so happy to see you. Where is Father?"

Lee Fung shook his head, his long black pigtail waving from side to side. "Misseh Scanlon no come. Velly, velly busy. Lee Fung he-ah. Missy Cece come home with Lee Fung."

Crushing disappointment filled Cece. Father had not come. Tears threatened to flow, but she sniffed hard a couple of times and took slow breaths to soothe her emotions. Well, he was such a busy man, after all. And he would certainly be home by the time she arrived.

Yes, perhaps their reunion would be better at home, at the new mill manager's house Father had described with such attention to detail in his long letters to Cece. Just the two of them, in the library. Cece loved the

Scanlon family's collection of books. Even in their old
small house they had had a library. The bookshelves, on
all four walls, had been filled with treasures. Books of all
kinds, on all sorts of topics, and in English, German, and
French, had delighted Cece throughout her childhood. She
remembered hiding behind the brown velvet Queen Anne
chair next to the fireplace and reading Lewis Carroll's
books. To this day, *Alice's Adventures in Wonderland*
and *Through the Looking Glass* were among her favorite
stories.

"Oh!" Cece exclaimed, feeling a tug on the fullness
of her jacket sleeve.

"Come, Missy Cece. Lee Fung get bag. We go."

Cece caught her bottom lip between her teeth. She'd
been woolgathering again. And in the middle of a crowd.
How embarrassing.

On the way to the ferry slip, Cece chastised herself
for her terrible habit, which everyone who mattered to
her had often attempted to break. But no matter how
hard she tried, her mind seemed to work all on its
own. It took off on private journeys to secret worlds.
Sometimes it would fly back into her memories; other
times it simply provided her with the most delightful
possibilities. Now if only she knew how to make those
visions come true . . .

The ferry crossing proved short and uneventful. Mrs.
Sanders introduced her doctor son to Cece, who responded
somewhat absently to the niceties. Her mind was on the
upcoming reunion with Father.

With a bump and a jolt, the ferry came to a stop
at the dock in Bremerton. Cece turned to Lee Fung
and urged the little man to hurry. Shaking his head,
his pigtail flying with each movement, Lee Fung went
to get the Scanlon carriage.

Lee Fung stowed Cece's luggage and helped her into
the vehicle, then climbed into the driver's seat. They
rolled away down the rutted road toward Port Gamble
to the north. Impatience grew in Cece. The trip, only
about fifteen miles, seemed to last nearly as long as
the voyage aboard the *Pacific* had. She passed the time

gazing out the window, admiring the endless rows of cedars. Finally they turned onto the main street—the only street—of Port Gamble. Peering out the window, Cece was astounded at the changes that had come about in the growing town these last six years.

"Silly," she mumbled to herself. She, too, had changed during those years. Looking down the street, she saw St. Paul's Episcopal Church. When they came to the end of the short road, they turned, and Cece caught sight of a number of new homes. At the far end of Main Street she spied the fire station and across from that the Country Store. At the sight of the store the butterflies in her stomach fluttered again. Father's letters had said the new house was located next to the store, right in front of the mill. She leaned forward to see better out the window.

Moments later the carriage came to a halt before what was clearly the rear of a rather stately house. With steeply pitched gables and dressed in millions of fish-scale shingles, the house faced the mill rather than the street. Father had explained that the house was being built in such a fashion so he could more easily keep an eye on the goings-on at the mill.

Even from the back, she could see it was a lovely house. Still, Cece felt a touch of homesickness for the plainer, cozier home she and Father had shared before she left for San Francisco. The unusually bright late-afternoon sunlight caught one of the many gleaming windows and splintered into tiny rainbows.

When Lee Fung opened the carriage door, Cece took a deep breath. The moment she had waited years for was at hand. Father was inside.

With a firm squeeze of her hand, Lee Fung helped Cece exit the carriage. "Good," he said, nodding. "Velly, velly good you home, Missee Cece. Good fo' Misseh Scanlon." He bowed in his customary graceful way and left to fetch Cece's luggage.

Cece quickly went down the sloping walk to the front of the house. Despite her preoccupation with seeing Father, she couldn't help but register the lovely

lavender-blue trim against cream-colored shingles. As
her heels clicked a brisk staccato on the front steps,
she admired the intricately turned cream-painted spindles
decorating the porch. At the polished oak door, she grasped
the brass knocker and clapped it down hard twice. Moments
later Mrs. Quigley, Father's longtime housekeeper, opened
the door.

Critical brown eyes took Cece's measure from behind
gleaming spectacles. "Miss Cecelia," Mrs. Quigley said.
"Welcome home."

Cece shook off the irritation the housekeeper's scrutiny
had caused. "Thank you, Mrs. Quigley. It is wonderful
to be in Port Gamble once again."

Mrs. Quigley nodded, then stepped aside, allowing
Cece to enter the spacious vestibule. As the housekeeper helped Lee Fung with the luggage, Cece stared
in awe, impressed by the magnificence of her father's
residence.

Beneath her feet, a richly patterned Oriental rug
covered a portion of the polished wood floor. An
ornate mahogany console table was set against the wall
opposite the door, a brass-framed mirror hanging above
it. A crystal chandelier sparkled overhead. Cece turned
slowly, taking in details of the opulent appointments.
She stopped, facing the mirror once again, and grimaced
at her reflection. Amid such loveliness, her travel-worn
appearance seemed even worse than it truly was.

"Your father is in the library, Miss Cecelia," said
Mrs. Quigley, interrupting Cece's scrutiny.

"And the library is . . ."

"There, miss," answered the housekeeper, her hand
directing Cece's attention to a heavy door a bit down the
hallway. Belatedly Cece pulled out her hatpin and removed
her straw boater. With nervous fingers, she attempted to
push the curls on her temples into some semblance of
order. Achieving merely an improvement, she shrugged
and decided her appearance was less important than seeing
Father. She rapped on the closed library door with her
knuckles.

"Come in," answered Edward Scanlon's deep voice.

Cece opened the door and slipped into a room of splendid luxury. Cherrywood bookshelves covered three walls from the floor to the high ceiling. To reach way up there, a ladder had been provided and was equipped with shiny casters to spin across tracks set into the shelves. The spines of hundreds of leather-bound books gleamed richly in the light of wall sconces placed at measured intervals between the bookcases.

A large window took up most of the fourth wall. Cece could see the mill from where she stood, as was surely the case with whomever sat at the desk in front of the plate glass. At the moment Edward Scanlon occupied the large leather chair and was engrossed in the perusal of an open book. Cece watched him for a moment, noting the new lines etched on his forehead, the tired set of his broad shoulders.

"I'm home, Father," she said with a catch in her voice. She had even missed the way he so solemnly studied matters pertaining to his business.

Startled, Father looked up. For a moment Cece thought she saw a strange emotion spark to life in his deep green eyes. And were his ruddy cheeks a bit paler than before she'd spoken? Oh, surely not.

Father cleared his throat. "Cecelia . . . Ahem . . . Was it a tolerable voyage?"

As Cece looked on, Father struggled to rise. The arthritis that knotted his hands had spread to his legs, he'd written, causing him distress at times.

Debating whether to go to his side, Cece responded, "It was lovely! The sun was out. No rain, you know. And the sky was a clear blue. The trees were greener than ever—"

"Fine, fine." With a nod, Father walked out from behind his desk and came to stand within a few feet of Cece. She waited, holding her breath, anticipating a loving embrace. It never happened.

"Er . . . Well," Father said, not even reaching for her hand, "supper is at half past six. Be sure to arrive on time. Mrs. Quigley does not tolerate tardiness." With another nod in her direction, he seemed to dismiss

Cece. He hobbled to the library door, opened it, and turned to face her. "I shall see you for supper. If you need anything, Mrs. Quigley will see to it."

Stunned, Cece forced herself to move one foot before the other and silently left the room. This was the homecoming she had so looked forward to?

A hollow feeling invaded her middle, accompanying her to the foot of the graceful staircase. There Mrs. Quigley waited to lead Cece to the room she had been assigned. She opened the door, allowing Cece to enter, then followed her into the room.

"Your father has taken into account the activities you are accustomed to, and has provided for them," Mrs. Quigley said. "Since he feels you should prepare a trousseau for the eventuality of a marriage proposal, I have obtained pillowcases and sufficient silk thread for you to embroider them." With a wave of her hand, Mrs. Quigley directed Cece's attention to a mountain of linen sitting atop a cedar chest below the window.

Cece restrained a moan. There had to be at least twenty pillowcases in the stack, maybe more. And she could no more embroider than she could fly. Clearly Aunt Prudence had been quite circumspect in the reports she sent home to Father. He had no idea of Cece's lack of sewing talent.

"And," continued Mrs. Quigley, unaware of Cece's dismay, "the piano in the salon downstairs is in excellent tune. You can continue to practice as you did at the convent."

This time the groan escaped. Mrs. Quigley gave Cece a startled look. "Are you all right, Miss Cecelia?" she asked.

No, she was not all right. Father had been too preoccupied with mill matters to spend any time with her upon her arrival. There was an enormity of sewing she knew her fingers were absolutely unsuited to tackle. And now she was told she was expected to continue to do criminal injustice to "Für Elise"! Perhaps San Francisco and Aunt Prudence had not been quite as bad as she had thought.

"Miss Cecelia?" queried Mrs. Quigley, concern and irritation mingling in her expression.

"Ye-yes, Mrs. Quigley, I'm quite all right. Thank you for the trouble you have gone to on my behalf."

A satisfied smirk appeared on the dour woman's face. "It is my duty."

Cece closed the door on the housekeeper's gray flannel back, relieved to be free of her presence. How could something so wonderful as coming home turn so awful so fast?

Her back against the closed door, she studied the room, noting its soft blue perfection. The reality of her situation struck her then. She was alone. All alone. Father was too busy with the mill. Mrs. Quigley had no interest in establishing a friendship with Cece. Even Mrs. Sanders would be happily engrossed in her doctor son's life.

Cece dropped onto the blue satin bedspread and allowed tears to fall. After a bit, she dozed.

A pounding on the door awoke her sometime later.

"Miss Cecelia," Mrs. Quigley called from the hallway outside. "Supper has been on the table for ten minutes now. It is becoming quite inedible and cold."

The censure in the housekeeper's voice jolted Cece out of her dream-filled state—not that she could remember the dreams clearly right now, but perhaps that was just as well. Her cheeks were awash with fresh tears.

"I—I'm so very sorry, Mrs. Quigley," Cece answered, straightening her skirt and tucking her shirtwaist firmly into neat array. "I must have fallen asleep." Steeling herself to confront the woman's displeasure, Cece opened the door.

Surprisingly the hallway was empty. She hurried to the staircase and ran lightly down the polished wood treads. In the vestibule she paused for a moment, not knowing which way led to the dining room. Soon the aroma of roasted meat beckoned her.

Cece sat at the place set opposite Father. Mrs. Quigley had put him at the head of the table and Cece at the foot. She shook out the heavy damask napkin and laid it on her lap, smiling apologetically. "I'm so very sorry, Father. The trip seems to have caught up with me, and I fell asleep. I didn't mean to make you wait supper."

Father looked up, and again Cece thought she saw a strange light appear in the depths of his eyes. He quickly turned his attention back to his supper, spearing a slice of roast with his fork. "Understandable, Cecelia."

Cece sighed, glad he would not be scolding her. "I shall make sure I am prompt in the future. I would hate to be a difficulty."

At her words, Father stiffened somewhat and glanced her way. He said nothing, though, and with a nod in her direction returned to ladling gravy over his mashed potatoes.

Cece reached for the platter of meat and helped herself. "The house is every bit as lovely as you said, Father. You must be quite proud of it."

"I am," he said.

Cece watched as Father's fingers fought to control his eating utensils. His arthritis was so advanced, she wondered at the effort he had expended in writing those long informative letters she'd so hungered for. About to thank him for his efforts, she caught sight of the lines around his eyes.

"You look tired, Father. Is there much work at the mill these days?" she asked, hoping to find a way to offer her assistance.

"I am tired," he admitted, hardly glancing in Cece's direction. "But the work is fairly constant."

When he fell silent again, Cece chose to follow suit. After all, he did admit to being tired. Before she could be of help to her father, she had to become sensitive to his needs. Then she would know how to alleviate his burdens, to become an indispensable part of his life.

Still, she couldn't help but feel disappointed with the way her homecoming had turned out. After relishing a wedge of the lovely rhubarb-and-strawberry pie, Cece begged off with a headache. She climbed the stairs slowly, trailing her fingers over the glossy banister. She would gladly trade the beauty of the mill manager's mansion for an hour of Father's company and conversation.

In her room once again, Cece found her luggage gone. She had expected to spend time tonight unpacking, but when she opened the carved cherrywood wardrobe, she discovered all her clothes had been hung there—the blouses on one side, the skirts next, and her two ballgowns on the far side.

Mrs. Quigley was indeed efficient, Cece thought. From the top drawer of the dresser she withdrew a nightdress. The housekeeper had drawn her a bath, and Cece indulged in a soak, then washed the residue of salt from her hair. She dried herself, pulled on the nightdress, and returned to her room. Closing the bedroom door, she looked at the bed, but was not ready for sleep. The window caught her attention, and she knelt on the chest before it, gazing out over the water of Port Gamble Bay while brushing her wet locks.

But looking through the glass didn't satisfy her. She dropped the brush, pulled and tugged at the sash until it gave, and opened the window to welcome the night air. Finally! She drank in the scent of home—salty air and freshly milled cedar.

Propping her chin on her hand, Cece leaned against the windowsill. A sudden glimmer of light amid the trees caught her eye. Someone had built a fire in the woods. Oh, how envious she felt!

As she watched the flickering flame she longed to share the warmth of that fire.

Early the next morning Cece determined to help poor Father. It had become all too obvious that he was over-worked. She washed quickly at the washstand, dressed simply in a forest-green skirt and a mint-toned cotton blouse, and tied her red-gold curls at her nape with a dark green bow. Certain that she looked efficient, she left the house. At the mill she let herself in and located Father's office.

He answered her knock with a curt, "Enter."

"Good morning, Father. I came to see how I could help you."

Father jerked his head up, startled by her arrival. "Cecelia . . ."

"I am sorry, Father. I didn't mean to alarm you, I merely want to alleviate your burden. Please tell me what I can do."

Father stared in silence for a moment, then shook his head. "There is nothing to be done. Nothing at all." He cleared his throat, clearing that strange raspiness his voice had borne, then waved his hand. "Go on, Cecelia. There is plenty to entertain you at home."

A sob rose in Cece's throat, and she fought to keep it from bursting forth. She succeeded, at the cost of a tear upon her cheek. "I—I shall see you at suppertime, then, Father," she managed to say, turning so Father would not see her weep.

She left the building, blinded by her tears. She only wanted to help him, to love him. How, Lord, how?

Outside, the trees beckoned. It was another astoundingly bright day, with none of the clouds and drizzle so common to the Puget Sound area. The lush green of the towering cedars was far more tempting than the empty mansion and Mrs. Quigley's company, and certainly better than crying herself to sleep again.

Wandering the dense woods around the Pope and Talbot company town, Cece finally felt the welcome she had so longed for on the trip up the coast. The forest wore a gown of springtime greenery and seemed to embrace her to its breast. The abundant Pacific Northwest rains had rendered the earth beneath her sturdy shoes soft, yielding, like a lush carpet extended for royalty. And mingling with the voices of birds busily building homes in the canopy of boughs above, the water of Port Gamble Bay gently roared its song of welcome.

She was truly home, and in the halls of her woodland castle Cece vowed never to leave this beautiful, wild land. After a while she lost track of time and just kept walking, trying to devise a plan by which to make herself indispensable to Father. She came to a halt before a particularly imposing evergreen and took a good look at her surroundings. She had no idea where she was.

Peering between the many tree trunks, Cece spied a rough shelter up ahead. Not knowing what she would find or, more precisely, who, she sidled close to the giant cedar and peeked around its girth.

Neatly aligned and tied rushes formed an unfinished shack of some sort. A spot had been cleared before it, and a small hearth of flat rocks had been laid out. Ashes filled the center, giving proof that someone lived here. The someone whose fire she had longed for the night before.

As Cece indulged her curiosity she became aware of a human presence. She looked to her right and gasped. She'd found an Indian. A nearly naked Indian.

The man strode to the fireplace, a wet fish in his hand. Droplets of water still gleamed on his muscular arms and on his powerful torso. Cece watched rivulets of water run down the man's body, mesmerized by her first glimpse of an undressed male. She could not call that . . . that—what did they call it? Oh, yes, a loinstring. Surely that did not count as proper clothing!

A curious feeling began in her belly, not unpleasant, just insistent, and very, very new. It grew as she watched the man cut and clean the fish, each of his movements bringing an abundance of firm muscle into sharp relief.

Cece gazed at the Indian's broad shoulders, their taut skin a rich bronze shade. His long straight hair was black, so dark that it looked nearly blue.

Brushing a stray ringlet from her brow, Cece appreciated the stark difference between herself and the man she watched. Her hair was light reddish gold; his was the color of mysterious midnight. She looked at the fingers that had smoothed away the curls from her forehead and saw milky white skin. She was so fair that she could easily see the fine veins carrying her life's blood through her. Lifting her head, she studied the Indian's exotic coloring. His copper skin revealed a virility that was dangerously appealing.

She well knew she was indulging in a dangerous pastime. She'd always heard how unpredictable Indians

were. Even after years of contact with whites, after
missionary schooling, after all the attempts to civilize
them, they remained foreign, different.

The Indian crouched, and Cece's eyes widened at
the sight of his thighs tensing and flexing with his
downward motion. His movements were graceful, sure,
and controlled. In painstaking fashion he built a fire.
Then he speared his fish onto a twig and laid the ends
across forked branches on either side of the blaze.

The man's untamed masculinity, so like the beauty
of the raw land that sustained him, introduced Cece to
the wickedly delicious taste of danger.

Chapter Two

—— • ——

Someone hid behind the massive cedar to the left of Matthew's camp.

It was a Boston—a white person—and a woman at that. But just as he knew he was being observed, he also knew she posed him no imminent danger.

Once his fish was slowly cooking, he returned to the rush shelter and continued to tie reeds together. He did not know how long he would need to rely on the shelter's protection. It did not matter; however long it took, it would be worth every minute. He sought a special *tamanous,* a measure of power from the spirits, and once he obtained it, he would be guided toward the right decisions.

Matthew worked on his temporary home, thankful for the continued mild weather. He took this unusual occurrence as a propitious omen for his spirit quest. He would succeed. He would receive the power to deal with Luke and advise the tribal elders. He would attain the power to cope with the Bostons. The tribe, his people, depended on his success.

A brisk gust of wind swept past Matthew's face, carrying with it the floral fragrance of the Boston woman. He wondered why she had strayed so far from the mill town, which he assumed was her home. Most whites felt intimidated by the woods, and the women were afraid of his people. Still, this one continued to spy on his actions.

When he had tied the final span of woven rushes to the rest of his lean-to, Matthew rose and stretched. He reached his arms toward the sky, relishing the pull along his back. He felt good to be done with that task.

The warm Pacific breeze blew by again, caressing every bit of him. Working out the twists the uncomfortable position had put in his body, Matthew wondered what the Boston woman thought of him wearing only his loinstring. Bostons were afraid of themselves, and they covered their bodies with heavy fabrics even in the steamiest heat of summer. Matthew had become accustomed to wearing white man's clothes while at the missionary school as a child. In fact, he'd had no choice but to adopt all of their outward trappings. Even his name, Matthew, was theirs, not truly his. But he had been called Matthew for so long, he had only vague recollections of the sound of his S'Klallam name.

Matthew rubbed his chest, glad of the freedom the forest afforded him. From behind the cedar, he heard a poorly muffled gasp. He smiled. She was shocked by his nakedness, it seemed. The streak of mischief he usually kept well harnessed came forward to tempt him. So she was curious about the Indian, but shocked by his "uncivilized" nakedness. Well, she was about to become just a bit more shocked and a lot less curious.

Deliberately Matthew turned to face the woman's hiding place, and without giving any overt indication of his awareness of her presence, he stared straight at the enormous cedar that hid her from his view. He again stretched his nearly naked body, proud that he was fit and strong.

He heard another stifled gasp, and then stealthy footsteps heading back toward the beach. Perhaps he had gone a bit far. But he had come to the woods to seek the spirits. The woman's presence behind the tree was the last thing he needed.

As he heard her gingerly make her way through the underbrush, the breeze brought another hint of her fragrance to him. She smelled of roses, sweet, lush roses. It was a young, innocent woman's scent.

Matthew wondered what she looked like. He wondered what she'd thought of him.

As her heart pounded furiously in her breast Cece tried to make her escape a silent one. The last thing she wanted was for that savage to become aware of her presence in the woods. Who knew what he was capable of doing to her, all alone out here in the wilderness.

The men she'd met in San Francisco were civilized enough to trust in most any situation. But this man was nothing like any of the gentlemen she'd met before. Why, to compare him with any of them—for example, Mrs. Sanders's doctor son—was absolutely laughable. Dr. Dexter Sanders was a tall and slender gentleman, his brown hair neatly trimmed, his black suit precisely cut and fitted. He had impeccable manners.

The barbarian in the forest was not particularly tall, but powerfully built. Broad shoulders tapered to a sinewy torso and a lean flat belly, all of which had been completely exposed. He obviously had no qualms about running about in nothing but that scant loinstring. Why, it had only covered the large bulge—

Cece quickly halted her train of thought as she felt her cheeks flush. She was mortified by her wanton behavior. But to be perfectly honest, she *had* stared at the Indian, mesmerized by the strong beauty of his very male body. Her normal curiosity about men in general had come very close indeed to being satisfied by her silent scrutiny of a particularly fascinating Indian.

When she stood about fifty steps away from her former hiding place, Cece stopped and leaned against another evergreen, a large Douglas fir. The resinous fragrance of the needles reached her nostrils, helping to clear the scent of the Indian's fire from her memory.

Nothing, though, would ever remove the image of his face from her mind. When he'd finished tying the reeds into a rough mat, he'd risen and stretched. Then, seconds later, he'd turned to face in her direction, allowing Cece a clear view of his features. His high, noble brow separated the blue-black gleam of his hair and the equally dark slash of straight eyebrows. Broad, chiseled bones created fascinating planes and hollows on his lean cheeks. His straight nose had led her gaze to his full unsmiling lips, and beneath them a blunt, uncompromising chin offered the opportunity for a good argument.

But the intense expression in the man's black almond-shaped eyes had impressed her most. She was sure, even without knowing him, that whatever he tackled he would do so with determination and passion.

The thought of the man's restrained power and passion unleashed an uncommon tremor down Cece's spine. The strangest tingling set up residence in the depths of her belly. She wondered if she'd ever see the Indian again.

"Oh, honestly, Cecelia Scanlon," she chastised herself in her best Mother Superior tone. "Spying. Such behavior is beneath any gentlewoman. Off with you." She started to walk again, hoping she was headed in the right direction. "Mrs. Quigley is probably beside herself worrying about tonight's potatoes drying out, or some other such nonsense," Cece muttered as she cautiously trod over the soggy mat of dead leaves and pine needles, avoiding the occasional tree root.

Careful not to make any sound that might alert the Indian to her presence, Cece picked up her pace. After a few minutes she came out from among the trees and found herself on the sandy shore of Port Gamble Bay.

A quick glance showed her she'd come all the way around the curve of the inlet between the mill town of Port Gamble and the village of Nuf-Kay'it, as she'd heard people say the Indians called it. She was actually on Indian land. And she had quite a ways to go to get back home.

The closer she got to town, the stronger her sense of discomfort became. Cece felt as if she were leaving home. In truth, she had felt far less welcome at the mill manager's mansion than she had in the halls of nature's palace. She would just have to return to the woods on a regular basis.

The clear water lapping up on the sand lured her; the rushing sound tempted her to join in the ocean's play. But she knew she'd already been missing from her father's house longer than she'd intended and she feared arousing Mrs. Quigley's ire.

"Tomorrow," she whispered, praying for continued good weather. Not that she could automatically expect a third cloudless, rain-free day. This was, after all, the Pacific Northwest. A wave crept to within inches of her shoes, and she planned to return to the beach regardless of the weather, regardless of everything.

When she finally reached her father's house, she noted the time on the cherrywood grandfather clock. Three o'clock. She'd been gone the better part of the day. Curving her hand over the satiny wood of the banister handrail, she began to climb the stairs to her room.

"Well," Mrs. Quigley said loudly from behind Cece. "It's about time you put in an appearance. Where have you been, Miss Cecelia?"

I don't believe it is any of your business, Cece thought. "Out walking on the beach," she answered, certain this response would be far better than the one she truly longed to utter.

"The beach, indeed," the housekeeper repeated, disdain evident on her features. "Had you not wasted the better part of the day, you would know you expect company for supper. Mrs. Sanders and her son will be joining you. Your father's assistant, Mr. Grimes, will also be here."

Cece wondered at the reason for the gathering, especially in view of her recent arrival. Mrs. Sanders was probably still tired from their journey. She'd have to ask Father when she saw him next.

She nodded in the housekeeper's direction. "Thank you, Mrs. Quigley. I shall be in the parlor by a quarter past five."

"See that you are, miss. Your father would not appreciate rudeness toward visitors."

"I have no intention of being rude, Mrs. Quigley. Rest assured."

Cece washed with the fresh water in the cream-colored pitcher Mrs. Quigley had set on her washstand, then dried herself on a soft cotton towel. From the mahogany wardrobe she pulled out a gold-and-black-plaid linen dress. Donning it, she smoothed the skirt over her hips and fastened the black satin sash at her back. With quick fingers she did up the large black buttons.

She glanced into the looking glass and adjusted the high lace-banded collar so that it lay comfortably against her neck. She also smoothed the rows of matching black lace at her wrists and on the caps over her shoulders. Satisfied with her attire, she took the time to pull her mop of curls into a knot at the base of her neck, adorning it with a black velvet bow.

Carrying a white lace handkerchief, Cece left the room and descended the stairs. She saw through the tall windows flanking the front door that clouds had rolled in. To be certain, the house felt much cooler than it had when she'd returned from her adventure. It was only June, and the weather could not yet be trusted. She hoped Mrs. Quigley had started a fire in the parlor; Father would appreciate the warmth, what with his arthritis and all. Mrs. Sanders, too.

Cece spared a moment of admiration for the white marble mantel in the parlor, where a small fire crackled merrily. Its drying heat offered a welcome pleasure in the formal room. Just as Cece sat on the elegant horsehair sofa by the brocade-dressed window, she heard the arrival of a carriage. Steps on the front porch and a knock on the door announced their guests. She wondered where Father was.

At the sight of her elderly friend, Cece jumped up, glad for the excuse to move from the unforgiving piece of furniture. She smiled. "Mrs. Sanders! I was so pleased when Mrs. Quigley said you were coming. Please join me. We have a lovely fire going."

Mrs. Sanders, one hand firmly grasping her cane, the other hooked into the crook of her tall son's elbow, took cautious steps to follow Cece. "Well, dear, Dexter's practice runs very smoothly, and his Chinese

housekeeper has his home in perfect order. I rested all
day, and when we received your father's invitation, it
seemed a delightful idea."

Cece looked up at the doctor and smiled. "Good
evening, Dr. Sanders. I'm so pleased you brought your
mother. Oh, and that you came, as well."

Dr. Sanders smiled back, his eyes lighting up with pleasure as he gazed at Cece. "So am I, Miss Scanlon."

Cece twisted her handkerchief between her fingers,
uncomfortable at the interest in Dexter Sanders's gaze.
She really had no interest in gentlemen—that is, in any
gentlemen other than Father.

A sharp rap on the front door's brass knocker had
Cece breathing a swift prayer of thanksgiving. She was
ever so glad for the interruption. She turned, anticipating
the recent arrival, and saw the rather nondescript man
she'd noticed at the timber-mill offices that morning.

Mrs. Quigley led the man into the parlor. "Miss Cecelia,
this is Horace Grimes, your father's assistant."

"Welcome, Mr. Grimes. I'm pleased to meet you."
So, thought Cece. This was Father's protégé. Funny,
from what Father had written, she had expected more
than the man's slight build, his thinning mousy hair,
and the round, gold-rimmed spectacles.

"The pleasure is all mine, Miss Scanlon," he answered,
taking her hand in his. The limp shake was another
disappointment, as was his nasal voice. "Your father
has mentioned you at times."

Cece didn't much care for the strained smile the man
gave her, either, so she gestured everyone to take a
seat. She walked to the mahogany piecrust table next
to the sofa and rang the small silver bell Mrs. Quigley
had placed there.

"You called, Miss Cecelia," Mrs. Quigley said, a hint
of annoyance in her voice.

"Is Father home yet?" Cece asked.

"Of course, miss. I was on my way to fetch him.
Supper is about to be served."

"Very well, Mrs. Quigley. We shall wait here for
Father before repairing to the dining room." Cece

nibbled on the inside of her lip. Mrs. Quigley was rapidly discarding all attempt at civility toward her. It was painfully obvious she resented Cece's presence in the mansion.

As the housekeeper reached the door Cece called out to her again. "Is there a fire in the dining room? My father's arthritis would greatly benefit from one this evening."

Mrs. Quigley stiffened as if stung, then, without facing Cece, answered in a stilted voice. "There is a fire in each of the house's five fireplaces, Miss Scanlon. Just as there is every chill evening."

Cece blushed in mortification. Mrs. Quigley had made certain everyone in the room knew Cece was not up-to-date on the matters of running the mansion. She dropped onto the sofa as gracefully as she could manage.

Mrs. Sanders laid her soft, blue-veined hand over Cece's. "Don't fret, child," she whispered. "You arrived only yesterday. She has surely been running your father's home for quite a while. You will assume your rightful place as mistress of the mill manager's mansion in due time."

Cece sighed. "Do you really think so? I'm afraid Mrs. Quigley will fight me every step of the way."

"Undoubtedly," answered Mrs. Sanders. "But I think you have enough spunk to match those lively red curls, and I am certain you shall give her as good a battle as that harridan could want. I have faith in you, child."

Cece chuckled, warmed by her friend's words. "She *is* quite a shrew. But you are right, she has worked for our family as far back as I can remember."

Mrs. Sanders nodded, a sage look in her pale blue eyes. "And she has no desire to be replaced. Even by the lady of the house."

The subject of their conversation appeared in the doorway. "Mr. Scanlon is already in the dining room. He invites you to join him."

The two men, whom Cece had conveniently forgotten while she spoke with Mrs. Sanders, hurried to her side, vying to see which one's arm Cece would choose. With gentle smiles to both, she turned to Mrs. Sanders and offered her arm to her friend.

The meal was excellent, as it was Mrs. Quigley's custom to prepare the very best. The lamb chops were juicy, the peas firm and sweet. Flaky rolls melted in Cece's mouth, barely needing the preserves Mrs. Quigley had provided. But during the entire meal, not one word of the men's conversation made any sense to Cece. They heatedly discussed something called the Dawes General Allotment Act, and as usual, politics failed to capture her interest.

" . . . Indians."

Cece looked up. She glanced from Father to Dr. Sanders to Mr. Grimes. When had they changed the subject? Or had they? She tried to follow the conversation, wondering why they'd mentioned Indians. But their talk was beyond her. Her mind took flight. . . .

What was he doing now? Was he cooking another fish for his supper? Or had he perhaps caught a rabbit or a wild bird?

She saw him crouch, tending something over the embers in his hearth, his blunt fingers gentle in their work. From her hiding place, she had noticed his hands—how powerful they looked! And he was by far the most capable man she had ever known. Why, he had built himself his dwelling from nothing more than reeds.

She saw him rise, his strong legs straightening, the muscles in his buttocks tightening into hollows. The absence of ordinary clothing had allowed her to study his lean masculinity. His back rippled with well-developed muscle; his chest was banded with ropy sinew. Every inch of him looked ready to spring into action. His skin, with that rich coppery color, looked smooth and firm. Cece wondered if it felt as warm as its sun-kissed hue implied. She longed to reach out and find out for herself. Her fingers tingled with the desire to do just that.

The strange delicious feeling she'd felt that afternoon rushed to Cece's middle once again. Each movement the Indian made strengthened the sensation, which in turn caused a warming low in her belly. Cece felt her cheeks flush. The oddest tingling began in her private womanly parts as she thought of her Indian, and she didn't know quite what to do about the heat that grew at the images in her mind.

Was this the wantonness the girls at the convent had whispered of? Was this what happened between a man and a woman? How could it be happening to her? All because of an Indian she'd seen in the woods.

Cece thought of the social affairs she'd attended with Aunt Prudence and of the gentlemen she'd met there. Not one had caused her the slightest tingle. Not one had caused her body to heat up. Not one had strong, capable hands or broad, muscular shoulders, or tight buttocks that made her want to—

"Cecelia?"

Cece blinked, stunned to find herself in her father's house, in the dining room, in the company of guests. *Oh, Lord!* The thoughts she'd been thinking!

The burning in her cheeks felt nearly as hot as the way the Indian made her body feel. At least her embarrassment was more acceptable than her wild imaginations.

"Cecelia!" She looked up at Father's insistent voice. "Are you quite all right?"

Was she?

"Ye-yes, Father. I'm fine."

"Come, we shall all go into the parlor. We must afford Mrs. Quigley the opportunity to clear the table."

Cece nodded and rose. On her way to the parlor, she glanced out a window. It was dark outside, dark as the Indian's hair, as his eyes, as the sinfully wicked fantasies he'd inspired. She wondered if she would ever get to know him and if she would inspire him to think similar delicious thoughts.

Halfway across the inlet between the village of Nuf-Kay'it and the timber-mill town of Port Gamble, a solitary man, consumed by his thoughts, sat near the heat of embers glowing in a circle of stones. Since the moment the young woman had run from the forest, leaving behind her sweet feminine scent, had she even once thought of him?

Chapter Three

———— • ————

Despite the drizzle, Matthew went to the beach early the next day and dove into the ocean. The chill of the water stunned him momentarily, but he pressed on and swam steadily. He refused to relinquish the luxury of his early-morning foray just because additional water flowed from heaven or because the water temperature was frigid.

He dipped his arms into the small waves, his body cutting through the crests, propelled forward by the strength of his muscles. Here Matthew was alone, all alone with the water, the sky, the spirits. The calm he needed to begin his quest was here.

He longed for a greater measure of peace. But ever since the Bostons had passed the Dawes General Allotment Act, matters had worsened. Some old-timers in the tribe believed nothing could be worse than the treaty of Point No Point signed in 1855. Matthew sensed deep in his gut that the Dawes Act could do even greater damage to his people.

When the treaty of Haud-Skus, or Point No Point, had forced the S'Klallam to relinquish all claim to their tribal lands, tracts of land had been placed in reserve for them, with restrictions favoring the white men, of course. The Dawes Act allowed portions of this land to be sold back to Indians. So-called surplus land was to be sold to non-Indians. Matthew sensed the danger in this.

After the enactment of the Dawes Act last year, Matthew had seen portions of trust land pass from Indian to white ownership. Many elders saw no difference between this and the Point No Point Treaty. He did. Back in 1855, land *had* been reserved for Indian use. Now the loss was permanent; private ownership left the S'Klallam no recourse but to buy back their own land, and they had no means by which to do so.

His friend Luke, hotheaded as he'd been even as far back as when he and Matthew had attended the missionary school, threatened to resort to violence—sabotage, as he called it—to prevent further loss. Matthew knew force was useless. There were far more whites than Indians. The Indian wars back in the 1850's had proven the supremacy of the whites. Although the coastal tribes had launched skirmishes against isolated white settlements and had even attacked Seattle, divisiveness among the different bands of Indians had allowed the Bostons to emerge as victors. His people numbered far less than the whites, and Matthew knew that Luke's way would only lead to more deaths. What would further bloodshed accomplish?

Matthew had always admired the great S'Klallam leader, Chet-ze-moka. He had had the wisdom to keep the S'Klallam neutral during the fighting. But now the news from the Port Townsend S'Klallam village where the chief lived was that Chet-ze-moka lay dying. His people were losing another great chief. It was imperative for Nuf-Kay'it to have a leader.

Matthew turned on his back, lazily propelling himself through the water by the motion of his feet. The sky above him was a steely gray with not a break of blue in sight. The light patter of drizzle on his face was not unpleasant.

Matthew thought of Luke's penchant for the Bostons' whiskey, certain that his litigious bent stemmed in part from indulging in the killing drink. Some elders were also guilty of overimbibing. Truth be told, Matthew thought, the guilt lay squarely on the white men's shoulders. Since they'd first reached Puget Sound, they had used alcohol to gain control of his people. How fitting that their methods could potentially turn against them if Luke lost control of himself.

Matthew couldn't understand the Bostons' love of intoxicants. He felt a compelling need for all his faculties at all times. He craved the feel of the wind, the wetness of water, the scent of flowers. . . .

At the thought of flowers, an unwelcome memory came to Matthew. The woman in the woods had smelled of blossoms, of beautiful roses. Each and every one of his dreams last night had been haunted by the remembered sweetness of her fragrance. What did she look like? he wondered.

Matthew was certain he could pick her out from a crowd merely by her perfume. Roses, mixed with her own indefinable, distinctively female scent.

"No!" he vowed. He would not allow her any further claim on his thoughts. He had no time to waste thinking of a woman, and especially not one of *them*. His heart lay with his tribe; his thoughts needed to be with his people at this time.

Turning over again, Matthew swam to shore. When his feet touched the sandy floor, he stood, sluicing water from his hair. Despite the rain, the morning was warm, which cheered Matthew. He didn't have to dress; he could wander about in his loinstring.

He smiled. The Boston woman had sounded shocked by the sight of him in his nearly naked state. Might she also have been pleased by his looks? He had been fascinated by her fragrance—against his better judgment.

In his quiet way, Matthew returned to his camp. Just before he reached the clearing, he took a deep breath. Were his senses playing tricks on him, or was she back? Following his instincts, he took a roundabout path and came through the trees to stand behind the large cedar she'd used for covering yesterday.

She used it again today. Matthew caught his breath. He had indeed guessed right. She was young, barely more than a girl. She was slender, her waist so narrow he could easily span it with his hands. The flare of shapely hips under her plum-colored skirt held an allure no male could ignore. But the wealth of fire-and-gold curls held his senses in thrall.

Rich ringlets cascaded down her back in sensual abandon. The breeze off Teekalet played among them, and they turned and twirled with a life of their own, catching what little light escaped the overcast sky. The misty rain brought out every bit of the wildness in the locks, and Matthew longed to bury his head in the rose-scented mass.

Apparently she had thought of him. After all, she was here again. A very male sense of satisfaction blocked out all common sense. He allowed himself to gaze a bit longer upon the girl's fragile, foreign beauty.

A hank of his own wet hair fell upon Matthew's cheek, and he pushed it back. Midgesture, he dug his fingers down to his scalp. He rubbed the thickness of his hair between thumb and forefinger, and compared its heavy, straight texture to that of her bouncy, curling tresses.

She turned her head a bit, apparently looking for him. The gesture afforded Matthew a glimpse of exquisitely fine white skin. He lowered his hand and looked at his skin. Compared to the pearly translucence of hers, his looked like tanned leather.

Awareness of their differences brought Matthew's pleasurable scrutiny to an end. She was a white woman, a Boston; he was an Indian, a S'Klallam. They belonged in two different worlds.

He took a step forward, out from the concealing shadows. "Who are you? Why are you here?"

She gasped and spun around. Her beautiful green eyes opened wider, fear evident in their depths. She took a step backward, stumbling against the trunk of the cedar.

"Oh," she exclaimed, her voice shrill with fright, and extended a hand as if to fend him off. Matthew had no intention of attacking her, but she obviously didn't know this. Perhaps he could play upon her fear to chase her from his camp.

"What are you doing here?" he asked again.

"No-nothing," she stammered, taking a tiny step side-ways, clearly planning to run.

"You were here yesterday. You are back again today. You must want something."

Her eyes opened wider, if possible. She shook her head again. "I—I don't want any-anything." She took another step sideways, looking away from him long enough to scan her escape route.

"If you insist," he conceded. "Who are you? Why did you return?"

She swallowed hard. Matthew felt a twinge of guilt. She had done nothing wrong, other than walk on S'Klallam land. And that was no crime. Her only crime was the theft of his sleep with her elusive scent.

"I am Cece. Cecelia Scanlon. My father is the Pope and Talbot mill manager."

Matthew stiffened. Her words presented all the proof he needed of the differences between him and this beautiful, curious white woman. With her round little chin tilted up in pride, she notified the world her father was the man responsible for cutting down the cedars in the woods, in the forest that grew on what once had been S'Klallam land.

"What are you doing on S'Klallam land?" he asked, his voice sharper than before.

Cece, as she called herself, lifted her hand to her slender throat, and Matthew noted a slight tremor in her fingers.

"I was bored at the house," she said, and Matthew heard the quiver of fear in her sweet voice. "And lonely. I decided to walk through the woods."

He hadn't meant to frighten her too much. He suddenly experienced a strange urge to cover those trembling fingers with his own. To tell her he meant her no harm, that he found her lovely, a ray of sunshine in the otherwise dim day. But he couldn't; he shouldn't. She was white; he was S'Klallam.

"If you were lonely, you should have known you would find no company in the woods," he said.

Cece shook her head. "I knew *you* were here—"

Matthew fought to stop the laugh her words provoked, especially at the sight of her fingers covering her pretty, rosy lips. He wondered if the moist flesh of her mouth was as satiny as it looked.

The corners of her mouth became visible on either side of her fingertips, and she soon gave up all attempt to cover her smile. "I did not mean to say that. As I'm sure you already know."

"Yes, I know."

Her smile was Matthew's undoing. There was no battling the charm of that bewitching, fascinating pink curve. Now he was certain the flesh was indeed satiny. Now every male instinct drove him with the urge to sample its firm sweetness, to taste the ripe richness of Cecelia Scanlon's mouth. He took a step toward her, then willed himself to stop. What was he doing? She would never accept his passion, his desire for a white woman.

Her youth, her beauty, were surely damning temptations.

He cleared the thickness in his throat. "You should not be here, you know. These are still reserved lands."

Cece did not respond. She gave no indication of having heard his words, her eyes slightly unfocused. Matthew took a better look at her, wondering if something were not quite right with the lovely Boston girl. "Cece? Cecelia . . . Are you . . . all right?"

When his fingers touched her hand, he felt a shock of heat pierce his heart. She was so smooth. . . . Matthew rubbed his fingertip over her wrist and was unable to stifle his whispered reaction. "Soft . . ."

At his gesture, Cece quivered. The slight shudder sent an aching tenderness to his heart, where the searing warmth had been only seconds before. His touch had affected her as much as it had him.

Her lovely green eyes suddenly refocused, and she dropped her gaze to where their hands met. Matthew felt her tremble again, this time more than before. Then she looked up, directly into his eyes.

The sound of misty drizzle kissing tree leaves suddenly
roared louder than waves crashing against the beach during
a winter's storm. The scent of musk-sweetened roses became
a stronger intoxicant than any liquor could ever be. The
slight breeze weaving through the tree trunks caressed
Matthew with a richer sensuality than any lover he had
ever known. All because Cece Scanlon's evergreen eyes
gazed into his.

Cece gazed into the Indian's midnight eyes. She must
be delirious. Just the touch of his finger on her hand
made her tremble like a wind-tossed leaf. His clean,
ocean-tangy scent had made her senses reel into another of her fantasies. But the depth of his unendingly
black eyes challenged her, tempted her to touch him
in turn.

His finger stroked her hand again, and Cece's middle
clenched with a pain sweeter than any she'd ever known.
With the pain came the sobering thought of danger. She
was alone in the woods with a man. A stranger. An
Indian.

She closed her eyes and shook her head. With more
reluctance than she would ever have expected, she
retrieved her hand and took a step backward. When
she opened her eyes and looked at him, she noted a
hint of red under the taut coppery skin of his cheeks.
Her fear dissipated in an instant. Somehow she knew
this man was incapable of any action that would ever
harm her. A newfound sense of pride filled her; he had
been affected by their simple touch, too.

"I—I don't even know your name," she whispered.

He swallowed. "Matthew," he answered, his voice
huskier than it had been before they'd touched.

"I'm surprised," she said, hoping to break the tension
between them, reluctant to leave his side. "Matthew is
not an Indian name."

He smiled, his strong teeth gleaming white against his
dusky skin. "You are right. Matthew is the name I was
given at the missionary school when I was a child."

Cece nodded. "That explains it. You speak English
as well as I."

Matthew laughed, and Cece felt his laughter touch the lonely corners of her soul. "I should hope so," he said. "After all the grammar classes, reading lessons, and compositions I had to write, I think Sister Mary Margaret would have died of apoplexy had I not learned."

Unwilling to allow him access to the feelings she knew were evident in her eyes, Cece stared at the ground. "I'm glad."

After a few moments of silence she heard him sigh. "Cece?" he asked. She felt his gaze upon her face, as warm as any summer's day.

She didn't look up. "Yes . . ."

"Why are you glad? Please tell me."

Shyness overcame her. How was she to tell him that after only a few moments together, he was now the closest thing she had to a friend? *Easy, silly, just tell him.* "Because I want to be your friend. And it would be ever so hard to be friends if you only spoke Indian, since I only speak English."

She hesitantly lifted her face, keeping her eyes focused on the carpet of dead pine needles until the last possible moment. When she looked at Matthew's face, the tenderness there took her breath away. Tenderness and sadness.

"Yes, Cece. It would be difficult to be friends if we spoke in different tongues." Matthew tried to control the rush of sentiment her innocent words had evoked, but he found himself considering her in a way he'd never looked at a woman before.

He discovered he wanted to be her friend and much, much more.

But he could never aspire to more than a pleasure-filled encounter. Ever. And he was sure Cece would never consider such contact with a man. So he chose to stifle his budding feelings for Cece and offer her his friendship. He hoped the spirits would help him because he felt too weak to control his desire.

He turned his back to her, looking for a way to break the pull of her appeal. But his shelter was built, he had enough dried fish and even some dried clams to eat later that day, and he had planned on spending the day in spiritual endeavors. With the intrusion of the earthly attraction that was Cecelia Scanlon, spirituality was now impossible.

Suddenly she spoke. "How did you make your house? What kind of plants are those? And how did you build your fire?"

Matthew laughed in relief. Cece herself had unknowingly provided for her own protection. "Those are just common reeds. I wove them together and tied the mats with leather strips. They will keep me quite dry since the water runs right off them. The fire was simple to make. I struck a match."

"Oh," she answered, and Matthew laughed at her crestfallen expression.

"You expected some sort of Indian secret for the fire, didn't you?" When she nodded, a wry smile on her pink lips, Matthew responded in kind. "Well, I am guilty of trading at the Country Store in Port Gamble."

"Oh!" she exclaimed. "That is right next door to my father's house."

Matthew nodded slowly. There it was again, that cursed reminder of their different worlds. "Yes, it is. And I trade for the matches I use."

"Well," she said, a thoughtful expression on her face, "I am certain you know many fascinating things. Why, I don't know anyone else who could live out here in the woods all alone like this."

Matthew shook his head. No, *she* didn't, but he did; almost anyone from Nuf-Kay'it, children included, could survive out here. Another unwelcome reminder.

"You know, Matthew, you could teach me all these things you know. I would dearly love to learn."

Matthew took a measuring look of the tempting beauty before him. "What good would they be to you?" he asked.

She drew herself up to her full height, and Matthew noted how tall she was—nearly as tall as he. They would indeed fit together perfectly.

At that impermissible thought, Matthew cursed and began to walk toward his clearing.

"Why, Matthew, learning for the sake of learning is a very valuable thing. Didn't your Sister Mary Margaret teach you anything? The sisters at the convent where I went to school were always telling us that."

He turned his head in her direction for a mere moment and caught a glimpse of her earnest expression. Intent on following him, she struggled with the awkward weight of her long, damp skirt.

He resumed walking. So did she. "No doubt they encouraged your insatiable curiosity, did they not?" he asked.

The *flap-flap* of wet fabric behind him came to a stop. Matthew dared another glimpse of his companion and nearly burst out laughing. Annoyance had replaced her eager expression. Her slender hands were balled into fists on her shapely hips, and a mutinous gleam brightened her intensely green eyes.

"No, Mr. Matthew, they did not. As I am sure you know." She took another step toward Matthew, and the seductive scent of roses teased his senses once again. His head spun as he breathed deeply of Cece.

"Just how is one to learn if one is not curious? You tell me."

This time no power on earth could have kept Matthew's amusement from bursting forth, and he relished the chance to indulge in jubilant laughter. He had had few opportunities to do so in the recent past.

"Matthew! Do *not* laugh at me. I am very, very serious."

After a moment he nodded. In between chuckles he answered her. "I know. You are also very, very right. I was mostly laughing at myself. I reminded myself of the nuns."

An impish grin brightened her features, but a doubtful look filled her eyes. "You did?"

He pointed at himself. "But I am the furthest thing from a nun, am I not?"

Cece studied Matthew. From his long, straight black hair down his muscular chest and belly, past his scant loinstring and his powerful thighs, all the way to his bare feet, Matthew looked nothing like a nun. He was a man. Cece felt a flutter in her middle, that unique shimmer she felt only when she became especially aware of Matthew's masculinity.

How could she not notice it? The man walked around the forest almost as naked as the day he was born. Any woman would notice a body so different from her own. Particularly if it was the first male body she'd had such a good look at.

She finally dared ask the question that had been swirling about in her head. "Do you never wear clothes?"

Matthew's gaze collided with hers. Cece noticed the intense light that had returned to the depths of his eyes, the very light she had seen glowing there when they'd touched and gazed at each other. A light that made the flutter in her middle spread and become a throbbing in her body.

He was nearly naked, a very virile man. They were alone in the woods. And she was a fool. This was not the time to point out his nakedness to a man who looked at her the way Matthew was looking at her. Unless she wanted to play with fire, the fire glowing in his eyes.

Cece twisted her fingers together, trying to think of a way to end this dangerous moment. She remembered how their earlier intimacy had ended when she'd begun to ask questions. She would try that again.

"Why are you not at your village? Why have you come here, all alone, to the woods?"

Matthew flinched. He closed his eyes and clenched his fists. His lips tightened and thinned, an expression of pain on his features. When he opened his eyes, the warmth was gone, replaced by an icy glare that frightened Cece in a way she had never experienced before, not even when he had come up behind her and surprised her.

"Matthew, is something wrong?"

He narrowed his gaze. "Yes, something is wrong. The daughter of the manager of the Pope and Talbot mill does not belong in the woods with a S'Klallam man. You must go home."

Cece gasped. His words hurt; they cut deep and caused tears to spring to her eyes. She had thought Matthew liked her. She had thought they would be friends. Apparently not.

He was as unpredictable as she'd heard all Indians were.

She firmed her shoulders and nodded. "I think so, too. Good-bye, Matthew." Without another glance behind her, she made her way back to the beach.

First Father, now Matthew. Was there something horridly wrong with her that caused the people she liked most to dislike her so?

She nudged a pebble with her sodden shoe and watched it roll into a wave. The water slithered down the sand, then returned to where the little rock was lodged. It then curled back to the depths, maintaining the normal ebb and flow of the sea.

"Well," Cece asked the ocean, "will *you* be my friend?"

The wave returned, coming all the way up to lick her shoe. As it swept away its splashing noise sounded to Cece like an invitation to sit and chat. She did. She poured out all her loneliness, all her sadness. She confided her fears and innermost longings to a wave that came, over and over again, to touch her toes. Finally, after talking about the new feelings she'd discovered at Matthew's side, Cece realized she had again been gone from her father's house most of the day.

Mrs. Quigley would not be pleased if Cece's absence for some reason disturbed her schedule. So with unusual alacrity Cece jumped to her feet and started back to her father's house.

Pausing on the front porch long enough to remove her wet, sand-encrusted shoes, Cece took a deep breath, hoping for the fortitude necessary to deal with Mrs. Quigley. After all, Mrs. Sanders had said, she, Cecelia

Scanlon, was capable of giving the formidable housekeeper as good as the woman gave. Somehow Cece
doubted that.

As she grasped the doorknob the door swung inward,
causing Cece to gasp in surprise.

"Well," Mrs. Quigley said, indignation etched on her
bony features, "I see you have decided to return. Where
did you disappear to this time?"

Cece shoved her shoes at the unfriendly woman and
entered the vestibule. "As you can see, my shoes are
wet and covered with sand. I went to the beach again.
Please see to them for me."

After Mrs. Quigley closed her mouth, she took the
shoes Cece had pressed to her ribs. She held the offending
footwear away from herself and gave Cece a look of
obvious dislike. "Do put yourself together once again,
Miss Cecelia. Mrs. Sanders has been waiting for you in
the parlor for some time now. I have prepared tea."

"Very well, Mrs. Quigley. I shall be down in ten
minutes. You may serve us then."

Oh, dear. Had Mrs. Sanders arranged to come for
tea today? Cece honestly couldn't remember much of
the conversation at last night's dinner. She flushed at
the memory of why she'd not listened.

In her room Cece hurriedly changed her very wet
clothes and soon gave up any attempt to tame her wild
curls. In just under ten minutes, dressed in a neat blue
serge skirt and white cotton 'waist, she ran down the
curving stairs and into the parlor.

"Mrs. Sanders," she said, extending both hands to
her friend in greeting. "I am so sorry I have made
you wait. I will confess, though, if we made a date
for this afternoon, I completely forgot about it."

Mrs. Sanders squeezed Cece's hands lovingly and
smiled. "Not at all, child. Don't apologize. You have
forgotten nothing. I decided to stop by and did so on
impulse. You see, I found something I wanted you to
have. It reminded me of you."

Cece sighed in relief. "You are a dear. How is your
arthritis in all this wet weather?"

Mrs. Sanders shook her head. "Not good, dear. Not good at all. But one must keep on in spite of these problems, right?"

Cece looked at Mrs. Sanders with a bit of skepticism. "If you say so."

"Tea, Miss Cecelia," announced Mrs. Quigley from the doorway.

"Thank you, Mrs. Quigley, I will pour." Cece placed as much dismissal in her tone as she was capable of mustering. Then she glanced at Mrs. Sanders.

A satisfied smile played upon Mrs. Sanders's lips. "Well done, child," she whispered as Mrs. Quigley left the room after sniffing her displeasure.

Cece smiled back, picking up the steaming silver teapot. "I am learning not to give an inch. I assume that is what you meant last night."

"A drop of cream, dear," Mrs. Sanders said, nodding when Cece complied with her request. "That is precisely what I meant, and I am proud to see how well you are doing."

The two friends continued to chat for a bit, enjoying the sweet cakes Mrs. Quigley had served with the tea. The cozy time went a long way toward salving Cece's wounded feelings. She now had a friend, a true friend. This time Mrs. Sanders was the one who had come to seek her out, not like when she'd gone into the woods to find—

Oh, dear, she thought again. She'd better not discuss Matthew with Mrs. Sanders. She would most likely disapprove of Cece's behavior. Still, she wished for someone to confide in, perhaps to ask for some advice.

Cece shook her head a tiny bit to clear away the painful memory of the afternoon. Mrs. Sanders helped distract her, as she had any number of entertaining stories, and kept up a steady stream of them.

" . . . So you see, child, it doesn't do to allow others to keep you from achieving your highest goals." Mrs. Sanders punctuated her sweeping statement with a pert nod. Bobbing her head again, she turned to the roomy bag she always carried and retrieved a parcel wrapped in brown paper. "Here, dear, your gift. I heard from my son that your father hopes you'll soon marry. I wanted to contribute to your dowry."

Cece took the parcel as a feeling of dread flooded through her. The dread soon turned to dismay as she stared at the contents of the parcel. "Lovely," she said to Mrs. Sanders. Her worst fears were confirmed when the plain white linen tablecloth unfolded, and a rainbow of embroidery silks fell onto her lap. Folded pattern sheets followed. Cece tried to muster some enthusiasm. "It will look lovely on any dining-room table."

As long as she had nothing to do with embroidering it, Cece thought.

Mrs. Sanders beamed. "I bought the cloth for my son's table, but once I arrived I discovered he had more linens than any single man needs. If only I could find him a proper wife . . . Anyway, this pattern made me think of you. I went with Dexter to the Country Store, and the gentleman there had just received these floral tracings. The roses reminded me of the scent of your perfume."

Cece smiled weakly. "What a lovely thing to say. I hope I do them justice." How dare she even say such a thing! She was utterly incapable of even coming close. She sighed.

Time sped by, and soon Mrs. Sanders took her leave. Cece went to her room, the tablecloth under her arm. Her conscience pricked her, and she decided she ought to make another attempt to embroider. After all the effort she had expended during the years at the convent, she really should have at least one complete project to show for her diligence.

She withdrew her hated sewing basket from the wardrobe. She traced the simple pattern of roses onto the fine linen and chose the silks she would need right away. After pressing an embroidery hoop around the first blossom and gathering the entire mass of fabric in her arms, she returned to the warm parlor.

By dinnertime she'd made acceptable progress on the first few rose petals she'd outlined in a simple running stitch. Laying down her work, she went to the dining room, praying Father would be less preoccupied with mill business and would spend time chatting with her.

But no.

She asked, "How was your day, Father?" and Edward Scanlon responded, "Busy." To "How is the arthritis now that the weather has changed?" he answered, "Painful." To "Pass the salt, please," he only nodded. Then Cece gave up. She had carried on a better conversation with the waves upon the beach that afternoon and experienced far less pain.

After the meal Father invited her to join him in the parlor, and Cece agreed, thankful for another chance to be with him. After checking that Mrs. Quigley had poured Father's after-dinner brandy, Cece settled herself on the horrid, elegant sofa and returned to her embroidery.

When Father entered the room, she nearly groaned out loud. He carried a newspaper, and his spectacles perched on the bridge of his nose. As he painfully eased himself into his leather armchair, she sought a subject with which to capture his attention before he dove into the news. Aha! She knew just the thing.

"Father, last night when we had guests, you and the gentlemen discussed something I knew nothing about. What is the Dawes Allotment Act all about?"

Father opened his newspaper, set it on his lap, took his brandy snifter in both gnarled hands, and swirled the aged distilled wine. Looking at Cece, he closed his eyes for a moment and sighed. He took a sip, then set the glass back down on the mahogany table by his chair. Picking up the newspaper, he shook it crisply before his face, then murmured from behind his cover, "Nothing, Cecelia. It is absolutely nothing for you to concern yourself with."

That was the extent of their conversation. For a while Cece struggled to fight the tears that burned her eyelids. Then she let a couple flow. Finally, in resignation, she picked up the tablecloth and began to outline roses again.

After a while the pain of Father's rejection subsided somewhat, and Cece allowed her mind to take flight. Sure enough, it went right back to her day in the woods.

To Matthew.

Chapter Four

————— • —————

Noise pierced the stillness of the dark.

Peering into the inky night, Matthew tried to discern who was out so late. "Who's there?"

No one answered. And he saw no one.

After a bit, he heard the slithering sound of a canoe entering the water of Teekalet—Port Gamble Bay. That was followed by the thunk of wood against wood.

"Who's there?" he called again, rising from his perch on a rock, curiosity prodding him to investigate.

When no answer came, he loped across the damp sand toward Nuf-Kay'it, the direction from which the sounds had come. Why was someone on the beach, loading a canoe at midnight? Clearly the person had refused to answer, if he had even heard his question.

He spotted the cedar *oo-okwst*—the canoe—first. Moments later, from the cover of the trees, Luke emerged, carrying an armload of torches and walking none too steadily.

"Damn Bostons," Luke muttered, oblivious to Matthew's presence. "Can't stay where they belong. Steal from us, an' when they leave us nothin', they come buy it away from us anyway."

He dropped the torches into the canoe, then bent to retrieve something from the floor of the vessel. It was a large bottle of whiskey, and Luke lifted it to his lips. He swigged great gulps of the fiery liquid. Matthew could almost feel the alcohol burning down his throat. How could Luke do that to himself?

Apparently with great ease, the ease of familiarity. Luke recapped the bottle, carefully placed it back in the canoe, and returned to the woods. When he emerged from behind the trees this time, Matthew saw the shotgun in his hand. He heard him mutter again.

"Well, I won' let 'em take it all. I'll show 'em. I'm gonna turn their lily-white hides red. I'm gonna build me one helluva bonfire. Then we'll all be redskins."

Luke laughed, seemingly amused by his witticism. His mirth caused him to stagger, so badly was his equilibrium impaired by the drink he had consumed.

Matthew winced at the sight. Despite the pathos in Luke's stance, Matthew knew his friend was quite capable of setting fire to just about anything. As was his intention.

"Luke," he called, hoping to halt his friend.

Luke spun in Matthew's direction and continued the spiral right down to the ground. He found his position hilarious and laughed hysterically. "Matthew, have a drink wi' an old frien'. Hey!" he exclaimed. "Why don'tcha come wi' me? I'm gonna buil' me a bonfire."

Matthew extended his hand to Luke and was dismayed at the strength Luke was still able to manage. This could prove harder than he feared.

"You don't want to do that," he answered, hoping logic might reach unimpaired areas of Luke's mind.

"I do." Luke nodded, then kept on nodding, the gesture obviously pleasing his inebriated senses, his long black hair marking the rhythm.

"And if you get shot? Or jailed?" Matthew asked.

" 'S better 'n dyin' without tryin'."

Matthew secretly agreed with this sentiment, but felt there were preferable ways to try than to go about burning Bostons. "Come on, friend. It is well past time for you to go to sleep."

Luke sagged against Matthew. "Don' wanna sleep. Sleepin's for elders and babies."

"Perhaps," Matthew said in a conciliatory tone, "but men who have celebrated too much are also in need of sleep."

Luke nodded. "I been celebratin', an' I'm gonna burn me some Boston hides. Soon they'll be red, too."

Matthew felt the anguish that had led his friend to this point but saw, too, the danger in the actions he was contemplating. As gently but firmly as was necessary, he managed to lead Luke back to the village. Unwilling to leave his friend alone, he took Luke to Uncle Soo-moy'asum's cedar-plank home. Uncle Soo-moy'asum—some Bostons had begun to call him King of England—took over the care of the drunken young man, since he was well suited to the task. The King of England was not only Nuf-Kay'it's shaman, he was also its leader, its *ssia'm*.

"Go, son," Uncle Soo-moy'asum urged Matthew. "Return to your quest. As you can see, much depends on the outcome of the next few weeks. You must prepare, strengthen yourself for the future. Liquor brings only false power."

Matthew glanced at Luke where he'd fallen asleep on a mat. "Yes, Uncle, I well know this. I offer you thanks for looking after my friend."

Uncle Soo-moy'asum nodded and waved Matthew on his way. "Go, Matthew. You are needed."

Matthew left his uncle's home and cut across the woods. When he reached his campsite, he made certain the fire would not spread, although, as damp as the evergreen needles still were from the earlier drizzle, he doubted they could catch fire. But it was far better to make certain than to lament later.

As he knelt by the still-glowing embers he caught sight of the massive cedar behind which Cece had chosen to hide. A certain sadness filled him. He hoped she would not return.

He wished she were still by his side.

Even though he regretted hurting her, he knew he'd done the right thing. The only thing. He must persevere with his plans. The village needed a new leader; his uncle was tired, disillusioned. Because of his family background and personal wealth, Matthew had the right to become *ssia'm*. But he was not willing to hold a potlatch celebration to proclaim his leadership until he was certain of his *tamanous*, his spiritual empowering.

For that he must forget the unforgettable Cece Scanlon. The spirits help him if she again haunted his dreams.

Cece hadn't slept a wink all night long. At least that was the way she felt when the faint light of dawn entered her bedroom window.

She rubbed her eyes, then looked outside to note another clear day. Pleased, she rose and opened the window, allowing the sea-scented air to enter her room. There was no other breeze like that which blew over the land from Hood Canal. It was clean, crisp, tangy. She had so missed it in San Francisco.

But now she was back to stay and had to find some way to fill her days. Otherwise she feared she might go mad.

Insanity surely lurked in her future, the way her thoughts and dreams kept turning to Matthew when she least expected it. All night long her rest had been disturbed by the memory of Matthew's black eyes boring into hers.

Before that, as she tried to finish the first rose on her tablecloth, she had found the red silk thread all a-tangle when she realized she'd been indulging in fantasies of Matthew and his exciting touch.

But Matthew had sent her away because he thought Father would not approve of her presence at the campsite. Although that was undoubtedly true, Cece felt she should have some say in deciding who she would befriend. She certainly wanted Matthew's friendship. She had never felt such an intense pull toward another person. Other than Father, of course. Father was her father, after all.

Oh, well. At least she could talk to Mrs. Sanders on occasion. And perhaps she would meet other young ladies in the company town. She hoped so. Otherwise life in Port Gamble, much though she'd looked forward to it, could become a jail sentence for her.

Cece dressed quickly and simply in a leaf-green-and-white gingham dress with long sleeves, trimmed in forest-green braid. She bound her hair in a chignon at the base of her neck and tied an emerald satin bow about it. With a final satisfied peek into her looking glass, she left the room in search of breakfast.

She found it, spared of Mrs. Quigley's presence, on the cherrywood sideboard in the dining room. Cece took a moment to admire the lovely piece of furniture with its graceful cabriole legs and rich patina. Father had excellent taste, and his generous income allowed him to purchase some very fine pieces.

Pulling out a chair, Cece sat down to a silent repast of eggs, bacon, and flaky biscuits. Delightful wildflower honey was a bonus in her steaming cup of Earl Grey tea.

After setting her used dishes on the tray Mrs. Quigley had provided for that purpose, Cece went to the parlor. There she sat on the sofa and picked up her sewing from where she'd left it the night before. Careful inspection showed the clot of red silk still hanging from the reverse side of the pattern. With tiny embroidery scissors, she trimmed the worst of the mess away and threaded more red through her needle's eye. "I *will* finish this tablecloth acceptably," she vowed. "Even if it kills me."

Lord only knew, it easily might!

After what felt like hours of struggling with wayward fingers, not to mention thoughts, Cece gave up on the roses. She thought to practice her music, but after one discordantly pathetic run through "Für Elise," she closed the instrument and sought the comfort of the library. A look at the polished brass clock gracing the mantel had her groaning. It was no later than eight o'clock, and she feared she might expire of boredom.

Nearly at wit's end, she sought some absorbing reading. Rummaging through the shelves, she discovered a copy of Shakespeare's plays and curled up to read of the ill-fated love between Romeo and Juliet.

When her eyes felt as if the clean white sand of the shores of Port Gamble Bay had settled under their lids and she could no longer bear to read another word, she closed the book and slipped it back into its place on the shelf. Just then a bird perching on a shrub outside the library window sang her an invitation to join him outdoors. She accepted.

Cece wandered the garden, not knowing quite what to do with herself. Father didn't want her at the mill. She didn't want to stay within close range of Mrs. Quigley.

And although the woods wooed her, Matthew would not welcome her.

Loneliness threatened to consume her, and when tears welled up in her eyes, Cece felt a pang of longing for her busy life in San Francisco. Perhaps she should not have been so hasty to leave Aunt Prudence's home. Although the social calendar Aunt Prudence maintained bored Cece, it would certainly have afforded her more excitement than languishing in Father's garden.

She had had such lofty goals, and they had been so summarily crushed.

Goals! That was it. Mrs. Sanders had advised her just last night not to allow anyone to deter her from her goals. And here Cece had been doing just that. Silly thing.

She looked toward the kitchen window and, not noting Mrs. Quigley's discouraging presence, took off in the direction of the woods, muttering at the absent Matthew. "Just you wait, mister. I have goals, you know. One of them is to become your friend. And I will."

Determination guided her footsteps, and within a short period of time Cece found herself nearing Matthew's clearing. A hint of nervousness landed in her stomach once again, then flowed into her now cold fingers. Would he reject her this time? Would he be hateful and send her away like a naughty child?

"Well, I won't go. And that's final."

"What's final?" Matthew asked from behind Cece, startling her with his silent approach. "Why are you here again? I told you to go back where you belong."

Cece whirled around, a fallen branch snagging the hem of her soft cotton skirt. She heard the fabric tear and bent to remove the wood before it did further damage. Then, branch in hand, she faced Matthew.

He laughed before she could say a word.

"You look ferocious, Cecelia Scanlon. Are you planning on doing battle? Against me?"

"If it comes to that, Mr. Matthew." Cece felt relief at his display of humor. Maybe, just maybe, he would allow her the pleasure of his company. "You told me to go where I belong, and to be honest I *am* where I belong.

In the woods, near the beach. My father's house is his, not mine."

Matthew took in the determined tilt of Cece's round chin. He also admired the flash of fire in her beautiful green eyes, their hue intensified by the reflection of the color of her dress and that of the trees. The girl was full of passion, passion he sensed had never been tapped. He envied the man who would someday do so—and acknowledged he would give his life for the privilege.

He damned himself for a fool. "I cannot keep you from walking by the water's edge, nor can I keep you from exploring the woods, if you so desire. There is too much forest for me to chase you from it all. But you should not follow me around. It would be wrong."

She took a step forward, a mutinous look on her face. Her clenched fists, one still gripping her dead branch, came to rest on her curvy hips. Matthew sighed. This was difficult; he must not only fight her, but he had to fight his own perverse desire for this forbidden woman.

"No, Cece. Listen to me. You are the daughter of the Pope and Talbot mill manager. I am a S'Klallam. We come from two separate worlds. And you surely know your people would frown upon contact between you and a S'Klallam. Your presence at my camp would cause a scandal. It would damage your reputation."

Cece took another step in his direction, then she exploded, gesturing in her anger. "Oh, fie on my reputation!" The dead branch came dangerously close to Matthew's head. He ducked, a reluctant smile on his lips.

"I don't care a fig about my reputation," she insisted, using the branch to punctuate her speech. "I am so bored, so lonely in that . . . that museum of a house. You are the only friend I have. So you can disapprove all you wish. I want to be your friend, and I shall not allow you to chase me away again."

Cece paused for a breath, then took stock of what had just transpired. Oh, Lord! Had she, Cece Scanlon, really stood up and fought Matthew down? The same Cece Scanlon Sister Marietta had called a "dreamy, quiet little thing"? What would the good nun think now?

But Sister Marietta was in San Francisco, and the silent man with a stubborn set to his square chin stood before Cece. He looked none too pleased with her outburst, but she had no intention of backing down. She did, however, deem it prudent to drop the menacing branch.

Glaring at him, she became aware of the objects Matthew carried. "What is that stick for, Matthew?" she asked, pointing to the item in his right hand. She decided to proceed with this friendship, to behave as if her outburst had never occurred. That would present him with less cause to argue.

Matthew gave her a funny smile and shook his head. "You surprise me, Cece."

Warmth suffused her. Although he had not said so, she could tell he enjoyed her unexpected strength. "Well? Are you going to tell me what that thing is for?"

"Yes, Cece, yes. Patience." Matthew extended the object in question toward her, and Cece took the long branch in her hands. Then he bent to gather the large basket by his feet, which she had not noticed until just now. His movement drew her attention to his behind. As usual, Matthew was clad only in his loinstring.

When she became aware of that fact, Cece felt the taut, exciting feeling begin in her middle. Trying to tear her attention away from Matthew's nakedness and her appreciation of it, Cece asked, "What is the basket for?"

"I am clamming. The clams are at their plumpest, juiciest best in June and July."

"Oh, how delightful!" she exclaimed. "I love clams. Can I come with you?"

Matthew chuckled, his teeth gleaming a bright white in contrast to his copper skin. Cece could not help but notice what a wonderful smile he had. The tingle in her middle intensified.

"I don't see that you have allowed me much choice in the matter, have you?" He answered her question with one of his own.

Cece smiled back. "None at all." Satisfied to have gotten her way, she followed Matthew to the beach.

There they spent the better part of two hours as Matthew showed Cece how to dig under the clam with the stick when she saw the bubbles they made in the wet sand. She soon became quite adept at flipping the creatures out of their nests so Matthew could pick them up and place them with the growing collection in the basket.

"Here comes another wave, Matthew. I want to dig out another one."

"Do we not have enough for a meal?"

"It is not the meal I was thinking of, but of the excitement in such a lovely day. And in the challenge of rousting the beasties from where they hide."

Matthew laughed. He feared he was lost. Cece was full of irrepressible joy and a zest for life. Her pleasure at running barefoot across the sand, sinking her slender little toes into the wet mess, had him craving to discover to what other sensual delights she would give herself so fully. She was driving him mad.

Just then a particularly large wave rushed up the beach and caught Cece unaware. The splashing water doused her, from her face all the way to her toes. At first she stared at the ocean, as if questioning its daring, and then she began to laugh. Matthew could do no more than join in.

Until she licked the water from her lips. The sight of that rosy tongue sweeping the fullness of her mouth made him hunger for a taste—a taste of sea salt and woman's sweetness. His gut clenched with the longing, the want.

He lowered his gaze and groaned, quickly realizing his mistake. Now his attention was riveted to the wet, sheer fabric of her clothing, half veiling, half accentuating her breasts. Full and round, her flesh pressed against her undergarment and the green-and-white-checked cotton of her dress. A berry-dark shadow was clearly visible, and Matthew longed to fully expose Cece's curves.

His longing grew, and his body hardened with need. She was beautiful, desirable. She was also a perfect companion, intelligent and challenging. He had never known another woman like her, and he doubted he ever would. How he wished he could make her his.

"Matthew?" Cece's feminine voice pierced his wayward thoughts, and he reluctantly looked away from her breasts. His gaze swept up her neck, admired her lips, and became riveted to the emerald sparkle of her eyes. There was so much life in Cece Scanlon. . . .

"I am sorry, I did not hear what you said." No, indeed, he had been too busy wanting her, indulging in a desire he had no right to.

Cece laughed, the sound tinkling merrily over that of the waves. Matthew cursed inwardly.

She lifted a shoulder, for mere seconds tightening the damp cotton across a breast. "I merely asked if we could eat soon," she said.

He cleared his throat. "Of course. Shall we go back to my camp?"

Cece nodded, a stray red-gold curl bouncing on her shoulder. "Will you show me how you prepare the wood to light a fire?"

"Of course," he repeated. He cursed the fire her beauty had lit in him.

At the campsite, Matthew showed Cece how he dug a pit and lined it with flat stones. Then he laid wood on the stones and lit the kindling. When he judged the stones hot enough, he carefully removed the fire, placing the burning coals in the center of his stone-enclosed hearth. He laid the clams on top of the hot stones. A layer of wet seaweed topped the shellfish, and the meal steamed for a while.

Throughout the process, Cece maintained a steady stream of questions, the most predominant being "Why?" Matthew was fascinated by her hunger for knowledge, dazzled by the ease with which she absorbed all he taught her. Finally, while they sat waiting for the clams to be ready, Matthew asked a question of his own.

"You said before you were bored and lonely in your father's house. How can that be? When I have gone to trade at the Country Store, I have seen women there in the early morning. That tall thin one with the spectacles and gray hair lives in the house, and the small Chinese spends his days caring for your father's carriage and horses. That seems enough people to keep you from being lonely."

Cece looked at the ground. She caught her lip between

her small white teeth, a tiny frown marring the smooth expanse of her brow. Finally she looked at Matthew, and the sadness in her eyes took his breath away, as did the tears pooling in the evergreen orbs.

"It's my father," she said, her voice so soft Matthew had to strain to hear her.

"I missed him so when I lived in San Francisco. . . . I decided I would return home when I finished my schooling and be of help to him at the mill." She twisted her slender hands in her lap. Matthew reached out and covered them with his own. She looked at him, then turned one hand and laced her fingers through his. The warmth and trust in her gesture reached Matthew's heart. He kept his silence, offering her the gift of his patience and understanding.

"You see, he is a very busy man. He always was. But now the arthritis has nearly crippled him, and his hands are so gnarled I cannot conceive how he managed to write all those long letters he sent me."

Cece's eyes reflected sympathy for her father as well as her own anguish. Matthew waited for her to continue.

"But he keeps pushing me away. He does not even speak to me, except to ask for the salt at the dinner table or to say good night. I—I have no one else, Matthew. . . ."

As her voice died softly Matthew longed to offer her a place at his side. He wanted the company, the support of someone so anxious to give, to love. But as he heard her story he was even more aware of the chasm between them. He was certain her father would have plenty to say if he suspected Cece was speaking with Matthew, never mind if he ever saw their hands twined thusly.

Matthew's gaze dropped to the two hands. The contrast between their skin illustrated his doubts. She was white, a Boston. He was Indian, a S'Klallam. He gently moved his fingers out of her clasp. Attempting to mask his withdrawal to spare her any further pain, he bent to the pit where the clams steamed.

Now he knew why she'd been so hurt when he sent her away. He also knew why she'd fought him this morning. She needed someone to care for, to care for her.

Much as he wished he were the man to do so, he could never be.

"Are you hungry?" he asked, hoping to distract his wayward thoughts.

A long trembling sigh escaped Cece. Matthew glanced in her direction and saw her square her slender shoulders. She smiled a brave smile for him, and his heart came close to breaking.

"Famished," she replied. "Are they ready?"

"Let us see."

With a long stick Matthew lifted the mass of seaweed he had set atop the clams to keep the steam about them, then drew out a couple of the hot delicacies. With a sharp knife he'd brought from his shelter, he pried one open and gave it to Cece.

"Here," he said, "try this."

Cece gathered a bit of her skirt in her hands to shield her fingers from the heat of the still-steaming clam. A bit of ankle peeked out from under the edge of her petticoat, and she noted Matthew's gaze riveted to the inches of pale skin. She blushed and rushed to smooth her skirt back with one hand, blowing all the time at the morsel in the shell she held in the other.

Hummingbirds seemed to rush into her middle at the heated look Matthew gave her—a look steamier than the clam she held. The liquid heat he'd inspired before overtook her, and she wondered if she'd ever be able to eat a bite. Her fingers trembled with excitement, and she dropped the shell.

"Oh . . ." she murmured, then bent to retrieve the clam.

Matthew had the same idea, and their fingers touched as each reached for the shell. He looked up. So did she.

In a second the forest about them seemed to hum with anticipation, as if all the animals and the plants longed for something, as if they were waiting for something momentous to occur. Cece felt the heat grow into a raging fire within her and knew without a doubt that only Matthew could douse the flame.

This was what the girls at school had spoken of in sly whispers. This was what Cece suddenly craved.

She smiled at him, certain her heart was in her eyes. He looked stunned by her smile, then took his hand away from hers.

Cece felt suddenly cold, bereft. Why? Why had Matthew backed away?

"Eat," he said, his voice gruff, and handed her a slice of what he'd earlier told her was camas and thistle-root bread.

Oh, no. She must have been too forward. Cece took the bread and stared at it. She had always been told proper young ladies did not show their feelings toward a gentleman. But she had been so sure Matthew felt the same way she did.

She ate swiftly and silently so as to escape from the now tense woods. She again fought tears. *Cecelia Scanlon, you certainly know how to make a fool of yourself.* Matthew had accepted friendship, and she had offered more. Something he clearly had no wish for.

"Well," she exclaimed, forcing a bright note to her voice, "I must be on my way back. Mrs. Quigley is never pleased when I disturb her routine. Thank you for the delightful meal. Oh, and for the lovely morning clamming also."

She turned and began to hurry from the campsite.

"Cece."

She turned. Matthew had stretched his hand out in her direction. "What do you want?"

Cece saw Matthew flinch as if she'd hit him. Then he swallowed hard.

"Take much care when you wander the woods," he finally said.

Cece nodded, unwilling to acknowledge the disappointment she felt at his words. She had hoped . . . Oh, never mind what she had hoped for. It was clear he had not hoped for anything.

"Yes, Matthew. I'm always cautious." Except with you, she thought, a sob tearing from her throat. With you, Matthew, I joyfully fling caution to the wind.

Chapter Five

———— • ————

The whispery sound of rain drizzling against her bedroom window awoke Cece early the next morning. She slowly opened her eyes and gazed at the sky. A pewter gray, it reflected the color of her mood ever since leaving Matthew's camp among the evergreens.

A trembly sigh shuddered through her. How amazing that the only color she seemed able to conjure was the green of the cedars in the woods. And perhaps the coal black of Matthew's eyes. Maybe even the deep bronze of his skin.

With a languid twist, Cece stretched against the mattress, moving every bit of her body in a slow, sensual motion. Just thinking of the warm tone of Matthew's skin brought back every exquisite feeling she had experienced each time he'd touched her. And when he'd held her hand . . .

The memory brought back the now familiar heat to her middle, and Cece straightened her legs under the covers. As she moved, the soft cotton fabric caressed her thighs, her nightgown a twisted tangle at her waist. The heat became a burn as she remembered the intensity in Matthew's eyes when he had touched her flesh, and closing her eyes, she saw how things could be between the two of them.

She saw the contrast between Matthew's dark rough-skinned hand and her own white satiny-soft thigh. She saw his fingers move, just the way they had against her hand, inching upward in a devilishly dangerous manner. She felt prickles of excitement everywhere his hand moved, nearer and nearer to her secret parts. *Oh, Lord!* The heat . . . If that hand were to reach its goal, would she be able to survive such a moment? Or would she just burn with longing, never reaching the unknown, craving the withheld knowledge?

She saw Matthew's broad, powerful chest and wondered how it would feel to lay her head upon his firm flesh. To rub her cheek, like a cat, against that gleaming expanse of manly muscle. To run her fingers over it, exploring the differences between her full curves and his chiseled planes. How would it feel to have that right?

With otherworldly clarity, Cece saw every intimate movement, felt every inner awakening. She gasped when the sting of desire spread through her body, claiming the sensitive flesh of her breasts. The fine handkerchief linen of her lightweight nightgown rasped against the tightened crests of her bosom and brought to mind the wicked wish to know Matthew's touch there. Trembling, she saw Matthew's dark hand cup her breast—

A sharp rapping at her bedroom door and Mrs. Quigley's announcement of breakfast abruptly broke into Cece's wanton thoughts, causing a stinging flood of embarrassment to rush to her cheeks. The daydreaming just did not seem to stop. This time she had indulged in thoughts of Matthew, *intimate* thoughts of Matthew, despite his obvious wish for no more than uncomplicated friendship. If he were to guess at the sort of fantasies she wove, he would most likely not want even the friendship they had discussed.

Sadness set in. What was she to do now? Not only did Father not want her around, but Matthew had made it abundantly clear that he felt she belonged in the mill manager's mansion. Everyone seemed to feel that way. How unfortunate that she did not.

"Oh, nonsense!" she exclaimed, sitting upright with purpose. With a quick glance around the room, she stood, looked out the window, and refused to allow such melancholy. "By da . . . da—" She listened for Mrs. Quigley, and hearing nothing outside her door, she firmed her fists on her hips and swore. "By *damn!*"

A hot flush filled her face, and she forced herself to keep from covering her lips at the swear word. This was the first time she ever uttered such a thing, and it had sure felt good.

"He-hell and damnation!" That felt even better.

She was not going to stand for being locked away in this eerily empty mansion. Wanting to feel the essence of Port Gamble Bay, she walked to the window. She opened it and took a deep breath, practically tasting the rich, damp earthiness created by the pervasive dampness outside. The leaves carpeting the forest floor would be squishy and matted down into the soil by the time she went back into the woods.

Leaning out, she twisted her torso to face the weeping sky. The gentle tears pouring from the clouds bathed her face, blessing her with their freshness. When she righted herself, a wild tumble of red-gold curls covered her face. As she pushed it back away from her forehead, she remembered the way the sunlight had polished Matthew's midnight-black locks. They had looked glossy, silky, inviting. Cece had longed to test that texture as she did now.

She shook her head at such foolishness. Lifting her chin, she squared her shoulders and frowned. "No more. He wants a friend. An occasional acquaintance, then, is what he shall have. *I* have better things to do than mope over a man."

Just what it was she had to do escaped her, but she was sure she should not waste time wanting what she would never be given. She would find something worthwhile to fill her life.

After such a momentous conclusion, choosing what to wear paled in importance. Uninterested in what she found inside her wardrobe, she pulled out a plain gray skirt and a white cotton cambric blouse with slim sleeves. Without much fuss, she donned plain white cotton undergarments, and then the colorless items she had chosen. Instead of leaving her hair loose, she tied it back into a severe knot at the base of her neck, forgoing her colorful ribbon ties. Her clothes would no longer color her life; purpose would now paint her days.

Bending to button her boot, she caught a glimpse of the tablecloth Mrs. Sanders had given her. With a baleful glare at the sewing basket next to the cloth, she refused to frustrate herself further and welcomed the growling in her belly.

In the silent dining room, Cece helped herself to a steaming bowl of oatmeal, grousing over Mrs. Quigley's uninspired choice. Then she smiled. The porridge was as interesting as the housekeeper herself.

Soon, though, Cece's displeasure turned to delight when she spied the covered bowl of fresh wild strawberries. After breakfast, followed by a bracing cup of Earl Grey, she decided to try the contents of Father's well-stocked library once again.

Time passed. The rain continued to fall. Despite the lure of Jane Austen's *Emma* open on her lap, and with the murmur of the rain at the window, Cece soon found herself lulled into a dreamlike state. When she gave her thoughts free rein, they rushed to Matthew, just as she longed to do.

How she wished to spend the day by his side—

No! Anger came in a flash.

"Cecelia, this just won't do," she chastised herself. "You can no longer mope and think of that man. Rouse yourself and *do* something."

She strode to the bookshelf and stuffed *Emma* back into her proper place. She then went to the window, but the dismal day helped her mood not at all. In frustration and fear of going stark, raving mad, she began to pace the highly polished hardwood floor. "You will not think of him again. You will not think of him again."

Again and again she repeated the words, underscoring them with her determined pacing. The more she paced, the more firmly ingrained Matthew's image became in her thoughts. If only there were something to capture her interest. But she was so alone, not a friend—

Mrs. Sanders! She would visit Mrs. Sanders. To be sure, the elderly woman was not Matthew, but going to him was an option Cece would no longer exercise.

Cece ran up the stairs to her room and donned her straw boater and a warm cape. Although it was late spring, the cool, misty drizzle bore an uncomfortable chill. She descended the stairs, fastening the navy cape's clasp at her throat. She stopped at the brass umbrella stand by the massive front door and took a black alpaca-cloth umbrella to protect herself from the inclement elements.

Dashing to the carriage house, her protective boots sinking stickily into the sodden ground, she came to a breathless halt. "Lee!" she called. "I need the carriage this morning. Could you ready it for me?"

In seconds, Lee Fung's face appeared around the side of Father's carriage, his good-humored smile the brightest part of Cece's morning. "Missy Cece! Velly good, you go. No good day. Lee Fung get horse."

Lee Fung's rather ragged chatter accompanied Cece all the way to the Sanders residence. "Please wait for me, Lee," she said once he had brought the conveyance to a halt. "I wish to visit with Mrs. Sanders, but I don't suppose I shall stay too long."

Lee Fung shook his head, his smooth braid swinging freely about his shoulders. "No wolly, Missy Cece. Lee fine in he-ah," he answered, pointing to the elegant carriage with its silver appointments and rich leather cushions.

Cece smiled, silently acknowledging how much she had missed Lee Fung's cheer all those years in San Francisco. Under the umbrella's protection she made her way up the short walk to the front door. The cold brass knocker, dripping with rainwater, slipped from her fingers, clattering loudly.

Moments later the door swung open. "Cecelia! What a pleasure. Do come in, child." Mrs. Sanders stepped aside, waving Cece in to the small entry hall. "Here. Hand me those wet things. On a day like today, you're likely to catch your death in this gray, wet wilderness."

Cece complied with her hostess's wishes, smiling at the older woman's dislike of her beloved Washington Territory. "Mrs. Sanders, I would wager that after you have been in Washington for no more than one year, you will have come to love it nearly as much as I do."

Mrs. Sanders lifted her silver head, aiming a sharp glance at Cece. "I very much doubt it, Cecelia. Very much."

Cece smiled. "And still I do not. But we shan't argue, let us just wait and see."

Mrs. Sanders shook her head but did not offer any further argument. She shook the umbrella over the small, flower-patterned rug that graced the dark wood floor and sniffed at the mess the water made. "May Li!" she called. "May Li, I am afraid I need your assistance once again."

Cece turned to see a rotund Chinese lady enter the vestibule, a large wad of rags in her hands. Her slanted black eyes twinkled merrily, and a smile broadened her already wide visage.

"He-ah, Mississ Sand-ell, I do it. You sit. Your bones bad today."

Cece was amazed at the gentle bullying the merry little lady could manage. Even more so, she was astounded at how well the rather formidable Mrs. Sanders took to being bullied. Then she realized the two women obviously understood and respected each other, which was clear from the caring look they exchanged when Mrs. Sanders made her painful way to the small parlor.

Cece watched her friend cope with her infirmity in a dignified manner, and her admiration for the lady grew ever more. "It is perhaps a poor day for me to visit, is it not?" she asked, worried that her presence might tax Mrs. Sanders too much.

Mrs. Sanders shook her head. "No, my dear. There will never be a poor day for you to visit me. Anytime shall be the right time. Please remember that."

After settling herself gingerly on the brown brocade settee, Mrs. Sanders slipped a pillow behind her back and placed her feet upon a needlepoint-covered footstool. A sigh of relief escaped her lips. With another of her characteristic nods, Mrs. Sanders turned to Cece, those pale blue eyes missing not a thing. "Now. What is it that troubles you, Cecelia? And do not try to deny that you are troubled, I clearly see it in your eyes."

Cece glanced up. Dare she speak to her friend about Matthew? She studied Mrs. Sanders, trying to divine her reaction. No. She had best not.

"It is, of course, this matter with Father. Last night I felt like an unwelcome stranger in what is supposed to be my home. I . . . I have become convinced I should have stayed with my aunt in San Francisco."

Cece looked down at her twisting fingers and forced them apart. At the first sign of a tremble on her lower lip, she caught the quivering flesh between her teeth and silently urged herself to remain calm.

Mrs. Sanders shook her head, *tsk-tsk*ing for emphasis. "Yours is a rather sad situation, my dear. But tell me, what do you really wish for with your father?"

The pointed question made Cece pause. What did she want with Father? She wanted to be his friend. To gain his respect, to feel welcome in his presence.

In spurts and starts, she put these thoughts into words. "I guess . . . I want a family," she finally said in summation.

Mrs. Sanders nodded her understanding. "You cannot be faulted for that." Leaning forward, she picked up a tiny silver bell, and with a slightly shaking hand she rang it, its clear tones filling the air with a welcome cheer.

In seconds May Li appeared at the doorway, a tray laden with cups, teapot, and tiny sandwiches in her hands. "Is velly bad day, no?"

Without waiting for an answer, she turned and left the parlor, closing the door in her wake.

Mrs. Sanders chuckled. "Now you can see why I did not need to supply my son with linens, or anything else for that matter. That lady knows everything, does everything, even before one knows one needs it."

Cece smiled. "She is a treasure, isn't she?"

"Pure gold," Mrs. Sanders responded. "Not like your father's Mrs. Quigley, I assure you."

Cece shuddered theatrically, then leaned forward to place a pair of the ham-filled diamonds on a plate. "As Sister Marietta would say, the saints preserve us, and heaven forbid!" Then she laughed, too.

Mrs. Sanders nodded. "That laugh, dear child, is the best thing I have heard today. I am glad you came. When shared, troubles are generally halved."

"When put that way, I must agree," Cece answered, her feelings for the elderly lady growing deeper each time they met. How she wished Aunt Prudence had been more like Mrs. Sanders. Or that Father were not quite so taciturn.

"Have you thought of perhaps taking over some task which is too bothersome for your father?"

Cece was startled by Mrs. Sanders's question. "No, I guess I haven't. Then again, I don't know if Father would accept my assistance. He has rejected it before."

"No, no, dear. I mean, just do the job and don't even speak of it to him."

Cece considered the scenario Mrs. Sanders painted. "Well. It *might* work, except that Mrs. Quigley is so efficient a housekeeper, she anticipates everything that must be done. Like May Li, but with a far less pleasant disposition."

"Too true."

Mrs. Sanders took a sip of her tea, and Cece bit into one of the delicate sandwiches on her plate. The smoky, salty flavor of fine ham filled her mouth, delighting her senses. With relish, she finished the tasty morsel, then the other, finally helping herself to yet another sandwich, realizing she'd spent so long moping in the library that the noontime meal had passed her by.

After draining her cup, Mrs. Sanders set it back on its matching porcelain saucer and continued to ponder the situation. "There must be something. . . ."

Cece shrugged and pressed the damask napkin to her lips. "I agree, but just what could I do—"

"I know!" Mrs. Sanders exclaimed. "I know just the very thing. He is retiring, is he not?"

"Why, yes, in July," Cece answered with a nod.

"And his work at the mill has always been uppermost in his thoughts, has it not?"

Cece nodded again, but before she had a chance to speak a word, Mrs. Sanders continued.

"Why do you not arrange for a retirement ball? A grand celebration of his years of faithful service to Pope and Talbot?"

Cece could not speak, the prospect so daunted her. After a few moments she regained her breath. "Me?" she squeaked.

"Why, of course, you. It is the best way to show your father that you have become a responsible adult. You can plan the entire event, become acquainted with the people he has associated with for most of his life. In short, show him how well you fit into his world."

Cece considered the idea, pursing her lips in concentration. "That sounds lovely, Mrs. Sanders, but the truth is, I would not even know where to begin."

Mrs. Sanders waved a blue-veined hand through the air. "That, dear child, is why you have me. I hosted numerous soirees for my departed husband. And although we find ourselves on the fringes of civilization here in this . . . this territory, I contend that a ball is a ball no matter where it is held."

Cece stared at Mrs. Sanders, half-horrified, half-fascinated by her preposterous idea. But the lady's calm assurance never wavered, and Cece began to gain confidence from her friend's absolute certainty.

"Do you really think I could?"

"Cecelia, my dear, you can do anything you set your mind to. Anything, child."

Cece felt a sudden pang. Anything? she wondered. Could she even win Matthew over to her way of thinking? Cece blushed, remembering just exactly what she *had* been thinking earlier that morning.

"Anything?" she repeated out loud.

"Anything," responded Mrs. Sanders.

"And you shall help me?"

"Every step of the way."

Cece drew in a deep breath. She squared her shoulders and ordered her mind to set stray thoughts of Matthew where they belonged. In the past, the soon-to-be-forgotten past.

It was time to face her future. "Very well, Mrs. Sanders. As long as you tell me what I must do, I am willing to try."

Mrs. Sanders shook her head. "No, no, dear. None of this 'willing to try' nonsense. You shall do it. Period."

"I . . . shall . . . do . . . it. I shall . . . do . . . it. I shall do it!" Cece chanted, each time gaining more confidence.

The door to the parlor suddenly opened wide, and in came Dexter Sanders. "Miss Scanlon! What a pleasure to see you again." A bright smile lit his fine features, and a gleam of admiration filled his golden gaze. "I could not help but overhear your assertion. Precisely what is it you shall do?"

Cece faltered, coloring at his obvious interest.

Mrs. Sanders reached over and patted Cece's hand. "Go on, dear, now that you have reached a decision, it will do you good to speak of it out loud."

Cece smiled thinly. "I shall host a retirement ball for Father, Dr. Sanders."

The doctor thought a moment, then dipped his head in a gesture of respectful acknowledgment. "A marvelous idea. He always has expressed pride in his career. A ball would be a fitting tribute to his work. And please call me Dexter. Dr. Sanders was my father."

Cece blushed again, uncomfortable with the offered intimacy, one which, due to her friendship with the man's mother, she had no acceptable way of refusing. "And I am Cecelia," she conceded, unwilling to allow him the more private Cece.

Dexter smiled in appreciation of her acquiescence. When he made a move to join them for the remaining tea and treats, Cece decided she would feel more comfortable taking her leave.

She rose, smoothing the folds of gray serge over her hips. "I must be off. If I am to plan this event, I must seek out Father and gather a list of the people he would most like to invite. And I must do so immediately."

Dexter stood. "Fine," he said. "Let me fetch my carriage."

"Oh, no," Cece answered, shaking her head, dismayed at the thought of having her plan so readily derailed. "That will not be necessary. Lee Fung brought me earlier and agreed to wait for me."

"Yes, he did. And that is what he told me," Dexter said. "But when I arrived, I told him to go on home. I need to stop by the Country Store today. Since it is next to your father's home, I can escort you home. Forgive my presumption, but I do wish to enjoy the pleasure of your company."

His earnest apology and visibly sincere wish to be with her smoothed the irritation she felt upon hearing of his high-handed behavior. And since the two other men in her life did no more than make her feel unwelcome, Dexter's attention was truly flattering.

Mrs. Sanders did nothing to hide her delight. "Do go on, Dexter. Escort the child home." She smiled, and Cece could almost hear the wedding bells ringing in her friend's mind. If she were not careful, this could turn troublesome. Especially since in Dexter Sanders's presence she felt none of the excitement, the heat she had felt from the very first time she saw Matthew. She now knew she craved that fiery sort of attraction, and she would wait until it came her way again.

"Well," she said slowly, "since you are going in that direction and you did leave me otherwise stranded, I have no choice but to accept your offer."

The smile on Dexter's face faltered as he registered her message of censure. Cece felt a surge of compassion. Only yesterday she had experienced the same sort of blow to her hopes, and she realized it must have been just this difficult for Matthew to find a way to extricate himself from her unwanted attention.

But now she was determined to face her future, and Matthew had no place in it. Once again she forced herself to put him ruthlessly from her thoughts.

After a flurry of good-byes, Dexter held the umbrella over Cece's head, and they splashed their way to the plain black carriage waiting at the street. They drove away, conversing idly about the misery of the constant Pacific Northwest drizzles, agreeing they posed the only detriment to the magnificent land they called home.

As Dexter slowed the horse upon their approach to the store, Cece remembered her latest disastrous attempt to embroider. She had hopelessly tangled the red silk for the roses, and since they were at the store anyway, she might as well purchase another skein. "I will come in with you, Dexter. There is something I need."

Her companion smiled. "Let me help you down," he answered, offering his hand.

Once on the street, Cece took the mahogany umbrella handle and held the covering over Dexter's head while he secured the horse. While she waited she looked around her, noting various new homes, their fresh coats of whitewash striped in rivulets of rain. As she turned toward the doorway of the Country Store, her stomach dropped as heavily as a pile of cedar logs, and she froze. Oblivious to the cool drip from the sky, four Indian men stood in a cluster by the door. She noted quickly that Matthew was not part of the group.

Her foolish heart beat in a rapid roll from just the thought that she might see him again. *Silly thing,* she scolded. As Matthew had said, they were too different, they belonged in two separate worlds.

Still, Cece could not stop the rush of warmth brought on by the rich memories of yesterday. The four strangers also had black eyes, which made her think of the most uniquely intense gaze she had ever known. Eyes that had told her Matthew wanted her company as much as she wanted to be with him. And yet that mesmerizing gaze must merely have been an Indian trait. Matthew had not had the same sort of longings she had.

Dexter's touch at her elbow startled her. "Shall we?" he asked, leading her to the door.

Cece felt the gaze of the four Indians send an icy quiver of anxiety trailing down her spine. At that moment she was infinitely glad of Dexter's presence at her side. Strange, she thought, she had never felt this sort of nervous discomfort around Matthew, no matter how piercing a look he had sent her way.

Then again, Matthew always bore an air of dignity, of inner strength and righteousness. A man such as he could always be trusted. Neither the color of his skin nor his heritage could change that.

Dexter helped Cece step through the doorway into the establishment. Her eyes took a few minutes to adjust to the dim lighting, but soon she was able to study the large room. The crowded jumble of items overflowing the shelves was familiar from her childhood days. So, too, were the rich scents of spices, damp wood, and fresh tobacco. Once again Cece felt the welcome she had longed for on that trip up the coast.

On their voyage about the store, her eyes came to a shocked halt when they reached the counter at the very

back of the room. There, his back to her, stood a man with
long, straight black hair. Loosely hanging to graze proudly
set shoulders, the locks looked as inviting as they had in
the woods the day before.

There was no mistaking that bearing, that inner strength
Matthew radiated by the simple virtue of being the man he
was. And even in a poorly lit crowded room, his masculinity
was almost tangible.

Cece stood still, helpless to look away, to move, even to
breathe, lest he leave and she find herself unable to drink in
the wonder of his presence. He was dressed in white man's
clothing today. He'd loosely tucked a plain white shirt into
a pair of dark blue trousers, but neither item of clothing
was able to hide the powerful build of the man who wore
them. Cece easily remembered how he looked without his
proper garb.

Then he turned around. It seemed to her as if he'd done
so in response to her perusal. After all, his gaze flew straight
to her, crashing instantly, heatedly, with hers. He, too, stood
motionless.

Matthew had felt someone's gaze on his back as if that
person had reached out to caress him, to touch him with a
tender caring he had never before experienced. He should
have known it was her. He turned, his eyes meeting Cece's,
and all the sensations he experienced on the beach the day
before came rushing back in swirling, frothing waves of
desire.

His body tightened, his loins hardened, and he was glad
to be dressed in Boston clothing today. His loinstring would
never have hidden his reaction to Cecelia Scanlon.

Because he did react to her, in a more powerful way than
he had ever reacted to any other woman. Damn! That he
should feel this way about a white woman . . .

For a small eternity all save Matthew and Cece ceased
to exist. The store, the shelves filled with staples, even the
people who had been at their side only moments before,
vanished, as if by an act of the gods. The world shrank
to encompass only Matthew and Cece in that moment suspended in time. Their eyes, one pair black as midnight, the
other green as the forest at high noon, locked in eloquent,

intimate communication. The echoes of unfulfilled passion rang off their furiously beating hearts.

Cursing, Matthew tore his gaze away from hers. He had once again fallen under the spell of the forbidden; Cece's pristine beauty had mesmerized him. What damnable manner of weakness was this that befell him each time he found himself in Cecelia Scanlon's presence?

When he saw Dexter Sanders place his hand upon Cece's waist, an unfamiliar burst of rage stole his breath. His insides roiled as he watched his friend touch Cece. Worse yet, he had to withstand the knowledge that his friend had the right to do so, when Matthew himself craved to be the only one.

Madness. Pure madness.

Through the boiling red haze of jealousy, Matthew heard his friend's voice greet him. He forced onto his lips a polite grimace—one could never call such a gesture a smile—and extended his hand in greeting.

"Dexter," he said. "How have you been?"

Matthew saw Dexter's gaze fly momentarily to Cece, and the smile that grew on the doctor's face caused the jealousy to twirl the coil of envy within his gut tighter. He clenched his fists.

"Fine," said Dexter, oblivious to Matthew's reaction. "Very, very well."

No doubt, thought Matthew, Dexter's well-being came from his intentions toward the young beauty at his side. And Matthew was helpless to stop the longing he felt for her.

With a nod Matthew acknowledged Dexter's words. He cleared his throat, hoping to ease the feelings of futile frustration tightening his voice.

"I have again spoken with my uncle," Matthew said when he felt sufficiently in control. "Although he is set in the old S'Klallam ways, he does listen to what I have to say. He no longer rejects all my suggestions."

"That is progress, Matthew. I believe we can convince him to allow me to provide medical attention to your people. I know I can help."

"As do I, Dexter." Undoubtedly many of his people's ways were far better than the Bostons' ways, but so, too, were many of the Bostons' talents worthy of acceptance. Matthew hoped to lead his people to where they could blend the best of both worlds.

Both worlds . . . Matthew looked at Cece and was surprised to find compassionate understanding in her expression. Her intelligence and the genuine interest she had in everything about her were merely two of her more endearing traits.

"Forgive me, Matthew, Cecelia," said Dexter, blithely unaware of the tension Matthew knew stretched taut between Cece and him. "I have been remiss in my manners. Cecelia, this is my friend Matthew. He is the future chief of the S'Klallam people in nearby Nuf-Kay'it. Matthew, this is Cecelia Scanlon, Edward Scanlon's daughter."

When he saw that Cece was about to announce their acquaintance, Matthew knew it was in her best interest that such a fact not be revealed. "A pleasure to meet you, Miss Scanlon. Are you visiting your father on holiday?"

Matthew watched Cece's eyes widen in surprise at his words. Then she clamped her full rosy lips into a tight red line and gave him a sharp shake of her head. "No, sir, I'm here to stay. Port Gamble is where I belong."

Matthew felt more than heard her determination, and recognized the message she had sent him. Perhaps she did belong in Port Gamble, but Port Gamble was a far different world than his village across the waters of Teekalet.

He nodded. "Welcome, then, Miss Scanlon."

With a regal tilt to her colorful head, fire flashing in the depths of her green eyes, she accepted his words. "Thank you, sir." Turning to Dexter, she smiled. "I must find red embroidery silk. I shall be but a moment."

Matthew watched her walk away and felt a lonely chill surround him. It was as if the sun had just left, leaving the world empty, shrouded in a colorless fog. Which was a fanciful absurdity, he thought, since the day had been misty, drizzly, and gray since early in the morning. But he could not quite shake the odd sensation her departure caused.

He managed a few moments of additional polite dialogue with Dexter, then with a final glance in Cece's direction, he bid his friend farewell. He went to the door and, with his hand on the fingerprint-mottled brass knob, pulled it slightly ajar.

A burst of raucous laughter greeted him. Luke and his three friends still loitered outside the store, ignoring the drenching rain. Each held in his hand a brown paper-wrapped bottle of whiskey, bottles that Matthew was certain were missing a goodly portion of their contents.

" . . . an' a tasty morsel she is, wou'nt ya say?"

More laughter answered Luke's assessment of the woman they were discussing. Matthew wondered for a moment who might be the current object of Luke's interest. But with Luke's next words, a chill of fear pierced Matthew's heart.

"She's mos' likely their sof'est spot." Luke swiped a hand across his lips, catching a glistening amber drop of liquid fire. "Bes' way ta teach 'em a lesson, I say."

Luke's companions heartily agreed with his observation. Matthew cast a glance behind him to where Cece stood by the counter at the back of the store, transacting business with Mr. Potter. Perhaps he was foolish to think Luke and the others spoke of her; not every man would find her devastatingly appealing. But the unease remained. As the manager's daughter, she could represent a weak spot in the mantle of power held by the logging company.

But when Matthew faced Luke again, he saw his long-time friend glance toward the back of the store. An unholy smile lit Luke's face as he nodded in silence.

After interminable moments he again faced his companions. "A ver' good lesson."

Chapter Six

———— • ————

Invoking all the curses he knew, Matthew stepped outside.

"Matt'ew!" Luke called in greeting. "Have a drink wi' us."

Before he reached his friend's side, Matthew smelled the acrid stench of alcohol, thick and heavy about the men despite the early hour. "The day is young for that. Or are you celebrating once again?" he asked, curbing his disgust.

Luke had the grace to look ashamed when reminded of the night he had invited Matthew to join his sodden celebration. He shook his head, waving the hand with the paper-wrapped bottle in a gesture that encompassed the mill town. "Nothin' to celebrate. They have it all. An' gettin' more, as I hear."

Matthew lifted an eyebrow. "What do you hear?"

"They're buying more forest. Bureau of Indian Affairs has been sniffing around," said one of Luke's companions, one who seemed less inebriated than the others.

"Damn Dawes Act," muttered another, lifting his bottle for a goodly swig of comfort.

Matthew felt before he saw Luke's gaze upon himself. When he met it, he was filled with compassion for his friend's anguish. Rage and fear battled in the depths of Luke's eyes.

"No," Luke said, his voice harsh, husky. He turned to look again in Cece's direction, and Matthew's insides tangled into knots of fear. "No," said Luke once again, a note of belligerence creeping into his voice. "Not so long's they have a lush . . . lush-iously delightful weak spot."

He raised his bottle to his lips and gulped down yet another measure of whiskey. Matthew, fearing for Cece's safety, fearing for his tribe's future, realized that in his current state Luke was beyond reason. He had to bide his time and speak with his troubled friend at a more propitious moment.

A far more pressing task was keeping Cece safe from a group of drunken avengers. The only way he knew to do this was to keep her in his sight until she was either safely back in her father's home or until Luke and his companions left the area. He felt certain Dexter Sanders would pose no deterrent when Luke decided to act upon his tortured emotions.

To this end Matthew found his way to the shrubbery on the near side of the mansion's gardens, next to the Country Store. A gigantic pine provided him with shelter from the strong wind that had kicked up since the time he entered the store. At least the drizzle had virtually stopped.

He did not have long to wait. Leaning against the tree trunk, Matthew watched Cece handily dispatch Dexter, not allowing him any intimacy the man might have hoped for. Matthew sighed in relief. He did not know how he would have borne witnessing a kiss between his doctor friend and delicious Cece Scanlon.

His gaze roving her curvaceous figure, he watched the object of his desire do exactly the opposite of what he would have hoped, not to mention what he would have expected her to do. Oblivious to the elements, Cece took a walk down the garden path.

After stroking a few early irises that waved wildly in the wind, she moved on to a lilac bush from which she tore off a fragrant cluster of purple blossoms. She brought the flowers to her face, to breathe deeply of their luxurious scent. Closing her eyes, she rubbed her cheek against the blooms, and Matthew would have given anything to have her rub against him in just such a fashion.

The familiar tightening in his lower body elicited a ripe curse for his weakness toward the woman who'd caused it. How could such an innocent evoke such a powerful reaction?

Slowly she lifted her eyelids, which appeared to be weighted down with the sensual pleasure of experiencing the flowers' perfume. In the brilliant green depths she revealed, Matthew found the answer to his question. Cece possessed an innate sensuality, all the more potent for its innocence. And it was to this untapped wealth of feeling that he so rapidly responded. She was magnificent, and he caressed her with his gaze.

With the sprig of lilac still held to her cheek, she took a few steps in Matthew's direction. She came to a halt at a bench no more than paces away. She was so close that Matthew heard the slight rustle of her gray skirt against the dark blue cloak she wore. He could smell the lilacs and the voluptuous sweetness of Cece's rose scent.

His senses came alive in her presence; her presence called him, drew him to her side like a foolish moth to a flame. He abandoned his shelter and without a word sat on the bench. She did not flinch, almost as if she'd been expecting him.

"Why did you not let me tell Dexter we'd already met?" she asked with a hurt look in her eyes.

Matthew met her gaze. "I told you before. It is best if the town does not know we are friends."

Her lips curved into a wistful smile. "Friends?"

Matthew understood precisely what she meant. He felt a pull for her far stronger than friendship, as he knew she did toward him. But it was wrong to pursue feelings that could bring disastrous consequences. "Friends," he answered, his voice firm with conviction.

She turned away from him, staring at the lumber mill sprawled across the shore before the mansion. She sat silently, still rubbing her face with the fragrant flowers.

Matthew's gaze followed the gallant line of her fragile neck, the shell-like curve of her ear, the tightly bound knot of hair at the base of her head. "Cece . . ." he whispered.

Ever so slowly she turned to face him. Her evergreen eyes swam in twin pools of tears, and her plump lips quivered. Matthew felt a rush of tenderness for Cece, an overwhelming need to hold her, comfort her, caress her.

Her sweet scent of roses sang a siren song to his desire.

He drew closer to her, finding a matching want in the secret depths of her eyes. Closer . . . closer to her seductive warmth, her tempting mouth.

With a gossamer touch, Matthew kissed those soft, soft lips. Again he rubbed his mouth across hers, watching her eyes drift shut, watching a blush paint her cheeks with passion. She sighed, her breath warming his lips, inviting him to come closer still.

He molded his mouth to hers, feeling the satin smoothness of her flesh. A tiny tremor shook her, and Matthew enfolded her in his arms. With the very tip of his tongue he explored the contours of her lips, tasting the essence of Cece.

Such pleasure! Just as her scent was sweetened with flowers, so Cece's taste was sweet with innocent passion. Matthew teased the sensitive inner flesh of her mouth, asking for entrance into the depths he craved to explore. At first her lips were pliantly receptive to his touch, but then, as he wooed her with tenderness, with passion, she opened up to him.

A ragged moan tore from Matthew's throat at Cece's welcome. Gently he explored her mouth with his tongue, intoxicating himself with her flavor. He felt the tremors in her slender body intensify, and he slowly and deliberately caressed her velvety tongue with his.

As the kiss went on and on Matthew felt consumed by the overwhelming need to delve ever deeper into Cece, to join their bodies as intimately as he'd fused their mouths. His body burned with the awareness of Cece's heated passion.

Out of nowhere a deafening thunderclap broke the moment, startling them into awareness of a different sort. The Pacific winds had picked up, turning into wild whips that lashed their bodies with the now rapidly falling rain. They had not felt the wind or felt the wetness. They had not seen the darkening sky.

A rare act of nature brought them back to reality, however. Thunderstorms were uncommon to the area, their power and energy occurring only a time or two each year. But just such a storm broke the sensual spell that had bound

Matthew and Cece in a blissful embrace.

Matthew brought his raging desire under control. He ran a trembling finger over Cece's kiss-puffed lips, then whispered, "You are a rare and beautiful treasure, one that must be protected against all harm. Go on. Go inside. The storm is rapidly worsening."

Cece took a dazed look around. Indeed the winds were whipping needles off the cedars and leaves from the shrubs. Wet strands of hair slapped her face while the cold water freshened her flushed cheeks. For the first time she did not feel rejected as Matthew urged her to leave his side. Oh, no. Not at all. This time she felt special, cherished.

She smiled. "I shall see you again—"

"Soon," he said. "Go. You should change into something dry."

"Good-bye," she whispered.

He nodded, never turning his intense eyes away from her. As she ran toward the porch Cece felt his gaze upon her, caressing her, heating her the way his fiery kisses had.

When she reached the porch, she paused to catch her breath and shake the water from her hair. As she grasped the brass doorknob she turned to Matthew one more time. He must have thought she had gone inside, for he stood still, his face lifted to the storm, his head and shoulders thrown back. She felt as well as heard the ragged cry that broke from his throat—a cry filled with pain and perhaps frustration.

Cece wavered at the door, wanting to run to his side, to throw her arms around him and offer him her comfort. But remembering the other times he had so ruthlessly pointed out the differences between the two of them, she curbed her impulse and opened the door, unwilling to suffer yet another rejection.

The ornate mirror in the vestibule reflected the tumultuous emotions she had so recently experienced. Her eyes sparkled with unshed tears of longing for Matthew. Her lips, swollen from his kisses, pouted for more of Matthew's passion. Her hair, pulled out from its severe knot, curled in a voluptuous cascade of golden fire down her back, just like the rivers of desire that had poured through her veins.

Her arousal was obvious; she looked well kissed. A sweetly secretive smile played upon her lips. What a joy to know Matthew's kiss! She turned toward the stairs, and with a hand on the polished cherrywood banister, she began the climb to her room.

"Hmmph!"

Cece closed her eyes, imploring God and all Sister Marietta's saints for the patience and strength to deal with Mrs. Quigley. With her hand still on the railing, she faced the older woman, noting the censorious expression on her pinched features.

"Was there anything you needed, Mrs. Quigley?"

"A bit more respect for your father's position, miss. You look like a wanton floozy."

Cece gasped, then gritted her teeth. Sparing another glance for the housekeeper, she resumed her climb. At the top step she came to a stop. Without turning, she spoke in a low, calm voice. "At least, Mrs. Quigley, I know myself to be truly desired. Something I take great pride in."

As she uttered the outrageous comment Cece realized it was true. Matthew had awakened not only her deepest, most sensual passions, but also an intense pride in her femininity. She walked to her room, shoulders back, head held regally high.

She was a woman, capable of igniting turbulent passion in a most virile man. She ran her tongue over her still-sensitized lips and drank in the mysterious flavor of Matthew. Her flesh tingled at the feel of the raspy texture of her tongue as she remembered the seductive roughness of his.

She laughed in exultation. She would always remember the velvety roughness of Matthew's desire.

His head thrown back, his face lifted to the skies, Matthew let out the cry of dismay that had built up in him since he had first discovered Cece. Now, after finally tasting the forbidden fruit, he craved far more than the heated kisses they had shared. He also knew that his position with the tribe and hers as Edward Scanlon's daughter would force him to deny himself what he so desired.

The wild winds whipped the water ever harder against his hot skin. The stinging sensation served to cool him some, but it did nothing to dampen the hunger he felt for Cece. A hunger he would have to set aside in favor of keeping her safe, of keeping his tribe out of danger.

You bear a great responsibility to the tribe by nature of your birth, his conscience said, burning with the fire of torn desires.

If he so wished, he had the right to succeed his uncle as *ssia'm.* But he had no right to do so if he indulged his longing for such an obvious representative of his people's enemies. A passion such as his was surely as dangerous as Luke's fiery temper.

Luke's rage had become a danger to himself and the tribe, not to mention the danger he posed to Cece. She was an innocent victim of an impossible situation. She was born a white woman, the daughter of the man who most vividly represented white rule in this corner of the S'Klallam world.

Matthew needed to think, to fashion a plan to protect all that he cared for. Perhaps advice would help as well. As usual, he headed toward Uncle Soo-moy'asum's cabin.

In the dark coolness of the forest, Matthew thought again of the way Cece had felt in his arms, how voluptuously she had filled them, how well her shapely curves had molded to his sharper angles, how delicious she had tasted.

He ran his tongue over his lips, still able to taste the caress they had shared, a caress as wildly heated as the fire in the bolt of lightning that had torn them apart, as passionate as the fury of the wind that had driven her into her father's home. Right where she belonged.

You should never have succumbed so readily to the lure of her pretty pink lips.

His conscience stung him with the harsh recrimination. He had to turn his back on his desire and face his future within the tribe.

But you will never find another woman to fill your arms the way Cece does.

"Noooo . . ." he ground out, cursing his taunting senses and his conscience. He *would* find a more appropriate companion for a leader of the S'Klallam. That is, he would once he got rid of memories of the scent of Cece, memories of her sweet taste, memories of the rich plumpness of her breasts swelling against his chest as his tongue had swept her mouth.

Damn the woman anyway. She wasn't even near him, and his trousers felt tight against his straining flesh once again.

He looked up, surprised to note he was almost at his uncle's home. He had best harness his renegade libido because his uncle was capable of reading him better than anyone else. He tugged at the waistband of his pants, trying to disguise his arousal, and not succeeding, he slipped his hands into the pockets, shrugging in defeat. "Damn," he muttered.

She makes your blood run hotter than any other woman and has you cursing more than you have in your entire life.

A wry smile began at one corner of his mouth, and soon Matthew was laughing in rich, sonorous peals. Although he did not have to act on his feelings for Cece, he did acknowledge that she was the most fascinating, tantalizing, and surely the most infuriating female on earth. His mischievous memory brought up a picture of Cece haughtily informing him that "Port Gamble is where I belong." He relished another laugh and thought of the saucy way she had of walking, how her rather plain gray skirt had peeped out from under her somber navy cape.

She is a treasure, he thought. But never to be his.

Cece would be someone else's to cherish, and he, Matthew, would make sure she remained safe enough to ensure that future for her.

He walked the last few steps to his uncle's home, his ardor doused by reality. He knocked. The door to the cedar plank house opened almost immediately. His uncle's leathery, heavily lined features softened into a smile. "Welcome, son," he said, standing aside to allow Matthew entrance.

Matthew nodded in greeting. "I need to talk with you. I hope I am not disturbing."

His uncle closed the door, then laid his thin, wrinkled hand on Matthew's shoulder. "No, son. You could never disturb me. Speak, I can see trouble in your eyes. It is Luke again, no?"

Matthew sighed. "Luke always seems to be trouble."

Uncle Soo-moy'asum nodded sadly. "Too many demons chase that young man. I am saddened to see he is unable to do battle against them."

"He does not want to try." Matthew shrugged. "What he does with his own life is his concern, but when he endangers the tribe, and other innocents as well, then it becomes my concern."

The King spread his hand in a gesture of resignation. "He battles the inevitable."

Matthew nodded. "I can sympathize. I, too, wish our situation were different, but there are more white men than there are of us, Uncle. Luke does not accept this simple fact. The power of their numbers, their wealth and weapons, leave us only the alternative of learning to live with them."

Matthew watched his uncle's eyes cloud over. The older man remembered days when the S'Klallam had truly owned their lands, their destiny. It hurt to see the beaten pride of a man to whom the gods had given a surfeit of the emotion. With his shoulders held firmly upright, the shaman walked to the middle of the cabin, stopping before the hearth.

Uncle Soo-moy'asum sat before the small fire, inviting Matthew to share in the warmth. As he sat down, Matthew felt overwhelming love and respect for his kinsman.

"So," the elderly man said, his piercing gaze intent on Matthew. "What has Luke done?"

"Nothing yet," Matthew responded, then went on to relate what had transpired at the Country Store. "I fear for him and for what may come of his uncontrolled rage."

The King of England stared at the glowing coals. "You are right, my son," he finally said. "Wild anger will bring that boy much pain. If he carries out his evil intentions, all our people will also suffer. That young woman does not deserve to become the object of Luke's revenge, either. You must see that she remains unharmed."

Matthew jerked his head up. "Me?" he asked, dread hitting him in the pit of his stomach. "How do you propose I do so?"

"Son, I see much you do not speak of. That young woman matters more to you than an innocent victim would. The light in your eyes changes when you speak of her. Protect her, for your sake and hers."

Shaking his head, Matthew stood. "I . . . I can't—"

"Yes, you can. And you must."

"But—"

"No, Matthew. Think clearly. Luke, despite his love of the Bostons' whiskey, holds you in high regard. If he is to listen to reason, it must come from you, even if you are rivals for the leadership of the tribe."

Matthew walked to the door of the cabin, relieved to be charged only with speaking with Luke. He turned to bid farewell to the King. "Very well," he said, willing to take on this relatively easy task. "I will talk to him."

His uncle's gaze stopped him. "More must be done, and you know so. Do not try to escape what the gods hold in store for you. Face your future, son. No matter how impossible it appears at this moment."

Unease rendered him weak for a moment. He hoped his uncle would not ask of him what he most feared he would. "What more do you feel I should do?"

Uncle Soo-moy'asum came to stand at Matthew's side, laying a callused hand on his nephew's tense shoulder. "This Cece, this innocent young woman. You must keep her safe. Do not allow Luke to get close to her, lest we all come to regret his deeds."

Matthew drew a shuddering breath. He knew what his uncle would ask of him. He also knew where his own baser passions lay. Proximity and desire would lead him down a path he believed would bring his own ruination. Yet he could not bear the thought of Cece coming to harm.

"How—" He cleared the thickness from his throat to try to voice the question he did not want answered. "How do you propose I do this?"

"You must keep her in sight until Luke comes to his senses. It is the only way. It is fortunate you are her friend already. Friendship will ease your task."

"Somehow, Uncle, I fear friendship will only make my task that much more difficult."

After a moment of thought his uncle spoke. "Perhaps. This may well be the test you need to show you the inner strength you possess."

His uncle's words still ringing in his ears, Matthew left the cabin. A test of his inner strength. Yes, he needed to know himself better in order to lead his people effectively. But how could facing the seductive temptation that was Cece show him the sort of chief he could become?

Were it only a physical attraction he felt for the mill manager's daughter, he was sure he could escape unscathed. But Cece tempted him on all levels. Yes, they shared friendship, as well as a rich consuming passion. But beyond that, he felt the need to comfort her when she was hurt, to protect her from harm, to share with her the special events that made life worth living, the feelings that made him the man he was.

These many layers of attraction frightened him. Lust was simple, easily sated. What he had felt on that bench in the middle of a rare thunderstorm was complex, insatiable. It had felt frighteningly close to another, deeper, far more potent emotion.

It was love he feared.

Chapter Seven

———— • ————

After an afternoon spent with memories and fantasies, Cece made herself enter the dining room in a far more sedate fashion than her giddy emotions would have had her do. She sat at her place and sniffed appreciatively. If anything could redeem Mrs. Quigley's other troublesome qualities, it was her talent with food.

"Dinner smells wonderful, does it not, Father?" she asked, determined to establish some sort of dialogue. "What do you suppose Mrs. Quigley prepared?"

She lowered her gaze to the napkin she was unfolding over her lap, and then glanced over at Father through the cover of her thick eyelashes. She noted his apparent surprise at her renewed attempt at conversation, but also saw that his scowl was not nearly as pronounced as on prior occasions. Perhaps he was becoming accustomed to her presence in his life.

Father cleared his throat. "Roast duckling, I believe." He lifted the silver cover off the platter and verified his guess. "Indeed it is."

Cece crossed her fingers under the table. Perhaps she could keep this exchange going for a bit. "Mmm," she murmured, "my very favorite. What is yours?"

Father continued to stare at the steaming poultry. Cece frowned. This was not the way the scene should be played, she thought.

"Father?" When he looked up, Cece noted once again that

odd expression in his eyes, but she was unable to fathom what it meant. Then Father shook himself and glanced in her direction.

"Yes, well. Ahem! You said something. . . ."

Cece crossed another two fingers. "Yes, Father, I asked what yours was."

Father shook his head, clearly mystified by her query, still bearing a hint of unidentifiable emotion in his eyes. "My what, Cecelia?"

Cece laughed. "How silly of me. I meant, I would like to know what your favorite food is."

Father stared at her, a quizzical look erasing all vestiges of that other disturbing expression. "Poached salmon, although why on earth you care to know escapes me."

Cece blushed, then sought to express herself as eloquently as possible. "I've been gone for such a very long time. I missed you all that while. Now I'm here, and I realize I hardly know you. And I want to. Very much."

Leaning over her table setting, Cece prayed her sincere emotion would reach her father, would perhaps touch his heart and make it respond in kind. Her plea had brought an irksome twitching to her nose and the gloss of tears to her vision, but she would not cry. No, all her tears had been shed in the privacy of her room.

She blinked hard, clearing away the moisture that had pooled in her eyes. When she did, she saw Father lift his deep green eyes to gaze fully at her, then close them rapidly. He kept his eyelids tightly shut; then his face blanched, and his lips tightened, as if he were holding something in.

Was she so ugly that even her own father could not bear the sight of her? Was that what kept him from treating her with greater warmth? True, she would never be the exquisite beauty her mother had been, but she had never noticed any horrible deformity on her face. After all, she only had a smattering of freckles. But to a man who had known beauty such as she had seen in Mother's portrait, perhaps freckles *were* a deformity.

She had to be sure to check in her washstand mirror when she went up to bed tonight.

Father slowly opened his eyes. He kept his gaze upon his

plate, then took a long, shuddering breath. "I understand, Cecelia. I, too, scarcely know you."

Cece winced at the ragged quality of Father's voice. What had she done to cause such a reaction? She had only asked for the opportunity to become better acquainted with him. They were, after all, father and daughter.

Then she remembered her plans. Perhaps with a more tangible matter to discuss, Father would feel more at ease around her. She took a deep breath, all the while sending a silent prayer of supplication to any of Sister Marietta's saints who might be inclined to offer Cece the assistance they always provided for the nun.

"I had the most marvelous idea," she began. "Well, *I* didn't, not just on my own, that is. Mrs. Sanders had the idea, but it is now my pet project."

Father carved a luscious slice of fragrant meat off the duckling's breast. "Yes . . ."

Cece held her plate out to him, breathing the rich aroma. "Thank you," she said, picking up knife and fork. "I know how you have loved the mill and working for Pope and Talbot all these years. Now that you are retiring, I—*we* thought it would only be fitting to hold a retirement ball in your honor. In recognition of all the years you have devoted to your work."

Father's eyes flew open, meeting Cece's expectant gaze with astonishment. So much astonishment, it seemed, that his hand trembled, causing him to drop the generous portion of duckling he'd been about to serve himself.

"Cecelia, how kind of you to think in such terms." Looking flustered, Father rapidly retrieved the meat, set it on his plate, then rang the small silver bell to beckon Mrs. Quigley. The housekeeper entered the room without a sound and, after Father's nod in the direction of the food stain on the tablecloth, proceeded to wipe away most of the juices.

Cece swallowed a mouthful of meat, dabbing at her lips with the heavy damask napkin. "Well, I do know you well enough to recognize how diligently and well you have always worked. I also know you take great pride in your work. It would stand to reason that you would like to celebrate the good in all those years."

Father cast another glance in her direction, this time without that strange gleam in his eyes. Cece set her napkin back in her lap and crossed some more fingers. If this kept up, she would soon have to start crossing her toes as well.

With a nod, Father picked up his wineglass and took a lengthy drink of the golden liquid. "It seems you are quite sensitive, Cecelia."

Cece blushed at his words. She would indeed take them in the form of praise. "Thank you, Father. I would love to share that special occasion with you, and I shall handle all the preparations myself. You need only be the guest of honor. Oh, and I need you to prepare a list of the guests you wish to invite."

A frown appeared on Father's brow. "Can you handle such an undertaking? You are young yet."

On the verge of a lie, Cece prayed for divine absolution. "Surely you know the good sisters prepared me to handle such affairs."

Father lifted his right shoulder, not quite seeming to believe, not quite seeming to doubt. "Prudence seemed to feel the sisters were quite thorough."

A smile bloomed on Cece's lips. "See? That is precisely what I just said. And Aunty Pru agreed." She really ought to send Aunt Prudence some gift; she had unwittingly aided Cece's cause in ways the fussy old lady never would have imagined.

"So," she continued, "we are agreed then? We will have a wonderful, lovely party?"

"Yes, Cecelia. It would be a great honor to have my daughter host a ball commemorating my years of service to Pope and Talbot. I shall draw up a guest list immediately."

"Oh, Father, this has truly been the most marvelous day of my entire life."

Father's ball and Matthew's kiss. What more could she want?

During the next few days Cece did not stray far from home. She divided her time between the library table, where she had set out all her lists, and the Sanderses' crowded little parlor. At first she found all the minute details that needed attention to be quite daunting. Then, with Mrs. Sanders's aid, she lost the fear she'd initially had for the entire undertaking. Too soon, though, all the work began to be just that: work.

At the oddest moments fragments of conversations she had had with Matthew would enter her thoughts, stealing her attention from the matters at hand. Other times the scent of damp earth would bring to mind the essence of the forest, Matthew's home. And, on this especially windy afternoon, the passionate gusts brought to her body the remembered heat of Matthew's desire.

On the mansion's porch, as she gazed out through the rain toward Matthew's camp, her body thrummed with unfulfilled desire. How she longed to be in his arms again. How she yearned for his touch, his hungry kiss. . . .

As she stared, wishing for something as unattainable as the moon, she thought she caught sight of someone in the bushes at the edge of the garden. Strange, she thought, who would skulk around in weather like this?

She walked to the top porch step, held on to a cleverly turned spindle, and leaned out into the rain, trying to get a better look at the shrub in question. She was sure the movement she had seen was not caused by the wild winds, and she didn't think any of the larger forest animals would be dumb enough to venture this close to town, much less in this gale.

A stronger gust of salty air slapped her face, drenching her with the drops it carried. She ran her hand down her face, wiping away some of the moisture, then licked her lips dry. The tang of sea salt on rain filled her senses.

A pin flew out of her chignon, bouncing down the front of her blouse, and a long wet ringlet of rosy gold hair followed it across her breast. Her skirt kicked up about her shins, whipping them. She shivered, then again wiped her hands across her face to push back the wet curls plastered onto her skin.

And she thought animals dumb to venture out? What was she doing if not braving the fury of the elements? But, filled with a certain reluctance to enter the house, she stayed on the porch a few seconds longer, admiring the untamed beauty of nature.

The steely-gray sky showed no sign of clearing. The pointed tops of the evergreens bowed to the power of the gusting wind while the oaks and maples relinquished to it much of their gay green garb. When she noted how far even the trunks were swaying, she thought of Matthew's rush shelter. How would he fare in this sort of weather?

With a last longing look toward the woods that hid his home, she began to walk to the door. But with her first step she stumbled, having noticed another jerky motion in the thicket by the woods.

For some strange reason she thought of the four Indians she had seen at the Country Store the afternoon Matthew kissed her. The shivers running down her spine felt the same as those she'd experienced when the four men had stared so closely at her.

At that thought she yanked open the door and rushed inside. She didn't quit running until she was in her room, before her wardrobe, surrounded by her safe, familiar belongings. How she wished she could talk of her feelings with someone.

But who could she tell that four Indians frightened her, but a fifth one made her long for his kisses? The presence of four Indians had made her press closer to Dexter Sanders, yet the other one had enticed her to escape the safety of her father's home to spend the day in his company. Who could she tell of the way the gaze of the four Indians had scared her speechless, whereas the intensely intimate looks Matthew had bestowed upon her were precisely what she most longed to see?

Matthew . . . When would she see him again?

Casting off the strange mixture of anxiety, fear, and longing, she changed into a quilted apple-green robe and cozy slippers. Picking up her hairbrush, she surrendered to the lure of the view outside her window and sat on her vanity stool, gazing idly into the trees, brushing out the tangles in her wet hair.

Another movement in the bushes drew her attention, and she caught her breath.

Matthew!

He took another step away from the cover of the shrubbery and stared toward the street, his fists planted squarely on his hips. The rain had completely drenched him, making his white shirt and navy trousers cling to his muscular frame.

Cece remembered how she had felt to have those powerful arms cradle her to his strong chest, how those thighs had felt rock hard when Matthew had drawn her closer for a kiss. As she watched Cece envied the raindrops. How she wished to caress him as they did, or at the very least to kiss away the wetness they left on his high cheekbones, his noble brow, his firm lips.

"Cecelia!"

She started at the sound of Father's voice, then turned away from the window, dropping her hairbrush on the floor. "Ye-yes, Father?"

"I have another name for your list."

"Coming."

She took a hesitant step toward the window for another glimpse of Matthew. Turning, she looked at the bedroom door and thought of the progress she had made with Father. Although she could not go outside and join Matthew—she did not know if he would even want her to—she longed to stay by the window and gaze upon him as long as he stood so near. To watch and dream of a time when they could again be together, share another embrace, another kiss. . . .

From the hallway she heard Father's labored steps. "Coming, Father," she said again, casting a last look of longing at the man standing in the rain.

Matthew stared through the rain, wondering where Luke had disappeared to so rapidly. He had been in the bushes, then he had vanished. At least Cece had had the sense to go back inside the house.

Perhaps now he could return to his shelter. His life was in an uproar; daily he spied on Cece, following Luke anytime he came near the mill manager's mansion.

After watching his friend, Matthew was fast running out

of sympathy for the man. Yes, he understood the frustration, but not everyone planned and plotted wrongdoing when life dealt them an unfortunate hand. That was precisely what Luke was doing.

On the other hand, each time Matthew caught sight of Cece, his feelings for her became stronger, his desire more heated. Watching her visit the Sanderses was torture of the most exquisite sort. The only thing worse was when Dexter escorted her home, and Matthew watched from the cover of the foliage to see if that dreaded kiss developed. So far, thankfully, it had not. But not because Dexter did not wish for it; Cece was adroit at avoiding the apparently unwanted attention.

Hardest to accept was how seriously she had taken his directive to stay away from his camp. In truth, he wished for her company in the privacy of the forest, in the shade of the evergreens. Fool that he was, he longed for the danger in Cece's nearness.

A movement in a window on the second floor of the elegant mansion caught his eye, and he started.

Cece!

There was no mistaking the gleam of fiery gold in her hair, the sassy tilt to her head. How lovely she looked, standing behind the glass, rivers of water silvering her image. The blurry sheets of rainwater lent her a mystical softness, making her look ethereal, like some creature the gods had created to shelter in a world of liquid sparkle.

Matthew smiled. There was something very special about a woman who was able to make him think along such fanciful lines. No doubt Cece was special, and that was why he was here in the first place. To protect her, keep her life safe so she could continue to be special.

With a final glance toward her window, he noted sadly that she had gone. He had to find Luke anyway, and perhaps try to speak to him before the man drank enough whiskey to get him into trouble.

Walking toward the Country Store, Matthew caught sight of the bench under the cedar, and his step faltered. For a second he allowed himself to dream of a time when he and Cece could perhaps be together again, share an embrace, another kiss—as long as he remembered that his dream must remain only a dream.

Later that afternoon, after the winds had died down, Cece peered over the rim of her teacup and nodded in agreement. She carefully set the translucent porcelain cup on its saucer away from the risk presented by the mountains of paper on the dining table, and smiled at Mrs. Sanders. "I think that is by far the best idea. We'd best go to Seattle and listen to the ensemble. How else will we know whether they play well enough to hire them for Father's party?"

"Then we have a date," Mrs. Sanders said, rapidly writing something in her small black notebook. "We should leave Thursday afternoon and spend Friday morning checking the progress on the special linens you ordered. And perhaps you can squeeze in another fitting for your gown?"

Cece thought a moment. "Why not? I realize Mademoiselle Monique is quite capable, and the good Lord knows the woman took the most detailed measurements imaginable, but a mannequin is not a woman, and I most certainly am."

Mrs. Sanders laughed in her soft raspy way. "You are getting there, my dear. Tell me, how are the responses to the invitations coming along?"

Turning to the sideboard by the dining table, Cece pulled out a carton. "Look for yourself. No one has declined."

"That is remarkable, dear. It means we shall be dealing with a good number of guests."

"And every last detail had best be just so, right?" Cece gave her friend a mischievous wink, having learned how precise Mrs. Sanders was. "That is why, on Friday evening, we will attend the the soiree at the Hotel Seattle."

A knock on the heavy door prevented Mrs. Sanders's response. Mrs. Quigley entered at Cece's acknowledgment and announced Dexter's arrival.

"He wishes to leave immediately," she added. "Something about an emergency, and he needs your assistance, Mrs. Sanders."

Flustered, the elderly lady stumbled as she reached for her silver-handled cane. Cece caught her friend's elbow, preventing a calamitous fall. "Thank you, dear child. I don't know if I shall ever become accustomed to Dexter's need for my help. I assure you I never reconciled myself to the need to aid my departed husband."

"Don't fret, I am sure he knows what you are able to do for him. And whatever the problem is now, you shall handle it admirably." Cece shook her head. Strange how such an able woman so easily lost her composure at the thought of dealing with ill people. But, she admitted, everyone had fears and faced them differently.

After Mrs. Sanders's departure Cece informed Mrs. Quigley of the plans for Thursday and Friday, noting the woman's continued poor disposition. Anything and everything brought frowns to her brow. Why couldn't Father have chosen a more cheerful housekeeper? After all, May Li was astonishingly efficient and a joy to know.

To Cece's surprise, Father decided to accompany her to Seattle, along with Dexter and Mrs. Sanders. At the last moment Father insisted on Horace Grimes's company as well. So on Thursday afternoon the odd group filled the Scanlon carriage as Lee Fung saw to their various pieces of luggage.

Sitting by the carriage window, Cece allowed her gaze to roam over the gardens, eventually lighting on the bench. As she stared at it she felt the longing begin. Several days had passed since the rainy evening when she'd seen Matthew standing at the edge of the woods. She wondered how he was, even where he was.

A burst of laughter at the door of the Country Store caught her attention. Almost as if in response to her stray thought, Matthew called out a farewell and stepped away from the store. He strolled down the street with a parcel in one hand. The tightly coiled strength of his body was evident. The swaying of his muscular arms, the bunching and flexing of his thighs, the breadth of his shoulders, all declared his strength, his masculine vigor.

The now familiar heat filled Cece, making her wish even more for Matthew's company. She watched him approach, wanting his touch, craving his kiss. When he came abreast of the carriage window, he turned, fixing his ink-black eyes on hers. She gasped.

Then she could not breathe, could not move. The carriage and her companions ceased to exist. Just as it had at the Country Store, the world around Cece and Matthew vanished, leaving them suspended in a sensual web of awareness too strong to break. They gazed into each other's eyes, mutely expressing what they were not free to voice.

Cece gasped at the rich emotion evident in Matthew's black eyes. It seemed to mirror the longing she felt, the need to be near him and share the feelings he awoke in her. Her gaze still locked with his, she gave free rein to her thoughts and imagined the conversation they might have.

I have missed you, Matthew would say.

As have I, Cece would answer.

I remember our kiss, he would add.

As do I, she would admit.

I want you.

So do I.

Only when the carriage jolted to a start, did her daydream abruptly end. Cece leaned out the window, striving for a last glimpse of the man of her dreams as the carriage rolled off. What she saw was not what she expected. The heated tender expression on his face had changed. In its place blazed anger, perhaps even disgust. What had she done to inspire such a look? Tears filled her eyes, and she wished to be done with all this nonsense of the ball. Then she would again be free to set things right between herself and Matthew, to erase the look of rage from his dear face.

In a haze of pure jealousy, Matthew watched the carriage drive Cece away from his side. He had watched Dexter help her inside, then climb in after her. He had noted, too, how her father's assistant had fawned over her, trying to insinuate himself between Cece and Dexter. Matthew had not been able to walk up to her and carry her far from both her would-be suitors.

His masculine pride wanted her for himself, but common sense told him he had no claim on her.

At least he had seen the longing in Cece's expression,

an emotion that mirrored his own feelings. He clung to the memory of desire blazing madly in her deep green eyes while the carriage slowly took her away.

Try though she might, Cece could not muster even the slightest interest in the evening's performance. For all she cared, the musicians could have played a series of sailors' ditties. All she could think of was those last few minutes by Father's house when Matthew had stared at her. She could have sworn she had read his every thought, his every desire in his midnight-colored eyes. And all they'd seemed to speak of was of his desire for her, only her.

Now here she was, caught between two arthritic dears and two perfectly acceptable men, longing for a third man Father would surely not consider suitable for her. Worse, she was forced to listen to music she would again hear in a few weeks. At least she had so far been able to decline to dance with both men; she refused to leave Father and Mrs. Sanders alone.

This ennui was all Matthew's doing. Even in San Francisco she had been able to take more interest in Aunt Prudence's social affairs than she was able to dredge up tonight. Despite the lovely room, sparkling with the light from an enormous crystal chandelier, and the gay crowd enjoying the excellent dance music, she was in no mood for a party.

"You look absolutely lovely tonight, my dear," said Mrs. Sanders for the third time when the musicians stopped for a much-deserved rest.

"Thank you." Cece thanked her for the compliment for the third time.

She glanced down at herself. At least she liked the gown she was wearing, Cece thought, and it did in fact look quite good on her. The mirror in her hotel suite had shown her how the deep green taffeta set off the color of her eyes, and the red in her hair had gleamed like polished copper. She wondered what Matthew would have thought of her in this elegant dress.

She jumped when she heard Father say her name. "Do go on, Cecelia. Dr. Sanders has asked you to dance yet again.

I assure you Mrs. Sanders and I can manage to entertain ourselves for a dance or two."

Much to her chagrin, Father cajoled and Mrs. Sanders teased until she acceded to one dance per man. Dexter was polite and quite an accomplished dancer. Mr. Grimes might not have been there. Given his rather weak leading, Cece could have just as well been dancing in the privacy of her bedroom.

After the dances, she exaggerated her exhaustion, only to see Dexter nearly trip over his own feet in his rush to fetch her a cup of punch. Cece fanned herself and sipped the oversweet drink.

Father, comfortably ensconced in a leather chair, turned to Dexter. "Well, Dr. Sanders, how is the health of Port Gamble as a whole?"

Dexter inclined his head in polite acknowledgment of the question and smiled. "Fairly typical, I would say. Most townsfolk are quite well. That is why I concern myself with the medical needs of the S'Klallam village."

Father started. A frown creased his forehead. "Those savages? Why would you waste your talent on them?"

Cece ground her teeth at her father's contempt for Matthew's people.

Dexter raised an eyebrow. "I find them to be far from uncivilized, sir. In fact, one of the more prominent men in the tribe, the man expected to be the next village chief, is quite insistent on convincing the tribe's shaman of their need for modern medicine."

Father waved Dexter's comment off with heavy disdain. "And well he would. I can see where he would find it quite advantageous to convince a fine physician to provide assistance to his people. I contend that one cannot deal effectively with heathens."

"Matthew is far from wild, sir." Cece noted Dexter's set jaw and the clenching of his fists. Apparently Matthew had gained quite a loyal friend.

Mrs. Sanders waved her lace hankie to capture the attention of the two men. "Edward!" she called reprovingly. "Matthew is a fine young man. He has been to our home on various occasions, and I am absolutely charmed by his wit, his intelligence, and his dedication."

Cece was so surprised that her mouth almost flapped open. Matthew? At the Sanderses' home? How had she managed to avoid meeting him there? Or did he avoid his friend's home when he knew she might be there? That possibility hurt.

" . . . quite well educated." Cece realized Dexter had continued his paean of Matthew.

"Very well read," chirped in Mrs. Sanders, nodding.

"Intensely . . ."

Suddenly she remembered the desire in Matthew's gaze as he'd looked into the carriage window. The passion blazing from the black depths after their devastating kiss. The intense attraction that had bloomed between them from their first encounter in the woods. And it was more than she could bear.

In the lull created by the intermission for the musicians, Cece stood. "Enough!" she cried. "I came here tonight to listen and find out if this ensemble is good enough for Father's party. It seems no one else is concerned with the tribute to his years of service to Pope and Talbot."

As she drew a breath she noted the deathly pall that had fallen over their corner of the room. "Furthermore I have heard all I care about this Indian paragon of virtue. If you continue to discuss your friend, I will make myself scarce."

She gathered a generous width of deep emerald taffeta and took two steps toward the salon's door. "If you will excuse me," she added for good measure.

Walking rapidly, nearly running, she fled the group. Like the length of forest green silk that fluttered about her heels, the crackling of the rich fabric of her dress followed her flight. A stranger or two turned their heads in her direction, but not finding anything of interest, they soon turned back to watch the musicians tune their instruments.

At Edward Scanlon's table, four sets of eyes watched Cece's disappearance in shock. Edward recovered his composure before any of his companions did. "Just what do you suppose got into that bewildering child of mine?" he asked.

No one knew what to respond.

Chapter Eight

———— • ————

Back in her bedroom the next afternoon, still fuming, Cece took just enough time to unpack the valise she had taken to Seattle, then changed into clothing appropriate for seeking out an elusive Indian.

She was damnably sick of being ignored by the important males in her life. She could swear by all the saints and apostles that Matthew had been avoiding her ever since that explosive kiss they had shared. And that was precisely the problem. How could he kiss her like that, then simply vanish from her life? That is, if she didn't count the time she saw him skulking in the bushes, and the time his hot gaze had scorched her in her father's carriage.

True, she had just about no experience with men, but she knew enough to sense that Matthew had liked that wild kiss just as much as she had. And the fire in his gaze had not been a figment of her admittedly overactive imagination.

She buttoned her pale green cotton blouse, tucked it into the waistband of her forest-green skirt, and took a quick peek into the mirror to verify that she looked acceptable. Not quite as elegant as she had looked last night, but she would do.

What would not do was for Matthew to avoid her. At the very least he had agreed to friendship. She was on her way to cultivate that friendship immediately.

She slammed the front door of the mansion behind her, hoping Mrs. Quigley's feathers would be duly ruffled. With purpose, she started off in the direction of Matthew's camp, but before she made it to the shade of the trees, she found herself nose to nose with the object of her ire.

"Well!" she exclaimed. "Skulking again, I see."

Matthew raised an eyebrow but did not answer.

"You know what I mean. I saw you that afternoon in the rain."

He shrugged. "Where were you off to in such a hurry?"

Cece planted her fists on her hips and glared at him. How had she thought that impassive face dear? "I *was* on my way to find a certain *friend*."

"I see."

She screwed up her eyes, trying to figure him out. She gave up. "What do you see? I was on my way to find you because I have a few questions to ask."

"Ask away," he offered without meeting her gaze, not seeming to care.

Cece was about to throttle him when she noticed him staring over her right shoulder. With a lightning-fast move, he grasped her arm and spun her to face the mansion. His breath hot on her ear, he spoke, his voice an angry growl. "You should never have come. Your father's housekeeper is watching."

More irritated still, Cece yanked her arm out of his grasp, waved to Mrs. Quigley, then faced him squarely once again. "So?"

Turning his face away from her, Matthew sighed, frustration evident in every inch of his masculine frame. A lock of gleaming black hair fell over his forehead, and before Cece could reach across to smooth it back, he raked rough fingers through it.

"You little fool," he ground out. "Your father hates Indians. Everyone knows that. And do you think for one minute that bat will not run to tell him she saw you speaking with me?"

A breeze off the bay drifted a stray curl down into her eyes, but she merely blew it away from her brow. "More fool you, Matthew," she said. "I told you once before that I don't care one fig who sees me talking with you. I meant every word I said."

She turned back, glancing at the window where the house-keeper had spied on them, but no one was there.

"She's gone," Cece said when she faced him again. "Perhaps now we can get on with my questions?"

Yet again, Matthew grasped Cece's arm. With firm determination, he led her deeper into the woods. If she didn't care about her reputation, not to mention her father's reaction, he did. He cared about everything that concerned the beautiful, irritating, maddening woman at his side.

He finally stopped near a fallen log and released her. "Ask me what you will."

Suddenly she seemed to lose all her fiery indignation. She sagged, reaching behind her to steady herself on the log, then sat down, spreading her skirt about her with jerky movements. She focused her attention on a pile of half-rotted leaves and bent to pick up a small stone from their midst. Delicate fingers traced its contours, and Matthew tried not to imagine how a similar caress would feel.

"Cece," he murmured.

She lifted her head, keeping her eyes shadowed by long, mahogany-colored lashes. "I . . . I thought you had agreed to be my friend." Then she sighed, and those ridiculously long lashes swept up, revealing crystalline tears.

Matthew felt her pain as if it were his own. "I did—"

"Then why have you avoided me?" she asked, drawing a shuddering breath. "I know you visit the Sanderses. I have been there quite frequently in the past few days. Surely we would have run into each other had you not expressly prevented it."

He couldn't avoid her now. She'd trained those brilliant green eyes on him, demanding—no, entreating—an honest answer. Yet he knew the only answer he could offer probably would not be acceptable to her.

He felt compelled to try. Sitting next to her, he clasped her hand between his. "There are many reasons why it would be best for you if we stopped meeting. Some of those reasons concern many more people than myself, so I cannot share them with you. But I know I would do anything to spare you more pain. I am afraid that because of the way your father feels, because of differences in our heritage, you would be hurt if our . . . friendship becomes known."

She blinked, and those brilliant tears drenched her eyelashes, bunching them into moist spikes. "You say you would spare me pain?"

Matthew nodded. This he could answer with all honesty. "Any way I could."

"What if you are the only one who causes me pain?"

Matthew closed his eyes. For a minute he could not face the sadness drawn on her features. He called upon the courage of his ancestors to help him continue. "Then believe me when I tell you I would rather cause you a small pain now than expose you to a greater wound later."

"And this is your decision?"

"Yes."

Suddenly she jumped up from her seat in her maddening, unpredictable manner. "You have nerve, Matthew! Do I not have a say in a decision that very much involves me?"

Her reaction left him speechless. The many facets of this woman would keep a man fascinated and exasperated for at least one lifetime.

"Your presumption puts me on a par with a doltish child. I resent your high-handed manner of making decisions. As an adult," she said, drawing herself up to her full height, "I take total responsibility for my decisions. And my decision is . . . ah . . . to go fishing today! With you."

Matthew shook his head, hoping that by doing so she might dissipate, like a figment of his fantasies. She didn't. She still stood before him, fists firmly on her hips, full pink lips pursed with determination, round breasts heaving with every breath she took.

She was magnificent!

And irritating.

And the most tempting sight Matthew had ever seen. He felt his loins stir at the same time a laugh built up inside him. He chose to indulge one reaction and stifle the other.

Cece watched Matthew throw his head back and laugh with a vigor that mesmerized her. Whatever she had done to earn such a unrestrained expression of joy was well worth her being its cause. "Does this good humor mean you will take me fishing? And you won't treat me like a leper anymore?"

She watched him slowly rein in his mirth. He graced her with a thorough, admiring look, then shook his head. "Yes, Cece, I will refrain from treating you like a leper, as you said. Mind, I never said I saw you as one. And yes, I will take you fishing."

Cece beamed with pleasure. "And you will show me how to cook what we catch?"

"As long as you share the meal with me." Amusement and resignation were evident on his face.

But at the water's edge, with a small harpoon in hand, Cece remembered their clamming expedition and wisely chose to set aside the weapon in favor of watching Matthew. After a few desultory attempts, he gave up trying to catch dinner. Soon he joined her on the warm sand.

Cece tried to hide the trembling thrill his nearness caused her by burying her shaking fingers in the dry sand. She scooped up a handful of the golden bits of crushed clamshell shot through with glittering crystals. Slowly she poured it into her other hand. The heat of the sun, captured by the tiny bits, caressed her hands.

Matthew's voice broke into her thoughts. "Where were you off to the other day?"

Cece's pulse quickened at the memory. "When you stopped by the carriage?"

Matthew nodded.

"To Seattle to listen to a chamber group. I needed to hire musicians for a ball to be held in Father's honor."

"You hired the ones you listened to?"

"Mmm-hmm."

"And matters are improving with your father?"

"Yes. Matthew—"

"Cece—"

Both looked up, their gazes locked, and intense feelings passed between them—remembered passion, unfulfilled desire, the sweet beginnings of need.

Matthew covered her hand with one of his, sending a shock through her now alert body. He pried each finger away to capture the sand she held. In a slow movement, a motion that seemed suspended in the clear sunshine, he extended his arm away from where they sat, opened his hand, finger by finger, and allowed the soft, warm grains to drizzle back to the ground. Cece's insides coiled tautly, her skin became sensitized, and her breasts tightened. A corresponding fullness deep in her womb made her feel ripe, mellow. And still she watched his hand.

With his other hand, Matthew gently wiped away stray fragments of glitter that clung to her fingers. "Cece . . ." he whispered, his voice, even to her inexperienced ear, filled with rich desire.

"Yes . . ." she answered, inviting what she had been craving for days.

Matthew didn't make her wait. With an expert ease, his mouth covered hers, heating her blood instantly, sending it flaming through her body in fingers of fire. Cece moaned at the welcome warmth, pressing her lips more intimately to his. Her response seemed to please him, for he growled low in his throat, then licked her lips with wild flicks of his wet tongue.

His pleasure emboldened her. She parted her lips, seeking the hot tip of his tongue with hers, touching then retreating, in a devastating dance. Matthew soon took the lead, and with pillaging ease he commandeered the kiss, sweeping her mouth at will, exploring secret places she never knew she had.

Moments later, when he nibbled at the corner of her mouth, Cece murmured her complaint, wanting more of the fullness of Matthew's kiss. She felt him smile, but he did not comply, so she felt compelled to slip her fingers into the thick richness of his long hair. She gripped handfuls of it and pulled his face back where it belonged.

Seeing how much pleasure his kiss had brought her, she took the lead this time, trying out her newfound knowledge on her teacher. She knew she proved to be an apt pupil when she felt the tremors running through his strong body as she plundered the depths of his mouth. Over and over again she savored his passion, and knew she would never get enough of the taste of Matthew.

Matthew welcomed Cece's boldness. Her sweet tongue

slipped into his mouth, caressing him with a thoroughness he had only dreamed of. Her passion was as heated and luminous as the color of her curls, as the brilliant green fire in the depths of her eyes.

Tightening his arms about her, he molded her closer to his body. Every inch of him was rigid with desire. He strained to take in all the passion she had to give, and she gave all a man could ever wish for. His loins burned for Cece, his flesh swollen and ready.

Cece whimpered softly when he sucked on her tongue, a sound so sweetly seductive that Matthew reveled in it. He felt the round richness of her breasts and knew he had to touch them. He caressed her side, sliding his hand ever upward, until he cupped one firm mound in his palm.

Cece stiffened at the new intimacy, but Matthew continued laving her lips with his tongue, and soon she was pressing more fully into his hand, the ruched tip of her breast taunting his fingers. He rubbed his thumb over her nipple, and Cece whimpered again, wriggling closer to him. He repeated the caress, then left off to undo the row of buttons running down her demure cotton blouse.

He took his lips from hers; he had to feast his eyes on the wonder of her nakedness. Through the sheer, lace-trimmed chemise, Matthew clearly saw the deep rose areolae surrounding the protruding tips. He cast a glance at Cece's face and noted the blush of passion on her cheeks, the swelling of thoroughly kissed lips, the desire in her heavy-lidded eyes. She took a breath, lifting the beauty of her breasts closer to Matthew.

He bent down and with hungry lips claimed the bud crowning her flesh. His mouth moistened the fabric covering while his tongue molded the cloth to her. He suckled, gently at first, and when she moaned her pleasure, with deeper, stronger pulls, he took her more fully into his mouth.

The scent of roses teased him. The pebbly texture of her hardened nipple taught him the extent of his hunger. The sound of the waves serenaded them while the sea gulls crooned above them. Matthew had never tasted anything so sweet, so seductive, so sensual. Cece's passion was full-blown, consuming, delicious.

Bit by bit a foreign sensation invaded him, from his feet, to his legs, then to his hips. He released the breast he had been feasting on and looked down.

"Damn," he muttered, frowning at the cold wave that had interrupted their pleasure. "Cece, it is getting late. The tide. Look."

Slowly she opened her eyes, desire still burning in her gaze. She reached a soft hand to his forehead, and Matthew closed his eyes to relish her touch as she smoothed his hair back. But too soon another wave lapped at his legs, reminding him of the time, their circumstances, and his responsibilities.

With a final look at the passionate beauty sprawled across his lap, Matthew shook off the dregs of desire. He slipped the pearl buttons on Cece's blouse back through the button-holes, helping her as her hands trembled too much to do the job. With a lingering touch, he placed a long curl behind her ear, not even trying to tuck it through the green velvet ribbon with which she'd tied the riotous mass away from her face.

He had to send her back. He had to go forward. And he could not find it in him to hurt her again.

"Go on," he urged. "I am certain the bat must have told tales about you already. We would not want the improvement between you and your father to go to naught."

Cece pouted. Matthew was right, though. If Mrs. Quigley had indeed run to tell tales to Father, she might have ruined all Cece had achieved so far. But she could not deny she would trade even that for the time she had spent in Matthew's arms.

"Even the loss of ground with Father would merely be a fair price to pay for the moments I spent with you," she confessed in a whisper, unable to speak any louder. The feelings Matthew had brought to life still rippled through her body. A brief breath of sea air rushed by her, sending a chill down her spine. She shuddered, allowing reality to set in. "You are right," she went on, a bit louder and steadier. "It would not do to anger Father any more than necessary. I shall see you again—"

The caress of Matthew's finger against her lips brought her words to a halt. "Don't, Cece. Do not make any sort of plans for meeting me. If it should happen, fine. I bear a great responsibility to my tribe, and at present that weighs quite heavily upon me. I *must* put the needs of my people before my own desires."

Cece felt the familiar anger at being pushed aside begin to boil up, but incredibly it was tempered this time by admiration for the man who selflessly turned his back on a passion as powerful as theirs. He truly was a strong man. She admired his strength, his integrity, but she didn't have to like the effect such admirable qualities had on her life.

She smiled sadly. "Very well. But if I wander the woods and should stumble upon you, I won't run away. Be forewarned."

The finger that had so softly rubbed her lips dropped away. "And I will not chase you off."

Taking a step forward, Cece stood on tiptoe and placed a gentle kiss upon Matthew's lips. "Thank you."

Noting the bemused expression on his face, she decided this was the best moment to depart. "And I will take care going through the woods."

At that, Matthew smiled, but said nothing. That was fine, she thought, he had already given her so much today. She'd spent an afternoon at his side, had received his kisses and caresses, as well as his promise not to chase her away. She would persevere to win his love and would not allow even him to turn her away from her goal.

He was her goal.

Matthew watched Cece walk away, and wondered if the sense of loss would ever ease. Strange that he should be so strongly affected by a woman he had known such a relatively short time. Nothing about Cece Scanlon fit any sort of pattern from his past experience with other women. He smiled despite the sadness he felt.

Needing to face the matter of the leadership of the tribe, Matthew walked slowly toward his camp. In Port Townsend, Chief Chet-ze-moka was dying. Before too long the S'Klallam would lose another leader. In Nuf-Kay'it,

Uncle Soo-moy'asum had stated his desire to pass the leadership on to a younger man, preferably Matthew.

Noting the lengthening shadows of the evergreens, Matthew pulled out some dried salmon and a chunk of camas-root bread. He spread a small amount of seal oil on the bread and began to eat. A handful of sweet, ripe strawberries finished off his meal.

He wiped the sticky juice off his hands, then lit the fire he'd earlier laid out in his stone hearth. Cool night winds came occasionally in June, making a man grateful for a smoldering blaze at his camp.

At the sound of a creak to his right, he looked up. What was that? At first he saw nothing; then Uncle Soo-moy'asum stepped out from among the trees. Relief swept over Matthew.

"Share my fire," he offered, gesturing.

Without a word, his uncle sat down and reached fragile hands toward the blaze. Then his bright black eyes focused on Matthew. "Come, son. Sit by me."

Matthew did so, wondering what had brought his uncle to his campsite at night. He did not have long to wait.

"There is trouble coming. The Bureau of Indian Affairs has sent two men to handle the sale of our land. Luke has spent the day drinking and making threats."

Matthew shuddered. "About . . ."

"Yes, about Miss Scanlon."

A sudden vision of Cece, bruised and disheveled with fear vividly painted on her face, took hold of Matthew's imagination. When he tried to breathe, he discovered a heavy pressure in his chest, as if someone had taken his lungs and squeezed all life from them. Nothing, nothing could happen to Cece.

With conscious effort, he relaxed. Tearing his gaze away from the small flames licking the charred chunks of wood, he faced his uncle. But the older man's expression was unreadable.

"That is unacceptable," Matthew managed to say in a rough voice.

Uncle Soo-moy'asum lifted his head briefly, then lowered it again in silent agreement with Matthew's words.

Matthew began to rise, dreading the thought of having to face a drunken Luke once again. But a firm hand on his forearm stopped him.

He turned to his uncle. "I am going to Luke. Why—"

"No. He is asleep in my lodge."

Matthew sat back down, surprised. Had matters become so dangerous that his uncle had felt the need to keep vigilance over Luke himself?

The grizzled head turned. The King of England's eyes pinned Matthew to his spot by the campfire. "He sought me, tried to convince me that his plan was the only way. He sat down and then fell asleep—which is fortunate, as I could not condone harming an innocent."

"Yes, fortunate," Matthew concurred. "But if all is under control, why are you here? You knew I was coming to you in the morning."

Uncle Soo-moy'asum shook his head. "No. In the morning you will go to Edward Scanlon. Warn him to keep watch over his pretty daughter. We cannot continue to bear the full responsibility."

A foul taste filled Matthew's mouth. Edward Scanlon. Cece's father. A dedicated professional at the Pope and Talbot mill. Avowed Indian hater.

Before he was fully aware of it, he began to shake his head. Then he consciously shook it so violently his hair whipped his cheeks. "No."

"You must."

"I see no chance at communication with someone whose mind is so completely closed to reason."

His uncle began to rise, a process hampered by a body worn by age. "As I already said, son, you must. By morning, I am certain, you will have come to agree with me."

"And I am certain I will not." Matthew hovered near his uncle, unsure whether to offer aid and run the risk of injuring the shaman's pride. In the end, his love for the King of England took precedence. Gripping his uncle's bony elbow, Matthew offered the needed support.

When Uncle Soo-moy'asum stood upright, his black eyes commanded Matthew's gaze.

"It has always been the most powerful part of your

nature, that which leads you to do what is right. Despite the price. It will be so this time as well."

His conscience arguing with his thoughts, Matthew watched the older man disappear into the dark shadows of the evergreens. True, he always sought to do his best, but dealing with Edward Scanlon went beyond the pale. In the midst of all the confusion reigning in his head, visions of Cece wafted from one thought to the next.

On the one hand, as his uncle had said, Cece was an innocent, and the tribe could no longer continue to bear the burden of keeping her safe from one of their own. Her father could provide her with all the additional protection she would ever need.

If the man was willing to listen to Matthew. Edward Scanlon was reportedly irrational in his dislike of Indians. So how was Matthew, a S'Klallam, to make Scanlon listen? How could he find the words to make the man take his warning seriously?

Damn his conscience! Matthew grimaced at what he believed was his greatest weakness. Here he was already thinking in terms of how best to deal with the bigot. He raked his fingers through his hair, frustrated by his own overzealous sense of duty. Then he smiled wryly.

Uncle Soo-moy'asum knew him only too well. After all, the man had raised Matthew, been the only father he had ever known. His father had died before Matthew turned one year old, and his mother had soon followed her husband. Matthew had never grieved for them; he had never even known them.

All his love and respect were held for the now elderly couple who had taken him in, loved him, and helped him to become a man. As always, his uncle's wisdom weighed heavily in Matthew's decisions, as did the shaman's uncanny knowledge of how Matthew's mind worked.

He laughed mirthlessly. Such irony. Tomorrow he, Matthew, would warn Edward Scanlon of the danger Cece faced. Matthew, the man who had come within seconds of stealing her virtue. Perhaps he should also warn Scanlon of *that* danger.

Crouching low to enter his shelter, Matthew rapidly took

off his shirt and trousers. He spread a thick bearskin over his bed of rushes and dropped heavily on it all. The scent of dried plants was a familiar one, as was the crinkling sound they made under his weight. The comfort of his uncle's lodge was undoubtedly one of the things he most missed since coming out to perform his mostly forgotten spirit quest.

At the thought of the reason for his presence in the woods, Matthew's conscience pricked him, making him determine to concentrate on his stated purpose immediately after the meeting with Scanlon. Once he laid the majority of the burden of protecting Cece where it rightly belonged, he would clear his mind of all but the future of the Nux Sklai Yem, the Strong People, the S'Klallam.

Concentrating on his responsibilities, he managed to avoid thoughts of Cece. Eventually he drifted off to sleep. But his dreams took over, subjecting Matthew to the most exciting, delicious visions of himself and Cece. He did not just dream of the two of them together, he enjoyed clear images of the most sensual of embraces, the most erotic of delights. The veiled glimpse of Cece's nudity that afternoon had merely served to whet his appetite for more of her.

Matthew awoke the next morning in a splendidly aroused and thoroughly frustrated condition. His daily dip in the icy waters of Teekalet did help a bit in calming his libido. But only a bit.

He dried himself off and dressed in his Boston clothes once again. A humorless chuckle escaped his lips as he thought of the reaction he would wrest from Edward Scanlon were he to appear at the opulent mansion wearing nothing more than his loinstring.

He thought carefully of how best to present the situation to someone who would not be the least receptive. If nothing else, Matthew knew he must maintain a calm demeanor, even if Scanlon lost control. The mill manager's temper was well known; he rarely lost it, but when he did, the results were universally devastating.

This time, though, Matthew knew that Cece's safety was at stake. That simple fact made his stomach writhe with anxiety as he went up the walk leading to the mansion.

He studied the newly built house. Despite his feelings toward the logging mill and his opinion of the manager, he admired the beauty of the mansion. The numerous sharp peaks formed by the roof were softened below by the graceful curves of fish-scale shingles. On the far side of the house he could just see the semicircular room that protruded from its main body. He wondered what was housed in that round room. He would probably never know.

Slowly he went up the front steps. At the top he grasped one of the daintily carved spindles and ran his fingers over the satin-smooth wood. With a gentle tap, Matthew let go the firm support for the porch roof and strode to the front door. Determined to succeed, he grasped the brass knocker. He rapped twice.

When the door opened, he saw the disapproving face of the woman Cece had called Mrs. Quigley. "I need to speak to Mr. Scanlon. It is urgent."

Matthew watched her raise her chin and study him down her rather long nose. She then sucked in her cheeks and pushed her lips out, almost as if she'd just bitten into an unripe berry. "You are the Indian who has been around Miss Cecelia, are you not?"

Matthew drew in a long breath. "We are acquainted, yes."

"Hmmph!" said Mrs. Quigley, then she muttered something that sounded like "Very well, I daresay." Matthew chose to ignore her very shrewish comment.

"I need to see Mr. Scanlon," he repeated.

"If it is about mill business, I suggest you wait until he goes—"

"It is of another nature. But, as I said, it is urgent." Matthew knew he had to get beyond this woman if he were even to try to deal with Scanlon. And from the way this encounter was progressing, the other would prove no less difficult.

Mrs. Quigley continued to stare at Matthew. Just as he was about to lose his patience, the woman waved him in, sniffing in a very irritating fashion.

Once he was inside the house, Matthew's step faltered. Nothing in his experience, neither at the village nor at the mission school, had prepared him for the extravagance of the mill manager's mansion. He turned his head from side to side, up and down. What he saw became spinning sensations of gleaming dark wood, brilliant-colored wool under his feet, a glossy mirror before him, and overhead, a lamp that sparkled like a million rainbows caught in a golden spiderweb.

The housekeeper took off down the hallway, her sharp footsteps alerting him to her departure, and Matthew hurried to follow. As he passed a highly polished dark wood credenza, the scent of the flowers arranged in a shiny glass bowl filled his senses. The fragrance of roses, a scent he associated with Cece, brought to mind the most inappropriate memory of the charms he had discovered under her plain green blouse.

He shook his head slightly in an effort to wipe out the image of Cece and took control of his wandering thoughts. He was here to accomplish something of enormous importance.

As Matthew wrestled with his thoughts he walked absently behind Mrs. Quigley, nearly running into her ramrod back when she stopped before a massive door. She knocked, and when Scanlon's deep voice answered, she pushed open the gleaming slab of wood.

"This . . . *man* insists upon speaking with you, sir," she said in a tone that told Matthew she fully expected her employer to refuse to deal with him.

Edward Scanlon's face flushed, contrasting sharply with his silver hair. "I see," he said, visibly trying to control the tone of his voice. He raked Matthew with a glare that bore only animosity and scorn. "And why would you dare disturb my peace in my own home?"

Matthew turned to face Mrs. Quigley, who stood by the door avidly absorbing all nuances and details of the meeting. "If you please? This is a confidential matter."

She jabbed her chin higher in the air and sniffed, then loudly closed the door behind her.

Matthew turned to Cece's father. He took a moment to relax his tense shoulders and unclench his fists. "This is about Cece—Cecelia, sir."

"The devil, you say!" Scanlon exploded, his face turning an even more alarming shade of red. "How dare you! What have you done to my daughter?" The man began to rise, struggling with his weak body.

Remembering his uncle's faltering movement by the campsite the night before, Matthew sympathized with Edward Scanlon for a moment. The feeling disappeared as the man's words sank in. A vivid image of Cece's nearly naked breasts flew to mind in unwitting response, and Matthew shoved that image aside, too.

"Nothing has happened to her. Yet. I came to warn you that a small number of the men in the village, angered by Pope and Talbot's intention to buy additional land, have begun to make threats. Your daughter's name has been mentioned."

Matthew became alarmed by Scanlon's condition. The man was nearly apoplectic. He lifted a gnarled hand and, pointing a shaking finger at Matthew, began to speak. "And you. Are you not also angered by the loss of lands? How do I know you are not the one cleverly plotting to harm my daughter? After all, how better to claim innocence than by citing this charade of an interview when the authorities come after you?"

Scanlon's reaction was worse than Matthew had expected. He swallowed his dislike of the man who had fathered Cece. "I have no reason to harm your daughter. I see no reason for anyone to harm her. Violence will only breed more of the same. I have come to inform you of what is happening in the village, and to urge you to provide her with additional protection."

Edward Scanlon grasped the edge of his desk with both hands, breathed deeply, then pinned Matthew with a venomous stare. "If even so much as one hair on my daughter's head is touched, I know exactly who to send the authorities after. If you value your freedom, make sure no one, not you, or any of your people, has an opportunity to hurt Cecelia. Because if, God forbid, she is hurt, I hold *you* wholly responsible."

Chapter Nine

———— • ————

After taking a moment to regain his composure, Matthew nodded and left the sumptuously furnished room. Instead of slamming the door behind him, as he so wished to do, he gently pulled it until he heard the latch click. In the hallway once again, he paused, wiped his hand down his face, then reversed his earlier steps.

Now the scent of the roses was sickly sweet, bringing to mind only the guilt he felt from the near seduction of an innocent. The excess of elegance evident in the hallway merely made more pointed the lack of material wealth he possessed when measured by the mill manager's standards. Sealskins and whale oil would hardly count here.

When Matthew reached the magnificent vestibule with its glittering chandelier and luxuriously thick Oriental carpet, he took a look at his boots crushing the velvet pile and felt in the depths of his Indian soul the earthiness of his heritage. He knew nothing but fierce pride in who and what he was.

A rumble of voices came from the back of the house, most likely Mrs. Quigley giving orders to one of the house-maids. Strangely enough the sound brought Cece to mind. Or perhaps that was not so strange at all. This house was the perfect showcase for her elegant delicacy.

Cece's milk-white skin had been protected by homes proclaiming her father's affluence. The fire of the sun had never baked her to a nut brown. Too, her fiery hair bore the sheen of red, which would most likely be leached out if she were constantly exposed to the elements. And her silky skin would have been leather tough had she been forced to wrest her living from the land.

No. Cece's pristine beauty, her satiny mane of hair, those sweet freckles that daintily frosted her nose, all attested to a pampered life of wealth. Matthew did not aspire to such a life.

All he wanted was the woman he had come to know and desire. The woman he was rapidly falling in love with.

The one woman on earth he could never have.

Juggling a stack of invitations, Cece pulled closed the door to her bedroom with the toe of her shoe. Lord, had she really chosen to host the affair of the year? It hardly seemed she could ever have been so naive. The amount of work—mindless, detailed work—the project entailed was irritating, especially since all she could think of now was the passion she and Matthew had generated. The moments spent in his arms had turned her from a lonely child into a woman, one who longed to return to her lover's arms.

Halfway down the stairs, Cece heard the front door open. She spared a curious glance to see who was leaving so early in the day, and gasped when she saw Matthew cross the threshold. What on earth had he been doing here in Father's house?

So far, to her surprise, Mrs. Quigley had not said anything to Father about what she had seen. Why? Cece had no clue, although she was certain Mrs. Quigley's silence was not due to the kindness of the woman's heart. After all, Cece was convinced the housekeeper had no more than a filthy lump of coal where that vital organ belonged.

But she was not a fool. She would not look askance at her good fortune. She would just continue to guard herself for what she was certain would be Mrs. Quigley's eventual attack.

In the vestibule, on her way to the dining room where she and Mrs. Sanders worked diligently on matters pertaining to the party, Cece glanced down and saw a fresh pine needle. She rushed to the dining table, threw down the pile of paper she carried, and hurried to collect that physical proof of

Matthew's presence in Father's home.

With the firm bit of greenery held between her fingers, Cece felt a consuming need to know the reason behind Matthew's visit. Had he come to see her? Quite apparently not. After all, she had been in her room, and Mrs. Quigley would not likely lie about her whereabouts. And he had no business with the housekeeper or any of the housemaids.

That left only Father.

As the frightening thought crossed her mind Cece heard the door to the library open sharply then close with a brusque slap. Next she heard Father's faltering steps and the tapping of his cane.

She looked down the hallway and caught the murderous expression on her father's face. She gasped. Never had she seen this side of Father. He had always been proper, controlled, every inch the gentleman. The man purposely pounding his way over the polished oak floorboards was a stranger to Cece.

"Father!" she exclaimed, unable to keep silent.

He looked up. Not a word breached his lips, but his furrowed brow spoke of his anger. The forest green of his eyes deepened nearly to black. Cece saw him swallow hard, then his jaw worked as if he'd been chewing a tough piece of meat.

Knowing how much Father disliked Indians, Cece now knew that Matthew had indeed met with him. The meeting must not have gone well. "Father," she called again.

This time he responded. "Cecelia."

"What . . . What is wrong?" she managed to ask in a somewhat squeaky voice. A spasm of fear ran through her body, and a sharp piercing pain shot through her thumb. She looked down. In her nervousness, she had stabbed the pointed tip of the pine needle into the soft flesh of her finger.

She pulled out the twig. "Ooohh . . ." The tiny exclamation escaped her before she knew it was on its way. A drop of bright red blood came to the surface of her skin. She brought her hand to her mouth and sucked, the tang of blood as unpleasant as the foreboding she felt.

Father's eyes narrowed. His gaze pierced her to the very marrow of her bones, and she could have sworn that he could see the damning intimate images flashing through her mind. Those eyes most assuredly could see Matthew's eyes blazing with passion, his mouth drawing hungrily at her breast. A blazing heat filled her cheeks, one she knew tainted her skin with the rouge of indictment.

Apparently, though, Father did not find anything unusual in her bright coloring, for he only answered with a tight, "Nothing. A very minor disturbance."

Cece drew a ragged breath of guilty relief. Matthew's visit must not have been about her. "Are you . . ." Her voice trembled so, she had to pause and start again. "Were you leaving for the office?"

A sharp nod accompanied his curt reply. "Of course."

"Then I shall see you at dinnertime," she said, expecting and receiving no response. When she heard the door close behind her father, she made her way down the hallway toward the kitchen. She longed for a cool drink but had no desire to call upon Mrs. Quigley to fetch one for her.

Taking slow, deliberate steps, she contemplated her predicament. She needed to know why Matthew had come to see Father, who was unlikely to offer any sort of explanation. Perhaps the visit had been about mill business after all.

But right in front of the library door, the sight of another pine needle brought her up short. She stared at the frond for a moment, then shook her head and bent to pick it up. How could such a small item take on so much importance to her? A strange stirring began in her middle. Unlike any sensation she had ever experienced, she could not put a name to it, could not even describe it. Still, the longer she stood outside the library door, the stronger the feeling grew. She soon had to acknowledge the power of guilt over a person's more rational capabilities. After all, despite her intent to question Father as to the nature of Matthew's visit, guilt mixed with fear had glued her lips, and she still had no idea what had prompted the unlikely visit.

Suddenly thirsting for answers far more than for any beverage, she whirled and ran to the front door. She yanked it open, only to let out a shocked exclamation. "Mrs. Avery! What a . . . a surprise."

The tall woman peered at Cece through her pince-nez. "Reverend Avery and I were speaking over breakfast this morning, and we both concluded I had been quite remiss in not welcoming you home sooner."

And what a dismal time for the woman to choose to remedy her error, Cece fumed inwardly. "It isn't as if I were a newcomer or anything, Mrs. Avery. But I do thank you for your kindness." Now, would she be equally kind and take her leave?

"I realize that with you being Catholic and all," Mrs. Avery said with her usual tinge of disapproval, "you are not true members of our congregation, but my visit is still the Christian thing to do."

Cece sighed. Clearly the woman was bound and determined to do her Christian duty by Cece, so all hope of cornering Father for an explanation was more than likely gone. Propriety demanded that Cece usher the minister's wife into the parlor.

She led the woman into the richly decorated room and sat as soon as her guest had done so. "Would you care for some tea?" she asked, hoping Mrs. Avery would decline.

She did not. "That does sound appealing. I find myself a bit thirsty."

Cece stifled a groan as she watched Mrs. Avery settle in for a long visit. Her foot softly marked each fleeing second.

The pastor's wife smoothed the skirt of her serviceable gray serge dress about her on the overstuffed sofa. Then she removed her kid gloves and set them just so on the intricately carved teak table Father had bought from a Chinese merchant.

As Mrs. Avery straightened, Cece heard her sniff then mutter something that sounded like "heathenish trappings." Cece stiffened, thinking of her very own heathen in the woods. Her missionary-raised, mostly civilized heathen. The only person in the world she wanted to see at the moment.

With what she believed to be an inordinate amount of patience, Cece listened to Mrs. Avery enumerate all the activities planned for the coming weeks at St. Paul's Presbyterian Church. Since it was the only church in Port Gamble, more often than not Father attended Sunday services there, asserting that any form of godliness was better than pagan disrespect for the Lord's day. Cece mounted a mighty struggle now to keep from checking the time on her pocketwatch.

Hardly interested in the conversation, she allowed her mind to wander. At the most inappropriate of moments, memories of her so-called savage's love filled her thoughts, and it was all she could do to keep from sending the woman on her way. Nodding where she thought best and shaking her head where it was warranted, she indulged in fantasies of Matthew—in Father's house, in the woods, in her arms, touching her as she had never been touched before. Matthew touching her in that way once again . . .

" . . . and the potluck dinner on the Fourth of July is just as popular as always," Mrs. Avery continued, oblivious to Cece's sensual thoughts.

When she could no longer stand the woman's droning voice, and the thrumming of arousal waged battle with the worries in her head, she stood. "I am so very sorry, Mrs. Avery. I find I am plagued with a violent headache." Cece grimaced and was glad she truly felt pain in her temples. It wasn't a headache as such, though, merely a response to the heated images she had entertained.

"A darkened room and a cool compress to the forehead should soon put you to rights," the pastor's wife offered. Mrs. Avery did mean well, and Cece figured it was not the poor woman's fault she was deadly dull.

Cece nodded. "That does sound good."

"I shall be on my way, then. I will look forward to seeing you at the Missionary Society tea."

"You can count on me. And I will bring some of Mrs. Quigley's delicious pecan tarts."

"Lovely," Mrs. Avery answered, tugging on the discreetly mended gloves. When she had arranged her plain black felt hat on her tightly braided knot of hair, she stood, making good her offer to leave. Cece squashed the rush of anticipation she felt.

She accompanied her unwanted guest to the door, then stood tapping the toe of her shoe in her restlessness, watching Mrs. Avery's progress up the walk, then down Main Street. Although Cece knew it had only taken the pastor's wife a very short time, she felt as if the woman's departure had been unduly drawn out.

As soon as Mrs. Avery was well away from the mansion, Cece slipped out the door and made a beeline to the trees. Father be damned! At his very best, he rarely said much to her, and this morning his mood had been so foul that she knew she would never wrangle an answer from him.

Matthew was another matter altogether. He had promised not to chase her away. Since she needed answers now, he had better provide them, or he was about to have permanent company in that cozy shelter of his.

As she walked through the woods she enjoyed her surroundings. The high-noon sun shone a mottled pattern of light and shadow on the ground. The sea breeze, not particularly rough today, caused branches to dance in the summer splendor. The closer Cece got to Matthew's campsite, the easier she felt inside, as if the beauty of the green palace she found herself in had taken the place of the ugly anxiety, guilt, and fear she had felt earlier.

She increased her speed. Soon she found herself running, feeling a sense of freedom in every movement she made. Laughing, she reached back and wrenched off the royal-blue ribbon she had used on her hair earlier that morning. Pausing only a moment, she raked both hands through the wild mass of curls swirling about her, remembering Matthew's wonder each time he caught sight of her hair. She knew it to be one of her best features, and she now took immense pride in how its beauty both lured and pleased Matthew.

She tossed back her head, then with impatient hands she bunched up the skirt of her blue dress and ran full tilt toward the man of her dreams.

Cece came to an abrupt halt at the edge of the clearing where Matthew had built his shelter. She took note of the deep silence of the woods, the stillness of the air, the charred remains of the fire in the circular stone hearth. She had no need to call his name; Matthew was not here. Disappointed, curiously deflated, but still determined, she followed her heart and the sound of the waves. Soon she broke through the trees to the brilliance of a sunny Puget Sound summer day.

White-crested waves rolled over the deep blue green of the ocean, surging over the sand to end in a bubbly gurgle. The sun, usually hidden by clouds and the misty drizzle that kept the Washington Territory the splendid green jewel it was, burned bright and hot in a pure blue sky. As it anointed the water with its presence the light caught droplets splashing over the waves and turned them into tiny rainbows. The sight stole her breath away.

Then in the distance Cece spied a black dot bobbing in and out of the water. Could that possibly be Matthew? No, surely not. Not that far from shore, she thought. It was most likely some odd flotsam.

But the speck of black did not randomly move with the flow of the water. It seemed to have an objective, a particular direction in which it went. She stood in its way. At that very moment Cece hoped and prayed that she stood directly in the path Matthew forged with his life, as he stood in hers. Matthew was her goal, her future, a future she could only conceive in terms of the two of them.

She knew the very moment he first caught sight of her. His steady progress toward shore stopped, his black hair glistening in the midday heat, his eyes unerringly finding her presence on the sand. Then, with renewed intent, he began to carve his path through the water.

Cece watched, excitement rushing to each corner of her soul. She so wanted to be with him that she grew impatient. Her breath became shallow. The heat of the sun burned into her hair, her skin, through her summer cotton clothing. She caught her bottom lip between her teeth, and the tang of sea salt invaded her mouth. Would his kiss be flavored with the elemental taste of the ocean?

She took a step toward the water, anxious for his arrival. Another pace brought her nearer, but not near enough. With her eyes firmly fixed on Matthew's approach, she bent and unfastened her boots. Heedless of propriety, she hiked up her skirts, then removed her stockings. He was only fifty feet away.

Still staring at the man she now knew she loved, she gathered her skirts up against her bare thighs and entered the waves. The shock of the icy swirl against the delicate skin of her thighs did not make her falter; she knew her heart. She took another step toward Matthew.

He looked up. Their gazes caught and held. Knowledge, infinitely old, basic, sensual, burned between them. He stood up.

Cece caught her breath at the sight of his sleek, bare chest, his flat, hard middle, bisected only by the thin leather thong holding his loinstring in place. The soft wet leather clung to his groin, delineating that which made him so consummately male. As he took a step in her direction his muscular thighs became visible, water sluicing down the ridges of sinew. Heat burned in Cece's cheeks, in her belly, her breasts, between her thighs. But she kept her gaze upon the virile body of her love and took another step toward her destiny.

As did he. Then, when only a few feet of chilly ocean separated them, he reached out a hand to her.

"Cece," he whispered.

Madness overcame them. He fought the water, his arms widespread. She reached for him, dropping her skirts, only to feel them swing into the water, the fabric dragging her down. The blood in her veins seemed to thicken, to slow, making her movements languorous, each gesture filled with sensual heaviness. High above them, the sharp shriek of a sea gull ripped through the air. The roar of the ocean mingled with the pounding of heartbeats, creating a symphony of passion. Matthew took the final step that placed him before Cece. She simply fell into his embrace.

They continued to stare into each other's eyes and held on as time seemed to stop.

Then, with a heartrending moan, Matthew's mouth claimed Cece's. A kiss, a possession, a claiming so deep, neither knew where their separate beings began and ended. All they knew was passion, desire, and need.

With feverish hunger Matthew's hands ran over Cece's back, stirring the most arousing feelings. His mouth made love, passionate, hungry love, to hers. His tongue claimed the deepest secrets of her soul, secrets she no longer felt she needed to keep. In turn, she made demands of her own. Matthew responded with an earthy honesty that made Cece crave more.

They tore apart for a second or two. Cece ran her hands up Matthew's muscle-carved chest to his solid shoulders. She flexed her fingers there, never taking her gaze from his bright eyes. When the drenched silk of his hair tangled with her hand, she tugged. Filling both hands with the thick locks, she pulled his mouth down to within a breath of hers. "More," she implored.

His eyes narrowed. His breath caught. Matthew felt the sweet caress of Cece's breath on his lips. He slid his tongue between his lips and felt her tremble as he teased her soft mouth. He smiled, for her response was more than any a man could ask for. Then she grasped the back of his head, pulling his mouth hard against hers.

He met her passion, innocent yet, with all the knowledge of an experienced male. He gave her what she'd asked for and took for himself what he needed. A tender bite brought her lower lip into his mouth, and he sucked gently, steadily. Running his tongue over her sweet flesh, he took in her gasp of arousal, her moan of need.

Needing to feel her more intimately against him, he molded his hands down her spine, pressing her abundant breasts against his chest. Her nipples, drawn tight with desire, burned into his flesh.

Down he moved his hands, reaching her firm buttocks. He tightened his fingers into the luscious curves and brought her against his hardness.

She froze. He opened his eyes and saw hers open with . . . what? Wonder? Fear?

But no. Against his lips he felt her smile, a smile ripe with the sinful knowledge of woman's power over man, and she molded her hips to his. There, in the cradle of her femininity, Matthew pressed his maleness, steely with need.

He shuddered, then slipped one arm up to circle her shoulders and lowered his other arm to her knees. The sodden fabric of her skirt made reaching her difficult, but he was driven by the fire inside him, the hunger in his loins. He dashed the skirt out of his way impatiently, wrapped his arm around the back of her knees, and swung Cece up into his embrace.

Her arms curled around his neck, forming a most welcome noose. Her kiss-swollen lips curved into a smile, and then she burst into peals of exuberant joy. He was mesmerized by the armful of womanhood he so willingly carried. She dropped her head back over his arm and shook her curls in wanton abandon.

The red-gold cascade caressed his naked flank, and a gust of wind blew stray locks across the front of his hips. Matthew caught his breath as his manhood hardened even more. Fire burned through him so fiercely that he was certain she could feel its searing heat. He had to have this woman for his own. Irrational possessiveness filled him for the first time in his life, and he feared he would never again be free from its grasp.

Her green eyes sparkled a message of love and desire to him, but the fairness of her skin brought him up short. He remembered the thoughts he had at her father's house, and knew that although their union felt right, their hopes for the future were wrong.

Trembling with need, and filled with pain greater than he had ever imagined he could feel, Matthew lowered Cece to the ground. The dry sand and sharp bits of clamshells bit into the soles of his feet. Reality had again invaded the dreamworld their desire created.

"Matthew?" she asked with a shy hesitancy in her voice.

"Shhh," he responded, tenderly touching her berry-red lips.

Because she was still pressed up against him, Matthew felt when she caught her breath, when she began to tremble. This time he knew passion had not caused her response. She was afraid of what had caused him to withdraw from her.

He tried to explain. "This is wrong—"

She cut him off. "No! Never." She shook her head with a vehemence born of youth and inexperience.

"This, Matthew, is the rightest thing in my entire life. *You* are the rightest thing in my life. Why do you always stop? Why do you always deny us what is so right for us?"

Matthew rose and turned his back to her. What he had to say was impossible to utter when the vision of her loveliness taunted him. Her hair, ruffled by the loving fingers of the sea breeze, was a sensual lure for any man, her lips gave testimony of her response to his kisses, and the flimsy cotton of her bodice, dampened by his own chest, clearly showed her tiny nipples hardened with desire.

"We must consider more than just our feelings, Cece. There is your father—"

Her fingers bit into his biceps and forced him to face her again. "My father, Matthew, lives in a lonely hell of his own making," she said, her voice husky with emotion. "I love him, but for some inexplicable reason—perhaps I'm too plain compared to my mother, or too doltish, or . . . whatever—he cannot or will not love me."

She looked where her fingers gripped his arm, and Matthew trembled at the beauty of that satiny, white skin holding his dark flesh. How many times had he fantasized about her fingers holding him, caressing him, taking him to the utmost heights of sensual delight? The fire began to burn hot within him once more.

He looked into her eyes and noted the pooling of tears. "Cece," he murmured, chagrined at being the cause of her pain again.

She shook her head the barest bit. "No, Matthew, I am not done yet." She let go of his arm. Her gaze pierced his very soul. "Matthew," she whispered, "when I'm in your arms, I feel real. I have reason to live. Your touch lets me know I'm alive. Your kisses make me want, and I know just what I want. I want you, to be yours. To be a woman, for you to make me one."

At her words, bold as any he'd ever heard, Matthew saw a flush of innocence fill her cheeks and knew that she was indeed his. But before he could act on that knowledge, he felt honor bound to tell her of the events of the morning. Of the way matters stood between him and her father. Between the tribe and her people.

"Oh, Cece, were it only a matter between the two of us . . ." He turned to gaze over the water and caught sight of a boat pulling into the dock at the mill. "Look," he urged, pointing at the vessel.

The wind blew strands of fiery hair across her face, but still she turned to gaze in the direction in which he had pointed. "The mill is your heritage. Your father has given many years to establishing a successful business there. But because of him my people have lost much of what was our heritage. Our lands are being sold even now to further the progress of the mill. Our children are wrested from their families and sent to be trained to be like your people. But we never can be. We do not look like you, we do not dream the same dreams. I am a S'Klallam. You are one of *them*."

She faced him, anger burning in her eyes. "Are you telling me you refuse to love me because I am white and you are Indian?"

"Perhaps that is the most basic way to look at this situation."

She gasped. Scorn spread across her face. Matthew would have preferred the anger she'd worn before.

She took a menacing step toward him, her fist waving before his face. "I cannot believe what I am hearing." One slender finger poked out from the fist, pointing in accusation. "If you mean what you have said, then you are no better than my blind, bigoted father."

"No, that is not the way I see matters, and I believe you have even said you cannot believe me guilty of such bias. There are other elements at work here, things you do not understand."

Both Cece's hands formed fists then opened again. She wrapped her arms around her middle, as if protecting herself from another blow. "Then, Matthew," she said, her voice carefully controlled, "for God's sake, tell me. Make me understand. Don't you see it is my life I am fighting for?

I have the right to know everything I must face."

The urgency in her voice made Matthew gaze more closely at her, study the emotions so rawly etched on her features. How he wished to spare her the fear she was sure to experience when he told her of Luke's threats. The anger she was bound to feel when she learned of her father's accusation. But as he gazed at her he also noticed something he had never seen before in her expression. Perhaps it had never been there, or perhaps he had never been so aware of the circumstances surrounding them. Cece was completely committed to facing whatever lay before her. The expression in her eyes was no longer that of an exciting imp, it was that of a woman, who, as she had said, was fighting for her life.

He extended his hand to her. "Friends?"

"Always, and more," she answered, the fervor in her words stunning him with the emotions she so openly displayed.

Holding her hand, he led her to the edge of the woods. On a sun-dappled patch of sand he sat, pulling her down beside him.

"The problem begins and ends with the difference in our backgrounds."

She snorted, a most unladylike sound, a very Cece-like sound. "Matthew, I already *know* that. You need to tell me what I do not know."

He began with the story of how the S'Klallam lands had been taken from the tribe and how no treaty had ever been upheld by the white man. At that, she became angry on the S'Klallams' behalf. Then he explained about the Dawes General Allotment Act and how it provided for so-called surplus lands to be sold to whites.

Her temper flared. "Who decided the land was surplus? Surely not the rightful owners. What gall!"

Matthew was hard-pressed not to laugh. She was charming, enchanting, and naive as many white women seemed to be. "You are right. We did not decide. Now the Bureau of Indian Affairs is processing the sale of additional S'Klallam land to the mill, and many of the young men are angered by this further loss."

"I should hope so. What are they going to do to stop this?"

He should have known that Cece would come to the heart of the matter in no time. "I am afraid that is what affects you most directly."

"Me?"

"Yes, you. Some of the hotter-tempered men have made veiled threats to your safety as a means to deter the mill from pursuing the purchase. I'm sorry, Cece. You asked, and there is no easy way to say such things."

She lost all the color in her cheeks. He felt her hands turn icy and begin to tremble. Her eyes opened wider, her fear clearly visible in their depths.

"But I have nothing to do with all this. Why, I think the government is completely wrong to break treaties and take what is not theirs. I—I would never hurt anyone or take anything from anyone."

"I know that. They know that. But those men wish to hurt your father. He is the representative of Pope and Talbot here in Port Gamble. They feel if they hurt him enough, he will stop the company from pursuing its ends."

Cece shook her head and grimaced. "It would do no good. Father does not care about me. I told you how he sent me away. I insisted on coming back, but he wanted me to stay with Aunt Prudence in San Francisco."

Matthew thought over the events of the morning. Something was not quite right, but one thing he knew. Edward Scanlon cared deeply about his daughter's well-being. He thought she should know, and he told her so.

Her eyes sparkled momentarily with hope, then dulled, and she shook her head in silent denial. He felt compelled to make her believe. "Had you seen the rage burning in his eyes at the thought of anything or anyone harming you, you would never question his feelings. Maybe he is cold-natured or perhaps he has difficulty showing his feelings. But be sure of one thing, Cece. Your father cares what becomes of you."

Cece sat frozen in the hot sand. Each of Matthew's words that proclaimed her father's love for her was a balm to her aching heart. So, too, was what Matthew had

not yet said. His very presence in the house of an avowed
Indian hater was mute testimony of his feelings for her.

Gathering about her the knowledge of those unvoiced
feelings as if they were the warmest cloak, Cece absorbed
strength and certainty—strength to battle Matthew's reser-
vations, and certainty that they were meant to come together.

She turned her hand in his, entwining their fingers. "You
care, don't you?" she asked, her voice no more than a
whisper.

He gazed out over the ocean. "Of course."

She tightened her grip on his hand, squeezing gently,
trying to communicate her turbulent emotions. She took her
other hand from his and, in a tentative gesture, reached out
to trace his high cheekbone. At the feather-light touch, he
shuddered. The evidence of her effect on him emboldened
her, and she repeated the action. Then she traced his thick
eyebrow, tucked a long strand of hair behind his ear, and
lightly rubbed his earlobe. Again she felt tremors shake
his body.

As her fingers ran over his dark bronze skin, she marveled at the sleek smoothness of it. Nearing his jaw, she
faltered, changed direction, and touched his lips. He turned
from the sea and looked at her. With his gaze upon her,
she deliberately traced the outline of his mouth once again,
leaving him no doubt as to how she felt.

"This solves none of our problems," he said.

"Oh, no. You're very wrong there. It solves one major
one. After today you will never see me as a child again. I
will be a woman from now on. Your woman."

Chapter Ten

—— • ——

My woman.

Cece's fingers danced over his lips one more time, and Matthew experienced the return of his earlier desire. With the tip of his tongue he reached out and caught one of those caressing marauders. He bit down gently on the fleshy pad, then brought Cece's fingertip into his mouth.

He watched her eyes grow impossibly big, then languidly close. Her breath grew shallow, and she panted little puffs of air across his cheek. A sweet flush rose over her features, replacing the earlier pallor of fear.

True, loving her would resolve nothing. But at this moment had his life been the price for such ecstasy, Matthew would gladly have paid it, and more.

"Cece," he whispered.

Her eyes opened, and he saw the widened pupils rimmed in evergreen. Her desire was clearly there for him to see. As they continued to gaze into each other's eyes, Matthew reached for her, cupping her shoulders in his large hands. He noted the daintiness of her form, the fragility of her bones. Mindful of the delicacy of her skin, he gently but purposely pulled her closer, urging himself to exercise whatever shred of control he still possessed.

The brilliant green light in Cece's eyes lured him ever deeper into desire. He lowered his lips to hers, wanting to savor the essence of her. He intended a light brush of lips, full of tenderness, but when they touched, when he felt her whisper-sweet breath against his mouth, every nerve in his body leaped into raging need.

He curved his palms over her jawline, angling her face below his, allowing his mouth free access to hers. He fitted his lips more fully over hers and pressed harder. Sanity offered a plea for restraint, but need, so long suppressed, refused to heed the warning.

In a breathtaking gesture, Cece began to return Matthew's caress. He felt the gentle, cautiously innocent probing of her tongue on his lips, his teeth, then on his sensitive tongue. His body clenched in fierce response, every muscle in his body relentlessly tight. He had to slow down or he would be rougher than she could tolerate.

Still relishing the depths of Cece's luscious mouth, Matthew slid his hand down the curve of her neck and rubbed the baby-soft skin under her firm chin with his thumb. In response, Cece arched her neck, giving him better access to that fragrant curve. Matthew tore his mouth from hers, gasping for breath. At the sight of the silky skin she so trustingly offered him, he moaned and buried his face there.

The sweet scent of roses filled Matthew's senses. He nipped the fine tendons running down her neck and became frustrated when he reached the impediment presented by the collar of her dress. He lifted his head and, with an intense look, asked permission, which she swiftly gave. He lowered his hand to the front of the soft, royal-blue cotton. In no time he took care of the seven buttons hiding Cece's beauty from him. The fabric, abundantly pleated at shoulder and waist, parted in the wake of his questing hand.

The daintiness of her undergarment fascinated Matthew. Before Cece, he had never seen anything so feminine and provocative in its innocence. Banded in fine white lace edging, her chemise was of the softest white linen. It was so sheer, in fact, he clearly saw the dark rose shade of her areolae through the white cloth. The material softly gathered over her breasts only emphasized their generously rounded shape.

With a hand that trembled with restrained urgency, Matthew unfastened the buttons of the chemise. As the fabric parted he laid gentle kisses on the creamy flesh he exposed. Each kiss was followed by a murmur of pleasure from Cece. He only stopped when he reached the belt at her waist.

With a gentleness he had never known he possessed, he laid her across his lap, freeing both his hands to continue their exploration. Her skirt, narrow at the waist and hip, flared over its length, ended in a goodly amount of now soggy cotton. Fortunately for a desperately aroused man, it was held together by only a handful of large black buttons, easy to find against the field of royal blue.

Under her skirt, her petticoat gleamed the same pristine white of her chemise. But by now Matthew's patience had vanished. He pulled open the drawstring holding the concoction together, and rapidly removed it from Cece's recumbent body, only to face the dilemma of her rose-satin-trimmed cotton drawers.

He uttered a curse under his breath and tugged at the strings on the obstructive fabric. "How do you manage to stay alive under all this . . . this stuff?"

Cece smiled. "This is only summer clothing. Winter is worse." She reached a tentative hand to his torso and caressed his belly. His breath stopped in his chest, and the muscles under her hand clenched in reaction to her tender touch.

"I envy the way you go about so unencumbered," she whispered.

Matthew frowned, the image of a nearly naked Cece not sitting well with him. After all, any other man would then be able to feast his eyes on the banquet Matthew meant to enjoy. "Perhaps I prefer you hidden by your suit of feminine armor."

Cece smiled. "I have no idea what you have done to me, Matthew, but I feel no shame. And I find it charming that you wish to keep me for your private enjoyment."

Matthew cursed again. The drawers were proving as vexing as the woman wearing them. "You are right. I care not to share," he muttered, battling a recalcitrant tie.

Cece's eyes glittered with an emotion Matthew was quick to identify. "Neither do I, Matthew," she responded, possessiveness strengthening her voice.

The cotton drawers gave way. He swept away the covering and gasped at what he found—the softest, most immaculate flesh he had ever seen lay bare for his pleasure. Pearly skin beckoned his touch, his caress, his kiss. And in the very middle, between her legs, lay a nest of reddish-gold curls, inviting him to touch and discover if they were as silky as they looked.

He gazed up her beautiful form. Her chemise, open but still covering her full breasts, lay ready to be removed. He continued his scrutiny and caught the smile playing over her lips. He noted the flush on her cheekbones, and finally he sought her eyes. The brilliant green had darkened with desire.

With her eyes firmly fixed on Matthew's beloved face, Cece felt his strong arms surround her as he picked her up and set her back down on her own discarded clothing. She moaned at the abrasion of cloth against her highly sensitized skin. All she wanted was to feel Matthew. His skin against hers, his lips wherever he wished, his passion consuming her.

She reached out again and caressed his thigh. Never taking her gaze from his, she was quick to note how his eyes seemed to sparkle when she touched him. To prove her suspicion, she repeated her caress. They did sparkle! She slid her fingers over his supple skin a third time, merely for the thrill of touching him in such an intimate way.

In response to her boldness, Matthew gently parted her open chemise and bared her breasts to the breeze. As the wind kissed her, her nipples darkened, and she felt them tingle as they began to tighten. Reverently he lowered his head and took one of the tight buds between his lips. Cece felt his light touch to the depths of her womb. When the tip of his warm, wet tongue lapped at the sensitive crest, rivers of heated passion began to flow through her body. As if he knew exactly what she was feeling, Matthew began to suckle her flesh.

"Ahhh . . ."

The sound of pleasure escaped her lips, giving form to the new sensations Matthew was teaching her. She wrapped her arms around his shoulders and lifted herself deeper into his mouth. Instantly his hands cupped the fullness of both breasts, embracing the flesh with his fingers. His caress became more insistent, the motions of his mouth stronger, the sucking deeper, drawing a moist response from her most intimate flesh.

Then Matthew's hand caressed her tightened belly, eventually slipping lower. Cece thought she would surely die from the pleasure of Matthew's arousing touch. But she did not die. Instead she came ever more alive. His fingers slid into the curls atop her legs, soothing her fevered skin. When she was gasping for release, he deepened his foray.

With incredible tenderness, he parted her flesh, insistently caressing the petals of her womanhood. A trembling began there and spread to every bit of her body. Matthew lifted his head, abandoning the breast he had so thoroughly loved. Cece, unable to speak, cried out her dismay.

He took possession of her other nipple, lightly biting into it. Cece's back arched in response. His fingers, ever insistent, found the very hub of all her sensation and plied it with tormenting touches. Cece's hips rose off the ground in reaction to the exquisite pleasure Matthew bestowed upon her body. As waves of delight rolled over her he slid his fingers away and slipped them between her wet folds to delve inside her.

Dear God, madness was pure ecstasy, Cece thought, quivering at the gentle invasion, along with his masterful touch, his talented mouth, his musky scent, the raspy sound of his breathing. She no longer existed as a separate being; she was being absorbed into Matthew.

Wanting to know him as he now knew her, she ran her hand over his chest, gently exploring the squared planes of muscle she found there. He felt so firm. Then, unexpectedly, he took his hand from her and set her own hand aside. Standing, he released the strap that held the bit of leather over his swollen manhood. When it fell aside, Cece gasped. He was indeed hard, his shaft engorged, obviously ready for loving. She felt a twinge of fear at the sight of that bold male flesh. Her stomach muscles tightened at the thought of being pierced and stretched. What if he hurt her?

"Don't be frightened," he whispered. "I will be gentle. There will be pain, but I will go slowly. I will try to make it as good for you as I can."

He kissed her again. His lips feasted on hers while his hands roamed over her nakedness. And all along, his hard shaft pressed against her thigh, allowing her to become accustomed to its presence. Curiosity and desire soon urged her to boldness. As Matthew's lips traversed the line of her collarbone, Cece slid her hand down his taut belly and beyond. Following her instincts, she ran feather-light touches down Matthew's manhood.

His hips bucked at her touch, his flesh quivering against her fingers. Cece sought his eyes, wondering if she'd done something wrong. The pleasure she saw in those ebony depths reassured her. She curled her fingers around the swollen flesh.

Matthew was hot and hard, his skin smooth as silk. Cece felt his blood hammering in her hand. She flexed her fingers, testing the firmness of him, and was shocked when he groaned, flexing his hips, rubbing the throbbing thickness against her hand. Gazing upon that intimate part of Matthew, Cece repeated the action and saw his hips move again, pushing his flesh up against her hands another time.

In wonderment, Cece sought Matthew's face. Exquisite ecstasy etched his high forehead, his deep-set eyes, his broad cheekbones, his full lips. She remembered how she felt when his fingers had caressed her intimately, and smiled. She now knew how to give him the same searing joy he had given her. She began to ply him with a tight, stroking rhythm, gently pressuring him with her fingers in counterpoint to the rough bucking of his hips.

His pleasure incited hers. When they were both gasping their need, Matthew raised himself on his elbow and with his other hand parted the flame-colored curls between her legs. His finger boldly claimed the depths it had earlier found, and he whispered praises to her uninhibited response.

He rolled over her fevered body and came to lie between her parted thighs. In a devastating motion, he brought his heated manhood to the portal of her femininity. He touched her burning skin with his, gently, insistently, until she moaned, wanting to experience the fullness of their loving, regardless of the pain it might cause. His lips claimed hers, his tongue delving, as he partially entered her.

Cece gasped at the foreign sensation, thankful that Matthew had paused, giving her time to accustom herself to having him inside her body. In a few seconds he deepened his presence. Inch by inch he probed her depths, patiently waiting for her to take all of him.

She looked up at his beloved face and was shocked to see the strain there. Only then did she realize what his patience and tenderness was costing him. A surge of rich emotion for her noble lover suffused her, and she quivered under him. He pressed deeper, and they found his progress hampered by nature's barrier.

"I'm sorry, love," he whispered through clenched teeth, then brought his lips to hers. At that moment he plunged fully into her, and Cece felt as if she'd been rent in two. She cried out, and Matthew took the cry into his mouth.

He was too big, too hard, too engorged for her to take. Tears glazed her eyes as she looked up at Matthew. The taut skin over his cheekbones glistened with a sheen of sweat, and beads of moisture gathered on his forehead. His control was greater than before as he obviously sought to spare her what pain he could.

Despite the fiery pain, despite the tearing burn, the thought of him leaving her body was intolerable. The sharpness of the sting inside her began to ease as she became used to his presence within her—his size, his shape, his heat. She moved a bit, trying to ease her hips into a more accepting position. Matthew gasped, and Cece felt him quiver within her. She stopped her movements, aware that what she had just felt was no longer merely pain. Repeating her earlier motion, she was gratified to hear Matthew's breath hiss out.

He began to move. Slowly, deeply, he plumbed her depths, setting up a rhythm she soon caught on to. Playing counterpoint to his thrusts, she was rewarded for her efforts by his fevered kisses, his gasping breath, the increased pace of his strokes.

The ebb and flow of his manhood matched the rapid beats of her heart, her heated blood flooding her body with the rhythm of passion. Matthew's chest pressed against her swollen, tender nipples, abrading her aroused flesh in much the same way his hips did below. The plunging grew deeper still, rougher, less controlled. And still she wanted more.

She cried out his name. Sobbing brokenly, she whimpered at the sensations spreading through her body, a body that was whirling through a vortex of the unknown. She clung to the only familiar thing. Her nails bit into Matthew's shoulders, and she clawed his back as her own hips bucked wildly, her muscles tightly clasping the hot male flesh that pulsed inexorably within her.

A tight spiral of sensation began to curl in that spot where she and her lover were joined. It coiled tighter. She moaned, tossing her head from side to side at the foreign, desperate longing that was overtaking her.

In her passionate fever she wrapped her legs around Matthew's thighs, deepening his thrusts. The coil of desire tightened ever more inside her. As the hot, hard tip of his manhood taunted her womb time and again, Cece felt the coil swell until suddenly it snapped. Bursts of flame exploded in her mind, blinding her, stealing her breath, leaving only the sensation of Matthew's presence deep within the most intimate part of her self, of being sweetly stretched to encompass him, the sensation of being only one.

Ripples of agonizing ecstasy whirled through Cece's mind and body. But before she could catch her breath, think of what she had just experienced, she felt Matthew increase his pace, his back muscles tensing to a point she would never have believed possible. Cece realized Matthew was on the verge of the same magnificence she had just experienced. Instinctively she increased the motion of her hips. She tightened her thighs about him, clenching his firm buttocks in her hands.

She felt him shatter the bonds of his own control. She felt shudders rack his strong body. She heard her name uttered on a tortured moan. Matthew slammed into her in a convulsive thrust, then bowed his spine, threw his head back, and let out a deep groan of intense feeling. His pleasure burst inside her body, and Cece watched the flush invade his cheeks, saw the expression of pleasure and pain capture his features. He stayed within her, pulsing throbs still detonating in her depths.

She smiled at her newfound femininity. She was a woman now. No child could give a man like Matthew the sort of pleasure she had felt him endure. No child could share it, knowing it firsthand in her own body. No child would anticipate the many times they would again seek satisfaction.

Smoothing her hands over Matthew's back muscles, she felt the tautness of climax leave his body. When he collapsed over her, she knew she had never known anything sweeter than to cushion her lover's spent body with her own. She nuzzled his neck, caressing his salty skin with her tongue. He trembled, and that tiny tremor moved her to awed pride. Such a minor caress could move a strong man so intimately, so measurably . . . and she, Cece Scanlon, was capable of moving a man to passion and completion.

"Cece," he whispered. "I am too heavy, let me move—"

"No," she uttered fiercely, determined to keep him with her. She tightened her grip, her hands, her legs, her intimate flesh. "You feel heavenly, and I quite like it. Stay with me. In me."

Matthew lifted his head at Cece's words. How could an innocent like her know the exact words to keep a man at her side? Then he smiled. He was not merely at her side. He was above her, around her, and so deep inside her they might as well be one person rather than two.

"Heaven, Cece," he whispered reverently, "is you. And like you, I quite like heaven. I believe, if you are willing to hold me in heaven, I shall stay a bit longer."

They rested silently, peacefully. The breeze off the bay cooled their hot skin, drying the beads of perspiration their loving exertions had caused to form. Their hands soothed, their lips met in tender communion. It was a moment of beauty, a moment of love. But neither spoke the word.

Love surrounded them, though. It was a presence in the silence of the woods, in the roar of the surf, in the voice of the sea gulls soaring through the sky above them. It filled every touch, every kiss, every breath they took. But neither one had the courage to voice their innermost feelings.

So soon the kisses became hot, sensual, arousing. Their hands no longer soothed, but sought to enflame. Matthew whispered intimate things in Cece's ear, told her how much he loved being inside her, how she felt to him, how he loved touching her beautiful body.

Cece felt him grow within her depths, swelling to the full hardness he had displayed so proudly when he earlier removed his loinstring. As she felt the change, she summoned an image of her lover standing before her, unashamed, aroused, ready to take her. Ready, as he was now in the wet depths of her body.

No longer ignorant, Cece joyously began the climb to completion, this time knowingly joining Matthew in their erotic dance of love. This time, when she felt the spiral begin to clutch her insides, she welcomed it and strove with every swirl of her hips, with every bit of her being, with every intimate tightening of her body, to heighten the pleasure both would feel.

As she reached that exhilarating peak a thin sound of release left her body. Her nails dug into Matthew, hanging on to the reality of love in that shimmering, pulsing maelstrom of giddy joy. And at the very crest of feeling she felt Matthew again go rigid from his own release. His final plunge inside her intensified every fragment of feeling coursing through her veins. His body quivered with the exquisite violence of emptying himself into her hot, loving depths.

After his world righted itself and he was again able to breathe, Matthew gazed down upon the lovely face of the woman in his arms. Every feature was indelibly etched in the deepest corner of his heart, even the glitter of tears flowing from the outside corners of her deep green eyes.

From the exalted look in the brilliant depths, he assumed her tears to be of joy, but Cece mattered too much for him to leave such knowledge to mere assumption. With the tip of his tongue, he laved a salty drop from her silky skin. "What are these for?" he asked, his voice husky with tenderness.

A smile curved her sweet lips, still swollen from their endless kisses. "They're for you. For me." She lifted that puffy mouth to his for a soft kiss, then ran a confident hand down his side. With an irreverent tap, she swatted his buttocks. "They're for us."

"For us," he echoed, his voice barely more than a breath of air. Gazing upon her beauty, Matthew was powerless to avoid remembering every nuance of her response to his lovemaking. The way her breasts had swollen into his caress. The way her intimate flesh had dampened for him. The way her inner muscles had caressed him to sublime joy.

No woman alive could give as Cece had given of herself were she not deeply in love with her partner. Male animal that he was, Matthew preened with pride at the knowledge. But, civilized male that he also was, he acknowledged the depth of the pain they were both bound to face because of their love.

Because they were in love. *He* was in love.

He could no longer deny them the beauty in the physical expression of that love. "I will never send you away from my side," he vowed.

Her slender arms tightened about him, and she cuddled closer. She nodded, an impish smile curving her mouth. "I know."

Despite her playful mood, reality had taken hold of Matthew's thoughts. He could not continue to put off telling her precisely how matters stood.

In a gentle fashion, he withdrew from her intimate hold. His hands lingered over the flesh he had so recently aroused and relished. He soothed her with his tenderness and his love.

"Get dressed," he urged. He reached for his loinstring, wishing for once for the security provided by his Boston garb. "We need to talk."

Cece pouted prettily. "I thought we had talked."

He shook his head. "Not nearly enough."

She dressed hastily, her movements a bit choppy as a result of the recent unfamiliar use to which he'd put her body. When she shimmied up her drawers, Matthew saw her wince.

"Are you very sore?" he asked.

A wry smile twitched at her lips. "Enough. My body had to stretch quite a bit so you could fit."

Matthew felt a surge of embarrassment rush up his face and wondered if the close proximity to this white woman could cause him to develop the habit of blushing. He hoped not.

Then he laughed. What a picture she made! In her demure cotton chemise and frilly drawers, she was every bit the innocent convent-bred miss. But underneath lived an earthy seductress who had given and taken her fill of passion. She was woman enough not to cringe from speaking of the act.

"You are a wonder, Cecelia Scanlon. And I must make sure you are completely safe."

Turning to retrieve her blue dress, Cece bent then rose again, the colorful cotton hugged firmly to her full breasts. Matthew noted the curves barely covered by sheer white cloth, and felt the tightening of his loins. Damn! They had just loved long and lustily, and still the minx was capable of enticing him again.

Before he acted on his instincts, though, she spoke. "I know just how to keep me safe."

"And how might that be?"

Her attention firmly fixed on fastening the large jet buttons on her skirt, Cece answered, "Simple. I spend my time at your side. *You* will keep me safe."

Her trust rendered him weak. Then the absurdity of her suggestion struck him along with the irony. "I am afraid that is precisely the problem."

"Problem? I see no problem, Matthew. While I am with you, the men from your village cannot possibly hurt me. And Father needn't know I am at your side. In fact, he would not even care enough to find out where I am."

The image of Edward Scanlon's livid features loomed in Matthew's memory. "Do not be so sure of that. When I tried to warn him this morning, he decided to ensure your safety by making me personally accountable for you."

She smiled, a most maddening act, or so it seemed to him. "Well, for once Father and I are in agreement," she said. "You have been chosen by both of us to keep me from danger."

Matthew cursed. Yes, both Scanlons had chosen him to protect Cece, but there was another issue at stake here. "I cannot turn my back on my responsibilities, Cece. I came into the woods to begin a spirit quest. You see, if I choose, I can become the next leader of the Nuf-Kay'it S'Klallam. My uncle, the current *ssia'm,* is getting old and has stated his desire to be relieved of the responsibility. Because of my family lineage and my personal wealth, I have a right to that position. The only challenge I face is Luke."

Cece gasped. "But he's—"

"Yes," Matthew answered. "He is unreliable. Before I assume leadership, I must seek a special *tamanous,* a powerful blessing. To do so, I must concentrate only on learning what the spirits have in store for my life."

Cece saw ridged creases line his forehead. She noted the serious light glowing in his black eyes. She watched those mobile lips, so recently softened with passion, as they thinned and tightened in determination. Above all, she heard the strong conviction underlining his words.

Matthew was S'Klallam.

As that thought crossed her mind a vision of Matthew's feverish embrace filled her memory. She felt the crush of his muscular arms about her. She felt the swirl of his tongue in her mouth. She felt the powerful thrusts of his manhood deep inside her. She heard his voice, ragged with emotion, call her name at the peak of his completion.

Matthew loved her.

Oh, he had never uttered those words, but sometimes they were unnecessary. Now she knew how much pain the confession of their love could bring them both. Matthew faced a dilemma she had no way of solving. And she stood at the very center of the entire mess.

Cece bit her lower lip, thinking through the ins and outs of the situation. Matthew loved her, but he had duties and responsibilities toward his tribe. She could only guess at the magnitude of their importance. He was the future leader of an entire village, of a people toward whom her father had repeatedly voiced an abiding hatred.

Yet, despite her father's bigotry, she could not bring herself to hate him.

Nor could she turn her back on Matthew.

She looked up with respect at the man she loved. "I now understand, Matthew. And I promise I will not interfere with your destiny. I only ask that you allow me a corner of that destiny. I cannot find a way to walk away from you. From us."

In that moment Cece saw the shadow of something intense, powerful, burning in the blackness of Matthew's gaze. She saw his throat work convulsively. His jaw tightened, and a muscle jumped in his lean cheek. He took a step away from her and turned his gaze toward the water of Port Gamble Bay.

Matthew's broad shoulders firmed, then slumped a bit. It seemed his burden was too great even for such sturdy bone and sinew. Cece longed to go to his side, to offer some bit of strength. But she bore the burden of being part of his troubles, quite possibly the greatest part.

In a voice that shook with emotion, Matthew spoke, never turning to face her. "I am not strong enough to send you away. Not now. Not after today."

Cece took a hesitant step toward him. She paused, wondering if her instincts were right. Then, throwing caution to the winds, following the desires of her heart, she went to stand behind him and wrapped both arms around his waist. She laid her cheek on his warm back, breathing in the essence of her man.

The waves of Port Gamble Bay kissed the shore in their eternal, unalterable rhythm. The breeze caressed the trees as it always did. High in the sky, a sea gull cawed, swooping gracefully on invisible currents of air, backlit against the ever-present blanket of cloud.

On shore, a man and a woman, torn by virtue of their birth, stood bound by a love neither dared confess. They gazed into a future fraught with fear, dark with danger. But in the midst of all the turbulence, a drop of hope flickered like a candle.

It was the light of love.

Chapter Eleven

———— • ————

Intense thoughts propelled Cece on her way home. Those thoughts chased each other, never giving her weary head a rest. What was she to do? She loved Father. She had come home to be with him. But fate had held something better in store for her. Even though they had loved a very short time ago, thoughts of Matthew and his passion quickened her body almost instantly.

Her nipples were still sensitive from the tender roughness of Matthew's mouth. And each time she took a step, her most intimate flesh reminded her of how it had felt to have him embedded deep inside her, how she had brought him the same pleasure he had given her. She craved another deep endless kiss from his talented lips and tongue.

But she had set in motion the preparations for Father's retirement ball well before she had had any notion of the riches the future held for her. She was not so irresponsible as to turn her back on a project she had undertaken, just because loving Matthew was infinitely more enjoyable than writing lists and overseeing the menu for the ball.

The clouds that earlier had resembled a silver blanket had come together in a shield of pewter gray, obscuring the cheer of the sun. The temperature had dropped some, and the wind from the ocean had picked up its pace. In spite of the threatening elements, Cece was reluctant to leave the woods, to emerge from the canopy of green into a world where all she had was the busyness of preparing for a ball. Now all the minutiae that once seemed so important had become meaningless, the party nothing more than a wretched nuisance. But she had to continue as she had begun.

For the next few frustrating days she did just that. She spent her time with Mrs. Sanders, going over a multitude of details. During that time she tolerated Mrs. Quigley's accusatory looks, knowing full well the woman did not have a Matthew in her life.

Even though she herself did, she respected Matthew's need for privacy and stayed away from the woods. Patience had never seemed so difficult to achieve, but she persevered and managed to accept the separation far longer than she would have thought possible.

She also made progress with Father, if she could call the polite responses she received to her questions "progress." Father did come out from behind his newspaper and ledgers to answer her queries, although he still did not venture any gestures of rapprochement himself.

Her ballgown was delivered. At the sight of the luxurious confection, Cece's thoughts immediately turned to Matthew. How would he react if he saw her attired thusly?

Cece quickly forgot her lists and dragged Mrs. Sanders up to her room. With Mrs. Sanders's help she tried on the dress this last time before the ball. The exquisite brocaded satin gleamed richly. The short, puffed sleeves, lavishly garnished with lace, added a whimsically feminine touch. The décolletage, showing off a generous expanse of white skin, ended its plunge in delicate silk rosettes. Cece had not been able to resist the soft fabric blossoms. The pale apple-green hue of the fabric showed to great advantage the red glints in her hair, and her eyes looked like deepest emeralds. Yes, somehow Matthew would have to see her wearing this marvelous dress. Somehow she would convince him to meet her in the garden on the night of the party after the guests were gone.

Still studying her reflection in the mirror, she turned sideways to get a glimpse of the back of her gown. The small, softly draped panniers over her hips made her figure seem even more womanly, and she took note of the fact. Proud to see that her looks matched the way she had been feeling about herself since the day she and Matthew made love, Cece smiled in satisfaction.

Mrs. Sanders patted Cece's hand, interrupting her musings. "You shall indeed be the belle of the ball, my dear. I should not doubt you will capture any number of hearts."

Instantly Cece thought of the heart she had already captured, not to mention other more earthy body parts she was now acquainted with. A raging flush heated her fair skin, and casting a nervous glance in the mirror, she saw the bare tops of her breasts turn a delicate rosy peach.

"I—I would just as soon avoid stealing anything at all, Mrs. Sanders."

The older lady *tsk-tsk*ed. "You do not wish to spend your entire life alone, my dear. I assure you, the company of a man, a loving man, is far better than solitude."

I agree, Cece thought. To Mrs. Sanders she offered a noncommittal sound and soon changed the subject to the safer matter of the menu.

Although Mrs. Sanders often sang Matthew's praises, something told Cece the older lady would hardly consider him a good candidate for marriage.

Matthew's lungs burned for air as his arms sliced through the waves once again. With just a few more strokes he would be close enough to shore to walk the rest of the way out of the icy water. It felt good against his skin, invigorating, and on occasion it served to cool off the remembered effects of loving Cece.

Setting such thoughts aside was essential to his purpose.

True, he had been raised by missionaries and had been well indoctrinated in the Christian faith, but he could never deny his heritage. He was S'Klallam, and the S'Klallam spirits called to his inner self. He had arrived at a melding of the two systems of belief, unorthodox in the eyes of most, perhaps, but infinitely meaningful and appropriate for him. To assume leadership of Nuf-Kay'it, he needed the empowering all other S'Klallam *ssia'm* had received.

The moment of decision was at hand. Early that morning his cousin Anna had run an urgent message to Matthew

from his uncle. Chief Chet-ze-moka, *ssia'm* of the Port
Townsend S'Klallam, had drawn his last breath. The loss
of another respected leader had cast the S'Klallam people
even more adrift, separating the villages from each other.

Already Matthew had begun the ritual cleansing and
purification the spirits demanded of a man on a quest.
Taking many baths, rubbing his body with hemlock twigs
to the point where it stung, and a fast of dried foods, were
some of the rituals needed to please the spirits. And he had
to do so to receive the final reserve of power that would
put him among the most fortunate men, those achieving a
special *tamanous*.

The spirits were everywhere; they surrounded a person
in the form of trees and animals, even in clouds and fog.
According to ancient legends Matthew had learned as a
child, before the missionaries had taken him to school,
the spirits inhabited villages much the same as people did.
They would choose certain men and grant them the secrets
to fishing, hunting, fame, and even the wealth necessary to
give successful potlatches, the extravagant celebrations that
more often than not determined tribal leadership. Since the
spirits hated the smell of camps and food, they only sought
a questing man when he was alone and purified through
fasting and bathing.

So Matthew strove to please the demanding spirits.

But he struggled daily with the desires of his flesh. He
craved Cece. Her softness was the bed he needed for sleep
at night; her laughter, the music to sweeten the work of his
days. Her conversation would provide the companionship
to forever banish his loneliness.

His toe struck bottom, and he exhaled a sigh of heartfelt
relief. Rising, he glanced at the overcast sky, wondering if
the rain would start anytime soon. Ever since the rainy days
he had spent with Cece, the damp trickle from the heavens
never failed to bring her to mind.

Hell! Everything brought her to mind nowadays, in spite
of his earnest attempts to concentrate on spiritual matters,
on tribal matters. And now Chet-ze-moka was dead.

Matthew remembered the stories his uncle told of Chet-
ze-moka's wisdom. How the chief had, through intelligence

and foresight, kept the S'Klallam from involvement in what the Bostons called the Indian Wars. The chief had understood that the whites were in the Pacific Northwest to stay, and if the Indian was to survive, the tribes had to learn the art of coexistence.

How he wished others, like Luke, were more of the same mind as the dead leader.

Unconcerned with his nakedness, Matthew squeezed the water from his hair and started off toward his camp. By the time he reached the shelter, his body had almost dried. He reached for his loinstring and covered his sex, glad not to have to dress in Boston garb just yet.

A crooked smile curved his lips when he caught sight of his other, now ruined loinstring. The day he and Cece had come together, thoughts of the bewitching creature had so heated him that he had run into Teekalet while still wearing the bits of leather. Leaving the water, joining Cece, he had made all his fantasies come true. But by the time Cece left, the leather had been stiff with sea salt.

Hungry now, he took a piece of dried salmon, one of the foods allowed on his fast, and sat to appease the ache in his stomach. Yesterday he had subjected himself to a ritual medicinal purge, an effective one at that, and today his insides demanded nourishment.

After a while he sat back and thought of what his uncle had said the last time they had spoken.

"Yes, son. It is only through mutual tolerance that our people stand a chance with the whites. We cannot defeat them; in truth, we are already defeated. Luke's tactics will only bring more heartbreak to a people whose hearts have already been rent in two. It must be precisely as you have said, Matthew."

Matthew had stared at the old man, the only father he had ever known. Uncle Soo-moy'asum rarely used his Boston name, choosing not to call him by anything other than the loving word "son." He felt the respect the older man held for him when he acknowledged the foreign name.

A presence made itself known, interrupting his thoughts. The air about him crackled with excitement. A lively squirrel scampered from behind a tree, its cheeks bursting with his next meal. Funny, Matthew thought, he could have sworn that yellow flower to his right had not been there before. The sea gulls raucously chattered at each other, their cries louder, clearer, more closely resembling a taunting conversation.

An unmistakable scent suffused the breeze.

"Come here," he said, smiling, extending his hand.

Cece gasped. "How—how did you know I was here?"

Matthew turned to face her. "The world comes alive when you are here. Besides, roses do not bloom in the forest, only on your skin."

She placed her hand in his, and at the contact Matthew felt the sharp shooting awareness of her femininity, of her sensuality, rush up his hand and pool low in his body. The sight of her, the scent of her, the sound of her voice all worked together to bring him to immediate arousal.

With a tug she was back in his arms where she belonged. His lips descended, plundering, reclaiming what was his, what had been denied him for many days. His hands ran restlessly up and down her back, lost in the sensation of cool silk over heated feminine flesh. Soon his hands met in front, and he expertly opened the many buttons on her blouse.

Cece was busy as well. Matthew felt those soft fingers searing paths of flame over his chest, his shoulders, his back. She grasped his upper arms, inhaling sharply as he nibbled on her full lower lip, then soothed it with the sweep of his tongue.

He tore his mouth from hers. "I missed you."

"Hush," she responded, touching his lips with a dainty fingertip. "I am here now. No need to miss me anymore."

"True," he said, the desire to claim her raging through his inflamed body, which soared to the heights of scalding bliss when her fingers found his hard nipples. At the arousing flicks of her nails, his manhood swelled, pressing hard against the leather pouch he wore. Soon he would remove the confounded contraption, but for the moment he hoped it would serve as a buffer, allowing him the control he needed to enjoy the bounty of Cece's body just a bit longer.

He cursed the pretty, lace-trimmed chemise he found once the blue-and-white-striped silk blouse was gone. In his haste a ribbon tie pulled too hard, and the gossamer cotton tore. He realized this, but lacked the patience to examine the damage. He needed Cece. He parted the fabric, and her full round breasts filled his hands, the deep rose-colored tips tight and reaching in readiness for his lips. He curled his tongue around one, pulling it into his mouth, then taunted the other with his fingertips.

The sweet taste of her filled his senses, the taut velvet feel of her rigid nipple telling him she wanted all he could give. Her hands, avidly exploring every part of him she could reach, found their way to the throbbing flesh that hungered most for release. Now she demanded what he could give.

His loinstring posed no deterrent to Cece's determined touch. Soon she and Matthew were naked, their hands teasing and stroking secret spots, mouths tasting and biting, raising the level of need to a nearly painful point. She tugged his hips over hers, settling his staff at the entrance to her aroused core.

"Now, Matthew, please," she cried, her demand turned to supplication.

No, he never wanted her to beg. He would gladly give her all she wanted. In turn, he would take what he needed for himself.

In a smooth plunge, he took her, burying himself in the deep, dark wetness of her body. She was so tight, so hot, that a groan of ecstasy was wrested from him. He held himself still, allowing her to adjust to his size, but before he knew what she was up to, her hips began to buck under him, her inner muscles relentlessly milking his flesh.

"Cece," he cried out, her name both a prayer and a condemnation. Gentleness be damned! He met her thrust for thrust. Deeper he plunged, thrilling to her whimpers, her gasps, her moans.

He felt her tighten around him, felt her hips convulse, heard her cry his name. And then that was all he knew, aside from pleasure so intense it must be forbidden to mere mortals. Their lovemaking was so powerful that he thought it surely would be his damnation. The pleasure soared on, claiming every drop of his essence, every throb of his shaft, each beat of his heart.

Their breathing returned to a normal rate very slowly. They could only murmur of joy and contentment; tender touches of lips and hands the only movement possible. After a while Matthew realized he lay heavily on Cece, and despite her protest he withdrew from her body, rolling onto his back. Never letting her go, he placed her head on his shoulder, and she did the rest. She pillowed her breasts against his side, then slipped a delightfully curved leg between his. She wrapped her arm around his waist and sighed.

Only then did he feel the rain on his hot skin. "The heavens weep for Chief Chet-ze-moka," he whispered.

"Is he the man who is dying? The leader who leaves the Port Townsend S'Klallam without a chief?" Cece asked.

Matthew nodded. "He died today. No one has stepped forward to replace him. The Port Townsend S'Klallam now have no real leadership." Matthew rubbed his eyes with his thumb and forefinger, his eyes suddenly feeling too tired to keep open. "Since my uncle has expressed his wish to step down, he has spoken frequently of his hope that I will follow him into the leadership of the village. I have *felt* his desire for me to become *ssia'm.* I can only consider doing so if empowered by the spirits."

Cece rose on one elbow, gazing quizzically at Matthew. "And how do the spirits feel?"

Matthew sighed, and rose, gently extricating his legs from the sweet temptation of her satiny thigh. He gazed out toward the water. He could not see it, only heard the rhythmic slap of choppy waves against the sand.

"I am not certain. I do know that if Luke decides to challenge me, and if he gains enough support from the villagers, there could be more bloodshed. There could be another tragedy, and we have already endured much misery."

Cece sat up, determination clearly visible in her features. "Then return to the village and take your rightful place, Matthew. What is so difficult about that?"

She was so intent on solving his problems that she had not heeded their surroundings, or even their state of undress.

Matthew stifled a laugh and sought to do the same with the spear of awareness brought on by the sight of her beautiful bobbing breasts.

Setting his mind on more serious matters, he lifted his face toward the canopy of pine boughs, letting the misty rain bathe his skin. "Yes, it is a simple matter to return, hold a potlatch, and declare myself the *ssia'm*," he answered. "But it is another matter altogether to present my tribe with a leader empowered by a special *tamanous*, one who can bring the differing factions together."

Cece crossed her legs, clearly seeking a more comfortable position. Unfortunately for Matthew, this position fully exposed the ruffle of flame-colored curls that hid her womanly charms. There would be no comfort for him while she was bare; indeed, there would be no further conversation if she did not hide from him what was no longer secret.

Matthew sat, trying to ease the tautening of his loins, and reached for her drawers. "Here," he said, his voice scarcely more than a growl. "For God's sake, cover yourself. Or I will spend the entire day indulging myself in you."

Cece gasped. Then she smiled. "What you have done to me, Matthew, is truly remarkable. Here I sit, naked as a newborn, carrying on a very serious conversation with you."

She shook her head, bemused by the changes she had undergone. Then she glanced down at Matthew's lap and burst out laughing. No wonder he wanted her dressed! His manhood, so recently spent, was again full and swollen.

"I do not see the humor in the situation," he muttered, his gaze firmly fixed on her own lap.

The hot carnal quickening shot straight through her, both at the sight of his ready shaft and at the lusty way he stared at her, fairly devouring her with his ebony eyes. "Well, Matthew, it seems you have another decision to make. Will we resolve this very immediate matter? Or shall we continue to discuss something we cannot solve quite so simply? We can do both if we take things in their proper order. . . ."

She reached out a finger and lovingly caressed the swollen tip. Matthew growled and tumbled her onto the ground, his mouth fastening itself to hers in a hungry conflagration. But this time Cece had no intention of just lying beneath him and allowing him to explore at will while she melted into rivers of sensation. It was his turn to burn, and hers to learn.

With strength that stunned her, she pushed him off onto the pile of crumpled silk she'd worn earlier. Matthew was quite cooperative and did not even comment on his wet mattress. Her damp garments, cushioned by the mat of pine needles on the forest floor, made a very adequate bed for their loving. Matthew's eyes never left her face.

Then she set to her delightful task. With gentle touches, she traced each line, each plane of Matthew's body. His chest, ridged with large plates of squared muscles, narrowed down to a lean waist and slender hips. His strong thighs, evidence of the power he'd gained swimming the waters of Port Gamble Bay, were taut with the control he exerted while allowing her free rein to explore. Between his thighs, his sex was full, ready for her, and she took advantage to excite him to a point of desperation.

Soon he had had enough, and he dragged her over his body. She raised a questioning brow as he settled her buttocks over his hips. The ridge of aroused manhood rubbed up into her moist layers, teasing her with what she wanted. She had an idea what he wanted, but did not quite know how to go about it.

He showed her. His hands tight on her hips, he lifted her, then brought her down on him, causing her to gasp at the sudden hot fullness. After a moment she moved tentatively and learned how much she liked the new position. At the same time she saw what her movement had done for him, and she repeated her action.

"Yesss . . ." he hissed, then with his hands he moved her again, bringing her down hard against his pelvis. Over and over he helped her, even though she no longer needed the help. She increased the pace as she felt her climax approach and saw the skin over his cheekbones stretch tight. Beads of sweat popped out on his forehead, and his jaws clenched with his attempt at control, at prolonging the delicious ride for both of them.

But she wanted none of his control, she wanted him as wildly lost to passion as she was, and she tightened herself about his flesh. He shuddered under her and his hips jerked up. Knowing she was close to completion, she repeated her movement, once, twice, then saw him shut his eyes and cry out her name. She felt him rise inside her to a depth he'd never yet sought. Then they shared ecstasy. Beautiful flames burned in her mind as the ripples of pleasure overtook her. The melding of two into one . . .

At the crest of bliss Cece learned the truth of love. This act was no more than the expression of the bond they had begun to build with their emotions, their feelings, their love. She could not tell where she began or where Matthew ended. They were one, bound by love, fused by the joining of their most intimate flesh. No power on earth could sever that bond.

A mystical silence surrounded them. After their heartbeats had slowed, Matthew helped Cece dress. Then he stepped into the shelter.

She watched him go, noting the smooth way he moved, the sturdy male grace of his body. He loved her. She knew it. And he was the leader of an entire people. The responsibility awed her. He was an admirable man, serious, dedicated, trustworthy. He might never be fully hers. She would always share him with his tribe, and that was fine by her, as long as he was willing to allow her to remain in his life.

She was not sure what sort of place she would occupy once he became chief, the *ssia'm*, as he had said. Surely not as his wife, since she was not S'Klallam, and the villagers were unfavorably disposed to whites, anyway. A stab of pain pierced her heart. It hurt so much that Cece fought to draw a breath of air.

Without needing to be told, she knew Matthew would take an Indian wife. When that happened, Cece would leave the Pacific Northwest forever. She could never witness the reality of Matthew with another woman. That would be an earthly form of death.

Before that happened, Cece vowed, she would live a lifetime of love with him. Before she had to relinquish the best part of her life, she would live it to its fullest. She vowed to take every ounce of joy, every bit of pleasure, every measure of love that grew between them, and savor each as a gourmet experiences a meal. She would treasure each caress, every word, every sensual, erotic moment, knowing she would have to turn them into memories to last a lifetime. She would be Matthew's woman as long as he allowed her to be, as long as his responsibilities did not wrench him from her.

Before their final parting came, she would create for Matthew the same sort of memories. If she could not be by his side, then at the very least he would have her in his heart, his soul, his thoughts. She would sear the image of their love in the essence of him, and it would endure for the rest of his life.

The ache threatened to bring her to her knees, but she stood strong. To stand at Matthew's side, even if only for a while, she had to be as strong as he. And she would have to find the means by which to weave her presence into his days without interfering with his destiny.

A sob tore from her, and tears burned behind her eyelids. Cece pressed a fist to her breast, where her heart beat out a symphony of suffering. For a moment she doubted her ability to withstand such stark pain. *Dear God, give me the strength to love him, then let him go.*

Matthew emerged from the shelter fully dressed. He wore a white cotton shirt buttoned to the throat, the long sleeves rolled up on his forearms in deference to the warm weather. Brown trousers encased his powerful legs, but did not hide the strength that propelled him forward.

Cece hastily wiped the tear that dampened her cheek and came to stand by him. Tentatively she touched Matthew's shirt sleeve. "This is the first time you have been dressed when we have been alone here."

A sad smile curved his lips. "So it is. But I must join my people at the village. There is the matter of the chief's burial. Too, I must test the mood of the men."

Cece frowned. "Tell me, Matthew, if you are so close a friend of this Luke, how is it that you choose peace between Indian and white, whereas he is determined to continue to fight?"

Matthew ran a hand through his hair. He shrugged. "I cannot be certain. I believe the difference lies with my uncle. You see, back in the 1850's, many of our people still tried to fight yours. Luke's father was killed in one of the uprisings, leaving his mother about to give birth. She was despondent over the death and never recovered after Luke was born. After she died, his uncle's family took him in. When he proved unmanageable, his grandparents gave it a try, but they were too old. Other relatives tried—all his relatives did. Luke's bitterness, even as a child, made him difficult to live with. He never forgave your people for his loss.

"My parents died in 1859. Smallpox stole them from me. I was only a few months old, and Uncle Soo-moy'asum and his wife took me home and into their family. I have never missed my parents, other than to feel an occasional curiosity about the two who gave me life. My uncle's family gave me love."

Matthew's simple explanation touched Cece's heart. He had no need to embellish his words; she knew what kind of family life he had had, what she had lacked. "You are so blessed, Matthew. You have a family, all the love anyone could need. I envy you that."

Matthew reached for her, and she willingly went into his embrace. Perhaps her childhood had been empty of the love she needed, but Cece knew she could make up her loss in Matthew's arms.

She looked up at his dear face. "You have set aside the anger you might have felt toward those who brought the illness that killed your parents."

"Perhaps," Matthew answered, lifting a shoulder in a dismissive shrug. "But I do not think I am quite so noble. My uncle deserves the praise. He gave what I needed. I never felt the anger since I never knew my parents. I did not miss their love because I had a family."

Cece cupped Matthew's hard jaw in her hand. "Have you any brothers or sisters?"

Matthew shook his head and smiled. "No, but I have a cousin."

"A cousin is not humorous. Why that smile?"

The loving bands of steel about her waist tightened in an affectionate hug. "Because this cousin is different. She is quite something."

Cece squinted one eye and studied Matthew's expression. "And you love her dearly."

"Yes, I love her dearly. In spite of herself."

Cece thought of what he'd said about his cousin. She was bound to be an excellent source of information on Matthew. Besides, the cousin might become a friend, something Cece missed in Port Gamble. "Hmmm . . . I do believe I need to meet this cousin of yours. She sounds most delightful."

With firm hands, Matthew set her away from him. A stern frown pleated his forehead. He shook his head. "No. Absolutely not. Anna is trouble on her own. And you are more trouble than any man can handle. The two of you together would be the end of me. No, you can never meet Anna. I will see to that."

Cece thought to argue, then realized it would be futile. Instead she smiled. He had said he would never again send her away. He had also said he loved Anna quite dearly. If that were the case, Anna would most likely visit Matthew at some point in his stay at the shelter. All Cece would have to do to make the acquaintance of the intriguing Cousin Anna was to frequent Matthew's camp. And since Cece was more than ever determined to live this miraculous moment in time with Matthew, visiting the camp would hardly pose a hardship for her!

"We shall see, Matthew. We shall see."

Chapter Twelve

———— • ————

After parting from Cece, Matthew returned to the village. A somber mood reigned, evidence of the respect and admiration the people had for the dead chief.

Chet-ze-moka had been his uncle's friend. A wise, honorable man, with a great understanding of justice, and full of personal integrity. Whatever he had promised, he did, and many men—both white and Indian—told tales of his boundless kindness.

Due to his position, Matthew knew he must travel to Indian Island, where the chief had lived. The islet by Port Townsend, near the mouth of Admiralty Inlet, was home to another group of S'Klallam.

Upon arrival at the town, Matthew stopped to express his sorrow to the grieving widows. Chet-ze-moka—called the Duke of York by his many Boston friends—had ascribed to the S'Klallam tradition of multiple wives, one Matthew had great difficulty accepting. See-Hem-Itza, affectionately known as Queen Victoria, and Chill-lil, who was called Jenny Lind, both deeply mourned their husband's passing. Matthew spoke respectfully to them, especially the elderly Queen Victoria, and let her know how much he would miss her husband's leadership as well as his peace-loving attitude.

Soon, though, some of the Duke's white friends took over what Matthew felt should have been a S'Klallam matter. The *Puget Sound Argus* carried articles about the chief's demise. A story in the *Seattle Weekly Intelligencer* soon followed. Frank Pettigrove, son of one of Port Townsend's founding fathers, started a fund drive to provide a burial for the chief. The white men made arrangements, and in two days the Duke's body was laid out for viewing at the county courthouse. He was buried, amid much pomp, at the Laurel Grove Cemetery.

Despite the flattering funeral—numerous carriages filled with the wealthiest and most influential citizens of Port Townsend followed the cortege—Matthew felt that matters had gotten out of hand. Chet-ze-moka's burial would have been best handled, in his opinion, by laying the man out on a traditional, raised burial canoe. But since the arrival of missionaries to the Puget Sound area, interment had become common. Matthew smiled wryly. In S'Klallam tradition, that sort of burial had been reserved for the lowliest of people.

A few days later, back at his camp in the woods, Matthew sighed. Lord Jim Balch, the chief of the Dungenness S'Klallam, had recently been murdered. Now Chet-ze-moka was also dead. No one had stepped forward to take their places, and the S'Klallam were disorganized. His people were losing their traditions, their identity.

While he believed survival lay in sharing the land with the whites, Matthew did not feel it was necessary to stop being S'Klallam to survive. To be sure, those of his people who had taken up the white man's drink were rushing down the road to destruction.

More pain would surely follow if Luke were to gain supporters. Matthew had to decide. Would he fill the empty slot of leader? Could he help the village?

Only the spirits knew. As yet, they remained silent.

Returning from the tryst in the woods with Matthew, Cece was aware of the changes in herself. First of all, she was indeed a woman now. Not just in the physical sense, by virtue of the act of loving Matthew, but also in the depth of emotion she had discovered inside herself. No child could love so fully, yet realize that love would most likely not last forever. A child would demand what she wanted, how she wanted it, and insist that she wanted it now!

Finally understanding Matthew's circumstances, Cece knew she loved him enough to walk away the moment her love became a burden to him—at enormous cost to her, true, but for Matthew she would bear the pain.

When the moment of separation came, she would still have Father. Knowing the depth of love Matthew had received from his uncle's family, Cece was determined to create a family of her own for the day Matthew was no longer hers. Father would never take Matthew's place, no one ever could, but at least she would not be utterly alone in the world.

And so, in the last few days before the ball, Cece worked ceaselessly to bring off an elegant soiree to honor her father. More than ever she was conscious of her behavior, endeavoring to embody the very essence of Father's idea of womanhood. As a result of her efforts, during those hectic days, Father seemed to take more note of her, and on occasion a faint smile hovered on his lips.

Triumphs! Cece relished each twist of that stern mouth as if it were a silver trophy.

But despite all she had to do, she found time to escape to Matthew's side for stolen moments of bliss. Their scintillating passion lured her to his side. His conversation also drew her to him. He always taught her something of value. He told her how the S'Klallam had used the bark of the enormous cedar trees to fashion capes to protect themselves from the persistent rains. That art was now nearly forgotten, and most S'Klallam wore Boston clothing, but they kept some of their traditional possessions, and a few even practiced the nearly forgotten arts.

Often Matthew spoke of his problems, of the sense of impending doom he felt. He frequently voiced his concerns for the future of his people. Cece felt honored that he shared such serious matters with her. He no longer treated her as if she were a child.

Two days before the party, having again escaped Mrs. Quigley's ill-tempered sniffs and snide remarks, Cece rushed to Matthew's campsite. Upon her arrival she was shocked to find a woman emerging from the rush shelter.

When the stranger looked up, Cece's heart began to break apart. So the time had apparently come. This lovely, raven-haired girl was the one who would share Matthew's life and his bed.

Cece studied the young woman. She was beautiful; Cece gave Matthew credit for good taste. The girl's dark copper skin gleamed with health, and her wrist-thick braid caught the light that filtered through the pine boughs. Her almond-shaped eyes shone with intelligence, and her full lips hinted at a sensual nature.

Slim, the girl was dressed in a simple blouse and gray skirt. But her clothes could never hide her proud heritage. She was S'Klallam.

Cece was not.

"Come on out," the girl called, startling Cece.

Instinct told her to run. She could never carry on a conversation with the woman who was to share Matthew's life. Sudden dizziness and nausea struck when a revolting thought crossed her mind. Had the S'Klallam girl already been invited to share Matthew's body?

Cece turned, her insides heaving at the images of the young Indian writhing under Matthew, pleasing him the way Cece had, as recently as yesterday. How could Matthew touch another woman the way he had touched her? How could he allow another woman's hands to caress him as intimately as she herself had yesterday? Cece thought she might die from the agony.

The girl's melodious voice broke through Cece's haze of pain. "Please, come speak with me. I know Matthew has been meeting someone out here. You must be very special to have captured his interest."

Matthew had spoken of the old S'Klallam tradition that allowed a man as many wives as he wanted. But he had also told her he hated the idea. Perhaps, when faced with two willing women, he had not found the prospect quite so hateful.

It was to her. She could not share her man. And yet this woman wished to speak to her. A swift rush of anger pushed the searing ache aside as she considered her position. If this fool was magnanimous enough to try to befriend Cece, she had formed the wrong opinion of Cecelia Scanlon. She would gladly scratch the silly thing's eyes out. Ready to do battle, Cece stepped forward.

"Ooohhhh . . ." The Indian girl's eyes grew round as platters. Her full lips formed a circle of surprise. "So *this* is what he has been hiding. Well, it's no wonder."

"And what, pray tell, is no wonder to you?" Cece asked, her voice sharp with animosity.

The girl waved her hand in Cece's direction, as if by the gesture she had explained all. Her black eyes, intently curious, never strayed from Cece's face.

Cece wondered if each of Matthew's kisses was blazoned on her skin for her rival to view. She hoped they were. She would gladly wear them as a badge of pride. That is, if the louse had not yet decided to spread himself between the two women. That was one bit of information she would come away with from this encounter, even if it was the last thing she did in life.

She narrowed her eyes in open challenge, then crossed her arms below her breasts. "You have yet to answer my question. What is no wonder to you?"

"Why, that you are white, of course. I would never have expected Matthew to make such a choice, but since you are so well acquainted with his camp, I assume you are the one who has spent time here with him."

Cece lifted her chin a notch. "I have."

The girl nodded. "Well, there you have it. You are the rose scent on Matthew's skin."

Cece gasped. This—this *floozy* had indeed gotten close enough to Matthew to smell her perfume on his skin, and flaunted the fact that she had. The nerve of the man to love Cece to distraction and then cozy up to this other woman. Just wait until she got her hands on him.

The girl did not seem to note Cece's incipient rage, nor had she heard her gasp of indignation. She continued speaking as if nothing at all were amiss. "It is about time he did something like this, though. He is twenty-nine. But you are not the sort I would have expected him to choose."

That did it! "No," Cece fumed through gritted teeth. "I imagine you expected him to choose someone like you."

She nodded.

Clenching her hands into fists, Cece took a step forward. "Someone *exactly* like you. Perhaps you yourself."

"What? Me?" The young woman laughed.

Cece knew she was on the verge of murder. "Is that not why you are here? To claim Matthew for yourself?"

The woman laughed on. After a bit, with obvious effort, she controlled her merriment. "Matthew? Mine? Oh, no. Well, yes, he is mine. But not that way. Never."

The humor in the situation still escaped Cece. "Precisely how is he yours, then?"

"He's my cousin."

This time Cece's mouth formed a circle of surprise. A foolish flush filled her cheeks. Wishing to die of mortification, she covered her hot face with her hands. "Then you are Anna," she mumbled through her fingers.

"Of course I am. Who are you?"

"If you will forgive my stupid assumptions and still care to make my acquaintance, I am Cecelia Scanlon. My friends call me Cece." Cautiously Cece peeked through her fingers to see how Matthew's cousin took her introduction.

Another look of surprise crossed Anna's face. "He does things the hard way, does he not? You are the mill manager's daughter, right?"

Cece took her hands from her face. She needed to face reality squarely. "Yes, I am. But let me assure you I have no animosity toward your people."

Anna giggled. "I should say not, or if you do, my cousin faces yet more trouble ahead."

From the knowing look Anna sent Cece's way, she knew Anna had quite a good idea of how matters stood between her and Matthew. She felt herself blush again. Perhaps those kisses were engraved on her face, after all.

Anna waved away the evidence of Cece's chagrin. "Oh, don't be silly, Cece. I shall call you Cece. You see, we *will* be friends. Anyway, I am not so young not to know why you come to Matthew. And I envy you."

At Cece's frown, Anna put out her hand as if to halt Cece's thoughts. "Oh, no," she said, "I don't envy you Matthew. I would never envy anyone my cousin. What I envy is what the two of you have found. If you are both willing to fight such tremendous odds, the love you feel for each other must truly be magnificent."

Cece bit her lip. New and private though her feelings were, they were too powerful to hide. Nor did she want to keep them secret. She looked at Anna and nodded. "It is. *He's* magnificent."

"Matthew? Magnificent? No, no. He is too serious, too stubborn." Anna rolled her eyes.

Cece laughed. She had been right when she suspected Matthew's cousin would be a delight. Now that she had no reason to hate the girl, Cece found herself warming to Anna. "He is a bit serious and far too stubborn for his own good."

"What about you, Cecelia Scanlon? How stubborn are you?" At the sound of the deep male voice, both women whirled in the direction of the large cedar at the edge of the clearing. There stood Matthew, clad as usual in his loinstring.

Cece longed to run into his arms, to seek those firm lips with hers, to feel his warm skin against her naked body.

But Anna was there, busy chastising Matthew. "Why on earth are you naked, Matthew? You have company, and you hardly look civilized."

Matthew shrugged easily and offered no explanation. Cece, again aware of the heat in her cheeks, wondered how Anna would react when she guessed how well acquainted Cece was with Matthew's body.

Anna looked from the silent Matthew to Cece, and back again. Cece knew Anna had noted her heightened color and Matthew's unwillingness to respond. Being no fool, Anna cast a sly smile at Cece and turned to Matthew with mischief in her eyes.

"Perhaps, cousin, this is *special* company. Someone to whom you wish to present yourself like a wild buck. Someone you wish to share *everything* with."

Cece dared a glance in Matthew's direction. The usually controlled man was furious! A stern frown furrowed his brow, and his black eyes snapped with anger. "Go home, Anna," he said through clenched jaws.

Anna looked at Cece. Despite her mortification Cece smiled. Anna had truly ruffled Matthew, something Cece herself had managed any number of times. Cece met Anna's gaze, and both laughed, sharing a moment of feminine understanding.

All this time Matthew had held a long stick topped by a wicked-looking prong. At the women's laughter, he viciously stuck the hapless utensil into the ground and stalked toward his shelter, muttering every step of the way. "I knew this would be the outcome. I should have stayed closer to home today. These two can drive anyone—"

Anna laughed louder, clapping her hands. "This is wonderful! Matthew is human, after all. *You* are wonderful," she said to Cece with a smile.

Cece smiled back. "Well, perhaps we are wonderful together."

Anna nodded sagely, mischief still in her exotic eyes. "I shall take that as an admission of what I suspect. And," she added, winking broadly at Cece, "as your estimation of his . . . efforts, shall we say?"

Cece shook her head, laughing helplessly. "You are as bad as Matthew said you are. And I need you as a friend." She extended her hand, certain of Anna's response.

But Anna again took her by surprise. She threw her arms around Cece and caught her in a fierce hug. "I am so glad," she whispered in Cece's ear, a catch in her voice.

After a moment the two women withdrew from the embrace, knowing they had forged a special bond. Anna gazed at Matthew's shelter, then turned to Cece. "I brought the stubborn mule some food. He takes this spirit quest of his far too seriously. But I shall make myself scarce. I know the two of you wish to be alone."

Cece tried to deny Anna's assumption, but found she could not lie. "That is true," she answered sheepishly. "But I do want to know you better. When will you return?"

Anna thought for a moment. "Tomorrow?"

Cece nodded. "There is much I need to know about a certain man."

Anna nodded, equally serious. "And there is much I need to know about a certain woman he has found in the woods."

With a quick good-bye they separated. And after duly teaching Cece the proper method of making a whaling harpoon, Matthew took her to heaven once again.

Things did not turn out quite the way the two new friends had planned. The next day dawned gray and rainy—not the usual misty Pacific rains, either. Winds gusted and rain lashed the ground in torrents.

Of course, the deliveries Cece had expected did not materialize. The ferry could not make the crossing from Seattle due to the rough seas, and Cece spent the day in a panic. Now they would only have one day for the last-minute preparations.

Despite the mishaps Mrs. Quigley, with a huffy sniff, assured Cece that all was well under control. The next morning, the morning of the ball, when the expected deliveries arrived, Cece began to believe perhaps Mrs. Quigley had been right. Everything did seem to be running smoothly without her direction.

So Cece managed to have the day of the ball to herself and spent most of it deep in thought. Although the ball meant a great deal to her, the scare she had experienced in the woods when she discovered Anna at Matthew's campsite was enough to demonstrate how deeply she needed to be Matthew's woman. His only woman. She now accepted her possessiveness where Matthew was concerned, willingly admitting she had no intention of ever giving up on the man she loved.

Somehow she would find a way to keep Matthew, help him unsnarl the matter of the leadership of the village of Nuf-Kay'it, and greatest of all three hurdles, maintain a semblance of peace with Father while she accomplished the first two.

Her first step, of course, was to broach with Father the subject of her feelings for Matthew. In her opinion, the best moment to do so would undoubtedly be when he was glowing from the success of the ball. So she planned to serve him an after-the-ball snifter of the finest cognac in the library. Then, after the certain explosion, she would run to meet Matthew and show off her enchanting toilette.

As the time for the guests' arrival approached, the butterflies in Cece's stomach took on the size of eagles. They soared and swooped in her middle, not because Cece anticipated the party itself, but because of the all-important meeting afterward.

At the first clatter of the brass door knocker, Cece descended the stairs, pausing for a second before the ornate mirror in the vestibule. As usual, stray curls had found their way onto her forehead. Fortunately the rest of her locks remained tightly anchored in an elegant upsweep, topped by a whimsical ostrich feather set among pale green satin ribbons.

A swift tug pulled the deep plunge of her décolletage up by an infinitesimal bit. At Matthew's side she felt no discomfort with her nudity, but here, quite fully dressed, a low-cut gown had her wriggling prudishly. Amazing what love did to a woman!

"Ready, Cecelia?" Father's voice at her elbow made her blush. She had been so busy considering the pleasure she'd experienced with Matthew that she had not even noticed Father's necessarily noisy arrival.

"Ye-yes, Father. As I'll ever be," she answered, nervously anticipating the meeting to come much later in the evening.

Father hooked the curved ivory handle of his cane over his forearm and leaned against the curving banister at the bottom of the staircase. They had decided to greet their guests there for the support the railing would provide Father's weakened legs.

The butler Cece had hired for the evening nodded in their direction and opened the door. From that moment on, a stream of handsomely garbed revelers poured through the doors. Cece's mind whirled dizzily at the number of faces she was hard-pressed to match names to. Eventually she gave up trying, and smiled and shook hands until her fingers ached.

She had not been able to eat much all day and now felt light-headed, so she demurred each time a servant brought the tray of chilled champagne to her. When Cece had greeted the last stragglers, she gladly escaped to the kitchen and poured herself a glass of iced water. Pausing to check that all was in order, she prayed to Sister Marietta's saints for the strength she needed this crucial night.

"Cecelia, my dear," Mrs. Sanders said the moment Cece entered the crowded dining room, "have I told you yet you look even more exquisite than you did the other afternoon when we tried on your pretty dress?"

"Yes, Mrs. Sanders," Cece answered, her patience with the lady's forgetfulness never seeming to run out. "But it is never a bother to hear that one looks well."

"You exceed merely looking well," Dexter Sanders said at Cece's elbow, startling her with his arrival.

Why did she feel so uncomfortable in Dexter Sanders's company? Cece wondered. He was always the perfect gentleman, even if he never let her forget he was interested in her. Perhaps it was because her interest lay elsewhere that she felt uncomfortable.

"Thank you, Dr. Sanders," she managed to say.

He frowned. "Dexter, Cecelia. Please."

A bit irritated by his renewed insistence, Cece nodded nonetheless. "You are right, Dexter. We did agree."

A pleased smile spread over his thin face, illuminating his pleasant features with hope—a hope Cece had no intention of encouraging.

"If you will excuse me," she said, "I see someone Father insisted I speak with."

Murmurs of polite acceptance followed in her wake. She paused to speak to a man Father had introduced to her as Captain D. B. Jackson, the man in charge of the Puget Mill Company's steamboats. After a few moments of chitchat Cece escaped to stand by an open window.

She stared into the black night, wondering if Matthew had lit a fire. More than ever she wished to flee from the mill manager's ostentatious mansion and share the bright simplicity of Matthew's hearth. She filled her lungs with the unique scent of Port Gamble Bay and leaned her forehead momentarily against the windowsill.

When she opened her eyes, Father stood next to her, wearing a concerned look on his face. "Are you quite all right, Cecelia?" he asked.

She nodded. "The crowd is just a bit much, don't you think?"

Father turned and studied the full dining room, noting the people seeking their place cards at the huge table. A proud gleam lit his deep emerald eyes. Then he turned to Cece and met her gaze for the first time she could ever remember.

The resonant notes of his voice were clear to her ears, even above the din of their guests. "You have done well, Cecelia."

Tonight was the night of that blasted ball Cece had endlessly spoken of. Whatever had possessed the confounded woman to conceive such a dangerous bit of frivolity? Now Luke would have a perfect opportunity to create a diversion and strike a crushing blow to Pope and Talbot.

Matthew knew influential members of Seattle society had been invited. He also knew a few of the managers from various Pope and Talbot operations had accepted the invitations. Some came from as far as San Francisco. Luke had been veritably salivating at the golden chance to act on his threats.

Somehow Matthew had to stop him.

To make matters even worse, the last time Cece had come to the woods, she had extracted a promise from him to meet her after all the guests were gone. True, it offered him the chance to be on the grounds, but if he were found, and Edward Scanlon decided to make good his threat, Cece's invitation would count for naught.

Edward Scanlon was highly unlikely to view favorably a midnight tryst between his beautiful daughter and the man he wished to blame for any disturbance that might occur. So, more than ever, Matthew had to be certain the festivities were in no way disrupted.

He watched the carriages pull up and the elegantly attired guests parade into the house. He watched the lights burn brightly inside, and heard the music of the chamber orchestra Cece had gone to Seattle to hire. He observed the extra servants she had commandeered for the occasion flit inside the mansion, serving the many people within.

But as yet he had not caught even one glimpse of the only person on earth he really cared to see.

Where was she? Was she still safe? Was she in there among all those strangers? Or had Luke already struck?

A sound in the darkness at the edge of the woods made Matthew whirl around in readiness. His sharp gaze caught sight of shadows among the shrubs, but he could not tell who was there. He could not see how many people there were, either.

A harsh laugh gave away the inebriated condition of the men in the shadows, and Matthew realized there were a number of them present. Fear invaded every pore of his being. What was he to do? He was alone.

"Pssst. Ovah he-ah!"

Matthew turned his face a fraction, trying to find the person who had called out. From the corner of the mansion, a small figure gestured wildly. "He-ah, Misseh Matchew!"

Matthew quickly found himself surrounded by a bevy of Chinese. He recognized the one who had called him: the Scanlons' carriage driver.

"Misseh Matchew, dose men no good." The little man jerked his chin in the direction of the bushes that hid Luke and his cronies. "My flien's hehp you. You an' Missee Cece."

Matthew caught the gleam of determination in the man's eye and forgave him the knowledge of his relationship with Cece. Clearly the man did not object, or at least not enough to permit any harm to come to her.

"You are . . ." he asked, needing to know his helper's name.

"Me Lee Fung. You Missee Cece's Matchew."

Matthew caved in and allowed himself a mild chuckle of irony. "Yes, well. We can agree on that." Whether he wanted to be or not, he was Cece's Matthew. Most certainly tonight.

"Misseh Matchew. What we do?"

Matthew's good humor disappeared. *He* had to decide what should be done here? Irony heaped upon more irony. He had felt a surge of relief when Lee Fung had stepped forward and offered him help. Matthew had hoped one of the members of the tiny army could provide an answer to this dilemma. But that was not to be. He was now faced with the need to deal with Luke, to protect Cece, and worst of all, he had a ragtag army of Chinamen to lead.

He ran his hand through his hair. How was he to protect the woman he loved while at the same time protect the tribe to which he owed his loyalty? How could he help both? He cursed his inability to turn from either.

Then the answer came to him. As long as Luke and his friends had their brown-paper-wrapped bottles, they would continue to drink until the last drop was gone. And perhaps they had already imbibed too much to carry out their plans.

"Lee Fung, you and your friends surround the house. All sides must be watched at all times. Those in the shadows will sabotage their own purposes with their weakness for whiskey."

At Matthew's words, Lee Fung's flat face wrinkled in distaste. "Pahhh!" he spit out as if just the thought of drinking whiskey brought a foul taste to his mouth. "Uncivilized ar-cohoh."

Again Matthew laughed. It was interesting to note what different peoples found civilized and not. With a nod of agreement he motioned Lee Fung toward his post.

With a few singsong phrases to his friends, Lee Fung sent his troops to guard Matthew's woman. Matthew walked with Lee Fung a few paces, then turned to his companion. "I will go to the men in the bushes. I need to learn their intentions."

Lee Fung nodded, his pigtail flapping on his shoulder.

Matthew continued. "When I return, we can decide what else to do."

"Velly good, Matchew. Velly, velly good."

With a few silent steps, Matthew left Lee Fung at his post and approached Luke and his friends. "Luke," he called.

"Matthew? Whatcha here for?"

The stench of whiskey drowned the fragrance of the roses blooming nearby. Matthew winced at the thought of the damage the men were doing to their bodies.

He took a deep breath to steady his nerves. "I thought I might find you here."

Luke nodded, then took another swig of the bottle in his hand. Waving the bottle in the direction of the mansion, he smiled at Matthew. "They're all in there. All at one time."

A knot formed in Matthew's gut. Did these fools plan on harming all the people in the mansion? Surely Luke had given up on his bonfire idea?

But Luke's next words proved his hope ill founded. " 'Member my bonfire? Well, it starts tonight. When they're all sittin' down to dinner. We'll burn wha' dey put on our land. 'S only fair."

"We brought whiskey ta make the kindlin' burn pretty," added one of Luke's friends.

Matthew clenched his jaw. They were insane. Who in his right mind tried to burn down a mansion with nothing more than twigs and half-empty bottles of whiskey? Although he hated the prospect, perhaps this time he would encourage his friend to drink his bottle to the end. The damage to Luke's body had been done a long time ago, and by allowing him to finish this particular measure, Matthew could perhaps prevent a greater wrong.

"After you burn the mansion down, then what?" he asked, hoping to gain more time, more ammunition with which to fight Luke's rage.

"It burns, das what," Luke muttered in response, a bewildered look on his face.

"Yeah, Luke," one of the others asked. "Do we get our land back?"

Matthew thanked the spirits for inspiring the drunken question. He could not have phrased the question better himself and was sure it bore more weight for Luke since it had come from one of his cohorts.

Luke stared at the man, then raised his bottle to his lips again. Tipping his head way back, he drained what seemed to be the last drops of the whiskey. Bottle still in hand, he swiped his mouth with his forearm and waved the empty flask in the air. "Dunno what we get back."

Ever the voice of reason, Matthew ventured a question. "And if someone catches you lighting the bonfire?"

Luke shrugged.

One of his companions yelped. "Hey! I won' go ta jail for a fire."

Two others merely shook their heads and drank long and deep of their whiskey.

Matthew laid a hand on Luke's shoulder. "Is it worth the risk if there is nothing to be gained?"

Luke wrenched out of Matthew's grasp, then turned and stared at the mill manager's mansion. Every inch of his body broadcast his anger. But not until he turned back did Matthew see the depth of Luke's pain.

The moonlight lit up a tear as it worked down Luke's lean cheek. A shudder shook his body, and Matthew watched his friend square his shoulders and fling the empty bottle onto the pine-needle carpet beneath the trees.

"They cannot take all our land," Luke cried, his voice rough with emotion.

Without another word he disappeared into the thickness of the trees, his friends following. In the silence of the night, Matthew heard Luke's anguished cry reverberate inside his head.

He, too, would fight with every bit of himself to keep from losing any more of what made him who he was, a S'Klallam, one of the Strong People, the Nux Sklai Yem. But he would not strike back with violence.

Chapter Thirteen

———— • ————

The crystal chandelier over the center of the dining room cast a scintillating brilliance over the scene before her. Cece's breath caught at the rare, awkward smile on Father's lips. She clung to his words of praise and could not turn away from that unusual expression of pride. Finally! Father had come to her, had offered her a smile, had given her a demonstration of approval.

"Thank you, Father," she whispered, reaching a hand to his arm. "You have no idea how much this means to me." Yes, her joy was all but complete. Perhaps God had just one more miracle in store for her. Later on tonight she would find out.

Father acknowledged her words with a scant nod. "Yes, well. We had best sit at the table. It would be wrong to keep dinner waiting for our guests. We have an eventful evening ahead of us yet," he said, obviously uncomfortable with Cece's emotion, subdued though it was.

But Cece was not about to lose the ground she had gained. She slipped her hand into the crook of Father's arm, and in the guise of helping him to the dais where the table of honor had been set, she made her presence at his side a fait accompli.

At the table she sat next to her father and unfurled her pristine napkin. Turning to her right, she caught sight of Mrs. Sanders's struggles with her cane. Cece realized she was surrounded by people who needed her, whether they were willing to accept her help or not. Fortunately Mrs.

Sanders welcomed her assistance.

"Ah, dearie," she murmured, "it is a nasty thing to grow old and infirm." Her twisted fingers worked to open her napkin, and soon she succeeded. She smiled at her minor triumph, then shook a thin finger at Cece. "That, Cecelia, is why you must always strive to achieve that which truly matters to you. Life leaves you before you are ready to leave it."

Cece nodded, accepting the merit in her friend's words. Then she smiled mischievously. "Even if the pursuit of what truly matters to you entails something as unbearable as moving to the uncivilized wilds of the Pacific Northwest?"

Mrs. Sanders turned her head sharply and wagged her finger at Cece, this time in warning. "Even then, dear child, even then. And do not think I don't know what you are about. I know you believe that within a few months I will have fallen under the so-called spell of this savage land. Well, I know myself, and I shall never do such a thing."

Cece merely smiled, thinking of the sort of spell savages could cast and how easily she'd fallen under such a spell.

Her thoughts came to a halt when the servants brought out the meal. A simple consommé was followed by a crisp salad, tangy with a piquant dressing Mrs. Quigley had created. When these dishes had been cleared the servants brought out succulent slices of roast beef, done to a delicate rosy turn. May Li had contributed her recipe for an exotic rice dish to accompany the meat, and the guests lavished much praise for the treat as they passed gleaming silver gravy boats brimming with thick meat juices.

Although her stomach had grumbled in hunger a few times, Cece found herself unable to swallow more than a few bites of food. The scent of beef and rich gravy made her queasy in the state she was in.

She dabbed her lips with her napkin and gave up on the meal. Carefully she folded the square of heavy fabric and was about to lay it by her plate when out of the corner of her eye she caught sight of Father whispering to Horace Grimes. To her surprise, she noted that each man had fixed his gaze firmly on her. When she nodded in their direction, acknowledging their scrutiny, both turned away and tried to pretend they had not been studying her.

A strange sense of dread came over her at that moment. What had caused that odd behavior? she wondered, and turned to Mrs. Sanders, hoping for some insight. She placed her hand upon her friend's arm and leaned close enough to whisper. "I just saw Father and Hor—"

Father's sudden attempt to rise put an end to Cece's words. She went to help him, but he brushed her hand away. With some difficulty he managed to stand on his own.

Cece's sense of foreboding and dread became fear when Father tapped his wine goblet to quiet the guests. When everyone was silent, he paused for a moment and cast an odd smile in her direction.

Then he spoke. "I wish to welcome all of you to my home and to thank you for coming. It is indeed an occasion of great pride for me, even if this ball represents the end of my career with Pope and Talbot. These have been good years, but regretfully I am not in the sort of health that would permit me to continue in the post of manager of the mill.

"As most of you know, my assistant, Horace Grimes, a very able choice if I may say so, has accepted the company's offer to become my replacement. Furthermore Horace and I have more personal news to announce. It gives me great pride to celebrate tonight the betrothal of my only daughter, Cecelia, to a man as fine as Horace. The wedding will be in October."

What?

Cece felt as if her blood had been drained from her head. The silence in the room throbbed around her. The fork she had been about to set aside dropped onto the porcelain plate, chipping the rim, the sound ricocheting around the room. In seconds, the pathetic sound died, leaving the guests once again shrouded in deafening stillness.

Then a few startled gasps could be heard, and a smattering of polite applause began in the far corner of the salon. The clapping picked up, a sound Cece heard as though from a great distance. Shock so complete she could barely move filled her, thoughts not even forming in her stunned mind.

The guests returned to their meals as soon as they saw she was not rising for further acknowledgment. Long moments passed. Finally Cece was able to look about her. The atmosphere in the room sent her senses reeling into a frozen wasteland of loneliness. No one in the gathering could possibly comprehend her devastation. Everyone had resumed eating, something she could not do. Her stomach had embarked on a violent rebellion.

How could Father do something like this without even consulting her?

She dared peek at Father and saw nothing odd in his expression. He looked just as he always looked—serious, unreachable, distant. Then she caught sight of her supposed fiancé. She shuddered. A man more nondescript had yet to be born to this world. And Father wanted to marry her off to him?

Soon the servants cleared away the dinner dishes. Cece gladly relinquished her plate, her stomach growing more mutinous by the moment.

Why would Father choose Horace of all people, anyway? Why not a more amiable man like Dexter Sanders? Or were the mill and the mansion that much more important than his daughter's happiness? Did he think to continue to control the business by marrying her off to the new manager?

What a despicable possibility! What a horrid probability!

Standing frozen in a corner of the room, Cece saw the two hired stewards remove the tables and clear the room for dancing. Utterly detached from the bustling activity, she could easily have been a bird, gliding by the chandelier, hovering above the scene.

She would not be able to escape. A small crowd had formed about her; strangers stopped to wish her well on her upcoming marriage. Marriage! Outrage set her thoughts awhirl at the very notion. Such a farce. A travesty. How could she consider marriage to that . . . that faded ghost of a man?

From within her fog of whys and hows, Cece heard Father introduce the musical ensemble and invite everyone to enjoy the dancing. At the sound of the first waltz, his gnarled hand appeared before Cece. Not knowing how to refuse without causing a scene, she grasped his fingers. Clinging to his hand, she stiffly followed his hesitant lead.

Still numb with shock, Cece was unable to utter a word, still unwilling to cause a scandal. How could Father have betrayed her?

She looked up into his face and noted a certain easing of the ever-present creases on his brow. Even his shoulders seemed less bent, as if a great burden had been lifted from them.

He was relieved! But how could he sell out his own flesh and blood?

Partway through the musical piece, through her furiously flying thoughts, Cece caught the sound of renewed clapping.

Looking around, she cringed. "No," she whispered, but no one heard. Her horror became reality as Father handed her to Horace Grimes.

A clammy hand clasped hers. A stringy arm curved about her waist. A thin body came up against hers to the exact distance prescribed by propriety. Cece's skin began to crawl. Her stomach quaked.

The sound of hands slapping against other hands finally broke through her daze, and Cece heard the echo of Father's voice ring through her mind. . . . *betrothal of . . . Cecelia . . . Horace Grimes . . . Cecelia . . . Horace Grimes . . . Cecelia . . . Horace . . .*

Fearing madness, Cece closed her eyes and shook her head in an attempt to clear the horrible litany of Father's words from her memory. She was stunned with the result. An image of Matthew's beloved face formed in her mind. She saw his dear features, the line of his high forehead, his bold eyebrows, his black eyes, his sensual lips. Just as he had looked the last time she saw him.

Matthew had leaned over her, his face taut with passion, claiming her body with his in a fever of desire. The image in her mind was so clear that Cece thought she could hear his breath, could feel the friction of his chest against her breasts, the pressure of his weight.

When she blinked, though, all she saw was Horace. All she felt was his repulsive touch. By now her stomach was so thoroughly upset that bile climbed into her throat, burning away at her. The impression of Horace's hand on her back disgusted her; Cece concentrated on taking deep breaths to keep from disgracing herself in the middle of a soiree.

Nothing, though, would ever make this man's touch acceptable. Only Matthew had the right to put his hands on her body. Especially if—

Then the music stopped. She squared her shoulders and extricated herself from Horace's unwanted embrace. Before she could say a word, he spoke.

"I cannot wait until October."

Cece gasped, then shuddered. "If—if you will excuse me, Mr. Grimes, I am plagued by a beastly headache."

Without waiting for his reaction, Cece grabbed fistfuls of apple-green silk brocade and rushed out to the vestibule, heading for the sanctuary of her room.

The entry was mercifully empty. Running blindly for the stairs, Cece caught her toe on the edge of the plush Oriental rug. She stumbled and fell, her glamorous gown forming a sea of shimmering green all around her.

The strain of her father's betrayal overwhelmed her, and tears began to flow. She moaned in an attempt to lessen the pain that welled inside her, not caring that she was still in Father's house. She did not care that there were guests about. She did not care that anyone might come upon her and find her in this condition.

Her own parent had betrayed her.

All she now wanted from life was a chance to share it with Matthew. But they had been torn apart by the accident of their births. She was determined to overcome that, even if it meant slipping into the woods at odd times to spend precious moments together. As much as she had wanted to be a part of Father's life, he had just shown her she was merely a commodity to him.

Why couldn't her father love her? Was she an even greater fool to believe in Matthew's love? After all, he had never spoken specifically of love.

Her shoulders shook as she began to cry again. Through the tears, Cece remembered Matthew's tenderness. She could almost feel the gentle warmth of his caresses. She remembered the respect in his voice when he spoke with her, how he always treated her as an equal.

No. She was a fool to doubt that Matthew's feelings ran deep. His behavior was far different from her father's.

And perhaps that was her destiny. To lose her father, her heritage, and make a life with the man she loved.

She raised her head. Dashing the dampness from her cheeks with a furious hand, she looked around her. All she saw were the artificial trappings of wealth that obviously meant everything to Father. But deep in her heart she acknowledged the poverty of emotion in which he lived. She knew she could never exist in such a deprived state.

The beloved image of Matthew's face flashed into her thoughts. She rose onto her knees, her heart beating stronger now. Since meeting Matthew, and loving him, Cece had discovered all the riches of love. She would never again live without the life-giving warmth of love. Matthew was surely the answer to her endless prayers. Gathering up her tattered self-respect, Cece started to rise, but a frail, cool hand upon her shoulder stopped her.

"Mrs. Sanders," she whispered, her throat still raw from the salty tears she had shed.

"Will you be all right, my dear?" The sweet, caring voice of her friend served to salve her aching heart.

"I—I think so," she answered. "I cannot understand why Father would do such a thing."

Dropping her cane, Mrs. Sanders leaned down to enfold Cece in a hug. Her sweet cinnamon-and-clove scent surrounded her with its homey familiarity, just as the slender arms wrapped her in comfort. "Hush now, sweet. Don't fret, don't even think another thought tonight. Go on up to your room. Bathe your face and eyes with cool water. Get yourself some sleep."

"Sleep!" Cece cried, pulling away to stare at the older woman. "I don't believe I shall ever be able to sleep again!"

Mrs. Sanders rocked Cece against her frail breast, crooning wordless sounds of love. "I know how it feels at this moment. But I can assure you everything always looks better after a good night's rest."

"Even a ruined life?"

Mrs. Sanders shook her head. "Now, Cecelia, enough of that nonsense. Your father is a highly insensitive and maybe heartless sort, but your life is hardly begun. Don't make the mistake of wasting one second of it because of Edward's calamitous announcement."

Mrs. Sanders's gentle scolding quickly cleared the fog of pain, leaving Cece in a better frame of mind. The elderly woman was such a wonderful friend. At least Cece could count on her. Smiling a somewhat watery smile, Cece looked up. "I do love you so, Mrs. Sanders. I thank God and all the saints for bringing you to Port Gamble."

Mrs. Sanders's sandpapery laugh seemed so normal after the lunacy of the dinner, the announcement, the nightmarish dance. And she was right. Cece had to focus on her goals and not allow even Father's cruelty to steal anything of value from her life.

She stood to her full height and hugged Mrs. Sanders in turn. "Your kindness has helped. I feel a tiny bit better. But I agree, I shall go to bed. I could never return to that . . . that debacle in there."

Bending quickly, she retrieved Mrs. Sanders's cane. "Here, we would not want you tripping and landing on Father's rug as I did. You could be hurt."

Mrs. Sanders's look of compassion told Cece that she well knew how deeply Father had hurt her.

As Cece took the first step up, Mrs. Sanders spoke again. "I shall speak with Edward. And I will return in the morning. We will see what we can salvage of this night."

Cece nodded, a pang of pain piercing her heart. She had held such hope for this night. She had planned to tell Father of her love for Matthew. True, she had not expected him to be overjoyed, but she had never thought her father had plans to sell her off before the ball was over.

Later she would have met Matthew to show off her gown. She took another step up and thought again of Matthew awaiting her appearance at the bench in the garden. Perhaps that was how she would salvage this night. She could still meet Matthew and spend some time with him.

She went up the rest of the steps feeling lighter with each one she took. Yes, she would wash away her tears, and when no one was about, she would slip out to Matthew's shelter instead of waiting until he showed at the bench hours from now.

When she reached the top of the stairs, she heard Mrs. Sanders's voice again. "Edward!" she called sharply. "Do join me in the vestibule. We must speak."

"Certainly, Edith."

"Don't you 'certainly, Edith' me, Edward Scanlon. What you have done this evening is contemptible."

Cece whirled at the blatant distaste in Mrs. Sanders's voice. That tiny lady could apparently bring a man to his knees. Cece leaned over the banister to catch Father's reaction.

Well, perhaps Mrs. Sanders could intimidate most men, but obviously not Father. A deep red flush reached his hairline, and a strange expression overtook his features.

"What do you mean, Mrs. Sanders?"

Mrs. Sanders shook her head. "So, now that I question the farce you have staged, I become Mrs. Sanders once again?"

"I have staged no farce. I am celebrating my retirement and my daughter's impending marriage."

Mrs. Sanders snorted. Cece was aghast! She would never have expected a lady such as Mrs. Sanders to respond in a manner more typical of Cece herself. "You mean your daughter's impending destruction."

Father flinched, then closed his eyes for a moment. When he opened them, that strange light Cece had noticed in his gaze on various occasions returned once again. He cleared his throat, then shook his head. "You sound just like the child. She tends to exaggeration and emotes over everything."

"Edward Scanlon, you listen to me. It is one thing for a father to arrange a suitable, advantageous marriage for a daughter. It is quite another to spring such news upon her in the middle of a ball. You never even informed the child, did you? Well, it is no wonder she has such a foul headache. Your actions have deeply hurt her."

Father drew himself up to his full height, squaring his shoulders. He looked for all the world like a man engaged in a bout of fisticuffs. He glanced away from Mrs. Sanders, then seemed to brace himself against further blows.

When he spoke again, it was in that odd gravelly voice Cece had come to despise, the tone he used when he was forced to speak. "I had no need to inform Cecelia of my plans. She is my daughter, not yet of majority. She . . . she is my responsibility. I make the decisions that concern her." He turned his back to Mrs. Sanders, cleared his throat, then spoke over his shoulder in a tired voice. "Cecelia insisted upon hosting this evening's event. She must do so. She cannot shirk her duties."

At the sight of the unyielding line of her father's rigid spine, Cece began to tremble again. True, she was not of majority yet. And, yes, she was under Father's jurisdiction, but surely that did not mean she would be forced to marry Horace Grimes. Did it? Her stomach churned once again.

Mrs. Sanders cracked her cane against the polished floorboards, the sound sharp and loud enough to be heard clearly over the music emanating from the dining room. "Her duties mean nothing, Edward. You have hurt your daughter. Leave her go. She is violently upset and will most likely succumb to the vapors if you insist on forcing her to return to your dubious festivities."

Without another word, Father left, his departure impaired by his infirmity. Shaking her head, Mrs. Sanders followed, the soft tapping of her walking stick a vivid contrast to the harsh thumping of Father's.

As Cece watched and listened she realized there would be no speaking to Father tonight. Perhaps there would never be a time or way to change his mind. And if he was right as to what he could force upon her, Cece was indeed lost.

Tears began to flow again, her heart aching from the pain. All she wanted was Matthew and to escape this ghastly house.

Gathering up her beautiful silk brocade skirt, she ran down the stairs. She rushed to the door, flung it open, and was hit by the cloying scent of the roses blooming by the door. The sound of the music behind her, the laughter of Father's guests, the thought of Horace Grimes's clammy hand holding hers suddenly made her stomach heave, and Cece knew she needed the shelter of a shrub.

She ran blindly to the edge of the woods, and her body emptied itself of what little she had consumed that day. Trembling, she retched miserably, feeling that she was about to fall. She swayed against the bush, wondering if there were anything left in her anymore.

From behind, strong, gentle hands encircled her waist.

Matthew!

Cece burrowed into his loving embrace, sobbing. She threw her arms about his neck, holding on forever. She knew she would never, ever let go of that sturdy column; she would never allow him to end this exquisite embrace.

In his deep voice he murmured her name, and his hands caressed her back with long, soft strokes that in time began to calm her. She nestled deeper in the strong comfort he offered, pressing kisses to his neck. She was so glad he had been there when she most needed him.

Matthew pressed his lips against Cece's temple. He was glad he had decided to stay after Luke and the others left. Cece clearly needed him desperately.

He held her close, unable to do more than whisper her name and gently rub her back. She needed comfort and love, and he gladly supplied both. It seemed as if she would cry forever, but after a bit her sweet lips began pressing soft kisses on his neck, and she whispered a soft, "Thank you."

He kissed her forehead in response. "Tell me, will you be all right?"

The silky curls on her forehead tickled his neck as she nodded. "Now that I'm with you . . ."

Silently Matthew led her to the birdbath in the garden and bathed her face with a handkerchief he wet in the fountain. Cece cleansed her mouth, grateful for the ever-present rains that had provided her with such luxury. Soon the nausea retreated, and she felt more like her usual self. As long as he kept his arms around her, she was certain normalcy would eventually return.

"Could you tell me what happened?" he asked, his gentle voice barely discernible over the sounds of the revelry inside the house.

A shudder tore through her slender body, making Matthew regret his question. But then her curls kissed his neck again as she said, "Yes."

"Come," he said, pulling her gently behind him. "Let us sit on the bench. It will be better for you than standing among the bushes."

Cece looked at the house and trembled slightly. Then she followed his lead and sat beside him on the bench where they had first kissed.

In spurts, she described the evening she had endured, pausing at the memory of the look on Father's face when he had discussed her with Horace Grimes. "I knew something was about to happen when Father and Horace stared so strangely at me. But I had no idea what was to come."

As yet, neither did Matthew, but he knew the incident had deeply disturbed her. He thought of his uncle and how the King always held Anna's and Matthew's feelings in such high regard. Obviously Edward Scanlon was not as considerate.

Cece resumed her tale in a shaky voice. "Then Father stood. He clinked his wineglass and announced that I was be-betrothed to Horace!"

Her words ended in a cry of pain. At first all Matthew felt was rage at Scanlon's insensitivity. Then the reason for Cece's upset sank in. The man had promised her to that . . . that worm who worked at the mill? His Cece to be touched by that . . .

"No!" The denial burst from his lips like a curse. "You will not marry that man," he declared. Then a painful thought occurred to him. "Unless . . . unless you wish to marry him?"

Matthew held his breath as he waited for her reply.

Cece's righteous anger was a most beautiful sight for Matthew. "How dare you insinuate such a thing!" she cried, her green eyes flashing defiance. He began to smile. But she still offered more. "I happen to love you. Only you. Although, after you suggested such a disgusting possibility,

I do not know why I should. All I know is that I do."

She twisted from his embrace and sniffed. He had all the answers he craved. Cece was truly his. And he was hers.

"Cece," he called softly, willing her to face him.

She made to rise, still fuming.

His hand reached for hers, and he pulled her into his lap. "Cece, please look at me."

Something in his voice must have reached her. She turned her luminous eyes upon him, and a gentle gasp escaped her rosy lips. She had to have seen the emotion in his gaze, the tenderness he knew was evident in his face.

"I love you, Cece. I have from the first time you disturbed the peace of my camp."

Tears flowed down her satin cheeks. "And you have disturbed my very existence," she whispered. "I am so very glad you have."

Matthew leaned down and kissed the dampness from her skin, thrilled when she sighed with pleasure. "I love you," he whispered again, for the sheer joy of repeating the words.

"I love you, Matthew. Forever."

"Yes."

Their hands caressed lovingly, and their lips expressed requited love. The moon poured silver gloss on them, and the scent of roses gently filled the air, no longer an assault to the senses.

Time lost all meaning, and the world was no more than the endless waves of love they shared with each other, a love each had feared could never be voiced.

The sound of the waves on the beach eventually pierced their tiny universe, the only sound that could be heard in the starry night. The guests had long ago departed from the mansion. Still, Cece and Matthew sat upon the bench with their arms around each other.

"You will have to go inside soon. It is very late."

Cece cast a glance at her father's house. A wave of revulsion stole her breath, and she shook her head. "I cannot go back there, Matthew. Please don't make me go."

"But you cannot stay here."

"Neither can you. Let me come with you to your shelter in the woods."

Matthew thought of the cramped space where he had been sleeping. The rushes upon which he lay his bear-skin each night were rough, and even the fur might irritate the silky softness of Cece's skin. In the morning she would not have the lovely amenities her father provided for her.

He shook his head. "It is too rough for you."

Cece squared her shoulders, and he knew, even though he would try to dissuade her, that she would dig in her heels and be as stubborn as she usually was.

"With you there, Matthew, it is pure heaven. That shack is a far more comfortable home than that empty museum my father has built. I am going with you, whether you like it or not."

Matthew smiled in defeat. He really did not want to be separated from her, and perhaps he'd enjoy the closeness of the shelter with her tucked against his side.

"Very well," he conceded. "But in the morning you must speak with your father."

Cece studied Matthew's face, intent on deciphering how serious he was. Determination glowed from those black eyes. He would not budge on this. He had compromised, and now she would, too. "Very well. I shall return to speak to Father in the morning. But I warn you now, I hold no hope for such a meeting."

Matthew shrugged.

Cece smiled. "You have gotten your way. Grant me my wish. Take me to your camp and let me sleep in your arms."

Matthew carried her through the woods, cuddling her in his arms, holding her close to his muscular chest. In the haven of his love, Cece dozed. When he laid her upon the rough pelt spread over the dry fronds of his bed at the camp, Cece smiled. She reached her arms up to him and whispered, "I love you, Matthew."

Matthew lay down at her side, enfolding her in his embrace. He pushed aside all thought of her father, of spirit quests, of the village of Nuf-Kay'it. This night was for the two of them. All other matters would intrude soon enough in the morning.

"I love you, Cecelia Scanlon."

Chapter Fourteen

———— • ————

Cece slept the deepest, most peaceful, most refreshing sleep of her entire life. She awoke in Matthew's arms, possessively held against his side.

She sighed, then breathed in lungfuls of fresh salty air. She could smell the scent of the rushes upon which she and Matthew lay. But most of all she enjoyed the rich, male scent of Matthew.

Cece rubbed Matthew's chest with her cheek, relishing the right to be by his side, to sleep with him, to touch him as she wished. Overpowering as their passion was, so, too, was the intimacy they had shared through the night— the privacy, the soft words they had murmured while half-asleep, the gentle kisses Matthew had rained upon the nape of her neck.

This was where she belonged. At Matthew's side. Oh, she had dreamed of making a place for herself in Father's life, and she still wished to share the sort of love reserved for a father and his child. But it was painfully clear that Father did not have it in him to feel such love for her.

She did not doubt that Matthew's love matched hers.

With fingers gentled by love, she outlined his strong features. She ran her nail through his thick eyebrows, followed the high curve of a cheekbone, and rubbed the sensual fullness of his lower lip. She was startled when his white teeth caught that wandering finger.

She smiled at him. "Good morning," she whispered.

Matthew swirled his moist tongue around the tip of her

finger, then smiled back at her. "Good morning."

She wriggled deeper into his embrace. "This is far better than waking up in that room in Father's house. There I am alone. Here I have all I need."

Cece's words struck a responsive chord in Matthew. He knew exactly what she meant. Her presence vanquished all the loneliness he had ever felt. But it was not time yet to bind her any tighter to him. He had extracted a promise from her last night, and he would make sure she kept it.

"It is time for you to return to the mansion. You need to speak to your father."

She groaned and dropped away from him, flopping onto her back. "Must I?"

Matthew rose, trying vainly to straighten out the wrinkles in his trousers and shirt. He noted the mess Cece's lovely gown had become. Out here in his world, no matter how lovely it was, the gown would never survive. He wondered if his delicate woman would.

Shaking off his gloomy thought, he extended his hand to her. "You must, and you know it. Besides, I have never known you to be a coward."

As he had expected, his veiled accusation stung her, making her jump up instantly. Then she paled and stumbled. She held her stomach for a few seconds, breathing slowly.

"You must be hungry after last night," he said, wondering what he could offer someone who had been so violently ill just a few hours earlier.

A glance at her face showed her features to be even more pinched than before. She shook her head. "Actually, I—I don't believe I could eat this morning."

She ran her hand through her tumbled curls, trying to set them back from her delicate face. Matthew wished for grooming tools fit for a queen, but all he could offer her was a simple comb. She gladly accepted, and sitting upon a log, she put it to use on the tangles of reddish gold.

When the silken mass was somewhat more controlled, Cece rose and handed Matthew his comb. A long, curling strand clung lovingly to the bone instrument. Matthew pulled it out and coiled it about his finger. He waited for her to speak.

She squared her shoulders. "You are right. I must speak with Father. This situation is absolutely impossible." She came to Matthew's side, rose up on her tiptoes, and kissed his cheek. "Thank you for the loveliest of nights, my love."

Every night should be like that, he thought. "It was your presence in my arms that made the night what it was," he answered. "Go now. Let me know what comes of this talk."

Cece nodded. "I will return as soon as I can."

He did not try to talk her out of it. "I will be waiting."

With a kiss full of promise, flavored with passion, they parted.

Sustained by the emotions evoked during the night spent in Matthew's arms, Cece crossed the woods in silence. The song of a bird in a tree kept her company for a while. Then she cut across to the water's edge, and the lapping waves marked her steps. She knew this would be a very difficult morning, and she took time to fortify herself with the glorious power of this splendid land so perfectly suited to the man she loved.

With heavy steps, she reached the mansion's porch. She turned the doorknob and was stunned to find it locked. She lifted the shiny brass knocker and rapped it sharply.

Soon Mrs. Quigley presented her disapproving countenance and blocked her entrance to the house. A wicked smile crossed the housekeeper's thin lips. "If you wish to see your father, you must do so at the mill."

Cece nodded. "As soon as I change."

Mrs. Quigley bent down to retrieve something just inside the door. "Mr. Scanlon was livid when he discovered you had slept elsewhere last night. Here is the case he ordered me to pack for you."

Mrs. Quigley shoved a valise at Cece, a smirk of evil pleasure on her lips. So, the nasty woman was living a moment of glory at her expense, Cece thought grimly. Fine. She lifted her chin. The joys of the night before would sustain her even through this embarrassment.

Cece took the bag, wondering what the woman had packed for her. Then she laughed. What did it matter? Any other clothes would be an improvement on the crumpled ballgown she wore at the moment. She would need those clothes for who knew how long. Father did not want her in his house after she had compromised herself by sleeping with Matthew.

In silence, she walked across the dewy lawn near the mansion. At the entrance to the mill she set her bag down by the door and went to Father's office. Each step she took felt as if she were walking blindly into a cavern in the wild. The unknown element of Father's temper frightened her. She felt stinging disappointment, too, knowing her youthful hopes of reconciliation would never come to fruition. Still, a corner of her heart harbored a drop of optimism. Perhaps the magnitude of her love would reach Father's heart.

Had Cece not been certain of her place at Matthew's side, the walk down the mill building's corridor to Father's office would have been the most difficult act of her life. The memory of Matthew's kisses fresh in her mind eased her way. She knocked on the heavy door.

"Come in," answered Father.

She entered silently, but not cowed. She would not allow her life to be destroyed. She had every right to her opinion and deserved to have her feelings respected. Certainly her preference in the matter of a husband had to count for something, and she would make certain Father understood that.

Father's detached look chilled her to the very bone. "I see you have decided to return." His voice matched his emotionless gaze.

"And was forbidden entrance to the house. I assume this has not changed."

Father swallowed hard. A strange emotion flitted in the depths of his forest-green eyes, but Cece was not able to identify it before he blinked, erasing all but certain anger. "You humiliated me and compromised yourself beyond redemption. Horace cannot risk his future by tying himself to such a woman."

Father lifted his gaze, only to turn it to one of the many shelves filled with books. Cece saw his throat work as he swallowed with difficulty. That quick glimpse of her face had greatly affected him. But if he'd been able to do what he had done to her, he could not have such strong feelings for her, could he?

As she turned the question over in her mind, Father spoke again. "Horace was the ideal husband for you. Now no decent man will consider you. Especially since the servants' gossip has by now ensured the destruction of your reputation."

Cece's formidable temper began to boil. "Is that all that worries you? My reputation? It never occurred to you to ask if I was hurt, just as it never occurred to you to ask if I was willing to tolerate your assistant's presence at my side for the rest of my life."

Father clutched the edge of his desk. "Your disrespectful chatter has proved all my worries over your safety unnecessary. I can see you are fine. No need for me to concern myself further. The impropriety of your behavior, though, greatly disturbs me. I expected the nuns and my sister to have taught you better."

He turned his back to her, his gestures hampered by his arthritic condition. After a breath deep enough to raise his shoulders visibly, he continued in the same displeased vein, not giving Cece another chance to defend herself. Finally he paused, apparently unwilling to continue discussing the matter.

Cece took her chance. "Does it not even matter to you where I spent the night?"

Father's shoulders shot straight back, then slumped, as if he'd suffered a blow to his stomach. In that tired tone his voice had earlier borne, he responded, his back still toward Cece. "What matters is that you were not where you should have been. But if you feel the need, enlighten me."

"Very well, Father. But I suggest you sit. What I have to say will not please you. Still, it must be said." Cece herself took a seat and gathered her courage.

She laced her fingers in her lap to keep them from shaking. When Father had sat down, never once meeting her gaze, she began to speak. "I spent the night with Matthew."

Father blanched. Cece was stunned by the sudden change. From a heated red flush, his face became paper white. He drooped into the depths of the scarred leather chair as if his strength had suddenly disappeared. But he uttered not a word.

At that moment Cece wished with every bit of her being that Edward Scanlon was like other fathers, someone who would reach out and cover her hand with his, one who might rejoice in the beauty of the love she and Matthew shared. But this was not to be.

She offered up a wordless prayer for strength and courage. Then she remembered Anna's words of envy for all that Cece and Matthew shared. Cece knew she could see this ordeal through to its conclusion.

Instinctively she reached for Father's hand, so knotted by his condition, as it lay on top of the ink-stained blotter. He flinched at the gentle touch, and his reaction cut her straight through the heart.

She squared her shoulders and continued. "You need to know this, since I now know I belong at Matthew's side. I love him, and he loves me. Too, if my suspicions are correct, you will become a grandfather in a matter of months."

"Who is this Matthew?" Father asked through clenched jaws in a voice icy with rage.

Who was Matthew? With a mature dignity born during the night, born of shared love, born in Matthew's arms, Cece answered, "You've met him but you don't know him, Father. He is one of the Strong People, the Nux Sklai Yem, a S'Klallam. I intend to marry him."

Edward Scanlon, the Indian hater, laughed scornfully. "Dexter's Indian, then," he said. "Such ridiculous nonsense, Cecelia. You are truly ruined, for no one in Port Gamble, or anywhere in the Washington Territory, will perform such a ceremony. You will have your little bastard in the woods."

Cece winced but did not desist. "Then we shall be married at Nuf-Kay'it, the S'Klallam village."

Father shrugged. "So be it. But realize you no longer have a place among your people, Cecelia. Decent folk will have nothing to do with you. It is a matter of personal pride."

She knew clearly at that moment that her life was about to change forever. She could still beg forgiveness and accept Father's dictates, choose to stay with him, and in time take up the place she had been born to. By doing so, she would turn her back on Matthew and their love. But even if she carried out his wishes, Father would not necessarily offer her love.

On the other hand, she could turn her back on the life she'd dreamed of as she grew up in San Francisco and build a new life at Matthew's side. Their love would sustain them, as well as their child.

When she thought in such terms, she realized she truly had no choice.

She stood. "If someday you decide your grandchild and I matter more than your pride, Father, you know where you can find us. We will be across Teekalet."

When Father refused to meet her gaze or offer a response to her challenge, Cece turned her back on the man who, until last night, had held the largest place in her heart. Head high, she left the office. Numbly she retraced her earlier steps, pausing only to retrieve her valise.

Outside, the misty drizzle served to clear her head, cooling the anger she felt. She doubted anything would ever erase the bitter taste of betrayal and the pain of Father's rejection.

She spared a final glance for the elegant mansion she had come to hate, and wondered if Father would find it an empty comfort when he was all alone. Out of the corner of her eye she saw the telltale shimmy of a curtain, telling her Mrs. Quigley had witnessed her ignominious departure from the mill.

The housekeeper's pettiness was negligible compared with her father's cruelty. An overwhelming sadness engulfed Cece, threatening to drown her in its enormity. Sadness? No, sadness was far too mild a word for what she felt. She felt grief, sorrow, a pervasive disconsolation she knew not how to dispel.

What would cause a father to distance himself from his only child? To build an unbreachable chasm between the two of them? Looking back over her childhood, Cece acknowledged Father's coldness toward her. Never once did she remember sharing an embrace. Never once had she experienced a fatherly kiss upon her brow. Never once had they shared a moment of closeness.

Was she so totally unlovable? She could comprehend his anger at a daughter who had stayed out the entire night. She could understand his displeasure at her departure from the ball. But the problems between Father and herself had always existed. She had no idea what an innocent child could possibly have done to make a parent withhold his love for her entire life.

Why would he promise her to Horace? Why in God's name had he not even mentioned his plans to her? How could he continue to share the same house with her without discussing the most pivotal change that would occur in her life? He simply did not care about her at all, she concluded.

Well, she thought as she took a shuddering breath, that part of her life was over. She had certainly burned her bridges behind her. She could only hope that Matthew did not turn her away. After all, she had nowhere else to go. Even though she had been unwilling to consider the thrilling, chilling possibility, she was now quite certain she carried Matthew's child.

The joy of bearing the child of the man she loved was so stunning, it stole her ability to breathe, to think. All she knew was how desperately she wanted to give Matthew a child—a child born of their love, created by their exquisite passion.

But the unknown element of childbirth and the uncertainty of her future cast a quick pall upon the feelings that so wanted to blossom within her. She still did not know what Matthew's reaction would be to the events of the morning. Nor did she have any inkling what he would do or say when she told him of the child they would have in a matter of months.

And Father would never know his grandchild. That saddened Cece as well.

Slowly she walked along the shore, feeling the ocean spray mingle with the gentle rain. The rains in the Pacific Northwest were merely dreary to some people, but rain had never bothered Cece. Now, after the events of this summer, she would always see rain as a reflection of the love she and Matthew had discovered under the tender blessing of a weeping sky.

She remembered Matthew's words earlier that morning. He had said he would be waiting for her. She smiled for the first time since she had left his side. She picked up her pace, anxious to reach him.

Yes, matters with Father could have turned out differently, but Cece still had Matthew. He had said he loved her.

She pressed a hesitant hand to her belly. Soon, she thought. Soon she would have their baby as well as Matthew.

They more than made up for what she left behind.

After Cece left, Matthew went for his morning swim. He needed the cleansing of mind and spirit he always achieved in the ocean water. He walked steadily until the waves slapped his thighs, then made a shallow dive into the next curl.

He would gladly kill Scanlon for the pain he had inflicted upon Cece. Yet Matthew knew there was not a thing to be done for her.

Rolling onto his back, he lay still, staring into the steel-gray sky. He closed his eyes, seeing Cece behind his lids as she had looked when he first saw her in that sumptuous gown. She was so lovely, so delicate. What could she truly see in a rough Indian like himself? Was it merely the challenge and the thrill of the forbidden? Matthew hoped not; to him she had become the very reason for living.

Cool drops on his face startled him, and he turned to swim back to shore. When he faced land, he noticed a small, animated figure at water's edge. Matthew squinted, trying to identify the person. Then he smiled. Little Johnny was trying to catch his attention. The child was the son of Uncle Soo-moy'asum's nearest neighbors. The scamp was always trailing after Matthew, whom he had cast in the role of hero.

Matthew waved at the little fellow, letting him know he was on his way back. In no time, Matthew was able to stand

and stride out of the waters of Teekalet.

"Matthew! Matthew! The King wants you to meet with the elders. Hurry!" Little Johnny caught Matthew's much bigger hand in both of his and dragged him in his wake.

Matthew was surprised; he wondered what had caused the elders to come together. He quickly dressed and, with his small shadow at his side, returned to Nuf-Kay'it.

Instead of going to the large communal lodge in the center of the village, Matthew chose to meet his uncle at home. The older man greeted him with a solemn look on his face.

Matthew became uneasy. "What has happened, Uncle?"

The King of England shook his head. "I am afraid you now must face another challenge, son. Luke is after you."

Matthew's eyebrows rose. "After me? What precisely do you mean?"

His uncle shook his gray-streaked head. "I have no details, son. Just what was told me. Luke says he has a matter of grave importance to discuss, and it involves you."

Thoughts of the events of the past evening filled Matthew's mind. Nothing had been said, but the vague feeling of impending doom he had had for some time now intensified. The dread in his gut deepened; fear tensed his muscles.

Through tightly clamped jaws, he spoke. "Then let us be on our way."

At the long communal lodge, Matthew saw that he and the King were the last to arrive. Luke, without his paper-wrapped bottle, stood at the front of the building. As Matthew and his uncle made their way in, voices died down. Dense silence filled the room, increasing Matthew's alarm.

Luke caught sight of Matthew, but did not meet his gaze. Instead he turned to the room at large and gestured to everyone to sit. When he was sure of the men's attention, he spoke.

"As you all know, our *ssia'm,* Soo-moy'asum, has stated that he is tired, that he wishes to give the leadership of the tribe to his successor. He has also stated that he wishes his nephew Matthew to follow in his footsteps."

Still without looking squarely at Matthew, Luke began to pace, continuing his monologue. "My childhood friend has gone into the woods, in his words, to begin a spirit quest, seeking a *tamanous* before assuming the position of *ssia'm.* I, too, feel I should assume the leadership of the village. I know there are those among us who prefer my more active approach toward the Boston thieves. I have been given a powerful *tamanous* and wish to lead."

From the far right side of the building, before all the men of Nuf-Kay'it, Luke raised his head and finally focused his eyes on Matthew, bold arrogance glittering in the black depths. "It would seem that a spirit quest is far removed from Matthew's mind. Instead he consorts with our enemies."

Matthew felt his stomach drop at the same time as many pairs of eyes converged upon him. Luke knew about Cece. He knew she mattered to Matthew. Their lifelong friendship was going to count for naught as Luke became consumed by his need for power.

He started to stand, wishing to halt the inevitable. But Luke would not be robbed of his opportunity. Anger and betrayal showed in Luke's face. Matthew felt a twinge of guilt take root in his gut.

"This morning," Luke said, his words tight with the control he exerted over his temper, "on my way to visit my old *friend,* I saw Scanlon's beautiful daughter leave Matthew's shelter, her costly ballgown wrinkled and her fire-colored hair tumbled over her face. They kissed, and she returned to the mill manager's mansion. Matthew, the man who mates with the mill manager's daughter, is unfit to call himself a S'Klallam, never mind to take his uncle's place."

With that, Luke sat down and watched the shock and anger spread across the faces in the room. The silence was deafening. Then, as if on cue, everyone seemed to have something urgent to say. One by one, in true S'Klallam fashion, each man stood and voiced his objection to Matthew's relationship with Cece.

Matthew wanted to kill. Luke's crude words, the way he had sullied Cece's name, sickened him, bringing to life a rage he had never before known. But his anger was not so much directed toward Luke as it was toward himself. He, Matthew, the man who had pledged his love to Cece, had exposed her to this sort of talk. He did not know who was worse: Luke for betraying the friendship of a lifetime, or himself for betraying the privacy and the trust of the woman he loved.

He rose, ready to battle any and all comers. But a gentle hand upon his forearm brought him to a halt.

"Sit, son. Let them all talk out their outrage. One cannot reason with anger."

Matthew looked down at the steady hand holding his arm. For all his slender build, Uncle Soo-moy'asum had a strength of character Matthew had always admired and respected. He did as his uncle bade him.

The King leaned closer to Matthew. In a voice too low for anyone else to hear, he spoke. "Forgive me, Matthew, for what I must do. As *ssia'm* I have distasteful tasks. But they are done when they cannot be avoided."

Gazing into the wise face he so loved, Matthew knew what his uncle's words meant. The doom he had felt so near had arrived.

Soo-moy'asum, shaman, *ssia'm* of Nuf-Kay'it, rose, and silence reigned again inside the longhouse. When everyone's gaze was focused upon him in expectation, he spoke.

"There is only one thing to be done. Matthew, you must choose between the Boston woman and your people."

Chapter Fifteen

———— • ————

In his silent shelter, staring at the fronds he had tied to
protect him from the elements, Matthew felt numb. The
fiercest of storms could have erupted over his head, and
he would most likely not have noticed.

The only thing he knew was a simmering anger and
complete disgust for himself. His selfishness had brought
him to this impasse. At a time when he should only have
considered the needs of his village, he had allowed his own
needs, his private hunger for a forbidden woman, to distract
him from his duty. In the aftermath, he had lost the respect
of his people and had left Cece vulnerable.

After today there was no possible way to keep Edward
Scanlon from learning of his daughter's romantic ties to an
Indian. By now someone from the meeting would have told
a friend, and that friend would have gossiped with someone
he met at the Country Store, and the someone at the Country
Store would surely have relished relaying the tale to one of
the mill employees.

Scanlon had been cold toward Cece before, and now
Matthew dreaded the thought of how the man's irrational
hatred toward Indians would cause him to treat his own
daughter.

All because Matthew had committed the sin of loving
her.

That was not his only crime, his overzealous conscience
reminded him. The people of Nuf-Kay'it no longer felt they

could trust a man who loved a Boston woman, not even if the man was the nephew of the King of England. Matthew saw the disintegration of his destiny as he closed his eyes. How could he choose between the woman he loved and his heritage?

Yes, he bore a duty to his people, but deep in his soul Matthew acknowledged that he bore a duty to himself as well. A man, even a leader, deserved a fulfilling life. The only way his existence had any meaning was with Cece at his side.

His thoughts seemed to swirl in his head, never ending, never changing. He had to relinquish Cece for the good of the tribe or turn his back on his heritage to pursue his personal future.

Damn.

A sound at the entrance to his shack brought his thoughts to a momentary halt. Then the scent of roses filled the air.

"Cece . . ." he whispered, smiling. The turmoil inside him could never reduce the pleasure her nearness aroused.

Seconds later her mass of tumbled curls poked through the rough opening of his shelter. Then partially bare shoulders followed. At the sight of the apple-green ballgown, Matthew realized he was not the only one with weighty matters to face.

The valise in her hand proved him right.

"Here," he said, "give me that." He took the bag and helped Cece to sit on the mat of dried grasses that had pillowed them through the night. He noted the redness in her beautiful eyes and knew again the desire to do intense bodily harm to any and all who caused Cece pain.

Especially himself.

When her bottom lip quivered, Matthew groaned. "Come here," he entreated, and without waiting for her to respond, pulled her onto his lap.

Cece nestled deep into Matthew's shoulder, breathing in the virile scent of him. With the warmth of his arms around her, the silence of the evergreen woods about them, she began to relax.

"I told you earlier I would come to let you know what

happened with Father. I don't believe you thought I would return quite this soon."

Matthew shook his head. Cece continued, telling him without leaving out a detail of the morning's events. "In essence, Matthew, he disowned me," she said.

When she finished talking, she dared glance at his face. His expression was fierce, almost as forceful as his embrace. Cece felt a moment of fear, but not for herself. She feared Matthew might vent his anger upon Father and later suffer the consequences. She reached a gentle hand to his jaw, tightly clenched as it was.

"Don't, love," she whispered. "It is over. He's in his museum, and I am here. *We* are here."

Her stomach flip-flopped when she thought of the other news she had for him. How would he take the idea of fatherhood? Well, Cece, she thought, there is only one way to find out.

Despite the intimacies they had shared, despite the love both had expressed, an overwhelming shyness filled her. "Matthew," she said, "I have something else to tell you. I—"

She flushed. A hot, burning prickle crawled up from the tops of her breasts to her neck, and all the way up her face to her hairline. "I—we . . . will be . . . that is, soon you and I . . ." She shut her eyes tightly and just pushed the words out. "We're going to have a baby."

In the stunned silence following her pronouncement, Cece did not dare open an eye. But when she realized Matthew hadn't moved, she lifted an eyelid a tiny fraction.

His face was utterly devoid of expression. Nothing showed on those sharply chiseled features.

Oh, God. "Matthew?"

A strong shudder ran through him. In a voice that shook a bit, he asked, "A baby?" Then, before she did more than nod, he went on. "Are you sure?"

Cece caught her bottom lip between her teeth. She had never in her life felt so vulnerable, so exposed, presenting the greatest gift she could offer to the man she loved. She prayed for him to accept it. "As sure as I can be this soon."

"A child . . ." This time his voice held a hint of awe, although his features still revealed nothing.

Her nerves got the better of her. Cece poked the solid chest before her with an impatient finger. "Darn you, Matthew! Say something. Do you hate me? Is it wonderful? Don't just sit there frozen and grim, saying only 'a baby,' 'a child.'"

A smile broke out on his lips. Then he began to laugh. The deep peals warmed the icy dread that had lodged in Cece's belly. Maybe, just maybe, things would turn out all right.

Matthew's laughter eased a bit, and he caught her gaze. "A redheaded Indian! This I must see."

Cece frowned indignantly. "I am not redheaded."

Matthew cocked an eyebrow and smiled. "If you insist. But to me you certainly look like a redhead."

Cece refused to let the matter drop. "I am a blonde. Perhaps a strawberry blonde, but I am a blonde."

Matthew's eyes narrowed. He studied her closely. He angled his head, then reached out a gentle hand to her head. "And will this blonde—excuse me, *strawberry* blonde—kiss this Indian?"

Cece caught sight of the banked flames in Matthew's eyes. Immediately the heat began to grow in her belly. She smiled knowingly and pushed Matthew flat on his back. "Anytime," she whispered against his lips, and proceeded to demonstrate.

As always, passion rushed over them, stealing their breath, leaving them no control. In the surging tide of sensual bliss, their mouths became supremely eloquent, their hands expressive, their bodies most articulate.

Love was the language they spoke. With hands that trembled in urgency, their garments flew off their bodies. Soon both were exposed to the loving torment only the other could provide. Intimate places were patted, soothed, aroused.

Cece whimpered from the ecstatic peak Matthew brought her so close to time and time again. But before she could demand that he give her what he so skillfully promised, he would subject her to yet another, more exquisite form of tantalizing torture.

"Matthew!" she cried, her voice ragged with need. "I need you. Now!"

He rose over her flushed, dewy body, nestling his manhood up against her nether lips, placing tender kisses on her pouting nipples, her neck, her eyelids, and finally her mouth. His tongue parted her lips as he slowly entered her drenched depths. She moaned at the beauty of the sensation he caused.

Soon the climb to heaven was upon them, hands grasping damp flesh, both gladly giving and taking. Two souls shared love; two bodies gave pleasure. In a fiery burst of perfection, both reached the heights of joy, crying out incoherent sounds of ecstasy.

In their quiet little shelter, peace reigned absolute. Their hearts beat wildly, and their breath came in rough bursts. Bit by bit, though, their bodies cooled, the damp flush of passion dissipated, and their breathing calmed. Matthew left Cece's body only to lie on his back and hug her close.

"I love you, Matthew."

He sighed. "I know."

Peace, that rare commodity, endured.

Days sped into weeks, the joy of shared moments blunting for Cece the pain of her father's betrayal. Soon, though, she and Matthew realized the rough rush shelter would hardly accommodate the needs of their tiny family, and Matthew began to build a cedar plank cabin. He insisted on doing all the work himself, frustrating Cece's every effort to help him.

The heat of late summer and the forced inactivity were driving Cece insane.

She wiped her forehead with her hand and turned back to argue with Matthew once again. "I cannot believe you will not let me help you more."

Matthew's face bore the same quality of a slab of stone. Finely chiseled, infinitely dear, but still, stony, and stoic.

"I am responsible for you and our child. I will carry these boards to the clearing. You can gather more berries, go clamming, or just wet your feet at the beach. *You* are building our child."

Cece snorted. "If I were not sick every morning, neither you nor I would even remember that. I feel useless and I want to do more."

"Then do as I say. Go clamming."

"But you yourself said the clams were best in June and July. It is now nearly September. You already showed me how to dry and store the clams we gathered earlier. Do you want me to dry tough clams?"

Matthew whirled to face her, all semblance of patience gone. "No! I want to get these cedar planks to the clearing so I can continue building our home. As you pointed out, it is nearly September. The cold damp of fall will soon arrive, and you carry my child. The two of you need a far better home than that rush shack. There is no one else to protect you but me. Let me do it, Cece."

His vehemence shamed her. He was right. She was being childish. But she felt so utterly inadequate, watching him work so hard on their new home, having nothing to contribute. He had felled the huge cedars, stripped them of their bark, and had split the trunks into long logs. Now he had begun to piece the cabin that would house them, and he needed to haul more logs to the site. All she ever did was prepare food at the necessary times. That left her with an inordinate amount of idle time.

Cece sighed in regret. "I am sorry, Matthew. You're right. I am behaving more like a spoiled brat than like the future mother of your child. Forgive me. Still . . ."

A noise to their far right, along the path they had worn to Matthew's logging location, prevented her from further voicing her frustration. Soon Anna's sleek black head appeared under the far-reaching branch of a Douglas fir. Cece smiled in relief. At least she would have some company for a few hours.

"I noticed the progress on the cabin. It looks like you are building a large lodge, Matthew." Anna's voice held admiration for her cousin's capabilities and maybe even a hint of concern.

"I do have a family now," he answered, returning to his stack of boards.

"Yes, but do you expect Cece to bear you a whole litter

at one time?" Anna asked in a mischievous tone.

Matthew stopped working, paused a moment as if considering something, then faced the two women, both struggling to control their laughter at the sternness in his gaze. He caught on to their mirth, threw his hands up in the air, and bent to the nearest cedar plank. "It will be a far cry from a mansion, in any case," he finally said, the words muffled by the effort he expended in lifting the long board.

At his words a soft cry of dismay slipped from Cece's lips. So that was why he was working like a beast of burden! He felt he needed to compete with what she had left behind. Tears filled her eyes, and she turned away from the two cousins.

She wrapped her arms around her middle and held herself, offering her battered emotions the only comfort they were likely to receive for a few hours. This was too private, too intimate a matter to discuss with Anna.

How would she ever make him understand that their rush shack was a castle fit for any monarch compared with the loveless beauty of the mill manager's mansion? All she wanted, all she needed, was his love. And their child. She slipped a hand over her still-flat stomach and smiled through her tears.

She turned to glance at Matthew and saw that Anna was still bent on haranguing him over some matter or other. Cece had stepped away from them to conceal her tears, and now she wiped away the evidence of her pain with a trembling hand. Matthew and their baby. That was the greatest treasure of all. Somehow she would find the means to let him know how she felt. She didn't need a mansion to be happy with him.

"Tell me, Anna," she called as she gingerly stepped over Matthew's tools spread out over the forest floor, "what can be done with all this bark Matthew has stripped from these trees? It seems such a waste to just leave it on the ground. He said the S'Klallam had many ways to use all parts of the trees."

Anna nodded. "Yes, of course we do. I am not the best at all of this, you understand. I went to missionary school when I was a child, but some things I do know."

Anna bent down and picked up a large length of the rough bark Matthew had cast aside when preparing the huge logs. She turned it over and showed Cece the inner texture of the wood. "My grandmother mashed the inside strips of cedar bark to weave fabric from the fibers. But I have no idea how she went about that. I do know how to make boiling baskets. We use them at home, and I think you and Matthew could put some to good use as well."

Cece smiled at the thought of making something of value for their home. "Then we will explore the possibilities of basketry," she decided.

Anna nodded vigorously. "Too, you can collect all this bark and start a kindling pile. It will come in handy in the cold months. You won't need to seek bits to start your fire when your condition becomes more advanced."

Cece felt herself turning red. Although she and Matthew often spoke of their unborn child, she still felt a bit embarrassed anytime Anna mentioned the evidence of the passion she shared with Matthew. It was silly, of course, but she could not help her reaction.

Ignoring her embarrassment, she nodded. "That is an excellent idea. I also like the thought of making utensils for our home."

Anna obviously liked the role Cece had cast her into. "Come along, we have to strip the stuff from these chunks lying about. We cannot let the fibers dry out."

As they went about their task Anna explained how they would tightly pack the strips together, so tightly in fact, she said, that the baskets would be watertight.

"How . . . can . . . that . . . be?" Cece asked, tugging on a particularly stubborn strip of cedar.

"It just is, as long as we make the basket the right way. You'll see. I have made dozens of these cooking buckets. I will show you."

When Anna deemed them to have the necessary amount of material, the two friends carried the load to the beachfront. On such a hot August day, with the sun shining hard overhead, the breeze sweeping over Teekalet was most welcome.

With painstaking care, Anna began to weave the framework of the basket. "It needs to be large enough so you can place hot stones in it."

Cece scrunched up her brow in puzzlement. "Why would I want to do that? I thought these would be for boiling our food."

Anna nodded, never taking her gaze from her swiftly flying fingers, tautly winding the strip of cedar around the frame she had made. "This basket will be for cooking your food. You heat stones until they are close to splitting, then you rinse off the soot from the fire and place them in the boiling basket filled with water. When that stone has cooled, you replace it with another hot one. After you have done this a few times, your water is ready to cook anything you wish."

Cece smiled, thinking of Mrs. Quigley's elaborate collection of copper pots. "How very ingenious! And I see how tightly you hold the cedar fibers, and how hard you pack them down."

Anna nodded again and went on with her work. "That is what makes your basket watertight. Here, you can't just sit and watch. Do what I did to make the framework and start your own boiling basket."

To Cece's astonishment, she learned enough to produce a decent bucket. Her triumph was complete when they filled it with water and not a drop escaped.

"There," she said, giving her cooking pot a pat of approval. "I don't feel quite as helpless as I did earlier."

Anna shook her head. "You are indeed as stubborn as Matthew said you were. Don't you realize you are doing the greatest work of all? You are building a child."

"It hardly seems like work," Cece answered. "Besides, if it weren't for me and the child, Matthew would have become Nuf-Kay'it's *ssia'm*. He could have been helping the village."

Anna waved her hand in Cece's direction, dismissing her concerns. "Hush now. Has Matthew said he has not decided to become the next *ssia'm*? Has he told you it is due to your presence in his life? I don't think so. Besides, my father always says the spirits know better than we what we need.

Perhaps at this time in his life Matthew needs you more than the tribe needs him."

"I hardly think so," Cece answered. "He would make a perfect leader. I feel I have stolen something precious from him."

Anna *tsk-tsk*ed. "You are *giving* my cousin something truly precious."

Shortly after uttering that sweeping statement, Anna left for the day, and Cece began preparing the evening meal. She thought about Anna's words. Could Matthew really need her and their child more than Nuf-Kay'it needed his leadership? Anna had an interesting way of seeing things, to be sure, but it did give Cece a different perspective to consider.

When Matthew arrived at sunset, Cece showed him her accomplishments. He praised her for her quick learning and hurriedly ate the meal she set before him. As he ate a handful of juicy blackberries he seemed distracted, as if he had much on his mind. And Cece could well imagine that he did.

Still, this mood did not hamper his hunger for her once they lay together on the fur-covered rush mat in the lean-to. In fact, every night ended in sweet, wild passion, leaving them both exhausted but satisfied.

Day after day, life followed a familiar routine. Matthew slaved over the construction of the lodge, and Cece knew she had to stop weaving baskets when she had nowhere to store those she had made. The pleasure she felt from living with Matthew nearly made up for the fact that he was so busy all the time. They spent time together at mealtimes and of course in the shelter at night. But inside their haven of rushes, there was virtually no occasion to talk. They would crawl in, and no sooner would Cece take the pins from her hair than Matthew would devour her with passionate kisses. Invariably they would make love and later fall asleep, content.

A slight niggling of concern began to bother Cece. They were no longer sharing long conversations about anything and everything, whether earthshaking or inconsequential. She missed the time they had spent together when Matthew focused all his attention on her. She chided herself for her childish selfishness and convinced herself he was merely being a good provider for her and their child.

Still, he never said anything about marriage.

Trying not to think much of his silence, Cece went about her days trying to keep herself occupied. She was glad Anna had become a frequent visitor to the camp under the evergreens.

One particular afternoon Cece heard the sound of something heavy being dragged along on the forest floor. She also heard Anna's ripe oaths.

Smiling, Cece went to investigate the cause for the noise and the curses. When she reached Anna, she found her hauling thick sticks along the ground, a large bundle strapped across her back. Her beautiful high cheekbones bore a flush from her exertions, and dewy perspiration dotted her forehead.

Cece shook her head. "What are you doing?"

Anna dropped her burden and blew a breath of air toward her forehead from the corner of her lips. "You're the one who has been bored silly, no?"

"Well, yes," answered Cece, staring at the items Anna had relinquished, certain she had no notion what to do with them. "But I'm afraid some sticks and a sack do not immediately bring to mind any sort of occupation."

Anna sat on a flat rock and pulled her skirt back to reveal her petticoat. She grabbed a handful of the plain white cotton and wiped her face with it. "You soon will, Cousin Cece."

Cousin Cece. The words touched her very soul.

"Would that it were so," she whispered, tears welling in her eyes.

Anna lifted her face and with narrowed eyes studied Cece's expression. "I have said something wrong, have I not?" she asked.

Cece shook her head. "No, you have not said anything wrong. It is only that . . . that Matthew has not spoken of marriage."

Anna closed her eyes briefly. When she opened them, she rose and reached for Cece. Cece gladly went into the embrace, tears spilling down her cheeks, sobs breaking from her throat.

Anna held her in silence, allowing Cece the luxury of weeping. When her sobs were spent, Anna's soft pats on her back offered Cece comfort. After a bit Cece pulled away and laughed self-consciously.

"I guess the old wives' tales about emotional expectant mothers are right after all." She smiled crookedly, waving an aimless hand in a gesture to illustrate her point.

"Nonsense! There is nothing wrong with wanting Matthew to marry you. After all, he lives with you as if you were already married, and you are even bearing him a child. It is my muleheaded cousin who bears blame here. I believe I know what is holding him back."

Cece gathered her courage and voiced her fears for the first time. "I know, too, what the matter is. I am Edward Scanlon's daughter. Not only am I not Indian, but I am the Pope and Talbot mill manager's daughter. The most unsuitable woman for him."

Anna nodded. "Like I said, nonsense. Anyone with eyes in his head can see that you are actually the only woman for Matthew. And if the leadership of the village is to be Matthew's, then the spirits will show him how to achieve it. He is a fool to risk the happiness you both have found."

"But he does not see it that way. He has not spoken of this, but from what he has already said, I would imagine he sees his actions as a betrayal of the tribe."

Anna bent again and picked up the items she had brought with her. She began to drag them the remaining distance to the clearing, and Cece rushed to help her with the load.

"Do not argue with me. I know I can help you carry these sticks. They are not too heavy for two." She felt that the burdens of a marriage were best borne by two as well, but Matthew maintained his silence over his situation, and there was nothing Cece could offer to help him bear his pain. He had not even asked to share the bonds of marriage with her.

Anna laughed. "You are determined, and I will not argue. But I will argue with my father and my cousin. Both are blind."

"Oh, no. Don't involve yourself in my troubles. I can only cost you the peace you have in your family. I am certain your father sees me as the terrible person who ruined the tribe's future."

With a sigh of relief, Cece dropped the sticks in front of the shelter. Anna slung the bundle from her shoulders and dropped it onto the ground as well. On mats of cedar bark that Matthew had in his shack, the two women sat for a well-earned rest.

Anna seemed lost in thought.

Moments passed. Cece wondered if she had offended her friend by speculating about the *ssia'm*'s thoughts. "Anna?"

Anna blinked, then looked at Cece, obviously startled out of her deep thoughts. "Yes?" she answered.

"I do apologize if I said anything wrong about your father."

Anna waved her hand. A frown creased her brow. "I was just thinking. I do not believe he sees you as any terrible sort of person, Cece. In fact, he was quite insistent at the start of all this that Matthew should stay constantly at your side to protect you. I think he even encouraged the attraction Matthew obviously felt for you. But his position as *ssia'm* had to come before his position as Matthew's father. It must have been difficult for Father when the elders could not accept your romance, and he was forced to put an ultimatum before Matthew."

Cece gasped. She had had no idea matters had gone this far. "So Matthew was indeed forced to choose."

Anna nodded slowly, sadly.

"Dear God," Cece murmured, anguish for Matthew overcoming her. "He was right, after all. He is S'Klallam, and he belongs here. I am white and I . . ." She allowed her voice to trail off. Looking around the clearing, she saw no evidence of her heritage. She thought of Father and the town of Port Gamble and could think of nothing there that would call her back.

"Oh, Anna," she cried softly. "Where do I belong?"

Chapter Sixteen

———— • ————

"Over here," Anna answered, her all-seeing gaze firmly focused on Cece. "I brought this loom for you, and you will help me set it up."

Before Cece could spare another thought for the problems she faced, Anna completely involved her in building the loom.

Cece grasped the sturdy stick Anna pointed in her direction. "Stab this one right about where you are standing," Anna directed. "I will set this one here, about five feet away from you."

Once the supports were up and had been given Anna's approval, Cece watched her friend slip the other sticks into holes already carved for that purpose into the uprights. Then Anna stretched on the loom a warp of the yarn she had brought in her bundle.

"I spun it myself," she proudly informed Cece. "It is very fine. I made it from the fur of the wool dogs and some goose down my mother gave me."

Anna's words piqued Cece's interest. "Dogs?"

Her friend nodded. "We have some small woolly dogs that grow a beautiful soft fur. We shear them often, otherwise their coats would become matted. That fur makes warm blankets. When you spin the wool with goose down, it comes out soft as a cloud. Here, touch the yarn."

Cece stretched out her hand and did find the yarn soft. "Do you think I could weave a blanket for the baby?"

Anna's smile was triumphant. "That is just what I had in mind."

Cece smiled back. The thought of making something for the baby gave her hope for the future. After all, she would have a wonderful bit of Matthew soon. And nothing, not a tribe or an irrational father, could ever take that away from her. "Show me what to do," she said.

Anna's deft fingers fairly flew over the two bars of the loom, slipping a small shuttle threaded with the downy wool through the threads of the warp. Soon the bit of fabric began to grow where Anna tamped it down firmly after she pulled the shuttle from one side to the other.

After Cece thought she had a good idea of how hard she needed to push down the yarn and how to work the shuttle through the warp threads, she turned to Anna. "May I?"

"Absolutely. The loom is my gift to you. The blanket is your gift for my nephew."

Emotion swamped Cece. Anna was wonderful, another treasure her beloved evergreen forest had presented to her. "Thank you."

Anna smiled. "You are welcome. It is a small gift."

"No. My thanks are for every bit of your friendship, your love, and especially your acceptance."

Anna looked down at her hands loosely clasped in her lap. When she looked up, Cece saw tears in her friend's eyes. "My parents were quite old when I was born," Anna said in a quiet voice that trembled just the faintest bit. "Matthew is eleven years older than I. He is my only brother, and now he has given me a sister."

At Cece's incipient denial, Anna held up her hand. "Please don't deny what you and Matthew have. He may be too consumed by thoughts of his duty toward the tribe to treasure your love properly, but I am certain that in time he will come around. He is a good man."

"The best," Cece whispered. "But I can't bear to see him suffer."

Anna lifted a shoulder in a shrug. "Perhaps his suffering now is what will teach him to value what you two share for exactly what it is worth."

"As long as it does not destroy him," Cece murmured.

"As long as the blindness of my people does not destroy his common sense," was Anna's tart retort.

Despite Matthew's efforts the lodge was not completed when the weather turned cold and rainy. Even as feverishly as he had been working, when the pervasive damp chill of the fall arrived, he became like a man possessed, redoubling his efforts to finish the house.

Cece helplessly watched as he exhausted himself day after day. The walls had been completed, but now the most crucial part, the roof, had to be laid down. Cece kept a wary watch all day as Matthew climbed the high walls, dragging behind him the boards that would form the gables.

"Can't you ask someone from Nuf-Kay'it to help you?" she asked one day when he seemed even more determined to finish his task.

When Matthew faced her, the haunted look in his eyes spoke eloquently of his pain. In that unguarded moment Cece learned of all the demons chasing the man she loved.

"No," was all he said.

She never asked again.

Cece felt a brief respite when Matthew asked her to collect soft moss with which to chink the cracks between the dovetailed wallboards. Finally she felt useful and went about her task with something akin to gratitude. Joy eluded her. Only when she thought of the life she carried inside did she manage to smile and feel hope.

Even when they worked together, he on the roof, she chinking the cabin walls, silence prevailed. Their evening meal that night was pure torture for Cece.

After she had stored the rest of the loaf of camas and thistle bread, and returned from washing their wooden bowls and spoons, she went to the shelter, her heart breaking in two. She sat just inside the opening of the shack, watching Matthew tend to the coals in the hearth. He wore a long-sleeved flannel shirt and trousers of brown corduroy.

Even covered by the sturdy garments, his body looked lithe and strong, and Cece could clearly see the tensile power of his muscles. He bent to the hearth, and his trousers tightened around his buttocks. He reached out an arm to grasp a long stick lying on the ground some distance away from him, and the flannel stretched across his wide shoulders.

The familiar sting of desire caught Cece unaware, making her wonder if tonight he would turn to her. He hadn't loved her in several days. He had worked so strenuously that he had fairly tumbled onto the rush bed, already asleep before his head hit the mat.

She still craved Matthew's loving. She still craved Matthew. The distance between them hurt, but the comfort of his embrace and the passionate sweetness of his caresses would express his love. It would tell her he still needed her. She turned around and went inside, silently removing her plain gray 'waist and skirt.

Matthew heard Cece moving inside the shelter, and every bit of him tightened with desire. He knew she was undressing, and he hungered for the intensity of her loving. He was the wrong man for her, she the wrong woman for him. Despite their love their future was troubled, strewn with painful hurdles along the way, and uncertain at best. But they both burned with the same hunger for each other.

Why had Cece's white God, the same God the missionaries had taught him to trust, and even the S'Klallam spirits all deserted him? Had his love for Cece offended them so very much? The irrational emotional parts of his soul wondered about this ceaselessly. But the reasonable parts of his mind told him otherwise. He had been forced to make a choice and he had complied. Cece carried his child, and he wanted both desperately.

The elders had been satisfied when Uncle Soo-moy'asum had issued his ultimatum. Matthew had seen only one possible action. He could not turn his back on the woman he loved, especially when she had nowhere to go and was expecting a child.

The complete severing of his ties to the tribe had cast Matthew adrift. He was still an Indian, would always feel the blood of his S'Klallam ancestors running through his veins. And regardless of how much he loved Cece, his loyalty to the the tribe was unsullied.

Could he not be loyal to his people as well as to his own heart?

With a deep moan Matthew turned to the shelter, needing the emotional sustenance he received in Cece's loving embrace. At the opening to the shelter he paused and saw her already lying on their bed. Her beautiful hair shimmered over the furry bearskin Matthew used to cover the rushes, its color a striking contrast to the dark animal pelt.

"Cece," he whispered, his love for her rushing into his throat, making it impossible for him to speak further.

Her eyes sparkled a green blaze at him, inviting him to join her. He had tried to deplete his strength day after day, hoping to find some way to resume his interrupted spirit quest. All he had accomplished was virtual exhaustion, and denying them both the rapture of their loving. No more.

He stripped his garments in seconds, glad for the autumnal breeze that cooled the evening. No rain had fallen today, and the air now bore a teasing nip that made the sensual heat Cece offered ever so welcome.

Taking care not to pull on her cloud of hair, he lay down beside her, his mouth coming straight to her rosy lips. With a moan of welcome, she parted them, and Matthew again tasted the sweetness of his woman.

Ravenous after days of denial, he kissed her like a man possessed. Over and over he plumbed the corners of her mouth, reveling in the flavor of Cece. His hands skimmed her body, unimpaired by her nightshirt. The fine cotton moved smoothly under his hand, adding a certain friction to his caresses.

But after days without the delight of her body, Matthew soon became tired of the fabric between them. He lifted the hem of the gown, and Cece raised her hips to help him. He took his lips from hers only long enough to pull the garment over her head. In that moment Cece sighed.

"Oh, Matthew," she whispered. "I love you so. . . ."

Her words, intense with every bit of her considerable passion for him, inflamed him further. With long strokes of his hand he swept her body, seeking to soothe and arouse with the same gesture.

Her satiny flesh was hot to his touch, and she quivered each time he touched her. When he placed his hand on her collarbone and began another sweeping motion, she writhed and twisted until the plump flesh of her breast came to fill his hand. She gasped when his palm covered the already beaded nipple.

Matthew left his fingers to linger there, placing a chain of kisses over her jaw, down her throat, and finally covering the tops of her breasts. She whimpered, and Matthew brought his lips to a taut, dark tip. With his teeth he gently nipped and teased, finally taking the firm little nub into his mouth. His tongue captured the flavor of Cece's skin in a burst of delight. He lapped at her, lathing the nipple with strokes of his tongue.

He continued his downward path, exploring the translucent skin under the fullness of her breast. It was soft and sensitive, and she moaned her pleasure when he stroked the generous mound with his lips. The firm plane of her belly beckoned, and Matthew kissed his way to the tiny indentation of her navel. The quick swirl of his tongue in the small well wrought a cry of delight from Cece and made her cross her legs tightly.

With a firm hand Matthew drew her silken thighs apart, refusing to let her hide any of her treasures. He rose on his knees and admired the splendor of her femininity. Holding her legs apart, Matthew lowered himself to her and nuzzled a kiss onto the curl-covered mound. She was totally, absolutely his.

He kissed her again, and Cece rose up sharply, crying, "No!"

Matthew placed his palm on her soft belly and urged her to lie down. "Trust me," he whispered. She hesitated, her gaze burning with passion but also filled with questioning curiosity. Seconds later she did as he asked.

With consummate tenderness he parted the tufts of hair between her thighs and found the tiny pearl of pleasure they hid. He kissed it gently. Cece quivered at his caress, but did not refuse him this time. Matthew continued to love her in this utterly intimate way.

She trembled from the pleasure he gave her, and his joy

grew. She was his, he thought again.

Cece's tremors soon became quakes, and Matthew knew she was close to release. With instinctive talent, he continued to caress her femininity until he heard her keening cry and felt her thighs tighten about him.

In a second he rose over her and plunged deep, feeling the spasms of her completion as he lovingly delved her core. The tight sheath hugged him insistently; his shaft caressed her demandingly. Moments later he, too, gave a cry of triumph and spilled his seed inside his woman.

"Mine!" he cried at the peak of ecstasy.

"Yours," she whispered in agreement when he collapsed over her.

In the splendor of the aftermath, they slept, not waking until sunrise, when Matthew reached for Cece, and they again loved, gently, slowly, tenderly.

A few hours later a chill rain began and did not stop for days. Cece stayed by the shelter, glad for the additional cover of the tall evergreens. Still, she could not avoid being damp most of the time.

When it seemed the rain would never stop, it suddenly did. But its damage had been done. Cece was unable to rise that day, her brow hot, her cheeks flushed with fever.

"Let me call Dexter," Matthew said, not for the first time, his concern for Cece at war with his guilt. After all, had she not been living here in the woods with him, she would never have been exposed to the inclement weather.

Keeping her eyes closed, Cece shook her head. "I cannot allow you to do that. I have no way of knowing what Father has told the townspeople, but I would spare him any further shame than that which he has already borne."

Matthew threw his hands up in surrender. "I cannot understand your consideration for someone who has shown none for you."

Cece lay silent for a moment. When she opened her eyes, Matthew noted the dilated pupils and the brittle glitter of sickness.

"He's my father, Matthew," she answered. "Hating what he did to me, I cannot allow myself to behave in the same fashion toward him."

"You are too tenderhearted," he said, the words sounding more like an accusation than anything else.

"Perhaps. But I would rather be tenderhearted than self-ishly heartless."

Noting the shivers racking her slender body, Matthew tucked another blanket around Cece. "Fine," he answered, willing to grant her this point, still intent on pressing another. "But you still need a doctor."

"I do not want Dexter Sanders brought out here."

She was becoming agitated, and Matthew realized that arguing would only harm her. "Very well. I will go along with your wishes. Just please get well," he urged, his voice husky with concern.

Cece placed her hand over his and squeezed gently. "I am trying, love."

Matthew kissed her and left to finish the final quarter of the roof. By the time he returned much later that day, Cece was sleeping fitfully, twisting and turning and moaning. He tried to wake her, knowing she needed liquid, but he could not do so. His concern turned to fear as her fever continued to burn.

He gave up working on the house the rest of the day, opting instead to stay by Cece's side, trying to rouse her frequently. On occasion she would mumble incoherent words; at other times, she called his name. But still she slept, and her fever raged.

He damned himself, knowing he had caused Cece's illness. Had he not allowed his body to overcome his reason, she would never have been forced from her father's home. She would not be expecting a child, an innocent who was surely suffering as much as she was.

He watched the color slowly drain from her fine skin. He lit a fire by the door to the shelter, hoping to offer her some warmth. It did nothing; despite the heat of her fever, she trembled visibly. He lay down beside her, offering her the life in his own body. Hers did not respond. He gazed at her features, pinched looking from the fever burning her, and still saw the beauty of the woman.

How could he live if he lost her? She had become more important to him than breathing. She was the woman for whom he had walked away from his tribe.

Still, she remained hot to the touch. Tremors shook her. She slept, never once waking, her body tossing in restless slumber. Bit by bit, though, she quieted, and her breathing became shallow, her sleep impenetrable. His fear turned to panic at the thought of losing Cece and their baby.

He wanted his child to be born. He wanted his child to live. He wanted to see Cece bring their baby to her full breast and nourish that new life. He wanted to gaze upon the face of a tiny being who was part Cece, part him. He wanted to hold his child in his embrace, to let that child know how precious it was, how precious its mother was. He needed Cece.

Matthew wished she had been more reasonable and had let him call Dexter, who was a good man and an excellent doctor. But despite his feelings toward Edward Scanlon, he respected Cece's goodness and envied her ability to spare the insensitive bastard any embarrassment. Matthew had not an ounce of forgiveness for the mill manager, no more than for the elders who had forced this exile upon him.

Dusk was near, and the dying light of day, the glow that made its way through the doorway to the shelter, illuminated Cece's pallor. Her fragile white skin looked transparent, the veins beneath it dark in contrast. The cinnamon freckles that normally were barely discernible now stood out clearly, vividly. They were no longer the charming evidence of her spicy redhead's temperament.

She had not moved for hours. Her breast rose and fell a small amount with each breath she took, barely stirring the blankets he had placed over her. Matthew ran a finger over Cece's flushed cheek and shuddered at the furnace of fever burning below the surface. There had to be something he could do.

He could not sit idly by and watch life seep from the woman he loved.

If he could not go to Dexter, bound by his word to Cece, then perhaps his uncle would consider caring for Cece. After all, Uncle Soo-moy'asum was a shaman, empowered to heal by the spirits. But to fetch his uncle, Matthew would have to leave Cece alone. What if on his way to seek help, she—

No! That possibility did not even bear thinking. He knelt by her side and kissed her forehead. "I will return in no time, my love. We need help."

With his heart in his throat, Matthew ran every step of the way to the village. He did not pause until he reached his uncle's home. He stopped long enough to knock on the plain door then pushed it open, not willing to wait for someone to let him in.

"Matthew!" exclaimed Anna.

"Where is your father?" he asked, wildly searching the shadows in the cabin for his uncle.

"He has gone with some of the other men to hunt deer," Anna answered. "What is wrong? Where is Cece? Are she and the baby—"

Matthew ran a hand through his hair, desperation clenching his gut. "She has run a violent fever all day. At first she tossed and turned and mumbled a bit. But now she barely moves, even to breathe."

From the shadows his aunt spoke. "How long now?"

Matthew spun to face her, finding her slight form silhouetted by the light from the fire in the central hearth. "Four hours? Five? I do not know for certain."

Princess Mary, as she was called, spoke again. "Anna mentioned a baby."

Matthew nodded. "Cece carries my child."

"You should have given your love to a strong S'Klallam woman."

His aunt's words were another indictment heaped upon his already burdened conscience. "Cece is delicate, too delicate for my kind of life. She has chosen to be at my side, though, and she suffers because of her choice. So does my unborn child."

Princess Mary rose, her small stature not diminishing her regal bearing. She waved her slender, wrinkled hand in the air. "You should have allowed one of our girls to tempt you long ago."

Matthew smiled ruefully. "After all the times you scolded me when I gave in to temptation, I cannot believe you are saying such things."

His aunt shook her head. "You never let those girls tempt your heart. Just your—"

"That does not matter now. Cece needs help. If she is not cared for properly, I will surely lose her and the baby. I—cannot bear that thought," he said, his voice thick with emotion.

He closed his eyes tightly and forced himself to take a few calming breaths. Then, feeling stronger, he cleared his throat of the roughness there and faced his aunt. "You know almost as much as my uncle about healing. Will you not treat Cece?"

Princess Mary turned her back to Matthew. After a moment, in a soft voice, she said, "She is not one of our own."

Matthew silently acknowledged the truth of her words, but his heart refused to give up. "Within her grows one of our own."

The elderly woman acknowledged Matthew's point with a tiny shrug. Matthew took her lack of further argument as a positive sign. He pressed on. "Without Cece I have no future."

His simple words seemed to reach her, where a more impassioned plea might only have made her more resistant. She left her place in the shadows and came to Matthew's side. "Your heart is truly caught, son," she said, placing her hand over his.

"Yes."

"You understand I cannot accept your love for the daughter of the enemy of our village."

It was Matthew's turn to respond with a shrug.

"You have not even married her," she added, heaping additional shame upon Matthew.

He gritted his teeth. Debating would not do Cece any good. It was not making his situation with the tribe any easier to bear. Marriage! If it only had been so simple.

"Can we be married according to my people's way?" he asked, a blatant challenge in his voice.

"No," she answered, her voice firm.

Matthew extended his hands in helpless capitulation. "There is the answer. We cannot be married in Port

Gamble, and we cannot be married in Nuf-Kay'it. Her father disowned her, and she is with child. Did you raise a son who would abandon his woman and his child?"

Matthew saw the effect of his words in the proud lifting of his aunt's chin. He had known her answer even before he voiced the question.

"No."

He allowed himself a brief moment of relief. "Then for my sake, for the sake of your unborn grandson, will you care for her?"

Princess Mary never spoke. She turned and crossed to the far right corner of the cabin, to the shelf where she always kept an assortment of medicinal mixtures and various healing herbs. With her usual economy of movement, she gathered various items, packing them in a large leather pouch.

She turned to Anna, who had watched the entire scene in silence, tears streaming down her cheeks, and gave her a pointed look. Anna nodded and watched her mother open the door. Matthew followed his aunt into the night, then led her to Cece's side.

Hour after agonizing hour, Princess Mary chanted for the spirits to come to Cece's aid. She brewed herbal mixtures of various sorts and, with a small wooden spoon, managed to pry Cece's lips apart and drip the healing liquids into her mouth.

Dawn crept in, lending light to the dark shelter through the opening in the rush wall. Still Cece lay motionless, her fever dangerously high.

When his aunt noticed the new day's arrival, she sent Matthew from the sickroom and urged him to resume the roofing of his cabin. "There will come a time when this girl cannot remain in this poor room. It is no wonder she fell ill."

"Do you think I am not aware of that?" he asked, a bitter taste in his mouth.

"Waste no strength on feelings of that nature, son. Work on providing your family a home."

Matthew studied his aunt for a moment. "Even if you do not accept my woman?"

Sadness filled her gaze. Slowly she nodded. "Even then, son. Even if she takes you from us, I do not wish her harm."

"Thank you," Matthew whispered. Careful not to disturb Cece, he bent to his aunt and kissed her creased cheek. The familiar scent of her herbs reached him and vividly brought to mind the times she had cared for him as a child. And in that moment Matthew knew without a doubt how deeply his aunt and uncle loved him. Princess Mary had gone against her convictions, had come to care for a Boston woman, just on the basis of her love for him.

He curved his hand over his aunt's slight shoulder and gently squeezed it. She laid her hand over his. "I love you," he said, then rose and went to work.

When he returned late in the afternoon, Cece showed no sign of improvement. Her breathing was still shallow, her fever still high. Her skin was even more transparent.

Matthew could not stop the anguish he felt at the sight of Cece covered in blankets, apparently lifeless. And how could the life within her possibly continue to grow when the one nourishing it lay ill?

From the corner of the shelter his aunt spoke softly. "No, son. Do not allow fear to steal your hope. You cannot stop believing the spirits will work through this."

Matthew dropped to his knees at the foot of the bedding. The contrast between Cece's deathly white skin and the dark brown bearskin was a painful illustration of how ill she was. Only days ago he had seen her vivid coloring highlighted by the nearly black gloss of fur, had enjoyed the beauty of the scene presented by her wanton desire for him. Today the woman on the bearskin could not feel desire, she could not feel anything but pain, and the scorching heat of fever.

A shudder ripped through his body. "She looks so . . . so frail. And she made the forest come alive. She made *me* come alive."

Princess Mary's only response was a penetrating look, then she renewed her chants.

In the morning, despite all his aunt's arguments, Matthew would not leave Cece's side. This was the second day she lay like this, and he could not bear the anxiety of being away from her. The house was worthless without her to fill it with her inimitable joy for living.

They continued their vigil, coaxing drops of different infusions between her colorless lips. Cece remained still, her breathing shallow, her skin dry and hot.

Then, late into the night, a ragged moan tore from her lips. Matthew placed a hand over her breast and heard the furious beating of her heart. His hand came away damp with the rivers of perspiration pouring off Cece's hot body.

Princess Mary pushed him away from her patient. "If you wish to help, fetch me a bucket of cool water. Some clean cloths, also. Hurry, son. Hurry!"

Faster than Matthew had ever known he could move, he did as his aunt had ordered. In virtually no time he was back with supplies ready to be used to help Cece.

Sparing a critical look for Matthew, one he chose to ignore, Princess Mary rapidly stripped Cece's damp cotton nightdress from her trembling body. She dunked all the cloths Matthew had provided into the watertight basket he had filled with the clear liquid from a well nearby, and with great care began to bathe Cece.

Another moan broke the silence. Matthew felt her suffering in the very center of his heart. He had brought her to this; his selfish, all-consuming desire for her delicate white beauty had grown into love. He had been unable to push her away from him, allowing her to love him, too. Because of him, she had lost her home. Because of him, she could lose her life. He closed his eyes, shocked by the prickling of tears behind his lids. He had not cried like this in many, many years.

When he opened his eyes again, he turned to his aunt but saw she had not stopped bathing Cece's now trembling body. Over and over the wet fabric cleansed the heated dampness from her. Over and over the woman who had raised him, the woman who could not accept his love for a white woman, tenderly and assiduously fought to beat the illness that held the white woman in its clutches.

A single tear slid down his face.

"Ma-Ma . . . tthew . . ."

He swung his head up sharply at the sound of that hoarse, reedy whisper and saw Cece's lips move again. "Ma . . . thew . . ."

"Here," he croaked, grabbing her limp hand. "I am here." His heart cried out to the spirits, to the white God. *Don't let her die!*

A sharp slap on his wrist caught him by surprise. "Pah! Get away, son. Let me do what needs to be done."

His heart beating erratically, he looked at Princess Mary. "Is she—" His voice broke. He took a moment to control his emotions, then voiced his greatest fear. "Is she dying?"

Princess Mary looked up at him impatiently. "Dying? No, son. She is getting well. Let the two of us make sure she does. Fetch me a clean gown for her. Soon she should stop this trembling, and the fever will go. She will need dry clothing."

Relief, sweet and piercing, robbed Matthew of the power to move. Yes, even the power to breathe. Then, dragging in a shuddering breath, he looked back at Cece, thoughts of thanksgiving filling his mind. She looked no better than before, but her breathing was deeper, and she was no longer deathly still. Tremors shook her body, and as he watched she turned her head just a bit. Her lips moved again, silently forming his name.

With the image of his name on his lover's lips, Matthew turned to Cece's valise and rooted around until he found another delicate batiste nightdress. The scent of roses surrounded him as he brought the fabric to his face. Cece. How could he question the rightness of loving her, even in view of the problems of the tribe? He needed her, just as crucially as she needed him.

That simple thought whirled through his mind as he turned to his aunt and placed the gown at her side. He noted a faint beading of perspiration upon Princess Mary's brow and only then realized the strain she had sustained, nursing Cece all this time without stopping her vigil. Again he realized how much the elderly woman loved him. He saw what a priceless gift a family was. And his heart broke for Cece's empty childhood.

He prayed their love, filled with hardships though it

was sure to be, would be enough erase the pain Edward
Scanlon's coldness had caused.

Just as Princess Mary had said, a bright flush soon
appeared over Cece's cheekbones. She no longer per-
spired, and the intolerable furnace heat of fever began to
abate. Cece's pulse became more stable, turning rhythmic
and even.

When they dressed her, she turned her head, whimper-
ing in protest. Cece was once again making her wishes
known. More than anything else, that gentle complaint,
that clear assertion of her desires, told Matthew that she
would recover.

Only one fear remained in his heart. Would their child
survive as well?

Although Matthew had never seen that baby, had never
felt the child move while it grew in Cece's womb, it was a
very real being to him. A person with a future. A little one
he wanted very much to get to know.

Unable to face the possibility of losing the baby, Matthew
ruthlessly crushed his fears, concentrating instead on helping his aunt with Cece's recovery. He did exactly what
the gifted healer told him to, his love and admiration for
Princess Mary greater than ever.

When Princess Mary took a few minutes to see to her
necessities, and to exercise her own limbs, Matthew took
her place by Cece's head. Ever so gently he traced the
delicately arched brows, the rounded cheekbones, the pert
nose, and her full lips. Although she was still flushed with
a light fever, color had returned to her lips.

As he watched her, his thoughts focused on her recovery,
he felt the slightest stirring of the hand he held in his. He
gazed down and saw Cece's slender fingers squeeze his.
Instantly he sought her gaze, and to his utter joy he found
the evergreen depths focused on his face.

A wan smile curved her cracked lips. "Matthew," she
whispered, somehow managing to imbue his name with a
magnificent wealth of love. "You look tired. Don't work
so hard on the house. We'll finish it soon enough. I'll just
sleep a bit more so I can help you."

"Hush. You just think of getting well. I will see to the

house." It humbled him to think that after her ordeal her first concern would be for him.

"Oh!" she cried with a startled look on her flushed face.

A twinge of fear gripped his heart. "What is it? Do you hurt?"

She shook her tangled curls, another weak smile widening her lips. "No, I do not hurt. I feel wonderful. See?"

Cece reached for Matthew's hand and placed it over her still-flat abdomen. To his delight, he felt the tiniest flutter. He shot his gaze up to meet hers, a question in his eyes.

Chapter Seventeen

——— • ———

Cece nodded, still smiling. For the first time since she became ill, Matthew found inside him the joy necessary to smile. Relief poured through him in waves that crested and swirled much like the waters did in Teekalet.

"I have been worried about you and our child. I did not want to . . ." Matthew cleared his throat, finally ridding himself of the heavy thickness that had embedded itself there the moment he began to fear for Cece's life. "I could not bear the thought of losing you."

"Oh, Matthew," Cece whispered, "I am so glad you feel that way. Although, because of our situation, it might have been best if—"

Rage pounded in Matthew's temples. "How can you say that? Never think such thoughts. Not ever again."

A tear slipped from under her lush lashes, trickling a damp trail into her hairline. Matthew felt her squeeze his hand again, and he returned the pressure.

"I love you," Cece whispered.

"And I love you."

A sound at the opening in the wall of the rush shelter made Cece glance up. A stranger, a S'Klallam stranger, bent to enter what she had considered hers and Matthew's private sanctuary. The elderly lady did so in a most comfortable, almost proprietary manner. "Who . . . ?"

Her voice trailed off as Matthew reached out an arm to assist the woman's progress into the cramped quarters. Matthew obviously knew her. But Cece certainly did not, and it peeved her to watch him usher someone into their shelter when she was so ill. About to chastise him, she fell silent when the woman spoke to her.

"You are very weak still. I will continue to give you the infusion I made, but you need to take some nourishment. Are you hungry?"

Cece felt her eyes widen at the stranger's familiarity with her condition. Who was this woman?

Then she heard Matthew chuckle. "I need to introduce you to my aunt, Cece. She is known as Princess Mary. She is Uncle Soo-moy'asum's wife and a gifted healer. We can thank her for your recovery."

Surprise was the first emotion Cece registered. Then she studied Matthew through narrowed eyes. Had he called Dexter Sanders while she was unable to stop him?

As if he had heard her silent speculation, he laughed louder, shaking his head. "You *are* recovering, but there is no need for suspicion. You asked me not to call Dexter and I kept my word. That is why my aunt is here. I know nothing about healing. I needed her help to keep you alive."

Cece turned her gaze toward the older woman. One glance told all. The lady carried herself regally, her pride as much a part of her as the multitude of wrinkles on her weathered face. Intelligence shone in her almond-shaped eyes and reminded her of Anna. This was Anna's mother, of course, and Cece immediately sought more evidence of that relationship. If she thought of the woman as related to Anna, she would be able to avoid seeing her as someone from the village that had shunned Matthew.

Mingled with the pride in her bearing, Matthew's aunt also managed to convey to Cece her disapproval of Cece's presence in Matthew's life.

She extended her hand to Princess Mary, silently cursing the weakness that made it such a difficult task. She had her pride, too. "I wish to thank you for all you have done on my behalf."

"I could not witness Matthew's pain."

Cece's eyes widened. This woman wasted no time in making her feelings known. Very well, neither would she. Without flinching, Cece kept her eyes fixed on the bright black eyes that spoke so clearly of broken traditions and dashed expectations. "Then my thanks are doubled. I would sacrifice much for Matthew as well. In fact, I have."

"Matthew has so said," Princess Mary admitted. The all-seeing dark eyes never wavered.

Cece felt the scrutiny of those eyes as if Matthew's aunt had opened her breast and examined her heart. She was unprepared for the woman's next question.

"Why take one of our men? Port Gamble has many."

Cece heard a strangled sound come from the direction where Matthew sat. He had clearly not expected this sort of attack either. She did not dare to look his way; she did not know how he was taking this exchange, and besides, this was her fight.

Matthew seemed to understand this, for he remained silent despite his reaction to his aunt's question. Cece wondered how long he would do so. Then she decided it did not matter. She had to deal with this matter before there would be any peace in the rush shelter. "There are men in Port Gamble, and there were many more in San Francisco. But there is none like Matthew."

The wizened head rose slowly, then dropped at the same deliberate pace. "Of course. That is why he must become *ssia'm*. There is none like Matthew."

Cece closed her eyes, knowing she was far from ready to deal with these issues, but it seemed fated, and Matthew's blunt aunt insisted on an instantaneous recovery on her part. "I do not wish to keep him from his destiny. I have not asked him to drop his responsibilities to the village."

"You did not need to ask. You lured him with your white Boston temptations. My son is honorable and will care for you and your child. But who will care for our village?"

Tears again welled in Cece's eyes. She wished for greater strength to battle such feelings but could not muster any more energy than was needed to lift her head slightly. "Why can he not do so still?"

Princess Mary waved a regal hand in Cece's direction. "Because you are the mill manager's daughter. We cannot trust his judgment now that he lies with you."

"Enough!" Matthew's voice tore through the wrenching words, leaving Cece to face her pain. He turned to his aunt. "You know how weak Cece is. This matter will be best handled when she is recovered. Go on home if her presence in my life so disturbs you."

Princess Mary shook her head, sadness in every movement. "No, son. I do not turn my back on my duties. Her health depends on my care. I shall leave when my responsibility is ended."

Cece gasped at the harsh indictment his aunt leveled on Matthew. She searched his face for his reaction. No change was visible in the stonelike cast of his features. But deep in his expressive eyes Cece saw what seemed to her to be agreement with his aunt's accusation. Her heart broke at the knowledge.

Cece turned her face away from the scene before her and allowed her tears to flow freely. She produced no great sobs or wailed lamentations. No, the all-encompassing misery she felt merely allowed for drop after drop of liquid heartache to eke from her eyes. The pain flowed from her at the same time the joy she had earlier felt at the movement of her baby left her heart, leaving her with only the leaden weight of guilt.

Through it all, she still loved Matthew; and if that made her selfish, then that was what she was, as she could not dredge up one ounce of regret for even the slightest moment of the beauty they had shared. The future, that great unknown blankness, left her saddened and frightened, however.

In the days that followed, Cece's strength returned with a speed that stunned both Matthew and his aunt. Cece took it for granted. She had much to accomplish, too much, in fact, to lie about feeling poorly. Only a few days after her fever broke, she was up and caring for her personal needs without the embarrassing assistance she had been forced to accept from Matthew's aunt.

Despite the woman's open disapproval, she never was anything other than solicitous and gentle with Cece. Her constant care did not once waver as a result of her inner feelings. For that Cece admired her, knowing that thanks to the woman's love for Matthew, Cece's child now had a chance to know life.

Always honest, Cece did not hold back her feelings, even on such a delicate matter. She could not. When Matthew's aunt came to ply her with yet another dose of a healing infusion, Cece placed her hand on the woman's shoulder. "Please. I must speak with you. I . . . want to thank you for all you have done. Not so much for me," she hastened to add, knowing full well how Princess Mary felt about her. "I thank you for my child. For Matthew's child. I know this has been difficult for you. And yet not once have you been careless or rough with me. I admire your courage, your strength."

Matthew's aunt kept her gaze upon Cece's hand, gently resting on her own forearm. "You thank me for your child. I care for you for mine."

Cece nodded, the bond of understanding from one mother to another bridging even the most elemental difference. "I know. I envy Matthew the love you give him. It is a precious gift from you to your son."

The grizzled head bobbed once. "Just as life will be a precious gift from you to your child."

Cece persisted. "Just as my life is a very precious gift from you to me. Please don't deny me the joy of thanking you. You have done much for me, you are still doing much for me, and I am truly grateful. Not even my father would do as much."

At her words, Princess Mary met her gaze. A question filled the bright black eyes.

Cece swallowed the lump in her throat. With no embellishment she described her childhood and ended with a recounting of the awful scene in Father's office the morning after the ball. Afterward she felt as weak as she had when her fever broke.

She had only one more thing to add. "Please believe me. I understand Matthew's responsibilities. I never wished to selfishly tear him from them. I only wanted to love him." Swallowing hard, she decided to say her piece, regardless of how Princess Mary might take her words. "Matthew suffers much as a result of your husband's demand that he choose between the village and us."

That endless dark gaze never left Cece's face. "I know my son's suffering. And I understand his heart. He will not abandon the mother of his child. His conscience would never allow him such a simple solution."

So intent was Cece on Princess Mary's words that she did not notice her movements until a gentle leathery hand covered hers. Cece's gaze flew to the spot where S'Klallam met white. She blinked and looked up into the elderly woman's face.

"I bear you no hatred. You love my son well. It is what your people have done to ours I hate. And what my son must abandon to have you."

"Cece, too, has given up a lot to be with me."

Cece spun her head around at Matthew's words. In his usual silent way, he had come up behind the two women without either one hearing his steps.

Princess Mary nodded. "But her sacrifice, my son, has not cost anyone any great thing. Your exile costs Nuf-Kay'it much." With a sharp glance in Cece's direction, Princess Mary bent and picked up her leather pouch filled with healing miracles. "It is time I returned home. Past time for you, son."

Without another word, the slight form of the formidable lady slipped into the woods.

Cece watched Princess Mary's departure, gnawing fretfully on her bottom lip. In desperation she called upon Sister Marietta's legion of saints, but did not hold much hope for their intervention. Just because she had seen Sister's prayers answered by the good saints, that did not mean that in Cece's hour of need they would swoop down from heaven and pull off a miracle for her. After all, it was Sister Marietta who had always launched into long discussions with the heavenly beings. It was Sister who received the answers she prayed for. It was Sister who had all the faith.

Secondhand faith would surely not serve a woman who had brought misery upon herself.

And she had. She was honest to the bone and could admit she had sought out Matthew, had relentlessly pursued him until he gave in to her wishes. And then, knowing the way she felt for him, particularly after that first turbulent kiss on the bench in the garden, she had doubled her efforts to carve a place for herself at Matthew's side.

He did not deserve ostracism from his people. He had warned her time and again of the unfordable chasm between them. She remembered his first admonition. *The daughter of the manager of the Pope and Talbot mill does not belong in the woods with a S'Klallam man,* he had said. And she had refused to heed his words. Now she had been sent from her father's house, which most likely was not a great loss. But worse, Matthew had been driven from his village, from the position his ancestors had decreed for him.

Now, too, a child's future lay in the balance.

Her hand gentle on her belly, Cece bit down harder on her lip.

"Don't," Matthew chided, using his thumb to release the flesh she had bruised between her teeth.

Cece looked at him, knowing full well her fears and self-recrimination showed in her expression. "I cannot help but feel it would be best if I went back—"

Her words were cut off by a crushing kiss. Matthew's arms pinned her to his body, holding her so closely she could not tell where her body ended and his began. Relentless, he kissed her over and over, as if by the passionate gesture he could make reality disappear, as if things would somehow be made right by the power of their love.

But inevitably the kisses ended. Lips swollen, breath ragged, they gazed at each other.

The breeze blowing in from Teekalet bore the chill of November weather. The sun rarely shone these days. Birds no longer sang cheerful songs in their search for the mates with whom to build their homes. The squirrels no longer stopped to chatter in their forays across the forest floor. No, they knew the barrenness of winter was just around the corner, an empty time when only what they had stored in better times would see them through.

Cece and Matthew knew they had sown the seeds of pain by crossing the boundaries of heritage. They now reaped a harvest of anguish.

*   *   *

After the painful moment of realization when his aunt left their camp, Matthew could not help but search his heart. He wondered how he would live knowing he had betrayed the trust the villagers had placed upon him. Now they were left with only a tired old man who had lost the drive to lead, and Luke, with his violent solutions to sensitive issues.

More than ever he needed to feel the empowering of the spirits, he needed to experience the strength of his *tamanous*, and perhaps then he would be granted the secret to ending his banishment—ending it without having to betray himself, his woman, and their child.

Each time he touched Cece, guilt ate at him like ants on the forest floor consuming any crumb dropped in their territory. In fact, he felt as insignificant as the smallest speck of food in contrast to the needs of an entire village. He felt so much anguish and anger that he reached for Cece less and less. He could not bear the bittersweet caresses.

He was wounded, too, by the look in her eyes. She noticed each time he pulled away. She realized it when he closed himself from her. He would not even take the loving she silently offered at night when they lay together in their shelter. Still, his damnable hunger for this white woman continued, ever greater, bitter in its consequences.

Consumed by his troubled thoughts, he finished the cabin. They moved their meager belongings into the structure, and before long Cece made her feminine presence known. On the large sleeping platform Matthew had built across the far wall, she piled the cedar mats he had used in the shelter, covering them with his bearskin. She placed her collection of baskets on another shelf, this one for storage purposes, and set among the containers two beautiful shells she found on the beach. Over the two small windows, Matthew had stretched thin skins that kept out the cold while allowing light to filter into the room. When Cece noted the utilitarian covering, she scrabbled in her satchel and pulled out a lacy petticoat, soon fashioning curtains of the fine yellow cotton to add welcome cheer to the home.

She set up her loom in a corner. Matthew's gaze sought out the contraption where she so diligently worked on a blanket for their child. He had built a structure, but Cece had made a home.

After a few days of sharing their new cabin, still perturbed by the thoughts brought on by his aunt's talk of duty and responsibility, Matthew reached a decision. As he watched Cece store the maplewood bowls and spoons on the proper shelf, he felt his heart twist with all the conflicting feelings it harbored. "I will return to my spirit quest in the morning," he said, without gently leading up to his announcement.

He saw Cece straighten, her spine stiff and proud. Without facing him, she posed a question he knew had cost her greatly.

"Will you be moving back into the shelter?"

He had given the matter much thought. "No. It is too cold to do that. I will return here each day. But please understand, I must not be—"

She turned to face him. Her eyes reminded him of the leaves reflected in the pool made by the spring not one hundred paces away. As the earth formed the pond to contain the water, so her will contained her tears and kept them from falling. He could not speak the words he had intended to say. He would not hurt her any more.

Instead she said what needed to be said. "I understand, Matthew. You must not be interrupted. I know how important this is."

Her gentle words were full of love and forgiveness. Marveling, not for the first time, at her generosity of spirit, Matthew could not help but be drawn to her warmth once again. "Cece," he whispered, surrendering to the feelings between them.

He reached for her, wrapped his arms around her, and closed his mind to the guilt that rose to taunt him. He concentrated only on the woman in his arms. For the first time since her recovery, he indulged the desire that always simmered under the surface. They loved gently, tenderly, with a passion so sweet it was not only Cece whose eyes gleamed with tears of wonder when they reached the pinnacle of joy.

Wrapped in each other's arms, they slept. In the bright

glow of morning Matthew rose, and with a soft kiss to Cece's brow, he left the cabin to resume the quest he had left unfinished.

When Cece awoke, she wondered if the night had been merely a dream. Had Matthew made tender love to her? Had his eyes filled, the beauty of their union so great it made a strong man weep? Had she imagined all that in her desire to be Matthew's woman?

When she stretched, she had her answer. The slight soreness between her thighs left no room for doubt that Matthew had indeed made their union complete during the night. But this morning he had left her side without a word of love.

When she went to the spring for fresh water, she clung doggedly to the memory of his fierce refusal to consider her departure as a means to solve his problems. He might not say the words, she thought, but he certainly found ways to show the emotions those words would convey.

A soft rustle of the dead leaves carpeting the forest floor let her know someone was approaching. "Who's there?" she asked, a frisson of fear running up her back. After all, that Luke person had threatened her safety, and she was all alone.

"It is me, Cecelia." At the sound of Princess Mary's voice, Cece's shoulders sagged in relief.

The older woman's eyes intently studied Cece before nodding in satisfaction. "You regain your strength. Have you been drinking the tea I left for you?"

Cece nodded, grimacing at the reminder of the tea's bitter flavor. "Every day. Could you tell me what is in it? It tastes terrible."

A tiny smile crossed Princess Mary's face. "It is made mostly from the leaves of the red raspberry. It will strengthen your womb."

That notion caught Cece's interest. "Really?" she asked. "That awful-tasting drink will help my baby?"

Princess Mary nodded, a hint of sadness visible on her creased visage. "I only bore Anna. I want to help you give life to Matthew's child."

Cece once again felt that unique bond, the understanding motherhood wrought between even the most unlikely female acquaintances. And she marveled at Princess Mary's willingness to help. She could not resist asking her why. "Even . . ."

"Yes," was the older woman's emphatic response. "Even if you represent everything I hate."

Cece turned her face aside, busying herself with moving the basket of water from one hand to the other. "Perhaps it will ease your concerns to know Matthew has resumed his spirit quest this very morning."

She spared a glance at Matthew's aunt with her last words. What she saw immensely pleased her. Princess Mary was unable to conceal her surprise.

The two women had been walking toward the cabin the entire time they had spoken, and just then reached the clearing. Princess Mary looked around but saw no evidence of Matthew's presence. "He is . . ."

Cece shook her head. "Not here. I do not know where he went. He asked that I not disturb him, and I respect his request. I respect your son's needs." *As he has respected mine.* Her unspoken words hung between the two women, both aware of the sentiment.

After a moment Cece, anxious to relinquish the weight of the bucket she carried, opened the door. "Please, come inside our home."

Stepping aside, Cece pushed the heavy door and held it fully open for Princess Mary. The older woman, in her stark black dress and hand-woven plaid shawl, entered the home. No sooner was she inside than she began to peer discreetly into every corner. She seemed to find nothing to comment about—until her gaze landed on the loom in the corner of the room.

With a birdlike movement she spun around to face Cece. "Is that my daughter's loom?" she asked, a hint of disbelief in her voice.

Cece hung the basket of water on a peg Matthew had stuck into the wall by her storage shelf, and her pent-up breath burst out in a lusty gust. "Why, yes. She brought it to teach me how to weave."

Princess Mary ran an expert finger over the almost finished blanket. "I did not know you two had met. Nor that you were the friend who wished to learn to weave."

Anna had a devious streak to her, Cece thought, and understood why Matthew called his cousin trouble. Cece cannily kept her thoughts about her friend to herself and gathered kindling to stoke up the fire in the hearth at the center of the house. "She was at Matthew's shelter one day this past summer. I—I had come to see him, and we found each other. I like Anna very much."

Princess Mary's words were slow and thoughtful. "That explains why she has been so concerned over your welfare. Yours and your child's."

Cece cast a glance at Princess Mary and smiled. "She has taught me so very much. I could not ask for a better friend."

A frown creased Princess Mary's brow. Despite the muted light in the room, Cece saw the hint of something powerful—perhaps pain, maybe anger—flicker in the depths of the black almond-shaped eyes.

"It would seem both my children have abandoned their people."

To her own chagrin, Cece burst out laughing. She sat back on her heels, fanning the growing flames with a large piece of cedar bark. "Hardly! Anna has worked diligently to teach me the S'Klallam ways. Thanks to her, I can manage to maintain a home like this one for Matthew and myself." The memory of her clumsiness during some of those lessons made Cece laugh again.

The sight of the loom, however, sobered her soon enough. "It is thanks to your daughter, and the wool you gave her, that I can make my child a blanket. For that I thank you, too."

Something in either Cece's expression or her words must have pleased Princess Mary, for she visibly relaxed and even sat by the small fire. She carefully set her leather pouch by her side and reached her hands toward the warmth.

Cece was glad to see Princess Mary lose some of her wariness. But soon her own rampant curiosity got the better of her. "That leather sack," she said, pointing to the object. "It contains your medicines, no?"

Princess Mary looked at Cece, her expression unreadable. "I carry herbs and an ointment or two with me."

"Are those the ones you used to heal me?"

Princess Mary shook her head. "I have more of the tea for you. I also have some bits of crab apple bark. Tea from it is restful to the heart, and I was asked to take some to a neighbor in the village."

Cece absorbed all Princess Mary said and found herself wanting to know more. She wondered if she dare ask the formidable matriarch to teach her herbal lore. *Well, silly, you won't know until you ask her.*

She stood, and taking a deep breath for courage, Cece looked steadily at Princess Mary. "I do not know much about medicine, ours or yours. But I am fascinated and would love to learn more. After all, your knowledge cured me." She certainly had Princess Mary's interest now, Cece thought. She plunged ahead. "Would you be willing to teach me? I truly wish to learn."

The creased cheeks hollowed as Matthew's aunt's jaw dropped in astonishment. Immediately her slight jaw clamped shut, and she frowned. Suspicion lit her gaze.

"Why?"

Cece shrugged one shoulder, then wrapped her arms around her middle. "Matthew has spoken of your wisdom. He respects your gift of healing, and I have experienced it. Anything you teach me can only enrich our lives."

"You wish to learn from an uncivilized savage?" Princess Mary asked, her voice ripe with bitterness.

Never breaking the nearly palpable eye contact, Cece shook her head. "I wish to learn from a woman far wiser than any other I know. White or Indian, Chinese or black."

A slow nod was her response. Then Princess Mary turned her attention to the fire. She stared into the dancing flames in peaceful silence for a bit. After a while she smoothed her skirt with a hand. With the other, she pulled the shawl tighter across her shoulders.

Nervous, not knowing what to say or do, Cece stepped to her storage shelf, planning to see to the matter of her midday meal. She pulled out a loaf of the bread she had baked the day before from the flour Matthew had bought at the Country Store. She sliced some with his wicked-looking knife and cut a wedge of creamy cheese from the wheel he had also bought. A crisp red apple completed her simple menu. She wondered if she should offer her guest some food.

Glancing at Matthew's aunt, and noting she had not moved from her position by the hearth, Cece decided against it. She gathered the stones for her boiling basket and set about brewing some tea. She opened the tin filled with her precious Earl Gray—Matthew's gift, an extravagance she had yet to understand—when Princess Mary chose to speak again.

"You are not what I expected. You do not hate."

The conciliatory tone of the woman's words so stunned Cece that she trembled in excitement. Perhaps the saints *had* listened. Perhaps love counted for something more than trouble and pain.

"Careful," said Princess Mary. "Do not waste the tea."

Only then did Cece notice the trickle of leaves flowing onto her dress. "Oh! I can be so careless at times."

Cursing her own distraction, she carefully placed all the tiny bits of the tea she could gather back into the tin and set it all on the shelf. Smiling, she went to sit at Princess Mary's side.

"Matthew still belongs at the village," was Matthew's aunt's final comment. She rose and left the house without another word, leaving Cece stunned with the suddenness of the statement.

Had it had a chance to do her any good, Cece would have howled at the unfairness of the situation. But the futility of the endeavor was not lost on her. Instead, to her surprise, she found herself thinking of her father.

The pain of his betrayal was still powerful, although in the aftermath of her illness it was no longer so sharp. Yet her heart came back to that infernal question: why?

She had seen the evidence of the love Matthew's family had for him. She was learning about maternal feelings each day her waistline expanded just the tiniest fraction, every time a flutter tickled her middle. And no matter how hard she thought of all these things, she failed to find a reasonable explanation for Father's behavior.

She had come to where she could accept her own share of the blame in the matter. She had known all along of Father's antipathy toward Indians, and she had been lured by a potent attraction to go against his tacit wishes. She had known he would violently object to her love for an Indian.

As to the night she had spent away from the house, it had been her selfish wish for Matthew's comfort that prompted her to sleep in his arms. No parent would condone such actions of a daughter, and she now accepted that truth.

Even if her very sanity had depended upon the love Matthew lavished upon her that night.

With nothing better to do, the house being neat and simple to maintain, and with Matthew intent on his spiritual journey, Cece decided to risk Father's wrath and try to establish some sort of contact with him. If not for his sake, or even for hers, then certainly for that of the child she carried. Her baby deserved a complete family, one in which the grandfather could tolerate the child's mother.

At the Country Store, Matthew had learned that Father had vacated the mansion soon after the ball. Horace had moved in, and Mrs. Quigley had kept her position as housekeeper. Cece rejoiced in the knowledge that when she arrived at Father's small New England–style home, she would not be met by Mrs. Quigley's disapproving glare.

Nodding to herself, approving her decision, she picked up the heavy woolen shawl Anna had given her when the weather began to change, and wrapped her growing girth against the biting cold of the late November winds. Taking care not to stumble, Cece began the walk to Port Gamble through the shadowed woods.

Her added weight made her progress slower than it had been during the summer, and she arrived in town later than she had anticipated. She was also more tired than she would have thought, but she had to consider her recent illness and that she now carried the burden of a five-month pregnancy.

She followed the directions Matthew had given her when he told her of Father's new house. At the swinging gate in front of the neat white house she paused, taking in the plain black shutters at the windows and the black-painted door with its brass knocker. The house was very like the one she and Father had occupied during her childhood. Nostalgia filled Cece and threatened to bring tears pouring down her cheeks.

She squared her shoulders and refused to yield to sentimentality. She had a goal in mind and no time for crying. She resolutely walked up the brick pathway to the two steps before the door. Deliberately she climbed to the stoop and, once there, gathered her courage and clasped the knocker in her trembling hand. The two precise claps reverberated in her mind.

From within, she heard the tapping of Father's walking stick. She took a deep breath and waited. Before long the door opened.

Father stepped up to the doorway, and Cece watched all the color drain from his face. The walking stick clattered to the floor unheeded.

"Abigail . . ." he whispered.

Chapter Eighteen

———— • ————

For a moment Cece was too stunned to move or say a word. Then the meaning of Father's exclamation became clear.

"No, Father. Not Mama. I'm Cece." Father's reaction showed what a troubled man he surely had become.

As unexpected as his initial reaction had been, the change that now overcame him was swift and painful to witness. A deep red flush rushed all the way to his hairline, and his eyes burned with anger and other unidentifiable emotions.

"Why are you here? Has your savage already tired of his white woman?"

She thought she had prepared herself for any abuse Father might level upon her, but this was too harsh, too cruel. Cece lowered her gaze to the forgotten walking stick, seeking to control her feelings. When she regained a measure of restraint, she met her father's green eyes.

What she saw there surprised her perhaps more than his prior behavior. Pain, gut-wrenching and all-encompassing, showed in the emerald depths, in the deepened creases fanning out from the corners of those eyes, in the twist of his mouth. Dear God, what had she ever done to cause such agony?

As she watched he regained his composure and blinked once. As if a broom had swept footprints off the sand, all sign of emotion vanished. His jaw worked once, jutting out in obstinate rigidity.

At that familiar sign of stubbornness, Cece called herself a fool for launching this failed venture. Father had no intention of listening with an open heart.

Fine! she thought. She still had her piece to speak. "No, Father, Matthew has not cast me aside. In fact, we have just finished building our new home."

That statement seemed to strike Father about as well as her sudden appearance had. This time anger, hot and bitter, was the dominant emotion on Father's face.

Cece went on, ignoring Father's obvious temper. "I came to speak to you on your grandchild's behalf. As you can see," she said, gesturing to her burgeoning belly, "my child grows daily. This baby deserves its entire family. And that includes its grandfather."

Father's shoulders slumped a bit, some of the anger leaving his features at the same time. "What sort of family do you speak of, Cecelia? You, who had no respect for me, my position in this community, or my personal wishes and deepest feelings."

It was Cece's turn to flush. "With time, Father, I have come to realize how badly I behaved toward you. I understand now that you have also been hurt. I should have had the courage to face you with my love for Matthew before the ball."

Father bent painfully, his stiff joints creaking their opposition to the motion. He picked up the cane and stared at Cece, that odd expression she had so often seen in his gaze those first few days back home vividly evident in his face. "Go, Cecelia. We have nothing to say to each other."

Cece felt as if she had suddenly been struck in her middle, so hard was it to draw her next breath. Enough! She could only take so much heartache at one time. "If that is the way you feel, then stay here all by yourself. I have someone to go home to."

She whirled away and would have run down the pathway, but heeding the constraints of impending motherhood, she forced herself to no more than stomp her furious way down the walk. At the gate she heard Father muttering behind her.

" . . . so very sorry, Abby."

She stopped. Had Father really spoken to her dead mother? she asked herself, turning to see nothing save the closed door. And in that pain-racked voice? No, she must not have heard correctly.

"No more," she swore. "That is that." She had done all she could this time. He certainly had made himself clear. He had no interest in even speaking with her.

She fought the cool wind blowing over the bay, and decided to forgo the walk along the shore. Usually that was her favorite path out of Port Gamble, but today she needed the cover of the tall evergreens.

As usual, the longer she walked under the canopy of boughs, the calmer she became. She was able to think more clearly of the recent run-in with Father. He was troubled. Very much so. Certainly a man who spoke to a wife, eighteen years dead, had a problem.

In view of what she had heard—those two times Father had mentioned Mother's name—Cece began to wonder if the trouble was not more within him than with Cece herself. Had he lost a bit of his mind when Mother died?

It seemed possible, she thought. Surely no sane person spoke to thin air, addressing it by a dead person's name. This mystery caught her curiosity, and she knew that no matter how much trouble Father gave her, she would be back. She would learn what lay behind Father's behavior, one way or another.

And her child would have a grandfather.

As determination fueled her pace, Cece fairly flew back to the cabin in the woods. Once there, she noted the deepening dusk and wondered if Matthew would return for their evening meal. Would he sleep by her side tonight?

In silence, thinking of ways to approach Father, Cece set out the dried salmon Matthew had said was one of the foods permitted during his fast. She also brought out a blackberry cake. She smiled, remembering the day she and Anna had gathered the ripe fruit.

Loaded down with large baskets of the sweet treats, the two women had returned to the camp in the woods. There Anna showed Cece how the S'Klallam prepared the blackberries for use during the cold winter months. Anna had taken a large stone and handed Cece another one. They had mashed the berries, mixing them with blackcaps, in the bottom of the baskets. When the juice ran freely, they had set the baskets by the fire to allow the contents to dry. Soon only sticky solids remained, and the two women shaped them into round cakes that Anna swore would keep forever.

Later that very same evening, Cece had discovered Matthew's special weakness for blackberries. After Anna left and Cece vowed never to look at another blackberry in her entire life, Matthew had brought a brimming bowl of the fruit inside the shelter. He proceeded to feed the luscious bits to Cece, licking away any drop of juice that escaped her lips. The game turned excitingly erotic, and berries and juice managed to land on the most outlandish of spots. The two lovers had been mighty solicitous about cleaning up the spills.

A sweet private humming began low in Cece's belly, fueled by memories of last night's tender loving. Perhaps the berry cakes would remind Matthew of the fruit's last appearance on their menu.

The sound of the closing door announced Matthew's arrival at the cabin. When Cece looked up, dismay rapidly replaced her anticipation. Matthew wore what she thought of as his carved-stone face, and she accepted that there would be no repeat of the night before. Still, she could not help but wish. . . .

Tossing off the heavy coat he wore, Matthew sat by the fire. He extended his frigid fingers, glad to finally come in from the worsening weather. Although he tried to ignore Cece's tempting presence in the cabin, her elusive rose scent captured his interest continually. For some reason, that bat of a housekeeper had packed a bottle of the fragrance in the satchel she had prepared for Cece.

And it was hell to avoid its lure.

He watched Cece place salmon in the two bowls, and before she served him anything more, he spoke. "That is all for me tonight."

She nodded. "I am having some of the dried blackberry cakes Anna and I prepared. Will you . . ."

Matthew stifled a groan at the swift, sensual image that invaded his mind. The day of the berries, after the two women had worked over the fire for hours, he retrieved the bowl of berries he had stolen from them and indulged in the most erotic of fantasies. He could almost taste blackberries sweetened by Cece's silky skin. In his mind he could clearly see the dark juice staining her breasts, her belly, her thighs. And he remembered the way she had covered him with strategically placed drops, only to lap them up with her soft little tongue.

Why would she choose tonight of all nights to bring the cursed fruit out? Just this afternoon he had realized his need for intense, uninterrupted concentration in order to succeed with his spirit quest. That precluded sating himself with the seductive pleasure Cece's body offered.

"No," he answered belatedly. The word came out more like a growl than a statement, and he regretted his gruffness. Cece's eyes showed clearly her surprise at his tone and the hurt he had inflicted.

He tried again. "Thank you, but I will take only the salmon."

Cece gave him a stiff nod, then placed his food before him. "Tea?" she asked.

"No, just water."

She fetched the enamel cup he had bought at the Country Store and, without touching him, handed him his beverage. Matthew was glad. Had he felt the heat of her fingers, he was not certain he would have been able to refrain from caressing her. Once he began that voyage, the destination was only too clear.

"I went to town this afternoon," she said suddenly.

Matthew started at the sound of her voice, so intent was he on avoiding contact with her. He met her gaze briefly and nodded.

He saw her bring her chin up a notch and knew she would speak regardless of his lack of response. He hoped he survived the evening.

"I went to Father's house."

Matthew's intentions began to crumble. "Why?" he asked.

Intently watching her face for her reaction, he felt his gut tense when pain appeared in the depths of her pine-green eyes.

"Because it was something I had to do," she answered, her chin squaring a fraction more. "In spite of what Father did, I realize I should have told him about you much earlier. That would have allowed him no opportunity to shock me with his announcement. Too, spending the night here in the woods with you was not the best way to respond to Father's actions."

Matthew cocked his head, trying to read the emotions swiftly succeeding one another on her expressive face. There was remorse, pain, sadness, but most of all he saw guilt. "You are not entirely responsible for the situation."

"Oh, no, Matthew, you are wrong. When two people argue, two people are at fault." She glanced down at her swelling middle, gently patting that precious mound. "It is only since our baby has been moving, and I have begun to make its acquaintance, that I have come to know how much I hurt Father."

Matthew clenched his fists. She was being charitable again, whereas he wanted to teach the old bigot a lesson in being a father. "He was wrong in what he did, Cece."

"Yes. Very wrong. But I would have reacted poorly if my daughter had slipped out to meet a lover she knew I would disapprove of. I would have been furious and ashamed had a daughter of mine spent a night in that lover's arms. And I daresay you would, too."

All his protective instincts had bloomed when Cece had been ill. He would have done anything, even faced Edward Scanlon, had that been the price to ensure Cece's well-being. Each time he had thought of their unborn child, the fear of any harm coming to that new life had been intolerable. Perhaps once again Cece's perceptiveness had brought her to the truth.

But the issue his masculine pride would not set aside was the one she had not addressed. "I would never force an unwanted spouse on my child."

Cece nodded, sadness etched on her sweet features. "Neither would I. And he tried."

Silence fell. Cece peeked at Matthew a few times and found nothing to relieve the uncomfortable atmosphere between them.

Finally, opting to give Matthew the evening alone, she slipped out of her garments and into bed. Sleep overcame her well before she felt Matthew join her on the sleeping platform. He stayed on his side, she on hers.

Having gone to sleep so early, she awoke equally early the next morning. There was sufficient water in her basket to brew a pot of tea, and she fed the fire to heat the stones. A bit of bread, toasted by the blaze, was all she felt like eating. She spread some wildflower honey on the warm bread and slowly savored her meal.

Soon Matthew awoke and stretched. Cece had studiously avoided looking at him while he slept, the unnatural strain of last evening still fresh on her mind. But this morning was a new day, and she did not want to believe he would continue to act so distant.

"Would you care for some tea?" she asked, ready to pour him a cup of the steaming brew.

"No, thank you." He rose and turned his back to her as he dressed. She was stunned and hurt. Matthew had never before hidden his nudity from her.

When he said nothing else, but washed with the water in a basket near their bed, Cece began to tremble. Had she offended him in some way? She searched her mind for the cause of his coolness, but could identify none.

Tentatively she rose. Wanting to go to his side, to feel his warmth, she took steps in his direction. "Matthew," she called in a soft voice.

"Yes?"

"Have I done something wrong? Are you angry at me?"

His back was still toward her, and she saw his broad shoulders rise and fall with the deep breath he took. "No. I am preoccupied with what I must do today."

She sought to pry another bit of conversation from him. "Your spirit quest, right? How is it progressing?"

Matthew's only response was a shrug. Cece's heart felt as if a giant hand had squeezed it. The differences between them loomed greater each day. Surely he would have shared details of his quest with her, had she been a S'Klallam. In painful silence she watched him don his coat and leave the cabin.

Only then did she indulge herself in the luxury of tears. As long as Matthew lived with her here in their cozy house under the evergreens, he would remain an outcast from his people. Their love formed an inpenetrable wall between Matthew and his heritage. This knowledge burned all semblance of peace out of him.

She, too, was an outcast as long as she lived with Matthew, but she was in the process of mending bridges with Father, and the suffering in his eyes had given her hope. Had there only been indifference in his gaze, she would have stopped trying to reach out to him. During the silent moments of dawn, she had come to admit that she had always harbored the tiniest hope for setting things right with Father.

How she would accomplish this was another matter. As her mind wrestled with the thought the memory of Sister Marietta's kind voice provided the answer. "In the Book of Romans it says you are to resist evil and conquer it with good," the wise nun had often said. "Give your enemy that which he wants, that way you can heap red-hot coals upon his head."

Cece had often wondered if Sister had memorized her entire Bible, so often was her speech peppered with quotations. But truth be told, this one sounded like a good plan. She just had to determine what Father really wanted or needed.

All he seemed to need was love, and Cece had plenty of that. Deep in thought, she carefully wrapped the teapot in a soft cloth, drying it for future use. As she set it on the shelf she caught sight of the large store of smoked salmon she and Matthew had. Father loved salmon, and Matthew had told her he had steamed theirs over a green alderwood fire. Whatever he did to it had left it flavorful and tender.

Following her instincts, she quickly wrapped a good portion of fish in a sheet of the newspaper Matthew had brought from the Country Store the last time he had gone for staples. The joy of a sound plan fairly bubbled within her.

She reached for her shawl and covered herself, knowing that the winds would be blowing a damp chill over the land.

Cece was on her way, and before the sun came close to reaching its zenith, she stood at Father's picket fence. She drew in a deep breath and nervously looked about. She noted the limp brown skeletons of geraniums that must have bloomed all summer long. Father's arthritis had kept him from cleaning the garden.

"Time to clean some trouble from your life, Cecelia," she said out loud, using her Sister Marietta voice. She pushed the gate open and strode with purpose up to the shiny door.

Once again her knock was followed by the tapping of Father's cane. As before, a slight hesitation on the other side preceded the opening of the door. Then, just like yesterday, Father's angry face met her gaze.

Before he could say a word, Cece thrust the package at him. "I only brought you a gift. I do not wish to disturb you."

His anger faded. "But you do, Cecelia, you do," he said, his words heavy with pain.

Cece gasped. This was the first time he had allowed her to glimpse anything other than his serious cool demeanor or his flaming temper. She was indeed making progress.

"I love you, Father," she whispered, then turned and walked back to the street. Although she strained to hear anything he might say, this time no sound came from the doorway, save the firm closing of the door.

Difficult though it was to witness her father's suffering, at least Cece now knew that he felt more than bland indifference toward her. And perhaps all that pain had a discernible cause. She clasped that hope close to her heart as she returned home, hoping also to see an improvement in Matthew's mood.

But she waited long hours in lonely silence. She forced herself to eat a small amount of food for her evening meal, more for the sake of the child growing inside her than to appease any hunger pangs. She felt none; an unusual numbness filled her heart, in a way shielding her from the pain of Matthew's absence.

Finally, exhausted and troubled, she slipped into bed and tried to find the comfort of sleep. That peace did not come. Neither did Matthew. When the signs of a rosy dawn began to show through the curtains at the windows, Cece was roused from the dreamlike state she had eventually fallen into by the sound of the quietly closing door.

When she lifted her head, she gasped. Matthew's face, ravaged with exhaustion and unnamed emotions, looked gaunt. The spirits had clearly not been merciful and had not brought his quest to an end yet. Cece wondered if what he sought was worth the anguish to which he subjected himself.

But she knew better than to ask. She lowered her head back onto the bearskin and closed her eyes. Listening avidly, she heard his heavy steps bring him to her side. In silence he stood still, most likely watching her. Although curiosity burned bright inside her, she held firm and allowed him the peaceful moment he sought.

When she thought she would surely explode, he sighed and sat down by her. Moments later she felt him recline, and soon his deep, even breaths told her he slept.

Unable to sleep, Cece rose, dressed and wrapped herself in her shawl, then went outside. Lured by the call of a lonely sea gull, she picked a path through the dank covering of soggy dead leaves and pine needles on the forest floor, emerging at the beach just as dawn broke. The sun on its journey upward cast spears of color onto the few puffy clouds that resembled roses in full bloom. Forcing her mind to remain blank, she sat on the dry sand and took in the beauty of the land she called home.

She lost all track of time. Sitting in silence, she wrapped her arms around her legs and propped her chin on her knees, as if to embrace her child. Its movements were the only comfort she found, and she enjoyed them fully. When it seemed her little one finally decided to nap, she released her legs and stretched them out flat on the sand.

At the sound of a soft rustle in the trees behind her, she slowly turned her head. A smile curved her lips, and relief swamped her. "Anna!" she called, overjoyed at the sight of her friend. Cece had not seen her since her illness.

Anna's joy seemed tempered by concern. "Cece? Are you all right? Why are you out here all alone?"

Cece could no longer inject joy into the twist of her lips when she offered Anna another smile. "In truth, I am less alone here than in our cabin."

Puzzlement creased Anna's brow. "What do you mean? I found Matthew there. He was sleeping, but he was there."

Cece nodded. "And that is the most company he has been of late. A silent, sleeping body. If I had wanted that, I could have found myself a great big sloth and saved myself endless trouble."

Anna clamped her fists onto her hips and glared at Cece. "Honestly, Cecelia, I do not understand what you say. What is a sloth?"

Cece grinned mischievously for the first time in a long while, and it felt ever so good! "A sloth, Anna, is a big, hairy beast from South America that barely moves. It spends most of its time sleeping. Your cousin reminds me of what I learned about such creatures in school."

A rueful moue appeared at the corner of Anna's full lips. "His spirit quest has not yet ended, I gather."

Cece snorted. "I doubt it ever will. And I do not know how long I can bear to stay in that empty cabin hearing the echo of Matthew's voice."

Her pique disappeared as she voiced her pain, and a tear slipped from her eye. Anna smoothly dropped to her knees at Cece's side and slipped a comforting arm around her shoulders. The gesture broke a dam. Cece's heaving sobs spoke of her pain and heartache as a flood of tears poured down her cheeks, a deluge she didn't even try to dry.

Anna held Cece's head gently against her shoulder. It had been so long since Cece had felt such acceptance, and she thanked God for Anna's friendship. After a while, when her eyes felt as though they had not another tear left in them, Cece lifted her head. Snuffling softly, she looked at Anna and caught her breath. Tears of sympathy gleamed in the morning sunlight on those lovely bronze cheeks.

Cece felt stunned by strong emotion and realized something of great importance. She offered Anna a watery smile then a swift, tight hug before she voiced her revelation. "I have been blessed through all of this. I cannot believe that God has finally given me the sister I always wanted. But here you are."

Anna nodded, fresh tears coursing down her cheeks. "Here *you* are."

The discovery left both of them with tremulous smiles, and they laughed trembly laughs. Cece wiped her face with the hem of her skirt and shook her head. "My life is so filled with irony. I wandered from my father's house to escape the loneliness there, only to find Matthew in the woods. Now my home with Matthew has become a silent, uncomfortable space I sometimes need to escape. When I do, I find you."

Wiping her face with the backs of her hands, Anna sniffed. "Oh, I am sure you won't need to escape your home with Matthew. The man, stubborn though he is, is far too wise to lose you. Just wait and see."

Cece tried to gain hope from Anna's words, but a niggling fear would not allow it. Avoiding Anna's eyes, she picked at a loose thread on her skirt. "I cannot help but see how much he has cut me off from him. He—he treats me as coldly as Father did when I first returned home. Our conversations are now all about the salmon he will eat and the water he will drink.

"It seems as if I am fated to lose so that I can gain. I lost Father to gain Matthew. I am loosing Matthew, but I found you. Must I—" Cece's voice broke as she tried to voice her growing fear. She lifted her head and forged ahead. "I wonder if I now must lose you in order to have my child. I am fairly going mad thinking about all this."

Anna gasped. "Oh, no. Never think that way. You have me, even if you don't want me." Anna laughed. "But as for Matthew, give him time. He has a lot on his mind. Give him time."

They fell silent for a bit, each busy with her own thoughts. Then they brought up less painful topics and chatted amiably for a while. Soon Anna had to be on her way, however, and the two women parted company. Cece, intent on taking advantage of the rare sunny day, set off for Father's home. This was the perfect opportunity to clean that garden of his.

She would not even knock on the door to let him know she was there.

Upon reaching the neat little house, Cece went right to work, ripping out the barren brown stalks with vigor. At times her anger at Matthew's silence got the better of her, and she yanked with far more strength than needed. The sodden ground squelched against her boots.

"You muleheaded . . . man, you!" *Squooosh.* "Can't even find the courtesy to inquire after your own child . . ." *Squooosh.*

As Cece stepped to the next bunch of dead plants, a slight movement caught her eye, and she fixed an intent glare on the window. Apparently Father had been watching her, for she was sure she had seen the curtain flutter.

She redoubled her efforts, tugging on a thick, stiff stalk. Pausing in her efforts, she patted her middle, unmindful of the streak of grime she smeared on her green dress. "I hope you are *not* another male. Lord save me from thickheaded blind men! First Father, then Matthew."

She stood to give her aching back some relief. Wiping some stray curls off her forehead, she realized her skin felt a bit warm. Perhaps she was straining too hard. She checked her cheek with the back of her hand, and it, too, felt slightly warm. She also felt the slick ooze of mud her hand left behind.

She had worked long enough. She was filthy and perhaps feverish. Fortunately there were only three more plants, all here under the window. She bent down and grabbed the first one. She pulled, but it wouldn't budge much. Eventually the dead root came out with a sucking plop. With a great sense of satisfaction, she moved on to the next one, but found it even more recalcitrant.

She blew out a puff of breath from the corner of her mouth, lifting the curls tickling her brow, and dug her heels deeper into the soft mud. "I shall name you Matthew," she informed the dead plant, by way of insult. "Come on, now, Mr. Matthew, cooperate!"

When the plant refused to yield, she grasped it with both hands and gave a mighty pull.

Suddenly the world began to spin. She saw the white clapboards sweep by, the window swirl within her range of vision, and her feet swing up toward the sky.

Panic gripped her. The baby. Oh, God, the baby!

"Help!" she cried.

Then, seeming to fly through the air, she could not speak. A soft whoosh of breath escaped her, and she landed roughly in a heap on the muddy ground.

Chapter Nineteen

————— • —————

Cece's head thumped against the squishy ground, making her senses spin. She fought for air but found she could not draw any in. Fear, cold and gripping, struck hard, and she tried to scream again. She tried to twist to rise but was not able to move.

When the world stopped spinning, Father's paper-white face materialized before her eyes.

"Cecelia, child, are you all right?" His gnarled hand patted her cheek, then worked its way to her neck, seeking her pulse. When he found it, he nodded, and Cece could see a fractional easing of his fear.

"Cecelia. Please answer me!" His voice was strained, and Cece opened her mouth to speak. All that came out was a sibilant wheeze.

Suddenly the weight that had lodged in her chest, keeping her lungs from working, seemed to ease, and she was able to draw in a rough, ragged mouthful of crisp air.

"Fa-father," she whispered, still unable to manage more than that.

Father closed his eyes tightly for a moment. "Thank God," he said fervently.

Cece blinked, wondering if the tender concern she saw displayed on his face was caused by a distortion in her vision as a result of her fall. She also wondered if the words she had heard were mere delusions of a love-starved person. She blinked again.

Father remained bent over her, worry evident in his

deep green eyes. "I fell," she said, then waved her hand, dismissing the inane comment.

Father rose laboriously, leaning heavily on his cane. "You did at that," he said, his voice losing some of its warmth. "What on earth were you doing in the garden?"

Cece pushed herself up on her elbows, grimacing at the gooey soil that hampered her ascent. "The garden needed clearing. I had nothing better to do today."

Rolling a bit, first to one side, then to the other, compensating for the mound of her child, Cece sat up. Slowly she gathered her legs at one side, then bracing a hand in the sloppy earth, she worked herself up to a kneeling position. With care, she stood, then glanced down at herself.

She laughed. "I look like a child who's been making mud pies. May I go inside and clean myself a bit? I'm thankful that I only had the wind knocked out of me."

Father frowned. "You are no longer a child. That fall could have had serious consequences."

"Father, please spare me the sermon. I am covered with this mess. May I go inside to wash up?"

He did not answer. In fact, Edward stared at Cece, his piercing gaze making her thoroughly uncomfortable. Sparking a bit of anger as well. Was he about to deny her the simple use of a washstand, some clean water and soap, and a towel to dry herself? He surely was not that petty.

Just when Cece was certain he would say no, he nodded jerkily and headed toward the door. He swung his cane up before him and cautiously negotiated the steps. Watching his deliberate, slow pace, Cece wondered how her father had reached her side so quickly after she fell.

She smiled. She had been right. He had watched her as she worked. Another measure of progress, she thought. This time, in spite of a nasty spill, she was going to enter his new home.

Without a word she walked behind him as he led her to the kitchen. Cece almost laughed when he cast a glance, ripe with distaste, at the mess smeared all over her. Some things never changed, she thought. Father still hated anything that was not clean, proper, and orderly.

She stole peeks at the tiny kitchen, noting its simplicity.

It had a stove, the enamel sink where she washed her hands, and a small gleaming table. She wondered who kept the place so clean for him.

Cece decided to risk Father's wrath. "I heard Mrs. Quigley remained at the mansion with Mr. Grimes," she said in a conversational tone. "Did you hire a new housekeeper?" She turned, her hands dripping wet, but at least free of soil. Father handed her a length of plain homespun toweling.

"No," he answered, with surprising willingness. "The Sanderses' housekeeper, May Li, comes twice weekly. I find I have no further need than that."

"How wonderful!" Cece exclaimed. "I find May Li utterly charming and quite efficient. I am so glad to know she is seeing to your needs."

Father only nodded. Perhaps he had exhausted his conversational offerings. Well, she was hardly done for the day!

Out of the corner of her eye Cece made sure Father was watching her. She lifted her hand to her forehead, prepared to feign a swoon. To her surprise, the swoon became nearly real when she felt how hot she had become. "Oh!" she exclaimed, wondering if she was having a relapse of her fever.

Father spun around. Cece caught sight of the involuntary grimace the sudden movement caused him. "What is it, Cecelia?"

She had gotten his attention. "I—I suddenly feel faint. May I . . ." She gripped the edge of the enameled sink, fear for her child truly making her knees weak. "May I sit and rest a spell?"

Father's eyes closed. Then he squared his shoulders and looked straight at her. In a strange way, Cece was almost glad for the apparent relapse. It was bad enough to plot to feign a swoon, never mind trying to pretend to worry about her unborn child. Causing Father an additional unnecessary concern would have been a cruelty she was not capable of. Besides, the piercing gaze would have uncovered any attempt at deceit.

The cane began to thump its way down the short hallway.

"Come into the parlor," Father said without turning. "The sofa is more comfortable than the kitchen chairs."

Cece followed her father, tentatively moving her hand along the wall with each step. When she reached a well-polished cherrywood grandfather clock, she leaned against it, the pendulum swinging in syncopated harmony with her heart. Dear God, she prayed, please don't let anything happen to my baby.

With a sigh of relief she reached the tiny parlor, collapsing gratefully on the sofa. She could not stop a smile, full of mischief, when she noted it was an old, comfortable brown velvet piece, soft and yielding. It was far better than the elaborate brocaded nightmare Father had purchased for the mansion. Horace Grimes well deserved the torture of sitting in it.

Her baby's swift kick caught her off guard. "Ahh!"

Father narrowed his eyes. "What?"

Cece burrowed her hips deeper into the welcoming piece of furniture and wrapped her hands about her middle. She was about to answer Father when she saw him blanch again. Every drop of blood seemed to rush from his face, leaving only a ghost of the man behind.

The abrupt change frightened her, and it was her turn to exclaim. "Father! What is it?"

Then she noticed what had caught his attention. His eyes, narrowed against obvious anguish, focused intently on her distended abdomen. He winced.

Cece extended her hand in his direction, as if to offer comfort. But he was too far to reach. "No, Father. Don't. This is your grandchild. No matter how you try, you cannot deny it. You cannot even ignore it."

Father shook his head. "You look so like Abigail," he finally said, the suffering heavy in every softly spoken word. "The last time I saw her, spoke with her, she was big. You were a large baby. . . ."

His words trailed off, and Cece waited in silence, her heart beating like a hopeful drum. A tear rolled down Father's cheek.

He cleared his throat. "I loved Abby, Cecelia. More than life itself. We dreamed of a child to make our love complete, but for many years none came. And then there you were, growing bigger inside her every day.

"Abby was no longer young, but no new bride could have been happier with the coming of her child than she was. We waited, impatiently counting off days. Abby made gowns and blankets, she knitted shawls and caps, she did everything conceivable to pass the time."

Father turned his gaze to the window, and his eyes took on a somewhat glazed glint. He seemed to be seeing Mama once again. "That morning, before I left for the mill, we sat in the parlor, drinking tea. She glowed with excitement. She knew she did not have long to wait. That was the last time I saw her alive."

His last word came out on a sob. Cece watched all of Father's strength ebb out. All that was left was a lonely man, still mourning the death of his beloved wife. Tears trickled down his face, and Cece realized she'd been weeping, too.

Together, for the first time, father and daughter mourned a woman dead eighteen years.

The silence grew less painful, and Father looked up. He pulled a snowy handkerchief from his vest pocket and wiped his eyes. He stood and brought the square of linen to Cece, taking a seat at her side.

"Here, child. It is the least I can do."

At Cece's questioning look, Father looked away, refusing to meet her gaze. "I never could overcome the loss. Abby's death is a wound inside me that has never healed. I allowed it to fester to the point where I could not cope with her absence. This has been my greatest weakness. I closed myself to all but my suffering and never learned to be a father to you. I chose to deal with you by ignoring your presence. Then I sent you away. The letters were the only way I could communicate with you."

Cece wanted to ease Father's agony by saying that none of that mattered, but she found she could not do so. It did matter. "A closer bond between us might have eased the ache, Father."

He looked at her in agony. "I have come to realize this now. Now that it is too late."

"It's never too late, Father," Cece said, believing this with every fiber of her being.

Again Father shrugged, his gesture full of skepticism. "Even when a fool cannot face a grown child whose face is the living image of the ghost that haunts his peace? Even when this child deserves respect and all he offers is rejection and a swift marriage to the first suitable man willing to take on the fool's responsibility?"

Cece swallowed hard, trying to dislodge the lump in her throat. Nothing would ever replace the lost years, she thought, but she could now face the future knowing the loss had never been her fault. "Even when that father has committed each one of those mistakes you have mentioned."

Father lowered his gaze to his hands. "I sent you away from the land you loved. I put you in Prudence's care when I was too weak to face your growing resemblance to Abigail. And upon your return, I surrounded us with others so I could avoid the pain brought on by your astounding resemblance to Abby. You never deserved such treatment."

Cece smiled her forgiveness. The gesture tightened her lids over her eyes, and she felt the burning pain of fever there. She raised her hand to her cheek once more. It was warmer than before.

She bit her lower lip and wondered whether it would be best to tell Father. She cast him a glance and, noting how upset he was, decided to spare him the worry.

"San Francisco was hardly torture, Father. Aunt Pru is no ogre, and neither were the nuns. In fact, some of the girls and I had outrageously hilarious times. I gather Aunty Pru never related our more ingenious escapades."

When Father shook his head, Cece laced her fingers over her middle and leaned back on the sofa. She proceeded to delight him with tales of mischief of all sorts.

At first he only managed a smile, then a soft chuckle. Encouraged by his response, Cece launched into the worst escapade of all. "I admit I am not too proud of this story, Father. But it was quite funny nonetheless. You see, Maria Magdalena Álvarez de Portillo is the most daring soul you might imagine. She is a tiny, blond imp, Castilian through and through, and quite a tease. She dared me, and I have yet to learn to resist a dare. If I were to pull off Mother Superior's wimple, she said, she promised to stop taunting the new pupils. What was I to do? I caught Mother Margaret sitting on the edge of the fountain in the courtyard, and when she least expected it, I yanked the wimple off. She was so stunned, she fell right in the water. All the girls laughed for hours when they caught sight of her shorn head."

After their laughter died, Father studied Cece again. "Cecelia, are you certain you are well? Your eyes have an odd glitter, and your cheeks are flushed."

Cece sighed. She might as well let him know. "I was ill a few weeks ago. I ran a high fever for two days, and I could be having a relapse. I should be on my way home."

Father winced. "This *is* your home, Cecelia. Please come back."

Cece bit her lip, tempted to continue building this bridge between her and her father. But at what cost? "With no conditions, Father?"

He closed his eyes and shook his head. "I am afraid I cannot do that. You shall always have a home, decent medical care, whatever you need, here at my side. But I cannot accept that savage. And I fear I must be brutally honest. I do not know that I can accept his child."

Cece felt Father's new rejection more deeply than any of his earlier ones. This one negated the choices she had made as a woman.

She stood. "I'm afraid I must refuse. I love Matthew, and nothing will ever change that. Just as you have always loved Mama. And I treasure the child I carry. I can never renounce either one of them."

Father rose, too. They walked in silence to the door.

With her hand on the doorknob, Cece asked yet another painful question. "Must I renounce you to keep them both?"

Her words hung in the air, heavy and meaningful. She dared not move or even breathe. This was the chance she had hoped for, prayed for. Would Father give it to her?

The ticking of the pendulum in the grandfather clock marked the passing time. Still, Father did not answer.

"Well," she said, pushing the word out from behind the lump in her throat, "it is past time I left. Good-bye, Father."

She pulled open the door and stepped outside. Taking a moment to tug her damp shawl tighter about her, she turned to close the door. Father's hand covered hers on the door handle, keeping the door ajar.

"I cannot embrace them, but you need not renounce me."

Cece turned her hand around and clasped Father's arthritic fingers warmly. "Thank you. Especially for my child." Standing on tiptoe, she pressed a soft kiss on his lean cheek. The gesture caught him by surprise. Without giving him a chance to say anything that might ruin the wonderful gift of hope he had given her, she turned around and walked toward the street with a lilt in her step.

"Cecelia," Father called behind her.

She turned around. "Yes?"

"Take off those wet things immediately when you get home, and drink some warm tea. Be careful. Please."

Joy burst inside her. A broad smile widened her mouth, and she felt so cheered she could have sworn she could fly all the way to the cabin. Instead she nodded and waved at Father. "I most certainly will," she answered, knowing this was an easy promise to keep.

Walking through the woods, Cece wondered at the strange turns life sometimes took. She had finally reached an acceptable relationship with her father, but now she felt an odd reluctance in going home. Would Matthew again be as cold as he had been during the past few days?

Ever since she had recovered from her illness and Princess Mary had voiced those harsh indictments against Matthew, he had begun to withdraw from her. He behaved in the cool, reserved manner he had tried to maintain toward her when they first met. Since he had resumed his spirit quest, matters had worsened.

Cece allowed herself to wonder if, after the spirits spoke to Matthew and he received the empowering from his *tamanous*, it would take him from her side. Worse, he seemed to despair of receiving a message from the spirits.

But could it be that he did not hear them because his heart was too torn by conflicting loyalties?

That unformed fear, lurking viciously in her heart, had shredded her peace the last few days. She had stubbornly refused to allow it to become a conscious thought. Now she knew she must. Beyond thinking about the matter, she had to bring it out into the open.

She would speak with Matthew; they would both have to state what lay in their hearts.

"How, God, how?" Matthew cried up to the heavens, seeking the white God as well as the S'Klallam spirits in his anguish.

After fasting and scrubbing his body with branches, Matthew was weakened in body and tired in his soul. Yet he had been granted no great revelation, no infusion of supernatural power to show him the way.

He did not know how he would ever send Cece away. He could no longer envision life without her. Not now after he had tasted the richness of loving her. Surely not after their child was born.

Still, the inner tug-of-war continued. After his uncle had forced him to choose between Cece and the tribe, Matthew knew that a number of Nuf-Kay'it's elders considered his loyalty suspect. And, through Anna, he also knew that Luke had been busy substantiating that doubt.

On the other hand, there were a few others, among them his uncle, who knew Matthew's loyalty had never diminished. But Uncle Soo-moy'asum, as *ssia'm* of Nuf-Kay'it, had been forced to set aside his personal feelings—even his faith in Matthew's loyalty to the tribe—and issue the ultimatum that had driven Matthew away. The man who had raised him had no doubt about Matthew's character; he would never question Matthew's commitment to his people.

He deeply regretted the difficult stance his uncle had been forced to take, all because of Matthew's love for a white woman. And he did love her. Just as he loved his people, his heritage, his destiny. And as God was his witness, he did not know how to choose.

If that made him selfish, then that was what he was. He would somehow learn to go forward with his life, knowing that his love for Cece stood between him and his rightful position within the tribe.

He wished he could be assured that an all-out battle with Luke would resolve the question. Were he to fight Luke—be it physically or verbally—and establish himself as rightful *ssia'm*, could he impose Cece upon the tribe? Could he subject her to the unpleasantness that was sure to be her lot for the rest of her life?

He could not find it in himself to bring her additional suffering. She had already borne shame, banishment, and illness because of him. He could not make the rest of her life the hell it surely would become were he to selfishly seek only his destiny with no consideration for hers.

No. Force was not the solution. Still, the matter of leadership had to be resolved. Matthew knew in his heart that he was meant to lead his tribe. He also knew that his only chance for lasting satisfaction was with Cece at his side. He was no closer to knowing how to achieve both since the unalterable reality of Cece's birth, her white heritage, immutably barred compromise. His people did not see her as an individual; they only saw a white woman, a Boston, the daughter of the former manager of the Pope and Talbot mill. An enemy.

He sighed and gathered his coat about him, then headed home. Home to another stiff, silent night, during which his greatest accomplishment would be avoiding Cece. He could not, *would* not, cloud his judgment with sensual pleasure at such a critical moment.

At the door to the cabin he paused, taking time to strengthen his control. After a deep calming breath, he pushed open the door. Closing it quickly against the wind behind him, he removed his coat and headed toward the hearth. There, her arms wrapped around her legs, sat Cece, silently staring at the cheery blaze.

Matthew knew her emotions were anything but cheery. The expression on her sweet features was serious, sadness evident in the slight downward set of her lips. Torn between what he felt he should do—avoid her—and what his heart wanted to do—comfort her—Matthew hesitated.

"We need to talk," she said, breaking the awkward silence. Then she looked up, and Matthew thought his heart would break. Her beautiful green eyes once again had that glitter of illness, and her cheeks bore an unnatural flush.

"Cece, you are ill. Again." He extended a hand to her, intending to lead her to their bed. But Cece refused his help.

"Yes, Matthew, I am not feeling well, and that is why we must not put off this discussion any longer."

Matthew sighed. He did not want to face the fear growing inside him, but he knew Cece would not allow him to hide. He had a strong suspicion that he was about to be forced to make another intolerable choice.

"What has happened on your spirit quest?" she asked, taking him by surprise.

Frustration gripped him. He ran a hand, rough with anger, through his hair, his fingers tugging at the long ends before letting go. "Not a damn thing," he said through gritted teeth.

She nodded, as if she had expected this answer all along. "I wonder if that is because I am at your side. Perhaps you cannot come to a decision about your future because your vision of that future is clouded by your feelings for me."

Matthew cursed. "No! The spirits—"

Cece rose and faced him squarely. "I don't believe you can blame the spirits for this one, Matthew." She swayed, and when he went to help her, she shook her head, refusing his help once again.

Matthew watched her walk to their bed and sit on the bearskin, refusing to allow his mind to replay the sensual images that threatened to engulf him. He concentrated on Cece instead, staring at her intently, noting her pallor despite the flush of fever on her cheekbones. As surely as he knew his name, he knew Cece was about to embark on another journey of suffering, another bout of misery brought on by him.

It occurred to him, not for the first time, that by keeping her by his side, he might be endangering her health and their child's. He knew Dexter Sanders could provide her with better treatment than his aunt could. If she reconciled with her father, the comfort of his home would allow her to have a more comfortable pregnancy than she would in this rude cabin under the evergreens.

If he set aside his forbidden love for Cece, his exile became unnecessary. His tribe needed him. Personal concerns had to be set aside sooner or later.

In a low, controlled voice he began to destroy his only chance of happiness. "I think you may be right. I have selfishly placed you in an unsafe situation, where you are repeatedly falling victim to illness. Because of my desire for you, I have also made my tribe suffer. I am no longer a child and must learn to deny myself pleasure in the name of the greater good."

He heard Cece draw a shuddering breath. Knowing that if he looked at her he would never finish what he must do, he turned his back to her.

"It is best for everyone, especially for you and our child, if you return to Port Gamble. Forget me. Repair the situation with your father and find a more suitable man."

A soft sob broke from Cece, but Matthew crushed the desire to wrap her in his arms and soothe her pain. "Dexter is an excellent doctor. He will care well for you and the baby. I have no doubt about that."

Matthew fell silent. The tightness in his throat threatened to betray his hurt, and he could not afford to let Cece see even the slightest sign of weakness at this time. With her determined spirit, she would battle down his fears until she extracted another promise from him, one he was no longer prepared to make.

When he felt sure he could speak again, knowing she was weeping too much to argue, he dealt them both the final blow. "It is as my uncle said. I must choose between you and my people. I choose my S'Klallam blood."

When Matthew finally fell silent, Cece stood again. She had been quite certain this encounter would end in the very manner it just had. But she had thought herself ready to face the moment of parting. She realized she had merely lied to herself.

In contrast to this pain, what she had felt the night of the ball was nothing. Every emotion inside her disappeared, leaving behind an endless void. She turned and cast a glance about the room, wondering what she would take with her. Then she realized she could take nothing. It was enough that she took Matthew's child and the eternal memories of their time of love.

She gathered her valise and haphazardly stuffed her few garments in it, unable to see her actions clearly through the veil of tears. Angry at herself for this pathetic show of weakness, she swatted her cheeks free of the salty drops. Stop it! she commanded herself. But her eyes refused to heed her order.

She smoothed the fur on the bearskin, rumpled where she had sat, and grasped the handle of the valise. She turned around, taking time to gaze lovingly at every intimate corner of the cabin, etching forever in her heart the memories it held. She had known her greatest happiness here.

She was living her greatest sorrow here as well.

Slowly, carefully, she walked to the door. She pulled the heavy wooden slab toward her and turned to Matthew one last time. He still stood firm as the stone she had often compared him to, his broad back toward her. How wonderful it had felt to wrap her arms about that sturdy back! How sweet the feelings those muscular arms had brought her when he in turn had held her close!

How painful to know she would never know those moments again.

Resolutely she faced the approaching dusk outside the cabin. "Good-bye, Matthew. Godspeed."

She closed the door.

At the soft, deliberate sound Matthew turned around, rage and misery battling within him. Hot bitter tears formed in his eyes, and he allowed himself to weep.

He wept for the empty years he faced. He wept for Cece's loneliness to come. He wept for his fatherless child.

After a while, his face drenched with his sorrow, he walked to the door. He opened it and saw the fiery glow of the setting sun on the horizon. Cece was, of course, long gone. But the memories remained. They always would.

Tomorrow he would return to the village. He had much to do there. Maybe he had a future after all.

But today, tonight, was for himself alone.

"Good-bye, my love," he whispered. Only the gathering shadows of the evergreens heard.

Chapter Twenty

———— • ————

When the polished black door swung inward, Cece almost broke down again. But during the eternally long walk through the woods she had shed enough tears to last her entire lifetime. Or so she hoped.

It was time to begin living her new life. "Hello, Father. I can no longer stay away. Does your offer of a home still stand?"

For a moment he stood watching her through narrowed eyes. Cece felt as if he were trying to gaze right through to her shattered heart. She blinked, hoping the broken shards of her love did not show too clearly in her eyes. Then, squaring her shoulders, she tried a wobbly smile.

"I have many more silly stories to make us both laugh," she said, disgusted at the weakness that made her voice break.

The stern cast on Father's features softened, and he stepped silently aside. He drew the door fully open and gestured to Cece to enter. When she stood at his side in the tiny vestibule, he closed the door behind her, and she felt she had truly severed her life in two. Before and after Matthew.

Again burning tears threatened to fall, but she battled her emotions, refusing to give them release. "If you tell me which room will be mine, I will put away my belongings. As you can see, I do not have much."

Father turned toward the stairwell, raising his eyes toward the top riser. "You have plenty, Cecelia. All you might need is in your room. I made sure your things were brought here when I moved. Go on up. You cannot mistake which room is yours."

Surprised by Father's confession, Cece spun her head about. "You hoped I would return? You really wanted me back!"

Father nodded slowly. "I was afraid you would return, given time, with your heart in shreds, as I can see it is."

Cece shook her head. Her feeble attempt at denial met only with Father's own shaking head. He lifted his hand to halt her words before she knew which ones to utter. "Don't, child. I do not wish to make your pain any greater. I, too, know how difficult it is to love and lose. I don't need to approve of the man you care for to feel compassion for you."

At his tender words, Cece broke down. She dropped her valise on the floor and wrapped her arms around Father's shoulders. No words came out; none were needed. All her pent-up anguish streamed forth.

She had not known how desperately she needed the comfort of her father's embrace. She had never suspected how stirring his acceptance of her pain would be. But here it was, all the love and compassion she could ever have asked for, and he finally offered it, thank God, when she needed it most.

Even after the tears slowed, even after the aching sobs came to a shuddering stop, Cece remained in her father's arms, soaking up the feelings he had withheld for her entire life. Both seemed anxious to make up for what they had missed. Cece vowed they would.

Her child would never miss as much as one ounce of love. Not even Father's love. She would find some way to make the stubborn old war-horse see the beauty and the worth in his grandbaby, no matter who had fathered it.

Firm in her resolve, Cece eventually relinquished the safe haven of Father's arms. "Have you decided that all I am capable of is watering at the eyes each time we speak?"

"Hardly, Cecelia. Our tears were long overdue." He reached out his gnarled hand and awkwardly patted hers. "We have to get this ordeal out of the way before we can move on to the business of the future. And, child, the first order of business is getting you into bed."

As Father spoke Cece realized how tired she really was and gave him no further argument. She began to climb to the second floor, but paused partway up the stairs. "Thank you, Father. Thank you so very, very much."

"No, daughter," he answered, causing Cece to look at him over her shoulder. A wry smile appeared on his lips. "You are more like me than I suspected. *I* thank *you* for your very stubborn love. It kept you trying to reach me, even when I was most unlovable."

Sadness stole a bit of the rueful humor from his features. Then he nodded and spoke again. "You are very like your mother, too. You inherited her enormous capacity to forgive. I owe you thanks for that as well."

Not knowing how to respond to Father's words, Cece said the only thing she could. "I love you, Father."

"And I you, Cecelia."

On those sweet words, Cece went up the rest of the way and indeed found her room. It was a miniature version of the lavish chamber she had occupied in the mansion, down to the blue satin spread on the bed. In the wardrobe, all her clothes hung neatly, a hint of rose sachet wafting to her when she opened the door.

Mrs. Sanders must have told May Li of her weakness for roses, Cece thought. Although she still liked the fragrance, she wondered if she would be able to continue wearing it, now that it was entwined with poignant memories of Matthew's love.

Haunted by the lingering hint of roses in the cabin, Matthew gathered a few essential items and left early the next morning for his uncle's lodge.

He strode purposefully through the woods, not allowing himself a moment of hesitation. He had let himself grieve for his loss, enormous as it was, all through the long night. Now it was time to face the needs of the village, permitting himself no weakness at all.

He feared that if he paused, the need for Cece would overtake him and send him running toward Port Gamble and the greatest joy he had ever known. He did not have the right to do that. He owed a special duty to Nuf-Kay'it; he had to prove himself loyal beyond any doubt.

He also owed Cece and the baby the right to the medical care he could not provide.

At the thought of Cece and their child, his step faltered, but he ruthlessly forced himself to continue placing one foot before the other, step after step, all leading straight to his destiny.

Somehow he would live the rest of his life without Cece's smile. He would continue to exist without knowing his child. And someday, when he grew old, he would look back and not regret the choice he had had to make.

At his uncle's cabin he knocked twice. Moments later Princess Mary opened the door. He met her questioning gaze with what he hoped was a sincerely steady one of his own. "I am home—perhaps, as you said, past the time when I was due, but I hope it is not too late."

His aunt stared at him, her wise bright eyes seeing more than what Matthew had hoped to show. So be it, he thought. I am in pain, but I will shoulder my responsibilities.

After what seemed like a small eternity, she nodded and drew back. "Come in, son. I do not believe it is ever too late. But you have much to do."

Matthew nodded. "I foresee trouble ahead with some of the elders, and Luke is a formidable adversary."

"You have never before turned away from the impossible, Matthew," Anna piped in from a dark corner of the large lodge. Matthew turned to meet her gaze and, at the sight of the reproach he found there, looked down at his boots. He knew Anna did not speak of the tribal difficulties that lay before him. She spoke of the impossible task he had just turned his back on.

He wanted to argue, to shout and curse, but found he could not. How could he reprove his cousin for stating what he had castigated himself with for days?

The morning after her arrival at Father's home, Cece awoke to the sound of a gentle knock on her bedroom door. "Cecelia, child, may I come in?"

"Mrs. Sanders!" she cried with delight. "Of course you may." At the sight of that dear lady's concerned countenance, Cece smiled and extended her arms.

Aided by her cane, Mrs. Sanders soon reached the bedside. She gingerly sat on the edge of the fluffy mattress and folded Cece into her loving embrace. The spicy sweetness of cinnamon and cloves filled Cece's senses, and she experienced an unusual sort of comfort when she breathed in the signature scent of her elderly friend.

Mrs. Sanders pulled away from the embrace first. "Edward sent for Dexter early this morning. I hope you do not mind that I tagged along. I have dearly missed you since you went away."

"I missed you, too," Cece answered honestly, wondering how much Mrs. Sanders knew about the events of the past few months. But Mrs. Sanders dispelled all possible awkwardness by squarely addressing the delicate matter.

"I am so very sorry you find yourself in such painful circumstances, my dear. Matthew is a wonderful person, but he does come from another cultural background. You cannot expect to bridge the differences when they are truly so great."

Cece heard the words and knew that logic was right. "I am beginning to consider that perhaps sometimes love is not enough," she said slowly, fighting the voice in her heart that insisted doggedly that love *always* was enough.

At the tremor in Cece's voice, Mrs. Sanders narrowed her eyes, closely scrutinizing her face. Then, allowing for the stiffness in her joints, she leaned over to plump up the pillows propped against the cherrywood headboard. "Well, dear, enough said. You have your sorrow, and I have mine. That is the way of life."

Setting down the carved cane, Mrs. Sanders settled herself more fully on the edge of the bed. "Now. Edward says you have been doing poorly. That simply will not do. We will see you and this little one to glowing health once again." She half turned toward the bedroom door and called out, "Dexter! We need your services in here, son."

From that point on, the three of them—Father, Mrs. Sanders, and Dexter—devoted themselves to her constant care and attention. So much so that a few days later, when all converged in her room, intending to serve Thanksgiving dinner there, she knew she had reached her limit.

Knowing she could not allow matters to continue along these lines, she took their feelings into consideration and placed constraints upon her temper. "Please! I can bear only so much coddling. I am not an invalid. I can walk down those stairs."

She watched the three of them exchange wary glances. Realizing the time for action was at hand, she threw off the bedcovers and slipped her feet into the blue satin slippers at the foot of the bed. "If you will all excuse me, I will be dressing now. This," she said, directing their attention to her rumpled bed and the wrinkled morning dress she wore, "is not all your fault. I have indeed kept to my bed for days. But I will surely go mad if I stay here another minute."

She went to the wardrobe, well aware of the looks the three of them cast in her wake. She swung open the doors and began sifting through her dresses. In the back corner she found a simple forest-green wool flannel with black braid trim. "Aha!" she cried, pulling out the garment. "This suits the holiday season nicely. It will only take me but a moment to be ready. I shall meet you in the dining room."

When none of them showed any inclination to leave the room, Cece boldly reached for the top button on the gown she wore and slipped it through the buttonhole. Her three guests hastily made their way to the door, without so much as a backward glance.

She smiled. It felt good to assert herself once again. Then she realized she had never really done so other than with Matthew. She had always been so desirous of Father's approval that she had bowed even to his unspoken wishes. Except for the fateful night of the ball.

That determined stance had gained her the most beautiful months of her life. She would long remember that lesson.

With a velvet ribbon holding back her curls, Cece felt ready to face the beginning of the season of cheer. She pulled her silk shawl tighter across her enlarged middle in order to cover the gaping back. Her little one was growing rapidly.

Now ungainly, Cece was forced to curtail her more physical activities. The Christmas season came and went, without much cheer on her part. She was agonizingly bored with all her idleness. Soon, though, the tedium brought to mind the tablecloth Mrs. Sanders gave her a while ago. The inactivity and her friends' frequent questions regarding the progress of the project drove her to attempt to embroider again.

One morning, after managing to tangle another sad amount of the colorful silks, Cece threw the confounded mess down and stomped to the coat closet, muttering as she went. "I have no idea what prompted me to try this one more time. I cannot sew. I was born with deficient fingers!"

She rammed her arms through the sleeves of her brown woolen ulster and was buttoning the roomy garment when a knock at the door brought her actions to a halt.

Still peeved, she roughly pulled open the door. A barely civil greeting for Dexter was all she managed.

"I feel fine," she responded when he asked about her health.

Gesturing toward her coat, Dexter stopped undoing his own coat buttons. "Were you going out or returning?" he asked.

Tapping her toe impatiently, wishing to be on her way, Cece finished wrapping a dull green scarf around her ears. "I was on my way to the Country Store. I have run out of some of my embroidering silks."

Dexter smiled, then stepped aside. "Allow me to drive you there," he offered enthusiastically. "It will spare you the walk in the nasty wind."

Cece shrugged. "Very well, let us be on our way."

Somehow Dexter managed to carry the entire weight of the conversation all the way to the store. Cece, peeping occasionally out the window, was glad. She had all she could deal with wondering if, once again, Matthew would be there.

When they reached the shop, Cece stole another glance outside. She swallowed hard and forced herself to face Dexter. As before, a group of Indian men stood clustered by the entrance. She did not look too carefully lest she find Matthew among them. She placed her hand in the one Dexter offered to assist her in exiting the carriage.

Standing by the front door to the Country Store, Matthew saw Dexter hand Cece down from the black carriage. Even such casual contact caused the usual possessiveness to surge hotly within him. Every muscle in his body tightened in readiness for battle over what his heart recognized as rightly his.

His mind, however, told him she would never belong to a S'Klallam man.

He gritted his teeth and clenched his fists. Without a word, not willing to offer an explanation for his reaction, he separated himself from the other men chatting there.

He would never have thought he'd be able to harbor such violent feelings toward a friend. But no reasoning would dislodge the jealousy and anger inside him each time he saw Dexter Sanders's solicitous attention toward Cece.

"She's mine," he muttered before he could stop the treacherous words. Witnessing the girth her coat covered, he felt possessiveness surge ever stronger in his soul.

Not that Cece's condition was overly noticeable—she merely brought to mind a plump partridge, swaddled as she was in that brown coat. He smiled, remembering how proud she had been of her tiny waist. She had never needed to wear a corset, and each time he would span the slender circle with his hands, she had smiled in satisfaction. She had never needed to voice her pride either.

Now here she was, stepping down from Dexter's carriage, the good doctor hovering anxiously over her, attending to her every need. Matthew crushed the urge to shove his friend away from Cece and to declare to the entire universe that she belonged only to him.

This was not the first time Matthew had seen Dexter dance attendance on Cece. In fact, the black carriage stood by Edward Scanlon's house more often than not, and Matthew knew that neither member of the Scanlon family needed that much medical attention.

No, Dexter's attention was of a most personal sort. Matthew could tolerate the sight no longer.

His movements stiff with tightly reined temper, Matthew strode down the street, heading toward home. To his chagrin, Dexter caught sight of him, calling a greeting.

"Good morning."

"Morning." Matthew forced the words through tightly clamped jaws.

Unable to stop himself, he looked at Cece. Although there was no surprise in her expression, deep in the evergreen pools of her eyes, Matthew saw the darkness of loss, the persistent sadness of an ended love.

Desperately needing the connection even a simple conversation would offer, he voiced the question foremost on his mind. "How are you and the baby these days? I trust you are completely recovered."

Cece's wistful smile and the sad look in her eyes told Matthew that she would never recover from the pain she had suffered. "I am no longer ill, Matthew," she said, and he knew she had carefully chosen her words. She continued. "How have you been? Have matters with the village improved in recent weeks?"

Matthew shrugged. "I am working on a solution to this delicate situation. It cannot be rushed."

Matthew watched Cece's throat work, and he wondered if tears threatened. She drew herself up, though, smiling sweetly. "How is Anna? Tell her I miss her. And Princess Mary?"

Matthew smiled back. "Both are fine. Anna misses you. She speaks of you often."

"I'm glad. I would hate to be so easily forgotten," she said, her gaze intent and meaningful.

A bitter laugh broke from Matthew's lips. "I doubt anyone who has met you could ever forget you."

She nodded, and her shoulders relaxed visibly. "Tell Princess Mary that I fully intend to hold her to her promise after my confinement. I still mean to learn all I can from her."

"She will be proud to teach you. She thinks quite highly of you."

"For a Boston woman, that is."

Matthew understood her implication and nodded. "Yes, for a Boston woman."

She turned toward the door, hiding her reaction to his words. But he could tell from the way she had stiffened once again that those words had dealt her another blow.

She placed her hand on the doorknob. "I must be about my business, gentlemen. Matthew, it has been . . . an interesting encounter."

Without another glance in his direction, she swept regally into the store. Matthew turned to Dexter, who had avidly followed every bit of the conversation, but at the sight of the turbulent emotions evident on his friend's face, he thought better of prolonging the meeting. Competition for a woman's love could easily destroy even the best of friendships.

Resigned to the loss, Matthew gave Dexter news of another kind. "My uncle has agreed to limited medical care on your part for the villagers who wish it. You should arrange to meet with him in the near future."

Dexter responded with a curt nod. "I will do that. Good day, Matthew."

"Good-bye, Dexter." Matthew knew he bid farewell to a friendship.

With saddened eyes, he held the door ajar and followed Dexter's path down the aisle of the store. When the doctor reached Cece's side, he placed his hand on the small of her back. The gesture burned the image of the proper white couple in Matthew's mind, and he knew he had just glimpsed Cece's future.

He could not bear to watch. Letting go of the door, he stalked off, calling himself every kind of fool. The slamming of the door only seemed to emphasize the finality of the moment.

Increasing his speed, he began to jog toward the beach, but once he reached the sandy ground, the wind off Teekalet felt far too bitter to his burning eyes. He swerved into the forest, seeking the cover of the evergreens. Picking up his pace, he ran between the thick old tree trunks, dodging roots and rocks on the ground. In a short while he found himself in the clearing where he had built a home for his small family. A home no one occupied.

After Cece left, he had not been able to walk into the clearing without feeling all the pain he had felt the day he sent her away. Even after all this time, he could swear he smelled the sweetness of roses nearby.

Refusing to give in to the weakness that brought a burning behind his eyelids, Matthew lifted his face toward the sky. Today it was pewter gray. Nothing relieved the sameness of the somber color, not a cloud, not a ray of weak winter-gold sunshine.

The expanse echoed the pain in his heart, never ending, dull, stretching into eternity.

He closed his eyes to the enormity above, blinking against the tears that threatened. Again he felt like crying. He had wept the night he sent her away, and now he again felt the gathering dampness. He lowered his head, shaking it in disbelief. Confounded woman had him crying even more than he had as a child, he thought.

He glanced at the sky one last time, and his breath caught in his chest at the majestic sight directly above him. An eagle soared sleekly on the currents of air, its wings spread fully out on either side of its elongated body. As Matthew watched, the exceptional bird seemed to pause over his head.

His heart began to mark an erratic beat, pounding the wall of his chest with each pulse. He drew in a shallow breath, not willing to move lest the animal be scared away. The awe, the admiration within him for this incredibly graceful, powerful creature swelled, warming every bit of his being. Then, with a graceful twist of its wings, the eagle swooped down, its white head leading the way.

It seemed to be heading straight for Matthew, and he had no intention of moving out of the way. For some reason, he knew the bird would not injure him. In fact, he felt safe, stronger than he had in a very long time.

At the last possible moment, the eagle turned, changing its direction enough to miss Matthew, its powerful wings whistling by his head. Matthew watched, entranced, as the bird again climbed to the heavens, carving a new path through the blank gray unknown. It had chosen its own voyage and needed no authority other than its own inner certainty to lead it to its goal.

The soaring eagle vanished from sight but left a glow in Matthew's heart and a smile upon his lips. It also left determination in his black eyes. He did not need to see it, he felt it, knew it was there, just as he knew the spirits had just spoken clearly to him. The sovereign eagle, a powerful creature, his *tamanous,* had shown him the way.

The great bird reminded him of a night when he had vowed not to let anything else be taken from him.

Forceful steps led him home. He arrived at Uncle Soomoy'asum's lodge and opened the door. Catching sight of Anna working diligently at a new loom, he called out, "Where is your father?"

She turned to face him, and her eyes showed her surprise. She must have seen something in his expression, Matthew thought. Later he would tell her of his experience, but right now he had more important matters to attend to.

"He is not here," she said. "He went to Port Gamble earlier this morning. He wanted to meet your doctor friend on his own ground."

Matthew's breath burst out in a frustrated gust. "Very well. I will not have the opportunity to tell him my decision ahead of time. He can hear it with the other elders tomorrow at the meeting I will call."

When Dexter finally took Cece home, she did not know whether she would give in to sorrow or anger, for the two emotions had busily traded places in her heart ever since she had walked away from Matthew.

She tried to concentrate on the silly tablecloth, but found she no longer had the slightest inclination to do so. She let her head rest on the curved back of the sofa and closed her eyes, forcing her mind to go blank.

When she opened her eyes again, she exclaimed in delight, "Snow!" Like an enthusiastic child, she scrambled to her feet, or at least she tried, falling back against the cushions several times until she allowed herself the twisting and turning required by her greatly altered figure.

Hurrying to the window, she stifled the urge to clap. Snow was fairly uncommon to the Pacific Northwest, and these scant, beautifully fluffy flakes were simply a blessing from a benevolent sky.

She watched the crystals fall for a few moments. Then impulsively she ran out to the vestibule and donned her ulster again. Shunning the somber green square of wool she had earlier used to cover herself, she swirled a cheery red scarf over her head, crossing it at the neck to protect her throat from the sharp winds. She had had enough of Dexter's excessive prudence. No one was going to treat her like an invalid again this morning. In fact, no one would *ever* treat her like an invalid again. As proof, she was on her way out to enjoy the snow.

Fortunately no one was around to offer an argument, and Cece took advantage of the situation. She had not had any more fever since moving to Father's house, and she felt reasonably comfortable in her heavy winter garb.

After a bit the evergreens, with their sugary sprinkle of pristine snow, posed too great a lure to overcome. Throwing caution to the wind, Cece gave in to the desperate need to visit the peace of the forest once again, to steal a glimpse of the place where she had loved Matthew so thoroughly.

The closer she came to the clearing in the woods, the slower and more deliberate her steps became. She needed to see the cabin again, but she knew she was still too fragile to withstand meeting Matthew alone. What would she do if he was there? Worse yet, what would she say if he spoke to her?

Despite the fear gnawing at her middle she continued, drawn by memories she could never overcome. Slipping behind trunk after trunk, she came close enough to see the long side wall of the cabin. Through the stretched skin on the window she saw the ruffled hem of the curtain she had made. At least Matthew had not erased every trace she had left behind.

Then he was there. Silently he stepped into the clearing and stood before the snug house, gazing steadily at it. His face, a bit thinner than before she left last fall, was set in that stony cast she so disliked. It hid all his thoughts and feelings only too well.

Her heart, beating faster than it had in her entire life, seemed ready to shatter. Just the sight of him here, by the home they had shared, brought her a pain too bittersweet to bear. Still, all she could think of was how much she longed for his arms to hold her, how much she needed his lips to kiss her.

Oh, Matthew.

She waited, silent tears chilling her cheeks, until he left the clearing. He had not made a sound. He had not gone into the house. He had done nothing but stare at it with that unreadable look on his face. Then he had walked away.

She followed suit, feeling frozen to the bone. It was not the wintry weather that left her shivering, it was the sight of Matthew, closed off to her, no longer attainable.

When she reached Father's little white house, she noted with a frown that Dexter Sanders's carriage was parked out front. Again. Surely Father was not ill. He had been in fine spirits this morning at breakfast.

Cece narrowed her gaze. Had Dexter come for a second time in one day to make his interest known to her? She hoped not.

But her hope was soon dashed.

"Cecelia!" Dexter exclaimed when she let herself into the vestibule. "I have been beside myself with worry. Where have you been?"

His assumption that he had the right to question her whereabouts grated on her nerves. But she let that irritation pass. "Hello, Dexter. How . . . nice to see you again. I went for a walk. Could not pass up the opportunity to enjoy the snow."

As Cece removed the red scarf from her head, Dexter virtually tore her coat from her back. He dragged her to the couch, where he made her sit while he rummaged through his black leather bag. "But May Li said she had not seen you for hours. It is now late afternoon. We feared something had happened to you."

Cece arched a brow. "We?"

To her amusement Dexter blushed. "Yes, well. May Li and I did not know where you were."

He pressed the stethoscope to Cece's breast, and she rapidly swatted his hands away. "Oh, Dexter, must you really? I feel quite fine."

Furiously wagging a thermometer in the air, he paused at the reproof in her voice. He frowned. "You were terribly ill only a few weeks ago."

Cece stood, ready once again to assert herself. "But I am fine now. Please put away that contraption. I do not wish to have my temperature taken."

Knowing she was a poor liar, she went to the window and faced the outdoors. "I went for a short walk, down near the mill. I was enjoying the snow and decided to sit on the bench in the garden at the mansion." Her voice quavered at the memories the bench brought to mind. But with a glance at Dexter Cece noted he was too busy storing his gadgets to have paid her weakness any attention.

Facing the window again, seeing no more flakes flutter to earth, Cece fell silent for a moment. "It is all over now, and I would not have missed a single minute of it," she said after a bit.

This time even Dexter could not fail to catch the melancholy lacing her words. Although the snow had stopped falling, only a fool would believe she spoke of frozen water. He snapped his satchel closed and walked to the door. "I can see I am not needed here. Good day, Cecelia."

"Good-bye," she answered, waving gently at his departing back.

Where had Matthew gone? she wondered. Had he continued fasting? Did that account for the gauntness of his face? Had the spirits finally spoken clearly to him? She hoped his torment was over. She would hate to think he suffered even as she did.

Suddenly overcome by exhaustion, she went to her room. She removed her boots and pulled the hairpins from her chignon. Not caring that she would rumple the satin cover on the bed, she lay down, running her fingers through the mass of curls that spilled over the pillow.

They had never made love on a bed like this one, she thought, her hand testing the coolness of the satin spread. How would it feel, she wondered, with the soft mattress yielding to the powerful thrusts of Matthew's virile body?

She would never know. She would never again know the ecstasy of Matthew's passion.

A tear rolled into the red-gold tendrils at her temple.

Chapter Twenty-One

———— • ————

Cece lay on the bed as sweet, sad images floated through her mind, until May Li called to her. "Time for din-nah, Missee Cee-cee."

Oh, no, she thought with a groan. If May Li were serving supper here, that meant the Sanderses would be dining with her and Father. Was she to be forced to fend off Dexter's unwanted attentions for a third time in one day?

She hastened to the mirror and checked her eyes. Slightly puffy from the tears she had shed, they did not look bad enough to beg off dinner with a headache. Then she shuddered, thinking better of the misbegotten notion. The last thing she wanted was Dexter palpating her once again!

She sighed as she walked downstairs. As the meal progressed Dexter was withdrawn, preoccupied. Edward, whose arthritis was acting up, offered little to the conversation. And Cece, bored to tears by Mrs. Sanders's detailed description of the complicated embroidery pattern she had purchased that morning at the Country Store, did not even try to follow what her friend was saying.

When the dishes were cleared away, Dexter came to assist Cece in rising. With a small formal bow he pulled her chair out from behind her, then replaced it under the table. Cupping her elbow to lead her from the room, he leaned far too close. "I would like a private word with you," he said, "if you please."

She frowned, but could find no reason to deny his request.

Father pounded in what Cece felt was the last nail on her coffin. "I am not fit company this evening," he said, sounding regretful. "It would be best if I returned to my room. Good night, all." As he leaned on his cane he looked so frail that Cece felt anxiety fill her heart.

Her fear must have shown on her face, for Father waved her on. "Go, child. Spend time with the Sanderses. I am fine, just stiff tonight."

Turning to Dexter, Cece placed her hand in the crook of his elbow, regretting the niceties of good manners that virtually demanded she do so. "Shall we, then?" she asked, checking on Mrs. Sanders's progress, hoping that her friend's presence might delay the private conversation.

Tapping a perky rhythm with her cane, Mrs. Sanders led the way down the hall. At the parlor door, though, she came to a stop, then turned to Cece. "I will be in the kitchen. I need to speak with May Li."

Cece groaned again, biting her lips to keep the sound from escaping her mouth. This bore all the signs of a staged scenario. Still, she said nothing, but allowed Dexter to lead her to the sofa for the second time in one day.

"Harrumph!"

Oh, dear, she thought. This *was* serious. It even entailed throat clearing. The look on Dexter's face brought a heavy reluctance to her middle, and she fervently prayed that her suspicions were wrong.

But this prayer, too, went unanswered. Dexter sat beside her, then clasped her hand between both of his.

"I had hoped," he said, "that after all this time you had come to suspect my feelings for you. I have not been particularly diligent in disguising them. I had furthermore hoped that you had come to feel favorably toward me."

Cece held her breath, hoping—praying—he would say no more. When he paused, she grasped the opportunity. "Dexter, please, spare us both the awkwardness. You, more than anyone, know of my condition. That remains unchanged."

He nodded. "You carry Matthew's child. Because I hold him in such high regard, I would be honored to raise his son as mine. It is also your child, and I can always love a child of yours. You see, Cecelia, I love you that much."

"Oh, Dexter," Cece said on a sigh. "I do sincerely regret this. I tried to stop you." As she paused to choose the proper words the baby kicked, startling her, but also giving her the assurance that she was doing the right thing. "I do not want to hurt you, although I fear I shall."

Cece stood and began to pace, her large abdomen making her movements somewhat graceless. "My body is filled by Matthew's child, just like my heart is full of love for Matthew. I will always love him. My feelings make it inconceivable for me to share my self, my life, with anyone but him."

Despite her words Dexter would not concede defeat. "Very well, love Matthew. Only allow me the honor of being your husband, your protector, even if in name alone, and therefore give your child a name. I can cling to the hope that someday your feelings toward me might change."

Cece wrung her hands, distraught at the pain she inflicted, but adamantly unwilling to consider Dexter's proposal. "Dexter, do listen to me," she urged. "My child will have a name. My name. And you deserve better than what you describe. This may sound trite, but surely somewhere a delightful lady is waiting for a doctor husband just like you."

Dexter swore under his breath and shook his head violently. "I do not want another—"

Cece laughed without humor. "Oh, yes, you do. I have it on excellent authority that I am more trouble than any man can handle. Trust me, there is a very right someone waiting for you. Go find her, Dexter."

"I cannot change your mind?"

"No.

"You cannot stop me from keeping hope alive."

"The sooner you stop hoping, the sooner you will stop needing to."

At that, Dexter's head jerked up, and he studied Cece's face, seeking something he clearly did not find. "You won't change your mind, will you?"

Cece lowered her gaze to the mound of her child, relishing the movements it made. "The love in my heart will never change."

Dexter turned on his heel and with a short "good night" he strode to the kitchen in search of his mother. Very soon Cece heard the front door close behind them. Breathing a sigh of relief, she climbed the stairs to her room.

With shaky fingers she tore off her dress, not caring that a few buttons popped off, not caring that she flung the garment onto the floor. Her slippers landed on the pool of fabric at her bedside, and a velvet hair ribbon topped it all.

Not bothering with a nightdress, she slipped naked between the sheets. Her body, overheated with the warmth of pregnancy, thrilled to the sensual coolness of the fresh cotton. This was how she had slept with Matthew until she became ill. Was Matthew sleeping now? Was he on their furry bearskin, naked as he always slept?

The image of his face, the way he had looked this afternoon, rose unbidden in her mind. The creases at the outside corners of his eyes had looked deeper. Were his troubles with the tribe still torturing him?

She was glad to have seen him again, even though it brought back the knife edge of her sorrow.

A whimsical notion occurred to her. She had come full circle to where she had begun. She was back to spying on Matthew from behind the cover of the huge evergreens.

Had he known she was there, as he had the first time?

Across the waters of Teekalet, on a mat-covered sleeping platform in the home of Nuf-Kay'it's shaman, Matthew fought to find the peace of slumber. No logic would convince him that Cece had not hidden behind a tree trunk by the clearing this afternoon.

Even when the breeze had not carried to him the sweet scent of roses.

All night long Cece tossed and turned, seeking but not finding a comfortable position. The baby, as usual, had woken up when she lay down, and still kicked continually. What few moments of slumber she found were filled with dreams of what her life might have been like.

Rubbing eyes made gritty by the lack of sleep, Cece cried surrender. The vivid images won the battle; peaceful rest lost without a whimper. When she opened her eyes, she saw the warm glow of dawn slip through the crisp white curtains on the window. Streaks of roseate sky bloomed between breaks in the clouds. Maybe today would be clear, Cece thought, walking to the window, both her fists pressed hard against her lower back.

"Only three or four more weeks, little one," she whispered, sliding her hands around to embrace her stomach. Not a moment too soon for her! She was ready to be slim once again, to move and bend and even run with the wind across the beach. Only now she would have company when she did these things.

A movement directly below her window caught her attention. "Oh!" she exclaimed in delight. Bathed by the coral-colored splendor of daybreak, Lee Fung held May Li in a fervent embrace, kissing the lovely little lady in a most passionate manner.

Cece moved from the window, allowing the couple their privacy. A chuckle escaped her lips. "This explains why he was quite content to wait for me each time he took me to visit Mrs. Sanders. He had his own visiting to accomplish," she murmured.

Cece rejoiced for her two friends, knowing the exhilaration they felt at this moment. She hoped, for them, that it would prove more lasting than it had for her.

Feeling strangely lethargic, she took her time dressing. She braided her hair and coiled it into a becoming knot on the crown of her head. Her face had plumped up a bit during the past few months, and the smooth line of this coiffure suited the rounded contours of her face.

Not particularly hungry this morning, she brewed her usual cup of Earl Grey, and for the sake of her little one, nibbled on a slice of bread. When she finished the tea, she sought Father's company, but he felt achy again and chose to stay abed.

"I'll visit with you later, Father. Is there anything you would like me to fetch for you?"

Father smiled one of his still-rare smiles. "Only a few of your school stories to make me laugh."

"Then I, too, have something to look forward to later this afternoon," she said, pleased to know her silly school-girl escapades amused him. But as she left his room she wondered what she would do for the remainder of the day. Especially when all she wanted was to return—

No! She would not think such thoughts. She would . . . She could . . .

She looked around the kitchen, then checked the hallway. When she was certain May Li was nowhere in sight, she stamped her foot. "Oh, damn! Damn, damn, damn!"

Knowing how childish her pique was, she ignored the mature side of her nature and indulged her frustration. She would *not* touch that despicable tablecloth. She would *not* spend her day sifting through the books in the small crowded library. She would most definitely, under no condition, dawdle about until Dexter Sanders decided to try to change her mind again. He was probably determined enough to persist, even after last night's conversation.

Seeing the sunshine outside, she crossed the room to the kitchen door, turning sideways to navigate around the table in the center of the room. Indeed the sun had broken through the clouds, which were soft and billowy, not the unchanging blanket of gray that had hidden the sky for days.

"Well, damn!" she cursed again. "I want to go to the woods, and I shall. I am the one who will shed buckets afterward. I can choose to cry." *And logic be damned!*

Moments later she entered the majestic halls of her ever-green palace. Diamond-bright spears of light pierced the solid green canopy, reaching the ground in random spills of glittering jewels. The silence of the trees sang sweetly of peace to her still-troubled heart. The crystalline purity of the crisp winter breeze was a balm to skin too long confined in overheated rooms, skin that had once reveled in the luxury of the winds from Teekalet.

She felt serene now. Her pace slowed, and she took the time to study the trees. The Douglas firs and the spruces, the alders and the cedars lined the woods with their heavy trunks, forming endless mazes for a person to wander around and investigate.

She would always revere this exquisitely wild part of her world. She felt blessed to have been granted the right to live within its green depths for the months she had. If only . . .

An odd sound to her right startled her, making her lose her footing, and she stumbled. Catching herself on a low-hanging branch, Cece pulled herself upright, staring intently in the direction the moaning had come from. But she heard nothing more.

The cabin in the clearing was not far, so she stood a moment longer, leaning against the tree. The misstep had shaken her, and she needed to feel steadier. She must not falter when walking through the debris on the forest floor; roots and fallen branches were easy snares.

Cece closed her eyes and leaned her head against the rough bark of the tree. Her back ached from the weight of her child. She took a deep, long breath of salty sea breeze, perfumed as usual with the sprightly scent of cedar. Then she heard the moan again.

This time she *knew* she had heard someone. Not something, but someone.

"Who's there?" she called, not certain that making noise was a good idea. If the person she heard was in pain, however, he was most likely harmless.

"Can you hear me?" she asked, slowly making her way to where she thought the cry had come from.

That was when she found her. "Oh, no! Princess Mary!"

Lying in a crumpled heap, Matthew's elderly aunt clutched her left side, tears of pain running down her lined cheeks. "Cecelia," she said on a gasp of breath, hurting too much to say more. "Help!"

Cece crouched by Princess Mary, spreading her knees wide to allow for her belly. "Don't speak. Just nod yes or shake your head no. Did you come alone?"

One brief nod.

"You fell, right?"

Another nod.

"Are your arms and legs hurt?"

One simple shake.

"It must be your hip. Am I right?"

A nod.

Cece fell silent for a moment. She peered through the trees in the direction of the cabin and breathed a sigh of relief when she spotted its walls at no more than one hundred yards' distance from where Princess Mary lay. "Put your arms around my neck. We are going to the cabin."

"No!" cried Princess Mary. "The baby—"

"The baby and I are fine," Cece insisted, determined not to show this rugged woman the slightest weakness. "You must get off the damp ground. Please, let me help you."

Cece's plea must have carried some weight, for two wiry arms wound themselves about her neck. She turned her charge sideways, allowing Princess Mary's right side to take the brunt of her meager weight. When she stood, pulling the added burden with her, a spasm of pain clenched her back, then spread to every bit of her body. *Dear God, I need help. This is Matthew's aunt. I cannot leave her here. And this time, Lord, secondhand intervention from Sister Marietta's saints will not do.*

Hoping this prayer, this very urgent prayer, was the one she was granted an answer to, Cece began to partly carry Princess Mary to the cabin in the clearing.

"Is Matthew at the cabin still?" she finally dared ask.

Princess Mary shook her head. "He left . . . when you did."

Another burst of pain broke in her back, this time curving around to her belly. Cece was afraid—was she harming her child in order to help Matthew's aunt? With characteristic doggedness, she forged ahead, refusing to consider that possibility for too long. It was utterly repugnant to her to leave an injured woman, an elderly woman, out in the woods.

She pushed forward, taking another series of short steps. To keep her mind off her fears, she spoke again. "Where has he been all this time, then?" She held her breath, dreading the answer.

"Home . . . with us."

Relief forced the air from her chest in a loud gust. In the few moments between revelations, she had feared learning of Matthew's possible marriage to a S'Klallam woman. Thank goodness she would not have to suffer that quite yet.

"Where is Matthew right now?" she asked. "Can I go to him for help?"

"Village," was the brief response. "Meeting . . . elders."

Oh, my, I surely choose my moments well, Cece thought. "Let us reach the cabin, then, before we fret over the next step. We are almost there."

When another hard knot of pain broke in her lower back, Cece faced facts. Dexter had warned her that on occasion the pangs of childbirth began this way. Her baby had decided to come today, three weeks early. And she still had to transfer Princess Mary to safety.

Gritting her teeth against the difficulty of carrying someone when her own body was already heavier than she could manage, Cece plowed forward, making progress by sheer force of will.

"Another step," she begged Matthew's aunt.

The woman complied.

"Another one."

Progress again.

"One last one, and we will be at the door," she whispered, another contraction clutching her middle.

Then they were there. "I cannot help you into the bed," she said, her voice conveying the apology she did not have the time or energy to speak. "I will help you lie here, then go find some covering for you."

She stood, took off her coat, and for the first time looked around the room. A tremor of awareness shook her, the coat slipping from her suddenly weak fingers. The cabin was intact! Matthew had not taken anything when he left. Her heart sped up its thumping beat. Had he found their belongings a poignant reminder of their loving time together?

"Well, thank heaven for that!" she exclaimed, reaching for the cedar mats on the sleeping platform to cushion Princess Mary. If asked, she could not have said exactly what she was thanking heaven for at that moment. Was her gratitude for finding the means by which to help Princess

Mary? Or was it for the possible evidence of Matthew's feelings for her? She ran her fingers over the bearskin, allowing herself only the briefest bit of melancholy.

Placing a mat beside her patient, Cece made a pallet near the hearth. "Here," she said, when she had the bedding ready, "we can make you quite comfortable." With care, and considerable pain on the part of both women, they got Princess Mary onto her makeshift bed.

Cece found her stack of cedar bark in the very corner she had left it months ago. Picking up two handfuls, she brought the pieces of wood to the hearth. "There is enough kindling to start a good fire. You need not suffer while I seek help."

In minutes she had a good blaze going. Slapping her hands together in satisfaction, as well as to dislodge the dust they had gathered, she stood and reached for her coat. She slipped one arm into a sleeve, then the other, sparing another look for the room. Amazing! It seemed as if she had left only days ago.

A strange sort of effervescence bubbled in her, unlike anything she had ever experienced. She wondered if it was caused by her labor and realized she needed help, and soon. Facing Matthew's aunt, she spoke quietly. "I hate to leave you—oh!"

This pain was one she could not ignore. The tightness gripped her belly for long seconds, making it impossible for Cece to move. When the pang eased, she let out a sigh of relief, then glanced at Princess Mary.

"Do . . . not . . . go," the older woman begged. "The . . . baby." Worry and fear clearly showed on her weathered features.

"I must," Cece said, then bit her lower lip. "I—I need Matthew."

At Cece's confession Princess Mary closed her eyes. She kept them shut for moments. When she opened them, a tear fell onto a withered cheek. "He needs . . . you, too."

Cece was stunned by the woman's words. Her breath caught as images of the heartrending parting Matthew had imposed on them burned in her thoughts. Then everything seemed to slow and stop. All she remembered was Matthew's rock-solid back. Not his face. He had been unable to witness her pain!

The tingling awareness became full-fledged excitement. Her heart refused to hear the caution her mind insisted upon. Still, she made herself verify what she had heard. "Did you say he needs me?"

The gray head rose and fell. "I am . . . sorry."

Cece's heart swelled with this apology. If Matthew's staunch mother could admit to being wrong and see his need for Cece, then surely anything was possible! Even convincing the man himself.

Smiling through her own tears, Cece pretended to misunderstand Princess Mary's words. "Well, I am not sorry. I am going after that muleheaded man, and I will get him to help us both. Then I shall sit him down for a long conversation. What do you say?"

Wise eyes studied Cece. When the scrutiny became prolonged, she twisted her fingers, wondering if her saucy statement had offended Princess Mary. About to offer an apology, she saw her nod slowly. Then the expression on the wrinkled features softened, a hint of mischief playing on pain-pinched lips. "Can . . . I . . . listen?"

Cece laughed for the first time in days, thrilled by the offer of friendship. "Oh, no. This time he is all mine. I will make him see reason, even if I have to hold him by the ears until he does so."

She blew a kiss at Princess Mary, then tightened the ulster about her. Her breath hissed out when another pain clutched her body. "Damn!"

"Be . . . careful," Princess Mary urged.

Cece made sure she caught her patient's gaze, then patted her belly. "With your grandson? Absolutely."

Slowly, stopping along the way to allow the contractions to pass, Cece crossed the unfamiliar part of the forest to meet her destiny. How or why it had taken this long for her to see the absurdity of languishing at Father's house, she would never know. Perhaps her illness had kept her befuddled too long. Perhaps the feelings of inadequacy caused by Father's rejections had resurfaced, usurping the place of common sense when Matthew sent her away. She admitted, reluctantly, that she had just given up the battle.

Yes, she was white, and Matthew was S'Klallam. Nothing either did would ever change those facts. But she had not caused his problems with Luke, and Luke had capitalized on her parentage. If Princess Mary could come to see her as an individual rather than as a threat, sooner or later the rest of the village would, too. She and Matthew could make it happen.

She did not know how. And right now she did not care how. She was done with the self-righteous nobility of giving up the father of her child so he could follow his destiny. From this day forward they would find a way to share that destiny.

All she wanted now was to reach Matthew, send help to Princess Mary, and birth this baby!

He needs . . . you, too! I am . . . sorry.

Princess Mary's words played a song of hope in her heart. The only ones sweeter were the ones Matthew had uttered in her ear each time he had made love to her. *I love you.*

She had forgotten those words, the feelings they expressed. Matthew had sent her where he knew she would receive the best medical care. Only now could she see that his overdeveloped sense of duty would force him to cut away his own joy in order to assure the safety of those for whom he felt responsible. And who was he more responsible for than his wife and child? In every way fathomable, Cece had long been Matthew's wife.

Now all she had to do was convince Matthew of that.

With that goal firm in her head, heart, and soul, Cece walked. She walked steadily until the next contraction made her stop. Once the pain released her from its bonds, she resumed her voyage to Nuf-Kay'it.

She refused to think of what she would do once she arrived at the village. She would be a foreigner there and was sure to draw quite an audience. Her ungainly gait and her distended belly alone would have done so. But she felt with absolute certainty that every resident of that small town knew precisely who Cecelia Scanlon was.

"You are about to come to know me far better than you ever imagined," she said out loud. She intended to keep

Matthew and their child, and Matthew would somehow prove that his loyalty had never suffered as a result of their love. She would do whatever it took, short of leaving his side again, to assure anyone that this was so.

"Thank God!" she cried when she spied a large lodge built along the same lines as the one Matthew had constructed. When she saw Anna slip out the door, her anxiety began to dissipate.

"Anna! Anna, please come." Cece saw her friend spin on her heel. When Anna saw Cece, a radiant smile bloomed on her pretty face. A smile that soon turned into a frown of concern.

"Cece, why are you here?" she asked, running to her side.

"Your mother," Cece said, still panting after the pain had begun to subside. "She fell in the woods. I helped her to our cabin. Her hip is most likely broken. She needs help."

With an arm around her waist, Anna began to lead Cece toward the house. She was glad for Anna's support; she was tired, more tired than she ever remembered being. The pains, and her exertions between them, had drained her. When the next contraction hit, a moan escaped her lips.

Anna pursed her lips. "My mother is not the only one in need of help," she said when the pain eased. "Come, let us get you home."

Cece shook her head. When she could speak, she cried, "Matthew! I need Matthew. Please, Anna, we must find him. Now."

Anna studied Cece with worried eyes. But something in Cece's expression must have expressed her determination to find Matthew, whether or not Anna complied with the demand.

"Come," Anna said. "He is meeting with the elders. My father is there as well. He will help Mother."

Surprised by Anna's strength, Cece allowed her friend to bear her weight. Scant minutes later they reached an enormous longhouse built of cedar boards, just like the one in the woods.

Anna threw open the door and practically carried Cece into the room.

Matthew's voice, raised in anger, reached Cece's ears. "I am still myself. And with my powerful *tamanous,* the eagle, I will lead our people through what may come. I will take my rightful place. I will hold a potlatch as the new *ssia'm.*"

Cece watched a stranger rise from where he'd sat in the circle of men. "What about that woman, your Boston lover? The daughter of the manager of Pope and Talbot? How much more of our land will you give to her and her father?" The questions were posed in a sneering voice, taunting Matthew.

Cece's gaze flew to Matthew's face. She saw him close his eyes and take a deep breath. *Oh, God!*

She wanted to scream. She wanted to cry. She wanted to throttle the fool who had asked such things of Matthew. Another contraction clasped her in its wicked embrace, and she did nothing. Through the fog of pain she heard Matthew's voice.

"I will be *ssia'm,*" he stated, his tone of voice brooking no argument. Matthew remained seated, as did the others gathered in the room. "Edward Scanlon is no longer manager of the Pope and Talbot mill. And even if he were, I would still marry Cecelia Scanlon, if she will have me. That matters not to anyone here."

Had she heard right? Cece turned to Anna, querying with her eyes.

Anna shrugged, smiling secretively.

Cece wondered what her friend knew.

The stranger in the crowd walked up to Matthew. "Traitor," he spat.

Cece gasped.

"No, Luke," responded Matthew, his voice as carefully controlled as the features on his rough-hewn face. He stood, bringing his eyes to the level of Luke's. "Just a man. One who sees reality as it is." Matthew's voice lost its edge of anger. "The white man is here forever. Our only hope lies in sharing the land. Fighting would be a vain endeavor."

Cece saw Luke clench his fists, and knew fear as she had never known it before. Was this man about to hurt Matthew?

Luke stood only inches away from Matthew. "Are you saying my parents' deaths were in vain?"

Matthew shook his head slowly. "Mine died of smallpox, if you will remember. It was a tragedy. Your father fought a battle lost before it even began. That, too, was a tragedy."

Luke's anger was palpable. "And yet you sleep with the enemy's daughter?"

Matthew shook his head. "She is only a woman. My woman."

Luke barked a mirthless laugh. "Betray us, then. My father did what he had to do. I will do what I must. There are others who agree with me and will see this through to the end."

"Not in Nuf-Kay'it." Matthew's voice bore the chill of warning.

"No, not in Nuf-Kay'it," agreed Luke. He spun away from Matthew and left the room.

Cece's contractions became stronger and more frequent, lasting ever longer. When the pain eased, she breathed a rough sigh and looked around the room. Where only seconds before the fury in Luke's and Matthew's voices had filled the room with tension, silence now reverberated. Matthew stood alone in the circle of mute, staring men.

With her gaze upon him Cece tried to stand on her own. Anna, perceiving her need to do so, helped steady her, then stepped away to allow Cece to stand tall. Somewhat out of breath from her effort, Cece cast her gaze about the room again, then took a step toward Matthew. She faltered, and Anna came back to her side.

Then, not ten feet away, two men rose to come to Matthew's side. From the back of the room another man made his way through those who remained seated. Finally Cece saw an older man, straight and thin, rise and look about.

At her side, Anna jerked at the sight of the older gentleman. "Father," she whispered.

Cece watched Matthew stand firm, receiving support, man by man. He held his head high with pride and self-assurance, his long black hair lying on his shoulders. Matthew would always be this man, his honesty and nobility as much a part of him as the wildly passionate side he kept private.

"Matthew," she whispered.

As if she had yelled his name out loud, Matthew jerked around to face her. "Cece!"

The torture of another pain hit her, and before she could brace herself, a flood of warm, slick fluid drenched her legs, pooling on the ground below her. The sudden rush, combined with the pain and her weariness, left Cece light-headed.

The room spun around. A bright burst of light appeared before her eyes. A rush of bilious acid climbed her throat. Everything faded into black.

Matthew watched her fall. With almost brute strength he swept the sea of men from his path. A cry of anguish left his lips.

"Cece!"

Chapter Twenty-Two

———————— • ————————

Her body's travail pierced the veil of unconsciousness. A new type of pain gripped Cece's body, this one more intense, sharper, and with a distinct downward push. When she opened her eyes, she realized she was in Matthew's arms, held high against his chest.

"What do you think you are doing, Matthew?" she asked, her voice peevish. "Do you want our child to just bounce out of me into the air? Do take me somewhere more—aaahhh!"

Another of those keen contractions caught her off guard, and its downward pull had her wanting to bear down with all her strength. "Would you put me down?" she screamed. "This baby will be born any moment now."

At her words she noticed the deafening silence in the room. Looking around, she saw only Matthew, Anna, and two other women. All the men who had been gathered in the place were gone. She also noticed the four pairs of black eyes firmly focused on her.

"Why is everyone staring at me?" Astonishment was the prevailing expression on all four S'Klallam faces. "And just who are those two women—"

Her demand was cut off by another convulsive clamping of her muscles. Matthew held her until the pain eased, then laid her down.

Although still casting cautious, questioning glances in

Cece's direction, Anna began issuing orders. "Bring mats for her. And water for the baby," she told the women. "Matthew, give me a clean knife, then go with the other men—"

"No!"

"No!"

The two cries came at the same moment, and Cece and Matthew shared a private look. Before she could smile at him, though, another tearing pang hit her, and she cried out.

Matthew tossed his sheathed knife at Anna, bending to wipe Cece's damp brow. He said not a word, only offered his support and tried to ease her discomfort.

One of the women returned, carrying a small leather pouch similar to Princess Mary's. At the sight of the bag, Cece remembered Matthew's mother. "Princess Mary!" she cried. "She fell and is injured. Someone must go to the cabin and help her."

"It has been done." Matthew's calm voice soothed Cece's fears like a balm on a burning wound. She wished something could ease the ever worsening pains of childbirth.

Cece relaxed a fraction, closing her eyes. A soft tap on her hand made her open them again.

The woman with the bag offered her something that looked like a leaf of some sort. "Chew it," the woman said. "The Indian plum eases pain."

Cece opened her mouth to take the offered relief. As soon as it was placed there, her jaws slammed shut with the force of the next spasm.

After the pain stopped, Anna turned to Cece. "I must check to see where the baby is." Without another word Cece felt her friend throw her skirts about her waist and spread her legs wide. Embarrassed by the indignity of the position, she turned her face into Matthew's shoulder.

"I will never forgive you for this, Matthew," she vowed through gritted teeth.

"Good," said Anna, ignoring Cece's discomfiture. "I see a nice little head with much black hair. And only seconds from birth."

Then, despite the leaf she had chewed, Cece screamed at the ripping sensation below. It was an inhuman sound, a gut-rending bellow. Her entire body tightened, bowing right off the floor in its effort to heave down, every muscle intent on expelling her child from her body.

"Short breaths, Cece. Little ones. Don't push so hard," ordered Anna.

The urge redoubled. "I—can't—stop—pushing."

"There! There it is!" Anna exclaimed, and Cece felt a huge slurp inside her body. Right upon its heels came a strange sensation of relief. She panted heavily, leaning forward to try to see over her skirts.

"Here," Matthew said, gathering the fabric out of her way. He placed himself squarely behind her and helped her up into a squatting sort of position. "Can you see the baby?" he asked, wiping her sweat-beaded brow.

Cece shook her head. Then another pain hit.

"The shoulders," Anna explained.

Bracing against Matthew's solid strength at her back, Cece bore down once more and felt her child squeeze its way into the world.

The chorus of excited exclamations faded when the thin, sweet wail of her newborn reached Cece's ears. She craned her head around, seeking Matthew's face. She gasped. Two silver tears slid down his bronze cheeks.

"Can you see it?" she whispered.

Matthew's gaze met hers. The intense emotions swirling in those midnight pools caused Cece to catch her breath. "Not it," he whispered, never looking away. "Him."

"A boy?"

"A boy."

They fell silent, still gazing into each other's eyes.

Their eloquent communication was cut short by the return of the powerful pains, indicating the arrival of the afterbirth. In no time Cece and Anna dealt with the matter. Through it all, Matthew was Cece's anchor. She turned to look at him, and her heart took flight at the overwhelming tenderness she saw burning in his eyes.

"Here," Anna said, interrupting them again. She placed the blanket-swaddled infant in Cece's arms.

Cecelia Scanlon fell in love for the second time in her life. With the same face. Anyone with eyes would know that the child she had just ushered into the world was Matthew's son. The tiny brow was broad like the child's father's. His black eyes had that same tilt. His miniature chin was as square and obstinate looking as that of the man who had sired him.

"Little Matthew," Cece murmured through the thickness in her throat. A tear splotched onto the baby's cheek, and his fist struck out. His almond-shaped eyes opened wide, and his mouth formed a perfect circle of surprise. When he frowned, he began to kick and flail his hands. Cece smiled through her tears and bared her breast. With a light tickle on his cheek, her son turned his mouth, seeking the comfort she offered. Seconds later the strength of the suction the tiny mouth created caused her to cry out.

"What is it?" Matthew asked, a worried look again on his face.

Cece shook her head, fascinated with the way the baby's cheeks worked as he nursed. "He surprised me, that is all. He is so strong."

Matthew nodded with pride in his expression. "He is a S'Klallam, one of the Strong People." Then he slipped a finger under Cece's chin and turned her face toward his. With a very intent look in his eyes, he spoke again. "And he is white. He is the future, for both our people."

Cece caught her breath. After what he had told the elders, and what he had just said, she dared almost anything. "Do you finally admit that you and I have that future?"

"Right before us. Together."

When she smiled, tremulous though it felt upon her lips, her breath hitched on a soft sob. "You know, I came ready to battle you. Even during childbirth. I told Princess Mary I would hold you by your ears and make you listen until you were ready to accept the truth."

"And that truth is . . . ?"

"That you are as much mine as this little boy and I are yours."

Matthew nodded. Slowly, as if he held the reins on time, he lowered his head to hers and sweetly rubbed her lips with his. Another sob broke in her throat, this one from the sheer beauty of the tender caress.

"Matthew . . . I love you," she whispered.

A rough tremor ran through his hard body, so strong Cece felt it. Matthew lowered his forehead to hers and just paused there. "I love you. You are my destiny. Without you at my side, I cannot go forward."

Cece sniffled and tried a weak laugh. "Then it is good that you will not have to try, right?"

His forehead rubbed against hers from side to side. "No, my woman, my wife. We will forge a new path, like this new life we created together. We will face the new world of Indian and white together. Married. Soon."

"Yes, soon—"

A knock at the door interrupted Cece's answer, and both turned to see who was there. Anna peeped around the wooden slab, smiling hesitantly. "May I come back in?"

Cece smiled. "I never noticed you had left."

Anna swept into the room, a knowing look on her face. "I noticed. You two only had eyes for each other and that beautiful little man."

Heated blood rushed to Cece's forehead. "Should I deny it? I will soon be your cousin by marriage."

Anna squealed in delight, but before either woman could say a word, another person entered the room.

"That is good, son," said the old S'Klallam man standing by the doorway.

Cece craned her neck to see Anna's father, Matthew's adoptive father, but only saw a shape in the shadows.

"Good, Uncle?" Matthew asked, disbelief in his voice. "This from the man who forced me to make an intolerable choice?"

The shaman walked farther into the large, empty chamber, coming close enough for Cece to see his

lined face. She thought she saw regret there. His next
words confirmed her suspicion.

"I never wanted to do that. My position left me no
choice. And as yet, you did not have your *tamanous*,
the power to fight for all you wanted."

Cece saw Matthew's uncle gesture toward the door.
Soon a small group of men gathered. She shook her
head. The entire moment seemed unreal. How could all
these strangers be surrounding her, only minutes after
she had given birth?

The shaman nodded his grizzled head toward Cece.
"Forgive us the intrusion, but these men must hear what
I say." He turned back to Matthew. "Son, you chose a
white woman. This was not what I would have wanted.
From the start I dreaded the pain your feelings for her
would bring you. But I know, because I know the man
you are, that your love for her never diminished your
love for your people. Remember, I encouraged you to
follow your destiny. She is part of that destiny. Until
you learned for yourself that you could love a woman
the tribe would reject and still be *ssia'm,* I could not
trust you with the leadership of this village."

Cece saw the black eyes narrow as the shaman
scrutinized Matthew. "After today, I would not think
to challenge your assertion that you will be *ssia'm.* I
would also not question your loyalty. I never did, nor
will I ever find reason to do so. I know the man you
are. These men," he said, jerking his head toward the
handful standing awkwardly nearby, "have come forward
to support you. They agree that although your choice of
wife is not one that pleases them, they know you are
needed in Nuf-Kay'it."

In the midst of such serious dialogue, all Cece could
think of was Princess Mary and her injury. Taking
advantage of the break in the discussion, she whispered,
"Matthew." When he turned her way, she gestured for
him to come closer. "What about Princess Mary? How
is she?"

The King of England, as Matthew had said his uncle
was called, turned his gaze upon Cece. "Yes, Princess

Mary. You cared for her even in your time of travail. She spoke of your courage and your strength. And your respectful compassion. She holds you in high regard."

Cece narrowed her gaze. She would again ask a question whose answer had hurt before. "For a Boston woman, that is, right?"

"For *any* woman," was the strong response. "I hold you in high regard as well."

Matthew slipped his arm around Cece's shoulders. "We will marry, and I will hold a potlatch to honor our marriage, our son's birth, and my position as leader."

Everyone nodded.

In the silence that followed, Cece noticed Anna's quiet movements, cleaning up all evidence of the birth. When she had gathered in her arms a water basket, an extra mat, the pouch with the useless medicinal leaves, and Matthew's knife, she turned to the men. Her bossiness returned, and she began to shoo them from the room.

"Can you not see this woman is exhausted? Go! There will be enough time to talk all these matters to death!"

When everyone but the King of England had left, Cece's shoulders relaxed. The old gentleman came close, and Cece removed the blanket from the baby's face. "Your grandson," she said, offering the only gift she could.

A wrinkled finger reached out to stroke the pudgy cheek. It trembled with emotion. Cece looked up, only to find a damp trickle gleaming on the old man's cheeks.

"Matthew's son," he said, his voice breaking.

"Cece's and my son." Matthew's words echoed through the nearly empty room.

The shaman whispered what Cece assumed to be a special blessing. He placed a wrinkled, callused hand upon her cheek and met her gaze. "Matthew's and your son," he said, then turned and silently left the room.

When they were finally alone, Cece turned to Matthew. "Am I to stay here? Could we not go home?"

"Yes, love, we will go home." In a very short while, after Anna had returned, a strange procession wended its way through the woods. Anna led the way, Baby Matthew cradled lovingly in her arms. Close behind, Matthew carried Cece in much the same way.

With a strong kick, Matthew shoved open the door to their cabin and carried Cece to the sleeping platform. Whoever had come to tend to Princess Mary had put the mats back in their place, covering all with the rich bearskin. He deposited his precious armful on it. Moments later Anna delivered the baby into Cece's arms.

"Matthew," Cece called, trepidation in her voice. "There is one favor I must ask. It is a difficult one, but it must be done."

Matthew turned to face Cece, his jaw clenching at the look on her face. He had feared this moment since he saw her in the longhouse. "No."

"Yes. You must fetch Father. This is his grandson,too."

"He is my son, and your father's hatred must not fall upon him."

Cece gazed at the sleeping infant. "I know how you feel. But you must give Father the same chance I gave your family. You must bring him."

A pall fell over the room. Matthew knew in his head that what she said was right. But his heart felt again the words Edward had used against him that day at the mill offices. And the child was S'Klallam.

"Don't forget, Matthew, that to your people I am the enemy's daughter."

Cece's words sliced through all the layers of pride and pain. She had faced the S'Klallam's disdain. She wanted her father to share the birth of her son. Matthew had no choice but to face the area's best-known Indian hater.

He released a ragged breath. He hoped he had the strength for this. Then he remembered the eagle. To have Cece and Baby Matthew in his life, he knew now that he could face Edward. He would do whatever he had to do.

"Very well."

Walking through the woods, Matthew dreaded that first moment of meeting Cece's father face-to-face. But he forced his thoughts to the beautiful scene he had left behind. Cece, nursing the baby, her face lit by the glow of the fire in the central hearth. Baby Matthew, his mouth making greedy noises, seeking nourishment from the generous flesh where his father had also sought much pleasure.

He smiled, filled with awe at the marvel of womanhood, at the marvel of Cece. When he looked up, he realized he had reached Edward Scanlon's house.

Squaring his shoulders, he strode to the door and knocked.

Edward Scanlon's ravaged face was the first thing Matthew saw when the door opened.

"You!" the white-haired man exclaimed. "What have you done to her?"

Matthew clenched his jaw before an unwise retort escaped. He swallowed hard, then sought and found Scanlon's forest-green gaze. "Nothing more than love her. Today she gave me a son, you a grandson. I would not have come, but she wanted you by her side."

A crooked finger pointed shakily at him. "You stole her! Where have you taken her?"

"I never stole anything." *Unlike what you and your people have done to us,* Matthew thought. "Cece went for a walk in the woods, and her travail began. She and our child are both well. She wants you at her side, and I have come for you."

Scanlon shook his head, burning rage turning his face a deep, mottled red.

Matthew tried one more time to make his point. "You should know that Cece and I will be married. If you value your daughter as much as you would seem to, it would be wise for you not to cause her undue grief. She loves you and she wants you to have a place in her child's life."

Matthew watched the man's emotions chase each other across the features that somewhat reminded him of Cece's in the intensity they reflected. Then the man's shoulders sagged. "I lost her mother," he said. "I cannot afford to lose her. Even if I must tolerate an Indian."

A harsh laugh escaped Matthew. "Do not forget I must tolerate you as well."

The shrewd green eyes studied Matthew for a moment. Then Scanlon nodded, a smile full of irony stretching his lips. "It is as it should be, then. Let us go to my daughter."

Matthew glanced at Scanlon's cane. "The arthritis?"

Pride broadened the barrel chest. "I will manage."

Edward Scanlon, uncomfortable the entire time he was at the cabin, softened long enough to smile when his grandson's fist curled around his index finger. And he kissed his daughter's cheek when he bid her good night.

Once Scanlon left and Matthew sent Anna back to the village, he turned to Cece. "Anna said you spent the time I was gone napping like our son."

"He did tire me out," she said, smiling gently.

Matthew smiled, then looked away. Her forgiveness shone in every feature of that beautiful face. Still, he owed her an apology. "I regret hurting you, Cece. I am sorry I sent you away."

"I know," she said, her voice a muted murmur in the peace-filled house.

"The problem was never you," Matthew continued, needing to voice all his feelings, once and for all. "I was to blame all along. I did not trust myself not to lose sight of my responsibilities when what I wanted was to sate myself with your love."

"You would never do that, you couldn't. You are far stronger than that."

Matthew sighed. "I know that now. I know I am strong enough to choose my own path, even during enormous opposition. I can pursue two seemingly disparate goals, without compromising either. I will always be a S'Klallam, no matter how much I love you, or how miserably I miss you. And I would rather love you than miss you."

"So would I, Matthew. Come," she invited, extending her hand to him. "Join me in our bed. It has been so long since you held me through the night."

"We will never be apart like that again."

Epilogue

The potlatch began weeks after the birth of Matthew Edward. For six days the feasting started at dusk and continued until late at night. Tonight the festivities would end.

When Cece saw the amount of gifts Matthew was to give away during the ceremony, she was astounded. Her husband was a rich man by S'Klallam standards, she noted with a wry grin.

The orange light of the fires allowed her to watch the events as she cradled her sleeping son to her breast. Satisfaction glowed bright in her heart.

She saw Father, stiff and uncomfortable throughout the entire ordeal, sit next to Mrs. Sanders. She, by contrast, seemed unable to understand all she wanted to, so to solve her dilemma, she befriended Princess Mary.

Dexter, on the other hand, stood to one side, watching everyone with a detached expression on his face.

Cece nodded. Both parts of her life had come together to celebrate her marriage, the birth of her son, and Matthew's ascension to the position of *ssia'm*.

"Oh!" she exclaimed, when an enormous yawn caught her by surprise.

"You have overtired yourself," Matthew chided at her side.

Cece turned to him with a smile on her lips. "No, I don't believe so. It is quite late, you know."

Matthew smiled back. "I know exactly what time it is."

The husky timbre in his voice told Cece that he knew just how old their son was, exactly how long they had denied themselves the radiant pleasure of their loving. He told her, without words, that their time had come.

He held out his hand to her. She stood, pressing the baby closer to her, then slipped her fingers between his.

Matthew led her across the clearing where the festivities were being held. "Let us say our good nights."

"But, Matthew, won't we seem terribly rude?"

He shrugged. Then he cast her a look over a broad shoulder. "Rudeness be damned. *I* need you."

A burning thrill ran through Cece's body, and she did not withhold her response. "I need you, too."

Matthew pulled her closer, wrapping a muscular arm about her shoulders. The alignment of their bodies produced a tingling friction she could not get enough of.

They stopped before Edward Scanlon. "We will go home now, Father. It is quite late, and the baby needs to rest."

Leaning heavily on his cane, Father rose. "So do you, child." He turned to Matthew, his features hardening a fraction. "As she has made her choice, I cannot but accept it. I know trouble has broken out as a result of the Dawes Act, and I do not want my daughter or my grandson caught up in it. I suggested to the mill that a section of the S'Klallam lands in question be returned to you. Perhaps they can become a permanent reservation."

At Cece's gasp of surprise, Father hushed her with a look. "I have no answer yet and cannot tell you how soon this could happen. It might, for all I know, take years to accomplish."

Cece rose on tiptoe and kissed her father's cheek. "What matters is that you have begun this. I love you, Father."

"Harrumph! Yes, well," Father said as he turned a bright shade of red. He faced Matthew once again. "Get these two to bed, now, young man."

Matthew nodded but did not say a word. He extended his

hand, his gaze firmly fixed on Edward's face. Cece held her breath.

For a moment Father stared back at Matthew, then nodded and gripped the extended hand. "Good night," he said.

"Good night," Matthew responded.

As they turned to leave, Cece saw Dexter approach. She wondered what to do, as she had not seen him since the night she rebuffed him. And he had been such a good friend to her husband.

"Matthew," Dexter said, holding out his hand. Cece squashed a nervous giggle. First Father, now Dexter. By the time she got Matthew to the cabin, his hand could be practically useless from all the shaking!

"Dexter," Matthew answered, clasping the hand extended in friendship.

Dexter lowered his head, then met Matthew's gaze. "I wanted to wish you both all the best."

They thanked him and began to walk home. After a few steps Anna's voice brought them to a complete halt.

"Dexter! I was looking for you. You never finished telling me how to turn a breech baby. . . ."

Cece and Matthew looked at each other, then at the two busily discussing difficult births. The intrigued look on Dexter's face spoke volumes, as did the determination etched on Anna's pretty features.

Matthew groaned. "Poor Dexter. Should I warn him?" he asked.

She laughed, shaking her head. "Let them both find their own way. Just as we did."

"Just as we will find our way home. Now."

Cece laughed again and allowed her husband to lead the way. Once they reached the cabin, she laid Baby Matthew in the cedar cradle his father had made for him. She moved silently to the sleeping platform and watched Matthew build a fire. His strong hands worked efficiently, just as they had the first time she saw him. When he stood, the muscles in his legs worked smoothly, flexing and extending just as they had nearly a year ago.

When he turned to face her, the intensity in his gaze stole her breath just as it had that first time.

"Come," she whispered. She undid the first pearly button on her leaf-green blouse. Before she reached the second, he was at her side.

"Let me," he whispered, and took over the task.

In moments both were naked. "Cece," he said, his voice trembling with emotion. She walked into his embrace. As one, they fell on the bearskin that knew so much of their passion, and renewed in the flesh the vows of love they had taken.

Overhead, the pines and cedars provided shelter to the love inside the cabin, a love strong and evergreen.

Author's Note

To play the kind of make-believe an author has the privilege of playing, I took bits of history and changed them to suit my story's purpose. The Walker Ames House, located in the town of Port Gamble, Washington, still stands and has always been a private residence owned by the Pope and Talbot mill.

I set *Love Evergreen* in 1888, however, and much of the story takes place in the mill manager's mansion. To provide historical accuracy, I must confess that construction of the lovely Victorian mansion was not completed until 1889.

I also played a bit with S'Klallam history. Chief Chet-ze-moka died in June of 1888, but there is no mention of any other S'Klallam chief after his death and that of Big Jim Balch. Matthew is only a product of my imagination.

Although any errors are solely mine, for research purposes I relied mostly on a collection entitled *Shadows of our Ancestors*, edited by Jerry Gorsline, and *Nux Sklai Yem, The Strong People*, a manuscript about the S'Klallam people by Stephen DeCoteau and Joseph Waterhouse, Jr.